"GIVE ME SOME HEAT, CLAUDE."

Claude loaded the HEAT round into the Carl Gustav gun, then dropped to the ground to avoid the backblast. Nanos tried to zero in on the light machine gun that was keeping them pinned down, but the next moment he was forced to duck. Plumes of snow were flung into the air by the stream of heavy projectiles coming their way.

He had to take the gunner out. Looking sideways, he caught Barrabas's eye. Barrabas was looking grim as he crawled forward, pausing now and again to squeeze off a shot. In that brief space of time, Nanos made a decision. Still holding Barrabas's gaze, he jerked his head in the general direction of the enemy. Barrabas nodded.

"Cover me," Nanos directed tersely to Claude before setting off at a crouch-run that took him in a zigzag pattern through the buzzing of hot lead.

He had a long way to go.

JACK HILD

THE BARRABAS BLITZ

A GOLD EAGLE BOOK FROM

WORLDWIDE®

TORONTO • NEW YORK • LONDON • PARIS
AMSTERDAM • STOCKHOLM • HAMBURG
ATHENS • MILAN • TOKYO • SYDNEY

First edition April 1989

ISBN 0-373-60103-4

Special thanks and acknowledgment to
Rich Rainey for his contribution to this work.

Printed in U.S.A.

THE BARRABAS BLITZ

CHAPTER ONE

Trondheim Fjord, Norway.

The ivy-covered institute, which looked as though it had been plucked from the hallowed heart of a university campus, was a protected site.

A gauntlet of tall spruce and fir trees shielded it from the winds howling in from Trondheim Fjord. The ribbon of driveway that looped around in front of the building was laden with gravel to announce the approach of vehicles.

From the moment Freda Stensgaard swung her blue Saab Turbo up the private road, she was a closely watched woman. Three armed men focused their eyes upon her.

Two of them viewed her on security monitors from inside a first-floor control room.

The third man, Karl Ostrander, observed her through the sidelight windows that braced the front entrance like a halo. Bullet-proof glass admitted an oval strip of fading autumn sunlight onto the plushly carpeted hallway of Trondheim House.

In its few years of operation Trondheim House had become almost invisible in the area north of Trondheim. To a casual onlooker it was just another civilian site, perhaps having to do with the university, but to a military eye it seemed like a brick fortress.

The white-coated "brains" working at the chemical warfare research center considered it just another job; they were simply building better mousetraps. Although the "mice" happened to be human, it was strictly theoretical. No one would ever be hit with any of these horrors, they reasoned. It was too unthinkable.

"You can relax," Karl said, turning toward the open doorway of the control room. "It's Freda."

One of the men laughed. "I'm afraid we'll still have to search her." While he spoke in jest, the desire lurking beneath the comment was evident.

"Sorry," Karl said. "That's my privilege."

Karl shrugged off their good-natured kidding. The three guards shared similar military and police backgrounds and had developed an easy camaraderie. And of course they'd drafted an unofficial set of rules and regulations to govern their private lives.

In the two years the men had worked at the institute, many women had come through the doors of Trondheim House, adding a covert spice to the long, dreary shifts where the biggest enemy was boredom. Freda was always a welcome diversion.

Karl watched the shiny turquoise-blue Saab as though it was a gift-wrapped package on wheels. It rolled to a stop in the small pond of gravel that served as a parking lot on the right side of the building.

A moment later, out stepped the prize.

Freda's bright blond hair drifted down her shoulders, ending in curling tendrils that spilled across the top of her bust. She wore a smocked gray flannel dress with white horizontal stripes. Racing stripes, Karl thought as he watched her lithe form slip out of the Saab.

The high-necked dress that clung to her body captured her curves, and held his hungry gaze. She wore white-powdered stockings and black open-toed shoes.

Oh my God, he thought. All this for me. I've died and gone to heaven.

Freda was more than beautiful. She was unearthly, and she reminded Karl of legends and myths, all that fairy-tale stuff that had been swept into dark corners of his mind until she came along. With a few quick strokes of a magic wand, she had brought those fairy-tale dreams back to life.

Karl still couldn't believe his luck in landing someone like her. Ever since that weekend they'd met in Oslo, she had been coming to see him regularly.

Freda was an artist, but not the starving kind. He gathered she was married to a rich old coot who didn't mind her weekend absences. She didn't like to talk about her husband, but he seemed to oblige her, content to play the rustic to his artist as long as the illicit weekends excited her.

Her timing was perfect, as usual. Trondheim House was always quiet after hours. Although by most standards the people who worked there were eccentric, they were quite traditional when quitting time came around. That's when their Mercedeses and Volvos paraded out of the lot.

Tonight only a couple of workers had stayed on.

Karl unclipped his computer-coded pass card from his breast pocket and slid it through the access slot above the brass doorknob.

After a buzz the lock hissed open and Karl swung the door inward. "Freda!" he proclaimed. "God, you look more beautiful every time."

"Only to you," she said, bathing in false modesty.

She darted to the open doorway and poked her head into the control room. "It's only me," she said, stepping in to flirt with the two men, one hand on her hip and with the other hand extending her soft gray suede purse toward them.

Both Lars Lindstrom and Eric Garstead stood up at her approach.

"Would you like to have a look?" she asked.

"We live for such moments," Lars said, reaching her first. The three played out the same charade every time.

She opened her purse for them and they gave it a cursory glance—as if a woman like her would have a weapon.

Lars smiled and closed the purse with a snap. "Looks fine to me." His eyes scanned her figure.

"You're such a sweet boy," she said. She patted his cheek, her fingers lingering long enough to turn the pat into a caress, and Lars Lindstrom into a little boy.

He backed away, reddening as if an untouchable pinup had come to life.

Karl gently tugged on Freda's arm, leading her out of the men's sight and into their fantasies.

They walked down the corridor to the guards' living quarters downstairs. Although it was Spartan compared to the rooms set aside for the white coats, the residence had one overwhelming advantage: it was totally separate from the rest of the institute—enclosed to form a world of its own.

Freda dropped her purse onto the low-slung couch while Karl poured two glasses of aquavit.

"To beauty," he said, toasting her.

"*And* the beast," she growled throatily.

ILSA KOENIG set down her Styrofoam cup of coffee on the gray-topped workbench and lit a cigarette. She turned her head to blow the smoke off to her right.

The small cloud passed harmlessly away from John Marsken, who sat directly across the table from her, his eyes throwing daggers at the smoke. Lately he'd been campaigning against her smoking, accusing Ilsa of waging chemical warfare against him.

It was a friendly battle. He was an ex-smoker and when he needled her it was with a certain compassion. Marsken made her feel guilty enough so she would cut down when she was around him, but wouldn't avoid his presence completely.

The two of them had become friends over the past year. Office mates. It was strictly platonic, and would most likely stay that way. They enjoyed each other's company, and that was one of the reasons they had stayed late together. The other reason was that both were ambitious, and once they neared the end of a project could not put it aside and leave it in the office.

Ilsa and Marsken were the only two staffers working in the lab that night. They would take their coffee breaks together, then go back to conduct their own separate wars.

As a research chemist Ilsa was looking for the equivalent of the philosopher's stone—a substance that would turn things to gold. She sought the perfect, all-purpose chemical. And John Marsken was an engineer. Once Ilsa found the philosopher's stone, it was his job to come up with the best way of throwing that stone at the enemy.

Marsken had several delivery and deployment systems on the drawing board: suitcases with aerosol sprays; dart guns and poison-tipped umbrellas; rocket loads and plastic-coated land mines; capsules, pills and powders.

The fact that their work was considered unethical, perhaps even illegal, didn't bother them. A slender thread of contracts and research grants connected them to the military and intelligence communities, for whom *legal* was a highly flexible word.

Consequently, their offices were filled with the forbidden fruits of their labor.

Ilsa had created dozens of analog drugs, synthetic variations of existing chemicals. At the moment her most promising was 2-CB-R, a variation of MDMA, the drug known as XTC on the street. The *R* in the 2-CB-R designation had a slightly wicked meaning: it stood for *Russian*. It was only fair. After all, the Russians added an *A* for *American* to many of their chemicals to indicate the intended target population.

In many respects 2-CB-R was a benevolent chemical. It wasn't fatal, and in fact, if used properly, the subjects who got hit with it wouldn't even know it happened. Ingestion of the chemical resulted in low-intensity hallucinations, telepathic perceptions, a bit of memory loss, and it induced talkativeness, making it ideal for interrogation.

Of course, with the right dosage 2-CB-R could turn the target population stark raving mad.

A work of art, Ilsa thought. And it was state-of-the-art. That was one of the reasons she had joined the staff of Trondheim House. They had almost unlimited resources, enabling her to work on the next generation of chemicals.

After a few minutes of idleness Ilsa started to get restless. She swirled her cup to stir up the sugar that had gathered at the bottom. Then she tossed down the coffee in one last gulp.

"I've got to get back to my office," Ilsa said.

"Me too," Marsken agreed. "People to kill, places to lace."

"What?"

"Nothing," he said. "Just a bit of conscience poking through."

"Don't let it happen again," she said with a halfhearted smile on her face. She picked up her empty cup and made a great show of wiping the tabletop clean.

Then, her moment of uneasiness purged, Ilsa Koenig went back to work on the weapons of war—a petite Frankenstein with several advanced degrees.

FREDA STENSGAARD was also going to work.

She drained her glass of aquavit, then placed it softly on the long, rectangular chrome-and-glass coffee table.

"Well," she said, stepping closer to Karl Ostrander. "What's the next course?" She looked into his eyes meaningfully, and once again cast a spell upon him.

Only too eager to be enchanted, Karl Ostrander stepped forward, his arms outstretched.

She locked her fingers together behind his neck, then pulled his head down to hers.

The taste of aquavit was still on her lips. He kissed her with abandon, his hands dropping down her back and sliding over the soft clinging dress.

Freda arched her back, snuggling her breasts against his chest.

"Ouch," she said.

"Mmm?"

"The clip," she said. "It pinched me." She daintily pressed the silvery thumb plates together, releasing the alligator clip fastening Karl's access card to his breast pocket. "We can't have that, can we?" She carefully laid the card on the sofa cushion, then renewed the embrace.

Karl's hands followed the dip of her back, traversing the gentle curve of her buttocks. He pulled her hips forward, the motion producing a whisking sound as the back of her dress hiked up her stockings.

Freda's breath was hot on his neck. Her hands prowled over his broad back, then down to his hips, her fingers grasping the smooth leather holster of the 9 mm Browning HP that fascinated her so.

He'd taken it out and shown it off to her many times before, watching with a dry mouth while she caressed the gun's sleek barrel.

It was always a real turn-on for her, and therefore for him.

She liked to play games. And tonight was no exception as she slipped her hand under the holster flap.

"Bang," she said, pressing her hips against his as she playfully squeezed the butt of his automatic.

He laughed.

His body stiffened slightly when she pulled the gun halfway out of the holster. Just like in the past it sent a fire up his spine when she did that.

She was beautiful.

A bit kinky. A bit dangerous. Always exciting.

Karl's right hand was still sliding up Freda's ample breast when she flicked off the safety on the Browning and lanced his brain. The 9 mm slug chomped through the right side of his head, entering just below the ear and slanting upward, the bullet coring through gray matter and skull in a spout of bone-specked gore.

Karl realized what was happening at the last possible moment, realized that she had begun pulling the trigger months ago when they first met and only now was it going off.

She was a goddess, all right, a goddess of death.

Freda was no artist, and there was no husband in Oslo.

As the sturdy husk fell to the floor, the last thought fleeing from his brain was that now there was no Karl Ostrander.

While the roar of the Browning HP turned into the yawn of eternity for Karl Ostrander, it turned into an echo of panic for Lars Lindstrom.

The young guard hurtled out into the hallway clutching his Browning HP in a tight-fisted grip. His heart beating fast, his breath trapped in his lungs, Lars raced headfirst into the chaos. The blood pounded out a steady rhythm in his brain, screaming "What-what-what?" with every step he took.

Freda backed into the corridor, a look of horror on her face. She gave Lars a dazed look. "In there!" she screamed.

"What happened?" Lars demanded.

"There's a man with a gun," Freda shouted. "Oh, God, he shot him, he shot Karl!" She backed away, covering her mouth with her hand.

Eric Garstead appeared in the doorway, amazed to find the panic-stricken woman retreating and his young partner stalking toward the living quarters.

He raced back into the control room, heading for the phone.

At that moment Freda Stensgaard spun around and slid Karl's liberated access card through the slot by the door. She silently twisted the doorknob.

The door opened and Magnus Koll came in, shoulder-length corn-yellow hair streaming behind him. At first glance he looked like a bohemian peace lover. But the weapons that hung so naturally from his stocky frame and the hint of a smile on his face said that peace was for dreamers.

Magnus Koll was fully awake and ready for war.

The Norwegian mercenary glanced quickly at Freda. She offered him two fingers in a V sign, then pointed one finger back down the hallway before motioning to the control room.

Magnus tossed a silver canister the size of a beer can into the control room.

The magnesium stun grenade struck like the hammer of Thor, blasting white light and ear-shattering shock waves into the control room. The flash-bang exploded at the exact moment that Eric Garstead realized the phone lines had been cut. He was still holding the dead phone in his hand when he detected the silvery canister out of the corner of his eye. The concussion knocked him senseless for ten critical seconds.

SOMETHING WAS WRONG, Lars thought. Something didn't fit. Karl Ostrander had been shot, all right. His skull was shattered and the ceiling was spattered with blood.

But there was no one else in the room. Karl's gun was on the floor right next to his outstretched arm. Suicide? No. It didn't make sense. Not with a girl like Freda coming on to him. And the girl had said a man shot Karl—

The girl!

"Noooo!" he shouted, running back to the hallway just as the explosion went off.

He saw a blond giant flying through the air toward him, arms outstretched.

Even as Lars aimed at the broad-shouldered assailant, a stream of 9 mm bullets scythed through his chest. The burst of automatic fire ripped him off his feet and dimmed the world for good.

Magnus Koll had landed in a prone position, his firing unhampered by the side profile of the 34-round magazine for the silenced 9 mm Sterling SMG.

He glanced at his target, saw blood on the wall and death in the eyes, then swung back in the direction of the control room.

The last guard staggered out, wild-eyed and bleeding from the mouth.

Magnus chopped him with a ridge hand to the hollow of his throat.

The guns were silent. Now only the "brains" were left.

Still prone on the hallway floor, Magnus glanced over his shoulder at Telik Wulfson, the backup man he knew would be there.

Wulfson had swept in through the main entrance behind Magnus, loaded for bear. His dark brown hair was cut short and high in front, giving his temples a craggy clifflike appearance. A long lock of hair was thonged in back just above his collar.

Like the blond leader, Wulfson resembled a phantom from the past, more at home in another time. But the weapons he wore were distinctly modern.

A Heckler & Koch MP-5 Kurz was strapped across his chest in a quick-release harness.

The short-barreled submachine gun was favored by pinstriped security men tagging along behind CEOs or commanders in chief. It was small and businesslike and could easily be concealed until it went to work.

But on this occasion Wulfson wasn't worried about concealing anything. In fact, the determined look on his face said he wasn't worried at all. He carried an Armsel Striker semiautomatic shotgun with a 12-round drum magazine, as well. The 12-gauge shotgun looked like the mutant offspring of a tommy gun and a small cannon.

"You're up," Magnus said.

Telik Wulfson nodded, ready for the next stage. He and Koll followed Freda through the door at the left of the main entrance. It had opened easily when Freda flicked the computer card through the access slot.

But the door at the end of the next corridor that led to the staff offices stayed silent and did not budge. She flicked the card through it twice more with no result.

In disgust she whipped the car down the hall like a Frisbee, and after a hard and low-angled flight it bounced to the cream-carpeted floor. "Dammit!" she shouted. "We need another card. I thought Karl used the same one on all the doors."

Freda paused to glance at Koll's eyes, wondering if he was enraged at the foul-up. She'd rehearsed it over and over, tracing every step of the move. On nights when there were no staffers in the building she had had Karl show her around. Just out of curiosity, she'd told him. He must have had two cards, or the access code had been changed. Either way she had miscalculated.

"I'll look in the office," she said quickly, and started to head to the control room.

Koll raised his palm and held her back. "Never mind," he said, unfazed by the setback. "Telik has his own passkey."

He nodded to Telik, swept Freda behind him, then backed up a few paces as Wulfson unlocked the door with the Armsel Striker shotgun.

With practice all twelve loads could be unleashed in three seconds. Wulfson had a lot of practice. Gripping the forward pistol grip with his left hand for balance, he pulled the double-action trigger with his right.

He fired three rounds through the access slot, and the 12-gauge blasts peeled the armor plate and bolt housing off the door. Then he stepped to his left and triggered several shots from floor to ceiling, tearing the hinges off the inside wall.

The metal-reinforced door jumped back several inches, still hanging precariously from the tortured hinges.

Magnus leapt sideways, planting his left foot on the floor before going airborne again and stomping his heavy right boot into the door just above the middle hinge.

The door fell free in a shower of plaster, flying nuts and twisted metal.

Magnus and Telik burst inside the office quarters, the Sterling SMG and the Armsel Striker scanning the maze of lab tables, glass-covered cabinets, partitioned offices and banks of metal file cabinets.

There was no opposition, but there was a lot of desperation.

Both of the late-night employees in Trondheim House had obviously panicked at the sound of explosions pounding their workplace.

After bolting the door they'd instinctively headed for the windows. Even now the man was trying to smash a chair through the unbreakable glass that broke up the expanse of the far wall of the huge laboratory, filtering dusky slivers of light into the room. But the metal-legged chair kept bouncing back, and the windows barely shivered from the impact.

The three invaders fanned out into the chemically tinged air of the lab, bringing a scary and stark reality into the harsh artificial atmosphere. It was like poking their heads into a poisoned well.

The hunted man turned from the window frantically. Sweat glistened on his reddened face. He snatched up a wicked-looking dart pistol from a desk top. He'd obviously been debating whether to use the weapon, but he was too slow and cautious, versed only in the theory of war. His combat experience was confined to the classroom.

Magnus Koll had done years of fieldwork.

With a fluid and barely detectable motion he turned, slightly raising the barrel of the Sterling SMG as he moved. He exhaled and triggered a 9 mm burst that splattered through the man's forehead, demonstrating with a bloody finality how it was supposed to be done—like bullets etching a path on a blackboard.

The "weapons expert" learned his lesson the hard way as he dropped stone dead on the floor, the graduation exercise hurling him into another world.

The small blond woman had been prowling along the windows, looking for escape, hoping that perhaps the designers of the building had overlooked one or two windows that she could open manually. Failing to find them, she kept glancing at the wrecked door the three marauders had stormed through. She was looking for rescue, hoping for the cavalry to come trooping through.

But a closer look at the quiet but ferocious presence of Magnus Koll made her think that any cavalry in the area was already dead and buried.

After studying the female invader and seeing no quarter in her hard eyes, she searched the gaze of the brown-haired man for any signs of leniency.

But mercy was alien to the mercenary's eyes.

Magnus nodded at his cohort, who headed for the gray metal bank of file cabinets to extract the deadly formulas and records of the Trondheim House experiments.

"What do you want?" the woman asked.

"What've you got?" Koll said, though he already had a good idea of everything the lab contained.

She shook her head. "It's just . . . it's just . . . chemicals."

"What are you working on now?" he said.

"2-CB-R," she said. There was a bit of pride in her voice, as if she was talking about her firstborn who'd just got all A's in school. She pointed to her workbench and rattled off as much as she could about the experiments she'd already performed with the drug. "It's an analogue of—"

"MDMA," Koll said. "Like the ketamine hydrochloride analogue."

She stopped, aware that he wasn't a novice in the pharmacology of chemical warfare. Koll fired several more questions at her about Trondheim House affairs and any other CW projects she knew about.

Finally he nodded his head with approval. She'd passed her oral exams.

"What's your name?" Magnus said, strolling closer, his voice calm and neutral, as if this was a chance meeting on a street.

"Ilsa," she said. "Ilsa Koenig."

"Goodbye, Ilsa Koenig." He ended all her hopes and worries with a 3-round spurt that spun her slight frame around.

Blood spouted from her punctured and torn torso as she whirled around. Her eyes had a pained, almost embarrassed look at the bloody mess she was making, red on white, red slick on the floor.

Then the pain came and hammered the surprise and life off her face as she went down.

Koll quickly scanned the laboratory, seeking out the silver-lined iron-and-steel canisters that housed small amounts of corrosive tabun and sarin, liquid nerve gases that shorted out the muscle-controlling cholinesterase in the human body, turning it into an uncontrolled dancing machine until the brains and lungs freeze-fried in asphyxia.

He and Telik carefully gathered canisters, vial cases and experiment records in the center of the lab. Then they stood by while a half dozen more of Koll's mercenaries streamed in from two vans that had just pulled up in front of Trondheim House.

The new teams of mercs brought in strips of C-4 explosive and carried out the treasure trove of chemicals selected by Magnus Koll.

A van loaded with chemicals finally pulled away, and Freda followed in her blue Saab.

Magnus Koll, Telik Wulfson and two other mercs made up the wrecking crew that stayed behind to place and wire adhesive-backed packets of radio-controlled C-4 charges throughout the institution.

When that was accomplished, the wrecking crew piled into the second van and drove down the gravel road.

Sitting in the front passenger seat, his right arm draped through the open window, Magnus Koll turned on a pocket-size remote-control detonator. "C-4," he said, "meet 2-CB." He thumbed the blast button.

Trondheim House belched fire into the Norwegian woods, the explosion sending a deadly mix of hallucinogens into the air around the rapidly vaporizing institute.

The sound was almost loud enough to be heard in nearby hell and back.

CHAPTER TWO

The black ship cruised down Trondheim Fjord in the dusk, seeming to grow a bit more invisible with each deepening shade of night.

This stretch of the fjord was relatively deserted. Only a few lights were shining from the distant shore. The forty-four-foot heavy-weather cutter had passed several of the more populated spots where footholds for civilization had been carved out of the woods, and the lit windows of secluded villas peered down at the fjord with lanternlike eyes.

After navigating an S-shaped bend, the ship cut its engines. Two hundred yards from shore it drifted slowly and quietly in the deep water.

It was a formidable craft. The flexible steel-alloy hull and aluminum superstructure were designed to take a lot of punishment.

A veritable tank without wheels, the search-and-rescue cutter jettisoned a very special cargo—Red Force commandos looking for Blue Force commandos on a Special Forces training exercise.

The five-man team of Norwegian Marine Jaeger commandos who made up Red Force headed for shore in an inflatable raft.

The scenario for this exercise called for the Red Force team to come in via Trondheim Fjord and pick up weapons at a cache in the forest, then carry out a mock assassination-and-sabotage mission near the medieval city of Trondheim. The weapons included 7.62 SVD sniper rifles favored by Soviet *Voyska Spetsial' nogo Naznacheiya*, the Soviet Special Forces troops known as Spetsnaz.

The Spetsnaz commandos were such a well-kept secret even in the Eastern bloc that most of their own comrades weren't aware of the existence of the elite troops, unless they happened to see one of their combat brigades in action.

Their training often included dry-run missions inside the borders of other sovereign countries, particularly in Scandinavia.

The fjords provided a favorite means of entry. Soviet commandos came in via minisubs, or more overtly, through "pleasure" yachts or freighters that left a few commandos behind in their wake.

The Trondheim exercise called for Red Force, in the role of Spetsnaz troops, to mimic the operations Soviet commandos routinely called out on Swedish and Norwegian soil and throughout Western Europe.

According to the scenario, Blue Force had been tipped off about the impending infiltration by one of the Norwegian surveillance agencies.

And so Blue Force had waited—not touching the cache in case it was booby-trapped or meant to signal the invaders.

The goal of the counterterrorist Blue Force was to catch the invaders red-handed, and if possible, take at least one of the commandos alive.

While waiting for the enemy to come by water, however, the Blue Force overlooked a much more hostile force approaching through the woods.

THE SPEAR that killed Marine Jaeger commando Johannes Krosett was nearly a thousand years old.

In its first incarnation the leaf-shaped spearhead belonged to a member of the Varangian Guard, Viking mercenaries who served in Constantinople before returning to Norway and putting their leader, Harald, on the throne.

In its second incarnation the spear also belonged to a member of the Varangian Guard. Nils Hendrik was a modern Viking mercenary who also wanted to put his leader,

Mangus Koll, on the figurative throne of power. The steel spearhead had been restored, runes were carved upon it, and it was fitted to a long wood staff.

Hendrik had carried the weapon in the woods for months, practicing until it seemed to be an extension of his long sinewy arm. He never went anywhere without the spear.

It had come from the private armory of Magnus Koll—from a collection the mercenary painstakingly gathered over the years. Most of the pain had belonged to the collectors of Viking artifacts Magnus had robbed.

Once again the spear was bathed in blood.

Johannes Krosett, a twenty-seven-year-old Norwegian counterterrorist, had little time to appreciate the spear's pedigree or craftmanship. All he knew was that something had ripped through his back as he crouched atop the banks of Trondheim Fjord on a training exercise that had suddenly gone live.

Perched like a troll among spindle-branched conifers and surrounding brush, the Norwegian Special Forces man had been almost invisible when the weapon hit him. It tore through the muscle and bone in his back with a violent thump, followed immediately by a ripping sound as the spearhead erupted from his chest.

Hendrik had thrown it with such force that the trauma of the spear thrust jerked Johannes Krosett to his feet, popping him up like a jack-in-the-box.

The Blue Force commando tumbled face first into the tall grass, his empty eyes looking out toward the cold blue waters of Trondheim Fjord, his head resting over the edge of the bank like a protruding statue.

The spear shaft stuck straight up, reminiscent of the flag of the Varangian Guards. But Johannes was only the first of the commando force to die in the sudden attack.

More unexpected intruders lurked in the woods—a cadre of armed men under the command of Nils Hendrik. Like him they were berserkers.

Every Viking chieftain had an inner guard of warriors called berserkers who worked themselves into ritual frenzy before going into battle. They functioned in the roles of assassins and shock troops and were highly feared adversaries.

The training exercise had now become a battle they'd lusted for, a very one-sided battle. Blue Force was ready to fight Red Force and not a group of berserkers screaming out of the black.

Spread out along the grassy ridge overlooking the fjord, the members of Blue Force were hit at exactly the same time by the rush of wild-eyed wraiths.

The need for silence had built up inside of the berserkers as they moved relentlessly through the forest, watching, waiting for the signal that would release them.

And when that sound—the explosion of the institute—finally came, the berserkers echoed it with their battle cries. They descended upon Blue Force like howling wolves with cold steel fangs.

Two more Jaegers were struck dead almost instantly, their eyes still trained on the serpentine stretch of water below them when all hell broke loose. First came the sound of the blast. It had erupted while they were looking for Red Force "enemies" in the fjord. In that moment of confusion they were rendered helpless and easily taken by the berserkers.

One of the commandos who'd been scanning the fjord in a prone position managed to twist onto his back just in time to see an apparition from the past bearing down on him.

The grim-faced berserker swung a razor-sharp battle-ax down toward him, scything at the commando's face like a free-swinging guillotine.

Raising his rifle like a club, the Jaeger commando deflected the ax with a clanking shriek of metal chopping into metal.

The rifle fell to the ground.

The berserker roared and raised the ax one more time.

Scrambling for his combat knife, the commando knew there was no escape, no retreat. Nor would there be any victory for the berserker axman. Even as the ax came down he snapped forward to meet it, at the same time plunging his knife blade into the man's chest and then yanking down through bone and muscle.

The ax head bit into his temple and blood colored his eyes, but it wasn't just his own. With an enlightened look of surprise, the berserker toppled forward, his blood pouring out of the path carved by the commando's knife.

Collapsing at the edge of the overlook, both commando and berserker tumbled down into the water below with heavy finality.

Two last commandos fully understood that they were under a bona fide attack.

Alerted by some barely registered clue or perhaps by their own subconscious as it whispered last rites to them, the remnants of the Blue Force commandos turned at the moment of impact. And they saw the berserkers of the Varangian Guard bearing down on them with a ferocity that had been strengthened by being spoken of in hushed thousand-year legends. Dormant and powerful forces appeared to have awakened and followed in their footsteps.

The Norwegian Jaeger unit had automatic weapons—but they were loaded with blanks. "Kills" were made with lasers attached to the rifle barrels that would hit sensor badges worn by both teams.

But instead of sensors to make them play dead when hit, the berserkers wore rune-marked amber medallions pledging their allegiance to the creator of runes and the power of chaos himself. Odin, the true god of war, the god of hanged men, sought baptism in blood.

The berserkers were his priests.

They swung long-handled battle-axes and razor-sharp swords to make their kills. Like their forerunners, they carried weapons wherever they went and always expected to use them.

The last Jaegers fell quickly to the expertly wielded weapons. The berserkers struck them down as easily as if they were chopping wood.

It was a flawless VG attack, patterned after the tactics of their ancestors. A quick, hard strike coming out of nowhere and then vanishing just as suddenly.

But there was one more action to do before they left the battlefield.

Nils Hendrik abandoned the tools of the past as he prepared for the most crucial part of the attack. He picked up an altogether modern weapon—an M-203 40 mm grenade launcher—that could penetrate light armored vehicles, or in this case, the lightly armored minds of the enemy.

He targeted the rescue vessel out in the fjord.

Hand-to-hand combat was over.

The chemical war was about to begin.

POWERED by two 185-horsepower diesels, the cutter turned toward the shore. The skipper of the search-and-rescue cutter and the three-man crew were prepared to act as observers during the training exercise. But now they had become participants, alerted by the distant explosion of Trondheim House and a warning flare that had been sent arcing in the sky by one of the Red Force commandos.

The comet tail of light signaled that the exercise was aborted and that authentic casualties had occurred.

The cutter probably would have reached some of the commandos in time if not for the grenade that thumped into the midship cockpit.

It went off like a hissing dragon, smoke and fumes billowing about the cutter in a man-made storm cloud seeded with chaos and madness.

Another grenade exploded, spraying cutter and crew with a brimstone of smoke and BZ gas.

Inhaled directly into the bloodstream, the BZ hallucinogen quickly wove dreams of panic, a panic accelerated by the sister compound simultaneously attacking both the heart and respiratory system.

Bursts of smoke and gas fell all around the cutter, drenching it in a steady mist of BZ.

The skipper went by instinct. The only thing on his mind was to save his crew and the commandos he'd brought into the fjord.

Unfortunately, in no time at all he was out of his mind, his heart racing and brain screaming as he tried to steer through a river full of hallucinations.

At first they were just wispy shapes, but once given life by his fevered psyche the hallucinations bloomed in hideous glory. Water spirits broke the surface of the fjord, growing like spouts.

Serpents hissed in the mist, their dragon heads balefully staring at the mortals who'd dared to venture into their domain.

And craziest of all, as the skipper was caught in a maelstrom of images, he thought he saw a horde of sword-wielding Vikings gathering at the shore.

THE RED FORCE Jaeger commandos were only fifty yards from shore when the exercise blew up in their faces. First they heard the sound of battle. Before they could fully react to the situation a rain of grenades thumped into the raft and the water around them.

The wet-suited commandos dove into the water, putting as much distance between themselves and the raft as possible. When they surfaced again, they stared up at the cliffs where the shrieking war cries and the screams of the dying had risen and fallen so quickly.

The echoes of the screams lingered like a bloody memory in the smoke-filled air that dispersed over the cold waters of Trondheim Fjord.

As the Red Force combat swimmers headed for shore, the bodies of Blue Force commandos were tossed over the edge of the ridge. Their lifeless husks made several loud splashes.

Then weapons sailed into the air, spinning end over end before sluicing into the fjord and dropping to the bottom.

The weapons were usually considered prizes, suitable booty for the victors, but this first engagement was special—the initial contact between the berserkers and the enemy had to be consecrated.

Both the dead and their weapons had been tossed into the fjord as offerings to the war god who had cloaked them so well in their first battle.

CHAPTER THREE

The white Lincoln limo glided north on the Baltimore-Washington Parkway at a soundless sixty miles an hour, heading toward Fort Meade, Maryland.

Tinted windows kept out the sunlight and armor plating prevented bullets from entering, though a long time had passed since anyone had shot at the occupant of the back seat of the Lincoln.

Outfitted with all the creature comforts a man could want, including telephone and television, the limo was perhaps the only sign of rank ever worn by the man who sat in the customized back seat.

Despite his massive size, Walker Jessup was an invisible man. He no longer held a military rank, and his intelligence background had been papered over by a string of jobs with overseas companies that could only be unraveled by Houdini.

And even if Houdini did manage to come back from the dead, he'd still need an army of accountants and ex-spooks to find one hint about who or what Jessup really was.

Jessup was known as the Fixer, a man who could get things done when all avenues seemed to be closed. One of the main reasons for this ability was his association with somebody who specialized in walking through those very same closed avenues. Nile Barrabas.

Colonel Nile Barrabas, ex-Special Forces, ex-military intelligence, was currently a soldier of fortune who fought on covert battlefields off limits to regular Western forces. Barrabas had a regular outfit of mercenaries working for him.

The SOBs, or Soldiers of Barrabas, all shared the same outlook, a strictly red-white-and-blue perspective.

The SOBs and his own innate skill at global gamesmanship were Jessup's ticket into some of the most fortified towers in the West, most notably the glass tower of the NSA in Fort Meade, Maryland.

Jessup's driver turned onto Savage Road, bringing the Fixer closer to the world's biggest secret, the National Security Agency. The NSA, often called Never Say Anything, dwarfed the CIA in size, scope and manpower, employing in one guise or another more than 100,000 people.

It was the ultimate repository of the intelligence community.

NSA listening posts were scattered around the world. NSA spy ships, reconnaissance planes and satellites scooped up data around the clock.

In the world of covert operations all roads led to Fort Meade. Intelligence was gathered and analyzed. And then, depending on the urgency of the information, it was acted upon.

Judging from the urgent summons that brought Walker Jessup to the agency, some very disturbing information had come into the Maryland house of glass.

He glanced out the tinted windows as he approached the headquarters. Electrified fences and barbed wire surrounded the complex and TV monitors scanned the grounds. As if there was something hidden inside, Jessup thought.

The dogs who now and then came into view were not named Spot or Fluffy. A biscuit or a juicy steak would not make them your friend, though perhaps an arm and a leg would.

"Here we are," Jessup's driver said. "Emerald City."

Jessup laughed. It was the only thing his driver had said since they had left his Wisconsin Avenue town house in Georgetown.

And in a way he was right, Jessup thought. Entering the huge complex built by the NSA was more than a bit like going to Oz.

"CZAR NICHOLAS" himself appeared in the glassed-in reception area to verify that Walker Jessup was indeed a welcome and expected guest of the NSA.

With his neatly trimmed brown beard and his Ivy League suit, he looked more like a tweedy college professor than a man second in power only to DIRNSA, the Director of the NSA. Teddy Nicholas was a graduate of the old school. He'd served in the Navy, in intelligence, and now rode herd over security for the largest intelligence agency in the Western hemisphere.

He'd picked up the Czar nickname because of his intense knowledge of Russia and his ability to speak the language like a native. This ability was demonstrated during an embassy affair when an eminent drunk from Capitol Hill was badgering the Russian attaché about religious persecution—always a good vote getter if it received press coverage. He hammered on and on about an obscure religious sect that had been driven underground.

Because of the senator's slurred words, the Russian didn't quite understand what he was talking about.

Nicholas leaned over and spoke softly into the attaché's ear, naming the obscure sect in Russian. He then went on to discourse on a subject that many a Russian had no knowledge of—the "People of God" sect referred to as the Khlysty, some of whom found salvation through self-flagellation.

The attaché nodded and calmly deflected the argument of the senator, who by then had already forgotten what the conversation was about.

It was just a simple moment, but Nicholas's command of the language and his encyclopedic knowledge hadn't gone unnoticed. The Russian realized that Nicholas was a man who took the dictum "Know they enemy" to heart.

The nickname Czar Nicholas stuck, but not only because of his command of Russian. Czar was also an appropriate title for the way Teddy did business. Very dignified. Very calm. And very single-minded. In a subtle but relentless manner, Nicholas would literally move mountains to get a job done, especially if that mountain was in the way of one of his listening posts.

After seeing that Jessup was equipped with the proper clearance badge, Czar Nicholas led him into the inner corridors of the NSA.

Although the traffic of NSA staffers in the corridors seemed on a par with that of any large company, there was a definite air of secrecy about them.

Different corridors required different levels of clearance and there were always guards on hand to make sure no one went where they weren't supposed to. Knowledge was a dangerous thing in the NSA, especially if you overstepped your "need to know."

But there were plenty of open-access areas. NSA headquarters could function as a self-contained unit, complete with stores, a bank, restaurants, hospital wards and, most conveniently, a travel agency or two.

Then there were the places few people saw—the offices on the ninth floor. Known as Mahagony Row, these offices were where NSA chiefs oversaw the empire that eavesdropping built.

The Czar ushered Jessup into his office and closed the door behind them.

At first glance the office had a spare and military appearance, but after looking around for a while visitors saw a very solid library. Unlike many other offices, the books hadn't been chosen because of their color or gold-trimmed bindings.

Technical treatises sat side by side with first editions of *The Journal of Albion Moonlight*, *Cannery Row*, and not forgetting the Russians, *Life and Fate*.

These books weren't part of the furniture: these books were read, as were the voluminous coded and condensed intelligence reports that were arrayed across the Czar's desk and shimmered from the computer monitor.

And what most visitors noticed were the brightly colored video game diskettes. *Conspiracy!*, which featured a war between alien and human intelligence agencies, was leaning against the computer.

It was possible to picture the Czar sitting here late at night after some emergency session, bathed in the glow of the monitor, calmly chasing alien agents through an on-screen maze, and perhaps speaking in their own language as though he were a native.

Czar Nicholas was human. He was approachable. People liked him. Even people whom he got rid of liked him, sometimes calling upon him to help find out who got them sacked in the first place. He also had a first-rate mind, both militarily and intellectually, which was why he occupied space in the ninth floor of the glass tower.

"You're looking well," Nicholas said.

"Don't sound so surprised," Jessup said, settling into a wide-cushioned settee across from the Czar. "It's part of my new regimen." As if he couldn't believe he was saying it, Jessup spoke with a reverential tone as he uttered a word previously unknown to him. "Diet." He paused, then, as if he were still reciting a sacred litany, he added yet another strange word. "Workout. You know, the usual."

"Wonderful," Nicholas said. "How's it going?"

Jessup smiled, thinking of the physical-conditioning expert he hired to outfit his town house with the latest hi-tech exercise equipment. "I've got every workout machine known to man installed. Now all I gotta do is figure out how to work them."

The Czar laughed.

He kept Jessup on a personal level for a while, making the small talk that came easily to two men who had gone to school together—the old-boy school of covert operations.

Except for their recent operations, they had never actually served together at the same time, but they recognized the kindred traits in each other. They were brothers under the skin, and though Jessup's excess yardage of that skin made him look like the "before" picture to the lean Czar's "after," there was no doubt about their affinity. They could do business together, both of them following the unwritten rules of their trade.

When a comfortable amount of time had passed, the Czar steered the conversation to the reason Jessup had been summoned to Fort Meade.

The invitation hadn't been earned by the charms of his personal company. It was for his *company*, the globe-trotting mercenaries who worked for him.

Nicholas couldn't have cared less about the offices in downtown Washington, D.C., on Pennsylvania Avenue near the DOD building, or the corporate suites that gave Jessup safe harbor throughout Europe. The Czar wanted him for only one reason.

Trust.

The Czar knew that if the job seemed impossible, Jessup's men would find a way to change the parameters of the mission until it was possible.

There were a lot of covert groups in the business, but not all of them could be trusted, and few of them lasted long given the nature of their work.

There were the cowboy operations, run by swaggering mercs who would blow a whole operation with a few drunken words to a bar girl—or blow away their own guys.

And there were the affiliates, security companies that appeared to be private intelligence entities for hire. They might actually carry out their assignment, but their real raison d'être was to infiltrate the companies or cabals that hired them and then pass on secrets to their real employers.

There were too many wild cards and too few aces out there. When you had aces like the SOBs, you played them.

The SOBs had reached perfection over the years. They lost many a good man in the process but always managed to walk away from the battlefield a winner. In many of those cases, winning meant walking away in one piece.

That kind of special-operations capability didn't depend on offices and salesmen and public relations, or on the availability of fancy hardware. It wasn't the caliber of the weapons that counted—it was the caliber of men.

And Czar Nicholas needed the highest caliber of men this time around.

"The reason you're here, pal," Nicholas explained, "is quite simple."

Having suckered many a man himself with that same pitch, Jessup leaned forward, blinders off. "And what's that?"

The Czar looked thoughtful for a moment, tapping the scarred cleft of his chin where his beard didn't grow. "Norway is at war," he said.

Jessup stared at Nicholas, looking for a sign that he'd just heard a joke. But the man's face stayed perfectly calm. It wasn't one of his pranks. "I like to think it's my business to know what's going on," Jessup said. "But dammit, it's news to me if Norway's at war. With whom?"

"With itself."

Jessup sat back, his broad expanse causing the leather cushion to wheeze in agony. He raised his hands in a help-less gesture. "Like the schizophrenic said—I'm not the problem, I'm the problem." When he saw that the Czar had kept a straight face, he said, "So who's going to win this war?"

"You are," the Czar said. "You and the SOBs."

He then took Jessup step by step through the series of "accidents" that had thrown a panic into the Norwegian Security Service.

"First came an attack on a chemical-warfare research facility near Trondheim. A facility which technically isn't supposed to exist." Nicholas then proceeded to explain Norway's position that, according to their own charter, no nuclear or chemical weapons would be kept inside Norway, nor would any foreign troops be allowed to be based there—unless Norway was threatened.

The key word was *threatened*, according to Nicholas. He then elaborated.

Russia had turned the entire Kola Peninsula into a veritable launching base for any conflict up to and including World War III, so there was ample reason to consider their buildup a threat. At the same time Norway had intentionally kept its major bases far removed from the Russian border, hoping to avoid an arms race that no one could win.

But Russia nevertheless conducted a one-man arms race, continuing to build up the Kola Peninsula, making Murmansk the largest military base in the world. In addition, Russian troops had been conducting exercises that revealed their intention to use chemical warfare against northern Norway as a prelude to taking over enough Norwegian soil to provide a buffer for the Kola Peninsula.

Finally Norway took steps to counter the threat. They received some stocks of chemical munitions from the United States, then put their own scientists to work at finding a way to counter newer generations of chemical agents.

At this point, the Czar said, "Let me add some more local color for you, before we continue."

Jessup smiled. He knew that Nicholas's famous crash course in the way of the world had just begun. The NSA man brought Jessup up-to-date on some additional chemical warfare developments that seemed to pertain to the Norwegian situation.

Contrary to the "never say anything" attitude that prevailed at the Fort Meade headquarters, Nicholas was of the opinion that excess knowledge could be a good thing. Overkill in background just might prevent someone from getting killed in the field.

He filled Jessup in on further complexities of the situation in Norway.

After taking a cold, hard look at the top-heavy presence of the Russians on their northeastern border, the Norwegian government concluded it would be suicidal not to take some precautions.

Russian missiles grew like trees in the forests of the Kola Peninsula with six thousand warheads branching out toward Norway. And one of the most common birds in the skies was the Backfire Bomber. Along with the jet interceptors that routinely screamed toward Norwegian airspace, the supersonic bombers were a steady reminder that Norway's future wouldn't be decided by Norway if the Russians had their way.

Russia's steady encroachment on the strategic Arctic islands of Svalbard was another potential flash point. The islands came under the sovereignty of Norway but by treaty Russia was allowed to mine them. And though the Soviets liked to refer to the thousands of Russians working on the islands as miners, for all the credibility they had, they might as well have called them ballerinas. The Norwegians believed the "workers" were there simply to seize the islands if conflict ever broke out.

With huge Soviet munitions stocks and special brigades in the Kola Peninsula poised for an attack on Norway, the government had to take some action.

Provisions to support a U.S. Marine landing were set aside in special areas of the country. Underground bunkers and abandoned tunnels were stocked with sufficient ordnance for the defence of the realm.

The airfields at Trondheim, Bergen, Rygge and other strategic bases could now handle increasingly sophisticated attack and reconnaissance aircraft.

Even while Norway stepped up its own surveillance capacity, it increased its joint projects with NSA and NATO. In some of the northernmost parts of Norway, the main employer in some towns was the NSA.

Walker Jessup consumed the intelligence provided by the Czar with the same appetite he usually displayed for fine meals. Although his massive frame was currently suffering under the temporary aberration known as a diet, his mental needs took the edge off his physical hunger. Jessup was only somewhat familiar with Norway's role in monitoring military activity on the Kola Peninsula and tracking the movement of the Soviet Northern Fleet at Murmansk, and he was eager to know more.

The Fixer listened attentively as Nicholas described how Soviet vessels had to pass through the Norwegian Sea before they could get to the Atlantic. With hydrophones mining the ocean floor, the listening stations in northern Norway could track Soviet subs. Lockheed Orion sub-hunting planes also scoured the Arctic waters, dropping sonobuoys and scanning Soviet intelligence ships poorly disguised as fishing vessels.

The information the Czar had gathered inside the NSA glass tower was far more specific than anything Jessup could have come up with.

Documents originally classified as Top Secret, Secret and Confidential had been shared with the U.S. The pooled intelligence on Norway's progress in defensive chemical and conventional warfare painted an accurate picture for the Fixer.

And now the Czar wanted the Fixer's repairmen to step into that picture.

After digesting the information and probing the Czar over a few areas that were unclear, Walker Jessup pushed aside the briefing papers.

"I appreciate the info you've given me," he said. "But from what I can see so far this is an internal security matter. Somebody stole one of their chemistry sets. It's Norway's problem, not ours."

"So far, I'd agree with you," Nicholas said, leaning back in his chair. "But now we've got to deal with something that officially hasn't happened. Although the 'accident' at Trondheim House made it into the papers, there was no mention of the bullets found in some of the bodies. The complex was described as a research clinic with no mention of chemical weapons."

Jessup nodded. "The Norwegians contained it."

"Yes," Nicholas said. "At first. But the attack on the chemical site was timed to coincide with a training exercise conducted by a Norwegian counterterrorist unit near Trondheim. The land-based team was killed to the last man in hand-to-hand fighting. With primitive weapons no less. Swords, axes, spears."

Nicholas silently clapped his hands together. Then he looked down at his locked palms and opened them slowly, as if they were revealing the secrets of the future. "If that's not crazy enough," he continued, "a team of combat swimmers were hit with a modern weapon. Grenades struck both the cutter and the raft they came in on. They were gas grenades. Not poison, but definitely incapacitating."

"Like the chemicals in the inventory at Trondheim House," Jessup said, putting the scenario together.

"Right," Nicholas agreed. "But the thing is, Trondheim House didn't have any such grenades at all."

Jessup exhaled slowly. He readjusted his bulk and found himself thinking of a long lost meal for a moment, but then he pushed the thought aside.

Nicholas stood up and walked around his office, arms folded behind his back. As he neared his desk, he stroked his beard, assuming the thoughtful persona of a college professor querying one of his better students.

"What do you make of it so far, Walker?"

Veteran of many a covert war, Jessup figured out what would happen next. "One newspaper will receive a phone call about the 'accident,' hinting at dangerous research into chemical weapons. Another newspaper will receive a tip about a reckless war game that got out of hand, endangering the public with prohibited chemical weapons."

The Czar nodded. "Several papers have already been called with anonymous tips," he said. "So far they haven't been able to verify a thing, but that'll come in time. Reporters are the same everywhere. They don't stop until they think they've got the real story."

"Homicidal Heroes Run Amok," Jessup said, conjuring a headline he didn't want to see.

"It won't be quite as bad as that," Nicholas said. "On the whole, the Norwegian papers are more restrained than ours. But they'll still have a field day with this, especially the papers on the left. This could endanger the entire counterterrorism program. It can also jeopardize Norwegian research into weapons that will be used against them. And that's just for starters. Ten to one there's a shipload of surprises sailing our way. Whoever dreamed this up sure as hell knew what they were doing."

"Spetsnaz?" Jessup said. The Russian Special Forces teams certainly had the capability. But it didn't have the earmarks of their style.

"No," Nicholas said. "If Spetsnaz is involved, we think it's more a matter of convenience than intention. They didn't launch the operation, but if they can make hay out of it, they will."

Jessup raised an eyebrow. "Who else is capable of launching an operation on Norwegian soil?"

"Vikings," Nicholas said.

"Uh-huh," Jessup said. "And they came back from the dead just for this operation?"

"In a manner of speaking, yes."

Nicholas told him of the one enemy casualty who'd been recovered from the fjord along with the bodies of the Jaeger commandos. He'd been dressed in the manner of a Viking mercenary from a thousand years ago.

"I've heard of guys being frozen in the ice and coming back to life," Jessup said. "But not for a thousand years. Are you trying to tell me that this guy's been around for that long?"

Nicholas shook his head. "No. This Viking was born in the twentieth century."

"Good," Jessup said. "For a minute there I thought you were going to tell me these guys are immortal. The SOBs are good, but even they have their limits."

Nicholas laughed. "Despite his appearance and his incredible physical condition, the Viking who died in Trondheim Fjord had a very modern incarnation. A fingerprint trace showed that he was a mercenary, a good one, too. A native Norwegian, he was involved in some questionable ops but no more than most. At the moment the Norwegians are trying to reconstruct his movements for the past year or so in the hopes of finding out a bit about who his playmates were."

"I wish them the best of luck," Jessup said. "But I still don't see the angle that brings us in—"

"We've been attacked, too," Nicholas said.

"The NSA?"

"One of our listening posts near the Norwegian/Russian border."

"The same crew?"

"Oh, yes," Nicholas said. "Unmistakably our Viking friends."

"How do you know?"

"Simple," Nicholas said. "The NSA station was attacked with spears."

Jessup snorted with derision, picturing a horde of barbarians attacking a heavily fortified NSA complex. His shaking jowls uncomfortably reminded him that he had a long way to go before anyone could call him svelte.

"Don't laugh," Nicholas said. "The attack was successful. It nearly put our post out of action for good. As it is, a couple of the people who were manning the station are still in the hospital. And I'm talking about a mental hospital. From all appearances they used the same kind of BZ gas on the listening post as they did on the commandos in the fjord."

Instead of being a reckless charge against an NSA post nestled in the woods, the attack was meticulously planned and carried out.

A fusillade of spears sailed into the cordoned-off grounds of the post when the wind was strongest. The spears weren't the traditional thin lengths of wood capped with a spearhead. They were rocket-propelled spears with long and wide reinforced wooden shafts with a heavy metal point—an iron-age warhead that could pierce armor with the right velocity.

The only armor that had been pierced was the mental armor of the staffers working at the station.

As the spears sailed over the station, the attackers ignited canisters of gas, dropping an airburst of chemicals over the ground. After the initial panic, the staffers moved about the grounds in awkward biochem suits, looking for the perpetrators.

By then the Vikings were long gone. But they'd left behind their calling cards—several rune-carved spears.

"The point is," Nicholas said, "these insurgents, these Vikings—whatever you want to call them—are damned good. They knew about the existence of Trondheim House. They moved from the middle of the country to the north without being seen, and they took out some of the finest commandos the country had to offer.

"Something tells me they're just getting started. And I want them stopped. I want someone over there who can meet them on their own turf—fight them with their own weapons."

Jessup nodded.

The SOBs were on board once again.

He stayed in the office of Czar Nicholas a while longer, conducting their usual negotiations and identifying their assets and contacts within the Norwegian security services.

The SOBs would be hired for their standard fee. Each SOB would get a fee of one quarter of a million dollars. That included burial fees.

On paper, Jessup had brokered the services of an executive consulting firm that was going to deliver a position paper on Norway. In reality, that "firm" was going to deliver a knockout punch to the underground army gathering in the North.

In a way there was no subterfuge. Jessup was providing first-class executives for this operation.

And once they reached Norway, there would be a lot of executive action.

CHAPTER FOUR

Nile Barrabas was on top of the world.

Almost.

He was actually about six feet from the top of what had become his world for the past two hours, a grim-faced cliff in Ausable Chasm.

The glacier-carved trench in the Adirondack Mountains was known for its breathtaking and occasionally life-taking scenery. It ran for miles through the wood-studded mountains, capped by lodges, mountain villages and a scattering of hillbilly homes straight out of *Deliverance*.

The Ausable River that raced down the chasm sometimes looked black and clear, and sometimes it spewed churning white foam. Right now it looked like a silver ribbon winding through a high-altitude relief map.

Although Barrabas normally stood out wherever he went, at the moment he was just a speck on a massive sheet of rock—a speck that clung to the steep cornice by means of sweat and willpower.

Like most successful climbers, successful meaning those who were still alive, Barrabas had studied the crags and crevices for a considerable amount of time before actually making his way up the face of it. He'd trained long and hard to keep his body in the kind of shape mandated by SOB operations, so theoretically he could make the climb.

But no amount of preparation could make the last leg of the climb a safe bet.

He was hanging from an overhang of rock that jutted out like an eagle's claw. The talon of rock curled downward, a gargoyle's finger pointing out the direction likely to be taken by anyone foolish enough to try to scale it.

A chilly noose of wind coiled around Barrabas's neck before it skittered over the summit. It was followed by a much stronger gust that plucked at his body in an attempt to fling him off the rock and make him airborne.

He pressed his face to the rock, clinging with feet, hands and heart as the heavy wind cooled his sweat-soaked headband. His smooth-soled climbing shoes inched to a tiny fault in the rock, seeking a better haven to withstand the nudging of the wind.

Barrabas ignored the cold that whipped through his Army T-shirt. The chill was unwelcome but not totally unexpected for this time of day—and at this height.

He'd blacked his face because of the sun when he first began the climb. No sense in being blind as well as dumb. But the sun was weak now. And in a sense, so was Barrabas. He'd used up almost all of his reserves in the climb.

Although he wasn't the type who pondered metaphysical questions, Barrabas found himself thinking, Why am I here? as he looked up at the claw of rock. Above it there was nothing but gray sky and a dull sun, a cloudy epitaph to his climb.

It was bad enough that people tried to kill him when he was on assignment with the SOBs. It was worse when he tried to do the same thing himself.

In a way, that's who his enemy was this time. Not the spire of rock, not the hazardous climb that got him this far—but Nile Barrabas himself.

He had to face down the fear.

He'd felt the challenge ever since the first time he saw the ridge when he was exploring some of the secluded Adirondack property he'd bought.

At the time he thought a man would have to be crazy to climb that peak.

Now, months later, he knew his first impression had been right.

Of course, he had no way of knowing that until he took the steps that brought him here—steps that had literally crumbled beneath him, adding another shock of white to his hair in the process.

He'd been halfway up the cliff when a six-inch-wide ledge, a veritable highway to a climber, crumbled under his feet. The ledge fell away from the jaw of the cliff like an ancient cracked tooth and Barrabas fell with it, until the safety rope looped into the wedge.

Dangling like a pendulum, he swung left to right in a shrinking arc that gave him a bird's-eye view of the chasm below. It was like moving in slow motion, every image coming into focus, slowly and clearly, even his shadow as it crept across the rock.

He hadn't panicked, although he did have a sudden reverence for the ropes he'd contemplated leaving behind.

Once the rope stopped moving, he caught his breath and began the climb again, moving slowly until he got to the top below the claw of granite.

The wind stopped.

It was time.

To get over the precipice, Barrabas had to be perfectly balanced. And with the carabiners, ropes, hammers and hooks hanging from his nylon-webbed shoulder sling, he was as balanced as the U.S. budget.

He unsnapped the sling.

The carabiners dropped free, sailing down into the chasm like weighted snakes, bouncing off rocks, then finally, silently, dropping into the river.

Barrabas could have hooked the carabiners in the rock in case he decided to climb down the face instead of trying to make it over the top.

But Barrabas wasn't coming this way again.

He was going over the top.

He exhaled and slowly stretched out his right hand, then his left, testing each grip before he moved. He had a solid grip around the spike-shaped rock, but there was no further grip. This was it.

Barrabas hung on to the crevice with all of his concentration embedded in his bloodied brawny fingers, wedding them to the rock.

He then performed the only maneuver that could get him to the summit, a maneuver he had practiced in his head a hundred times.

He pushed his legs slowly free from the rock. He hung suspended from the overhang by the strength of his hands. Then he did a slow-motion leg lift, his body almost in a jackknife position.

He now rocked from left to right.

The motion picked up speed in an infinitesimal arc. Barrabas rocked farther, his lower body swinging out like a second hand on a watch counting down to oblivion.

When his body was swinging fast enough, Nile Barrabas let go. He sailed into the air, hundreds of feet above the waiting chasm. His legs curled up and over the saw-toothed summit like those of an acrobat dismounting a gymnasium horse. Barrabas's upper body thumped onto hard, flat rock. The jarring impact felt as soft as falling into a bed full of feathers.

He'd done it.

Nile Barrabas had defeated his most impossible enemy— Nile Barrabas.

He lay there on his back, chest heaving, heart pounding as he looked up at the heavens he'd come so close to visiting.

The gray sky seemed a dozen shades whiter now, and the clouds were no longer floating epitaphs heralding the airborne funeral procession of Nile Barrabas. Now they were more like smoke signals announcing his triumph.

Nile Barrabas felt alive.

True, he'd almost killed himself to feel this way, but it had been a while since he'd butted heads with fate.

He stayed flat on his back, arms stretched over his head while he closed his eyes and caught his breath. The stress had ceased, allowing his body to register the cuts and scrapes where the rock had bit into his skin. The aches and the stretched muscles suddenly announced themselves now that Barrabas wasn't calling upon every ounce of energy to save his body. But Barrabas took note of it with pleasure.

He'd been on R & R so long that it was starting to get stressful—until today's climb burned out the pressure inside of him.

There would be no more climbs for a while.

Still unmoving, Barrabas savored the incredible solitude of the granite summit, far removed from the hue and cry—until a soft female voice broke the silence.

"Why don't you just walk up here like everybody else?"

Barrabas tilted his head back and opened his eyes, looking up at the plaid-shirted presence of Hilary Diamond. The tails of her shirt were knotted in front, providing a glimpse of smooth flesh.

"I might get lost on the trail," he said. There were easier ways up to the top of the ridge. Several trails and wide mountain roads led up to the summit. "Besides, I needed a little adventure."

"If you're looking for adventure," the auburn-haired woman said, "I can think of something a lot more interesting to climb."

Barrabas lunged forward and grabbed her ankles. "Careful," he said. "Or I just might take you up on that." His eyes scanned her statuesque full-figured frame, until he saw the light in her own gaze. "What equipment would I need to make that climb?"

"I think you're outfitted quite well," she said, her voice laden with the flirtation the two of them had shared for so long now.

Her smile made him glad that his mountain retreat wasn't all that secluded after all. A man could only be alone with nature for so long. It wasn't natural. A woman like Hilary made the idea of communing with nature a hell of a lot more attractive.

The first time he saw her she reminded him of a Daisy Mae in high heels. She was a Manhattan refugee who'd come up north to run Diamond Lodge, one of the last great camps in the Adirondacks, the kind of hideaway favored by Rockefellers, Posts, and in the recent past, Nile Barrabas.

He'd stayed at the lodge, fell totally in love with the area and perhaps a little in love with Hilary. Then he'd purchased a more down-to-earth hand-hewn log cabin perched close to the edge of the chasm. It had all the amenities a man could want, except for a phone.

But that was no great hardship, especially when a woman like Hilary Diamond agreed to forward any of the messages that came into her lodge down the road.

And though she had obviously come here with some news for Barrabas, there was another kind of message in her brown eyes. She flicked her fingers through her hair, winding several brown strands around them. Her hair curled inward in the sixties fashion, the post-beehive, all-natural love child look.

Of course, back in the sixties she was taking prep-school proms by storm, while Barrabas was storming bamboo palisades in Vietnam, getting his baptism in blood.

He felt her muscles tense as his hands slid slowly under the hem of her blue jeans and up her calves.

Although she was electrified by the touch, she tried to gloss it over. Their flirtations had never passed to the next stage. Even with just what little she knew of him she sensed there were a lot of uncharted areas to Nile Barrabas, areas she was a bit afraid to explore.

His shock of white hair had nothing to do with age and everything to do with travel. He'd been a tourist in places where average people didn't dare to go.

It was obvious from in the way he walked, in his military bearing and in the cold steely gaze she felt settle upon her now and then.

A certain kind of unspoken knowledge passed between them, hidden by words that didn't quite cover the attraction. But there was something that kept them apart, a barrier that he wasn't ready to give up yet.

Perhaps it was a woman somewhere.

Perhaps it was a war.

Barrabas had always sensed the hesitancy that tended to tamper down the desire in her, and so he'd never taken her to the edge she was leaning toward. He was ready for her, but he was leaving it up to her to decide when and if *she* was ready.

Hilary gently shook her head back and forth, softly scolding him. "Aren't you supposed to have a partner with you on these climbs?"

"Yes," Barrabas said.

"And ropes and ice picks and St. Bernards with barrels of whiskey hanging from their collars?"

"It might help."

"Nile, there are rules you're supposed to follow when you're risking that—" she cleared her throat and gazed at his prone form "—that slightly in-shape body of yours."

"Play by the rules, you get knocked out of the game."

"Uh-huh," she said. "Well, Nile Barrabas, whatever they may be, I think you've played some pretty interesting games in your time... Ouch."

Barrabas gripped her calves as he arched his back, then snapped his legs out and jumped to his feet and turned to face her.

He was half a head taller than her, and a world away. "You didn't come up here to talk about games," he said.

She laughed, a throaty and lighthearted laugh that was full of promise.

"Not entirely," she admitted. "There was a phone call for you down at the lodge."

Barrabas nodded his head. He knew he would not have to seek out death sports for a while. Death would seek him. No one else would call him here but Walker Jessup.

"He sounded like a substantial man," she said.

"*Substantial* describes him well. What did he say?"

"Something about a party you were invited to. And he said you'd know what he was talking about."

"Yes," Barrabas said. "But can you recall his exact words?"

Jessup was a master of double-talk, always using pet phrases to clue Barrabas in as to what was really going on behind the innocent facade of conversation.

Hilary nodded. "He said to tell you that you were invited to a class reunion. A full-dress affair."

Barrabas exhaled a gust of pent-up air, feeling like he'd been holding his breath for weeks.

The SOBs would be reuniting again. "Full dress" meant that it was a sanctioned military operation. Wherever it was they were going, the powers that be wanted them there.

Often when the SOBs went into action, it was right in the middle of an undeclared war and ended up with both "undeclared" sides shooting at them.

This time only one side would be gunning for them.

"You're going away, aren't you?" Hilary said.

"Yeah," Barrabas said.

"You coming back?"

"Sure." He smiled. "If I have a say in it."

Hilary folded her arms in front of her, trying to gauge the hard gaze of the man in the torn Army T-shirt. "It's going to be a while, isn't it?"

"Yeah, it is," Barrabas said. "Maybe you should help me pack." He nodded toward the thick spires of pine that marched up the steep incline to his distant cabin.

"Maybe I'd better," Hilary agreed.

She took the hand he offered as he guided her to the private road that led to the private life of Nile Barrabas.

CHAPTER FIVE

Majorca was sinking. And Lee Hatton didn't intend to go down with it.

The premiere playground of Spain's Balearic Islands was getting too crowded for her. Convinced that sooner or later the weight of tourists and jet-setters would plunge Majorca to the ocean bottom, she was looking for another island paradise to escape to whenever Majorca seemed too confining.

She'd found it on Lanzarote, the closest of Spain's Canary Islands off the west coast of Morocco.

The place offered everything she needed. The unspoiled beaches, palm trees, warm sirocco winds and volcanic moonscapes made it an intriguing haven.

With the right man, it would be the ideal place to find herself stranded.

Unfortunately, the right man hadn't landed yet.

Enthroned in her café chair, a short-haired Cleopatra in sunglasses, Lee Hatton had already fended off several would-be Mark Antonys since she'd arrived at the oceanside hotel a short drive north of Arrecife.

Now she had another potential suitor on her hands. Unfortunately she had invited this one herself. She needed someone to handle her rather complicated finances on Majorca and Lanzarote, and despite his ermine approach Elisio was the best man for the job.

The hot afternoon sun and several glasses of wine had convinced Elisio, the Madrid-born financial manager and year-round resident of Lanzarote, that it was his duty to see to her physical as well as her fiscal well-being.

"You are such a stunning woman," Elisio said, hovering behind Lee Hatton's chair to personally pour another glass of wine for her.

Naturally he took the opportunity to peer down the bodice of her white sundress, perhaps seeing if there were any bathing-suit lines spoiling her overall tan.

"Keep it up," she said, "and you'll find out just how stunning I can be."

He laughed, thinking he was getting to her at last.

Lee Hatton, combat medic, SOB, and current object of Elisio's affection, was thinking that a short backfist to his aquiline nose would sufficiently blacken the eyes whose avid gaze traveled uninvited down her cleavage.

But that wouldn't do. She wanted to fit in with the natives. It would be unseemly to deck him in public. The right moment would come sooner or later, she thought. It always did.

He beamed at her as he sat back down, unaware of the chilly gaze shielded by her dark sunglasses.

"Back to business," she said.

Elisio shrugged and smiled. Courting a deal was as much of a thrill for him as courting a beautiful woman. If that was what she wanted, then he would oblige.

"Now," he said. "About the properties you're interested in, I think we can find a way to..."

As the financial wizard spoke, Lee drifted into a semitrance state, only half listening to the figures and percentages that poured so fluidly from his tongue, as if there was a numbers-crunching spreadsheet program embedded in the circuitry of his brain.

Money bored her. Spending it didn't.

But the most important part about her money was the way it was earned.

The covert side of Lee Hatton was the side that excited her the most. This life, this pleasant but balmy life on the islands, was a beachcomber's dream. But it wasn't her only dream. After a while she had to wake up and get back to work—the solitary work that only the SOBs provided.

Despite the ease with which the raven-haired woman moved through the high echelons of society, Lee Hatton was worlds apart from the landed gentry.

She belonged to a different society entirely—the killing kind, a warrior society that had its own rules and its own way of life. It was a society that had accepted her because she was one of them.

Lee had been groomed for the life-style. Her values, her visions, were shared by the SOBs and so they were her buddies, her comrades-in-arms.

"And there we are," Elisio said. "Simple as that." He snapped his fingers, announcing the completion of his mental gymnastics.

There was a dreamy look in his eyes as if he'd just recited a love sonnet to her, pouring out his heart and soul to her. And in a way he had. Elisio's world was governed by endless figures and the odd but eternal romance of the deal.

Her world was governed by the need for action. For weeks now there had been an insistent voice in her mind, calling out almost like a privately chanted prayer for the kind of action that demanded the most from her.

"And now that we have met the challenge, we have to celebrate," Elisio said, sounding like a twentieth-century conquistador who'd rescued his fair damsel.

"I thought that's what we were doing," she said.

He shook his head sadly. "Ah, there is so much you have to learn, so much I have to teach you."

Lee lifted her shades and raised her eyebrows, staring at Elisio. He was an attractive man, and to some women he would make quite a catch.

But to Lee Hatton he was too small to keep, another one caught inadvertently in her net. Sorry, Elisio, she thought. I've got to throw you back.

While she was figuring out the politest way to extricate herself from Elisio's wine-laden pursuit, she saw a waiter in crisp whites carrying a phone toward their table.

Elisio faced the approaching phone as though it was an old friend who couldn't be ignored. He nodded to Lee and gestured apologetically with his manicured hands. "Please excuse me," he said. He lifted the receiver before the surprised waiter even had a chance to set the phone onto the table.

"Hello," Elisio said in a slightly bothered tone of voice.

His reserved expression was suddenly shattered by whoever had spoken to him on the other end of the line. With his face turning red, he handed the phone over to Lee. "It's for you."

Conditioned not to notice such gaffes, the waiter vanished from their table.

The stunned look on Elisio's face almost made up for the boorishness he'd displayed. She managed to contain her laughter as she cradled the phone. "Hello," she said. "This is Lee Hatton."

The unmistakable voice of Nile Barrabas said three magic words. "I need you."

"It's nice to be needed," Lee said.

"Are you available?"

Lee glanced at her companion. He was tanned and had a sleek look acquired by frequenting gymnasiums, but his muscles were soft. "To the right man I am."

"Good," Barrabas said. "If you're ready to make a house call, something's come up that needs your diagnosis."

"Who's the patient?" Lee asked.

"I'll tell you in Copenhagen," Barrabas said, giving her the name of a hotel in the Danish capital where the SOBs would rendezvous before moving into Norway.

"Then I'll see you there," she said.

She hung up the phone.

"This man is close to you?" Elisio said. "An old friend?"

"Close, yes. Old, no." Lee summoned the waiter for the check, then glanced at Elisio. "Look," she said, "I've got to go. Put everything we discussed down on paper, meet me here at six, and I'll sign off before I leave."

Elisio noticed the change in her manner. Gone was the idle-rich pretense. In its place was a much more vibrant woman, a commanding woman who was in truth far beyond his reach.

Elisio raised his glass in toast. "To a safe trip," he said.

Lee graciously accepted the toast, although she had no doubt that the trip would be safe. It was after she got there that the danger would start.

LIAM O'TOOLE dwarfed the wooden bar stool in the center of the stage.

Rather than sit on it like everyone else had, the red-bearded Irishman lifted his right leg and planted his foot on top of the stool.

He waved a sheaf of papers in front of him, maneuvering them under the single spotlight on the Club Exo stage. Either the lone spot was all the club owners could afford, or they thought it suited the downbeat boho ambience.

When the bar bands played the club on weekends, usually only the lead singer or guitarist was visible. The rest of the band stayed in the dim background, their splits, sneers and pogo jumps unseen and unsung.

But the light seemed just right tonight. It was Poetry Night, the regular midweek wordfest that featured proven draws like Mona Magnum—who billed herself as the "Bleached-blond, bleached-brained anti-poet," who used to dance at the club when it was an exotics place.

The club also featured relative unknowns like Liam O'Toole, who had stumbled into the bar one night weeks ago by accident and found himself right at home in this midtown maelstrom.

Tonight was his debut at the Manhattan club.

"Louder!" shouted a wise-ass skinhead in leathers. "We can't hear you." The poetry lover emphasized every word he spoke with a sharp rap of his half-filled beer bottle on the stained black café table.

"I haven't started yet," Liam said in a soft low-key voice. "That was a dramatic pause."

"Fuck the pause," suggested Mona Magnum, who'd already done her bit for the night. "Hit Fast Forward and get it over with."

Liam studied the cute young leather-clad part-time dominatrix.

She had mascara-splattered raccoon eyes and brightly rouged cheeks. The Irishman speculated that her blond rooster spikes had been coiffed either by sticking her tongue into an electric socket or by a man with a grudge against women. Beneath the filmy noire that coated her, she was an attractive woman.

"First let me dedicate this one to you," he said.

Mona shrugged and despite her demon-may-care attitude, her glossy black lipstick formed the glint of a smile.

"It's a poem about ghosts," Liam said, banishing the hesitant smile.

Instead, she nodded, a queen to her court jester. Mona was the supreme arbiter of taste in Club Exo.

"This one is called 'Agincourt Alley.' "

Liam had been weaving the ballad for months now, sewing it together in his dreams.

"The archers are among us still," he shouted, his voice bellowing out a warning. Several of the listeners in the front row stepped back as if they had been slapped. Good, he thought. He had them. Maybe they were scared. Maybe they were interested. Either way he wasn't going to let go.

He continued reading the poem, alternating between a soothing, almost reverent tone for one line and a violent shout for the next.

The poem was about a medieval army of British bowmen at Agincourt who slew five times their number when the French attacked the invaders with all of their nobles. After slaying the attackers, the archers were ordered to shoot and bludgeon all the prisoners. They did, and they kept on marching across France.

Long after their deaths they kept on marching in ghostly ranks. They fought in battle after battle, year after year, continuing to march long after death, setting up their order of battle.

Their ghostly ranks were seen advancing upon the Germans in Belgium at the Battle of Mons.

They were seen marching over the French countryside, pursuing foes who'd long fled the field.

The archers were doomed to come back again and again, fighting in every battle.

Liam wrote the poem after he'd visited the battle sites at Agincourt and Mons, where he'd sensed them himself, sensed that there were certain men who were fated to fight unending battles.

Men like Liam O'Toole.

Liam caught his breath as "Agincourt Alley" built to the climax.

By now nearly everyone in the audience realized that the man delivering the poem was one of the bowmen, that he too was doomed to haunt battlefields forever.

"Look through my eyes," he said softly, "and see . . .

"The archers are still among us."

The audience jumped back once more, retreating from the steady gaze of the battlefield bard.

Liam scanned the room.

There was a loud stillness in Club Exo.

Drunks who'd wandered in earlier in the evening and were wondering what he was raving about, nodded their heads just the same.

A young couple in love, who looked like they got their street gear from a Sid and Nancy catalog, held each other's black-gloved hands over the sticky tabletops.

Blank faces, intrigued faces, skeptical faces stared at him.

Liam O'Toole stood before his motley judges.

Mona Mangum jumped to her feet. "Nice shooting!" she crowed, clenching her hands in fists and waving them over her head like an underworld cheerleader.

Then came the applause. It was a smattering at first, but then it built into a loud chaotic wave.

It was followed by some catcalls and loud dissent.

"Fascist Neanderthal!"

"Warhog!"

Liam O'Toole bowed.

He wondered if he should quit now—while they loved him and hated him in the right ratio. He didn't want everyone to go for his stuff. Perhaps just a talent scout or two—if there were still any left who actually went out to hear the poetry in its natural lair.

Whenever he read his material, like any other poet, Liam always scanned the audience for that face that one day would be there.

The face of the muse herself.

The muse of Club Exo was a small press publisher who had discovered Mona Magnum right here in this downbeat club. Although at first he thought Mona could have just as easily been discovered under a rock, after hearing one of her readings, Liam knew she was the genuine article.

Now if only Liam O'Toole, aspiring poet, awe-inspiring SOB, could earn that same stamp of legitimacy.

As he read his second poem, Liam scanned the audience for the muse who held that license.

She was frequently in attendance at Poetry Night, although in her subtle manner she usually slipped into a seat at one of the back tables.

Toward the end of his next poem he saw her, nursing a glass of Club Exo's high-priced cheap wine.

She was hard not to miss, fulfilling nearly all of the requirements he'd expected in a muse. She was a round-hipped, silken-haired, poet-loving siren in a jet-black sweater. And she was known for issuing widely read and respected poetry anthologies, rather than stillborn vanity-press tomes read by no one but the poets who had to pay huge fees to appear inside their suspect covers.

Subconsciously Liam found himself turning toward her, projecting in her direction. But even after he realized what he was doing, he kept his gaze fixed on her. For the moment, she was his audience.

She would lift Liam O'Toole from the horde of would-be poets with their addled odes, the five-and-dime rhymers who sat down on the spur of the moment and dashed out some doggerel and considered themselves masters of the craft.

It took time to master the craft and even then there was no guarantee. Real poets went on and on, stalking their art with a hunter's patience until it could be caught, tamed and exhibited to the public.

But, judging from the gaze meeting his from the back of the club, his exhibition was due for a quick closing.

The muse looked bored.

Liam O'Toole, ex-Army captain, scarred by booze, war and wrecked romances on several continents, shuddered inwardly.

He'd always fought for the chance to be recognized and now it was here at least. What if rather than being recognized, his disguise was unmasked tonight? That he wasn't a poet, but a poseur?

Maybe despite the temporary adulation from the Club Exo crowd after his first poem, Liam wasn't one of the real ones. Maybe he was just another deluded wordspinner.

Perhaps the crowd was just taking their cue from Mona Magnum, whose whims and fancies were as legendary as her borderline X-rated performances in this very hall.

No! he thought. It was impossible.

Liam believed in himself even if nobody else did. Whether they chose to be enlightened by his art or stay living in the dark ages of the soul was up to them.

Liam finished his second poem, and it received a lukewarm response.

He felt adrift now, gripped only tenuously by the last poem he planned to read.

"This one is called 'The Nite Rites of Deacon Bretwald,'" Liam announced. "It's about a place full of the troubles."

Waiting until they had settled in quietly, he unleashed his poem in a howling cadence.

"God's got a gun in Ireland . . ."

Liam was off again, inhabiting the poem and possessed by it in turn, while he provided the audience with a glimpse of life in the Emerald Isle.

The audience applauded loudly when he finished—except for a young woman in a crisp new beret that marked her as either a legionnaire or an habitué of Fifth Avenue. Wearing a soft chamois shirt with gold-trimmed epaulets, she denounced him for his militaristic attitudes.

"You're glorifying war."

He looked at her. She was perhaps twenty, world-wise and weary, a woman who had seen it all, if only on television.

"I have no apologies," he said. "But I'm not glorifying war—the glory goes to the warriors who have to fight them."

Liam bowed to the audience then skipped off stage. He went over to the bar and collected his performance fee from the bow-tied bartender—a shot of Irish whiskey.

"Another postcard from County Antrim," Liam said, tossing down the shot glass of Bushmill's.

Another poet took his place on stage. She was a somber girl in ripped T-shirt and jeans that showed plenty of skin and ribs, the result of the self-imposed concentration camp she lived in.

As she recited her death sonnets, she chewed upon a shard of glass, occasionally spitting out blood-specked splinters onto the dusty wooden stage.

If this shrieking violet got applause, he thought, then he was definitely in the wrong place.

Even on the best of nights, Club Exo could be considered the wrong place. In its former incarnation it had been a strip joint. When the new owners were looking for a sufficiently trendy name and a chance to save some money on a new sign, they took advantage of the Exotic Dancers sign, removing all the letters until only EXO remained.

After printing up several leaflets and advertising Club Exo in the nightlife tabloids as a place with minimalist ambience, the doors were opened. The club was a success right away, conjuring up images of exorcists, aliens and other exotic life forms like rockers and poets.

Liam O'Toole had tumbled into the walk-down club on one of their poetry nights and had become a midweek regular ever since.

He'd absorbed the atmosphere, learned the faces, almost as if it was a battlefield and needed a strategic assault. Tonight he'd staged his first major operation.

But even with the rounds of applause that had come his way it was hard to tell whether he'd taken Club Exo by storm.

The glass-chewing poetess abruptly finished her nearly incomprehensible set and walked off stage before the crowd could respond to her poems. A smattering of applause followed her out of the room and into the hall.

During the break between readings, Liam nonchalantly studied the crowd from his perch at the bar.

Nearly half of the men had buzz-saw cuts, looking like stand-ins for Zippy the Pinhead. The women were a bit more decorous, many of them wearing Salvation Army get-ups or S & M inspired outfits of glossy leather and ratty bandoliers.

But the one he studied most was the muse. Clad in black, her hair a bit mussed but still in, she looked like an exile from academia. A highly educated woman with beatnik sensibilities. She had to be, he thought. Otherwise why else would she dare to enter the East Side haunt.

The muse caught his gaze. She stood up and headed toward the bar. Either she was thirsty or Liam O'Toole was about to be discovered.

Perhaps both.

She walked right up to him and said, "Hello, I'm Gloria Gehlen."

Liam smiled. "I know the name," he said, "but it sounds nice coming from your lips. Can I get you a drink, Gloria Gehlen?"

"No," she said. "Let me get you one."

Liam raised his bushy red eyebrows. "Thanks," he said. "Let me warn you, though. I could get used to that."

After whiskey and wine arrived, she sipped from her glass, peered over the rim and said, "You were strong tonight."

Liam knocked back his Bushmill's, then appraised her with a calm eye. "Is that good?"

"Strong is strong. Good is good," she said. "There's a certain brute force in your poetry, and that's rare. As for your technique, well, that could be improved. The important thing is, you tell a good tale."

God in Ireland, he thought. This is real.

Gloria nodded at the side of the stage, where several cardboard cartons were stacked waist-high. "Do you have anything up there?" she asked.

"Not yet," Liam said. "Just what I carry about here." He reached inside his leather jacket for the scrolled-up sheets of paper that bore his poems and handed them to her.

Some nights the stage behind Club Exo looked like a warehouse, piled high with cartons full of poetry volumes, chapbooks and photocopied stapled sheafs for sale. For many of the poets it was the only place they could sell their work. It was either that or they would have to go out on the street to sell their poems by the page or by the pound.

It was the same when the bar bands played. Every weekend they lugged their cartons of albums, recorded and produced with their own money in one of the small studios that had sprouted up around Manhattan. After their sets they'd sell the albums, complete with amateurish jacket art, to the wowed or stoned patrons.

Liam O'Toole was determined not to print anything by himself. With his SOB contract fees he could easily have printed tens of thousands of copies of his poetry books. But he was determined to have someone else do it for him. Someone legit like Gloria Gehlen.

"I think you're on the right track," Gloria said after scanning Liam's work. "Do you mind if I look at these for a while?"

"Is the Pope Catholic?" Liam said.

"What?"

"Never mind. That's just a fool's way of saying yes, of course you can look at them. I've got copies."

"Good," she said. "I want to read them again, let them sink in."

"I'd be honored," O'Toole said. "It's not every day a poet gets a chance to have someone like you consider their work."

"Poet hardly seems the right word," Gloria said. "Combat correspondent seems more like it." She shuffled his poems like a deck of cards, riffling through them faceup before deciding which one to play. Finally she selected one and laid it down on the bar.

"Poems by Liam O'Toole," she said, testing the title with her lilting voice. "I think I'd prefer something like *Dispatches by Liam O'Toole* instead." She tapped her index finger on one of the poems, tracing the words as if they were a map. "These places you write about—these battles. You've been out there in the thick of it. Haven't you, Liam?"

He studied her, wondering for a moment if the fascination was for him or the poems he'd written. "I've been a lot of places," he said. "Those poems come from where I've been. You can call them dispatches if you want. But don't plan on trotting me out like a dancing bear to do tricks. My poems have to stand for themselves. The last thing Liam O'Toole wants is some PR schtick like Guerrilla Goes Ape Over Poetry. Being a soldier, being a poet—those are things I am. I take them both seriously."

"So do I," she said, shrugging her hair back over her shoulders. "And I think you know I feel that way. Otherwise we wouldn't be talking here, would we?"

"Right you are." Liam lifted his shot glass as he said, "Here's to talking." He tossed it down. "And to drinking." He ordered another round for the two of them, basking in the glow of the fine Irish whiskey and the attention of a genuine major Manhattan poetry publisher.

After reading through his poems once more and then setting them neatly aside, she asked, "Do you know Robert Service?"

Liam nodded. "'There are no pockets in a shroud,'" he quoted Service. The Canadian poet's work always brought the trenches of World War I to Liam's mind. "Can't say I know him personally, though I have been pretty close to him at times." He recalled that the poet died sometime in the late fifties, far away from the trenches and close to the Yukon that he wrote about so well.

O'Toole considered the numerous times in his past years with the SOBs that he had chanced a visit to the dead poet's abode—risk was his life and his work. The Irishman was a free-lancer in the original medieval sense of the word. A lance for hire to the right cause and commander. The cause was the West and the commander was Nile Barrabas. Many a time it had only been because of Barrabas's skill that the Army captain, weapons expert and bard of the battlefield had made it home to write of his exploits. There was little he wouldn't do for Barrabas.

"I think you can reach the same size of audience that Service did," Gloria said, interrupting O'Toole's musings. "In time."

"In time," Liam repeated. "That's the operative word here, isn't it?"

"I like your work, Liam O'Toole," she said. "And I like you. I think *in time* we can accomplish something, something grand. But I need more than this." She patted the small stack of poetry as if it were a purebred canine that had taken second place at the dog show.

"It's a new style for me, a new frame of mind. I'm just stepping into it."

Gloria nodded. "Then step fast, Liam. You've got to put more of this together. Sure, we might be able to get a couple of these out in a quarterly or an anthology." She picked up his poems and waved them about as if they were tickets to glory. "But that would dilute their impact. Give me the whole story, Liam. Capture it all. Give me something that will slay everyone—not just me. Do you hear what I'm saying?"

Liam laughed. "You're saying I'm good but not good enough. Close, but no cigar."

She reached out and patted his shoulder.

The touch was electric. Liam felt off balance for a moment. This woman wasn't reaching out to Liam O'Toole, the hearty Irishman, the hard-drinking, hard-dying hell-raiser who attracted women and trouble in equal parts.

She was reaching out to Liam O'Toole, the poet.

"You've been there, Liam. When you're reading the poems I can see the fire in your eyes. And that tells me that not only have you been there, Liam, you're still there, living it every moment. Now, your task is to help *us* live it. I can work with you on this. We can really make something happen here."

It was nice being discovered, Liam thought, but it couldn't be compared to what he thought it would be. It was like everything he had hoped for, and more. He felt as though he were walking around in his own dream, calling out the shots.

And then, just as another poet on the night's roster took the stage, the dream burst.

In through the door of Club Exo came a man who would only care about the muse if she was wearing a string bikini or maybe a conch shell or two.

Alex Nanos, the one-man Greek armada who could pilot anything from a pair of water wings to a supercarrier—as claimed by him during ouzo-fueled evenings—had not come to New York for sight-seeing.

"Is something wrong?" Gloria asked.

"Not wrong," Liam said. "Just not right, either." So far Alex hadn't seen him, but the Greek's eyes bounced over the crowd quickly, then zeroed in on Liam.

Seeing that Liam was talking to a woman, which in the mind of the tanned, weather-beaten Greek was a religious experience, Alex had obviously decided to give the poet a few more moments of his sacrament.

But Liam knew the ceremony was as good as over.

Usually Nanos could only be found on one of his yachts, trolling for models and starlets in the Florida Keys or the Hollywood Bars.

The fact that he was on foot, adrift in Manhattan's Lower East Side, meant that he had a different quarry in mind. He'd tracked down Liam himself through the poet's network of regular bars. And judging from the cheery glow on Alex Nanos's face, the Greek had bought many a drink from many a bartender to find out where Liam O'Toole could be found.

"Is that a friend of yours?" Gloria asked, looking to the far side of the bar at the Greek.

"At times," Liam said.

"And what about the tall black guy, the one in the long leather coat? Looks like an actor or someone I know."

Alex Nanos was not the only SOB who had come into the bar. There, in the flesh, was also Claude Hayes, a very smooth underwater demolitions man who always reminded Liam of a Moorish warrior, one of the great Carthaginian mercenaries who'd attacked Rome.

The leather coat he wore dispelled that illusion, but the soldier's soul was still apparent.

Claude Hayes and the other SOBs were the characters who made their way unannounced into Liam's poetry. They wore several guises and perhaps they wouldn't always recognize themselves but they were in there, exactly as Liam saw them. His poetic license sharpened a few of their words and magnified some of their deeds, but in essence his poems were true.

And despite the incredibly bad timing, he was glad to see his friends, though what to do next left him baffled.

"If they're friends of yours, why don't they come over here and join us?" Gloria suggested.

"Uh, they probably think I'm making time with a beautiful woman, and they don't want to step in and spoil it."

She laughed. "Well? Are you?"

"I'd like to think so."

"Keep thinking along those lines and you'll do just fine." She smiled in Nanos's direction, then waved.

It had the effect of a magnet.

Nanos and Hayes came over and helped them prop up the bar. The Greek's approving eye studied her as if she were sculpture.

Claude Hayes was friendly but a bit more guarded. Gloria was thrilled at the chance to meet Liam's friends, unaware what their presence meant.

"What on earth does this dive have to recommend it?" Nanos said. Then, before the insult was in striking distance, he turned to Gloria and said, "Except, of course, for the beautiful women who come here?"

"It's a place where people come to give poetry readings."

Claude Hayes understood. "You've been doing us proud?" he questioned.

"I made a stab at it."

Claude looked at Gloria. "What do you think? I know he's good, but I'm a—I'm a traveler, not a critic."

"He's excellent," Gloria said. "An original. A unique talent. He's going places."

"That he is," Nanos said. "Sooner than he thinks." He looked around Club Exo at the barcrawlers, brawlers and especially at the blond spike-haired Mona Magnum, who was sharing a table closest to the stage with a male rooster-haired counterpart. "Look, I know you poets have to suffer for your art, but it looks like the audience has been doing a lot of suffering on their own."

"So you think our man here really knows how to stack up his words?" Claude asked, liking what he heard. "That calls for a drink."

"Everything calls for a drink in this outfit," Nanos said, but didn't stop Claude from summoning the bartender for another round. "By the way, Liam, in case you haven't guessed, Nile has sent out the call."

Liam nodded. "I kinda figured you weren't here for the weather. It's too gray up here for a Mediterranean man."

"The way I see it," Claude said, picking up his conversation with Gloria, "Liam is another Sun Ra."

"Who's that?" Gloria asked.

"Sun Ra is an intergalactic jazz musician. Solar powered soul. You should listen to him sometime. He'll remind you of Liam—without the red hair, that is."

"I'll take your word on it," Gloria said.

"No, take his word. He's the poet."

Almost, Liam thought. Almost a poet. He'd been found by the right person. But now he was going to be lost a while.

"Drink up," said Nanos. "We who are about to be saluted—"

"You've got that wrong," Liam said. "But never mind. I know what you mean."

Nanos shrugged and finished his drink in tandem with Claude. The two new arrivals at Club Exo pushed off from the bar and said their good-byes to Gloria.

Then Nanos spoke to Liam. "I'm going to try and make another call to Billy Two. Our meditating madman's flown the coop again, off on another one of his pilgrimages. I tried to send a telepathic message to him but nobody was home."

Liam smiled. William Starfoot II was a full-blooded Osage Indian known to the SOBs as Billy Two. He had become part mystic, part madman after the Soviets zapped him with an overkill of an intravenously administered drug that tampered with his brain circuitry.

Ever since then, with a few short circuits along the way, Billy Two had been trying to rewire his head.

Liam felt he understood Billy Two more than the other SOBs—except perhaps for Nile Barrabas, who gave Billy Two the room to roam on earth and in space.

Nanos nodded his head one more time at Liam's longhaired muse before turning back to the Irishman. "Sorry, but it's gotta be tonight. We'll wait outside."

"Okay," Liam said. There was no question about his turning down the operation. Nile needed him. It was that simple.

After Nanos and Hayes left them, Gloria moved closer to Liam, as if she sensed her new friendship walking out the door with the two men.

"Who are they?" she asked.

Liam took a deep breath, then exhaled, his barrel chest feeling awfully tight. "You could call them archers," he said.

She stared at him uncomprehendingly at first, but then he could see that she remembered his poem about the soldiers fated to move from one battlefield to the next.

"You're going away with them," she said. Her face suddenly seemed older.

"Yes," he said.

"How long?"

"As long as it takes. A week, a month...a lifetime."

"My God," she said. "It's real. It's all real. I was almost hoping that you were just a good conjurer, imagining all these things you write about."

Liam eased away from the bar, pushing away his empty shot glass. "Thanks for being here tonight," he said. "You've done a lot for me."

"We could have done a lot more," she said.

"Made some poetry of our own," Liam said.

Gloria folded her arms around her to fight off the chill of another friendship lost.

"Where are you going?"

"Where else?" Liam said. "To get some more material."

As she stood there with his poems in her hand, he leaned down and kissed her, his whiskey-tinted lips tasting the wine and want on hers.

"Wait," she said as he started to walk away. She fished in her purse for a moment, then came out with a light brown card. "Here," she said. "It's got my number. For when you get back."

"I'll be back," he said to the muse who had been about to launch him into the stratosphere of published poets. On his way out of the bar he tucked her business card into his pocket, taking a rain check on his dreams.

CHAPTER SIX

William Starfoot II was lost.

The Osage tracker, cartographer and survival expert was lost in a place where there were no geographical coordinates and no contour lines.

The topography was totally unknown and uncharted. Even if the Marine Corps vet could have charted a map of the territory, it would have soon proved useless.

He was in a place where the terrain changed at will, sometimes in slow, molten drifts, other times in quick, sharp snaps as fault lines opened beneath him.

Physically, Billy Two was in quite familiar surroundings. He was on his secluded Oklahoma ranch, lying on a hill beneath the hot sun and a dry wind that scoured his face.

His long black hair snaked like tendrils in the wind. His face was painted with symbols that, should a visitor have stumbled onto the land, would have made him seem like a man from another world—a man cast there not by his choice.

Jagged lightning bolts seared his face, striking across his cheeks.

Bright red sunspots formed a half-moon from his chest down to his ribs, bracing a harvest of blood red spears.

He was a warrior, a dream warrior. And without the symbols or the mental constructs that drew their power from the symbols, he would have been a lost man.

Billy Two wore the paint to help stake himself to the sacred ground of his ancestors. The paint was the only salve left for the wounds that had never healed.

The mental wounds would open suddenly, catching him without warning. Then once again he would be stricken by the unseen stigmata that cut him apart from the rest of the world—even, at times, from the SOBs.

The SOBs tried their best to understand him, but when Billy Two often couldn't understand himself, he could hardly expect anyone else to.

When he was on operations with the SOBs they were continually checking on him, just to make sure he was still there with them. His skills had never suffered. In fact, some of them were heightened. He was more of an instinctual soldier these days.

Still, potentially Billy Two could jeopardize an SOB operation if he wasn't mentally sound for the duration of the mission.

Madman, messiah, or the old Billy Two, the SOBs were never quite sure who was holding court inside his body at any given time.

After that mission when the strapping Osage Indian had been taken prisoner by the Russians, Dr. Lee Hatton had done her best to bring him back to the real world, but she had provided no guarantees.

Even after the tireless ministrations of the SOBs' doctor, Billy Two was a patient at risk. It wasn't a physical risk. His body had recovered from his imprisonment by instinct, and the full-blooded Osage had returned to his native roots, careful to evade the traps of wealth that had so easily ensnared his father. When oil had been found on Osage land, the gods had been lost, swept away in a thick black flood. With their departure many of the tribal traditions had also been lost.

Back home, Billy Two had reacquired the Osage feel for the land, honing his body on treks through the wilderness, treks that helped ease the chaos in his mind.

But there were still times when he was suddenly thrown back into the purple haze, baking under a psychotropic sun.

At those moments there was no one to turn to, no one who could ride the storm—no one except the entity inside him, the entity that made itself known as Hawk Spirit.

Sometimes the spirit came unbidden during Billy Two's most lucid moments. Other times the Osage had to find Hawk Spirit on his own. Only that entity, the essential Billy Two, knew how to navigate in the world of chaos.

Now Hawk Spirit was in hiding.

Or Hawk Spirit was dead.

Billy Two had no way of knowing. He was meditating, he was hallucinating. He was hunting, he was hunted.

Dreamer and dream had become one. Unless he found Hawk Spirit, he might not wake up as Billy Two ever again.

His latest psychotic episode had begun days ago when he was swimming beneath a clear waterfall on his land, letting the cool stream flow over his near-naked body.

And then he heard voices.

At first it seemed like the gurgling of the stream. Then it seemed like the insistent hissing of snakes. Finally he could make out the spirit voices. They were hallucinatory heralds, auditory invitation to the madness he could never quite escape.

Billy went off on his own then, roaming the wild-eyed blue yonder, trying to catch up to the echoes of the Pied Piper of his soul. It was a sound he'd heard before. The sound of the Piper at the Gates of Dawn. The Piper at the edge of the abyss.

Billy Two had gone too far to come back in one piece. He'd come back in several pieces at once, all of them different. Some were shadows of his former self. Some were like gods. But they were untamed gods, uncontrollable manifestations of Billy Two.

He'd been away from the main house for three days, walking beneath the sun, fasting, walking again in the directionless state of a man in a trance.

But now his wings, his legs had given out. Physically and mentally, he was crash landing.

Billy Two exhaled, trying to bring himself back to earth. He stretched his arms flat out on the ground, his fingers clutching at the grass.

Then, through his closed eyes, he looked for Hawk Spirit. At first it was like trying to catch water in his cupped hands. The image of Hawk Spirit stayed there for a moment, but then slipped out of his grasp.

Control the dream.

The thought came unbidden.

The dream is like the hawk. Though wild, it can be tamed.

Billy Two mentally summoned the hawk. As he raised his hand, he pictured the hawk flying down to him.

And suddenly there was a shadow across the sun, passing over his shuttered eyes.

Hawk Spirit had come.

It perched on Billy Two's hand. He could feel the weight—the weight of a winged spirit.

He raised his hand higher. Hawk Spirit flew away. And Billy Two watched it through closed eyes for the direction home.

Finally Billy Two opened his eyes for real, snapping awake for the first time in days. He'd been walking during that time. But it was a form of sleepwalking and of dreaming while awake. Now the dreams were gone.

He stared up at the sun, watching the silhouette of a hawk fly straight up.

The image lasted only a moment, making it seem like his eyes were playing tricks on him.

But the world that Billy Two gazed upon was a very concrete world. The hills of his ranch surrounded him on all sides. The hills were still, no longer seeded with hallucinations. And the sky above him held only one very bright sun, not the constellation his inner eye had been watching for so long.

His fever dream had broken. Billy Two was back in the real world, free of the asylum that every now and then his consciousness checked into.

He sat up slowly. There was sweat pouring down his chest. His eyes were tired, as if they were exhausted from too many visions.

And he had a terrible headache, a splitting sensation that probed the back of his skull. But at least it was real.

He was home.

Billy Two stood up slowly. He walked down the hill, circulation gradually returning to his feet, the blood spreading with every step he took.

The unbidden ceremony was over. "Goddamn," he said. "Or damn god." It was as solemn an oath as he could muster.

Billy Two walked back toward his ranch, thinking of the dreams that had come to him this time. Hawk Spirit was not always a friendly god.

But the Hawk Spirit totem was always with him. Always at the back of his tortured mind he could hear the flapping of wings. And so, like it or not, he followed the entity called Hawk Spirit.

During his last dream journey, Hawk Spirit had shown him glimpses of the future. They didn't make sense to Billy Two. Not yet. But they would in time.

The strange dreams were about shadow spirits, about an ancient enemy he had met once before—dream warriors who marched side by side with their god of war next to them.

He dreamed of serpents and oceans. He dreamed of places where dragons waited. Dragons and black wolves. But worse than those beasts were the warriors themselves.

In the dream the warriors were as crazed as Billy Two.

He pushed the wispy Hawk Spirit dreams out of his mind as he headed home.

An hour after he came back from the shadow world of the Hawk Spirit, Billy Two stepped through the oval portal of his white stone gate.

He felt like sleeping genuinely now. In a bed. He wanted to dream the normal dreams of everyone else in the human race.

But as he headed for the low-slung platform bed in the back bedroom, he noticed the signal light on his answering machine.

Despite his return to his ancestry, Billy Two hadn't gone all the way back to the days of smoke signals.

As sure as Hawk Spirit was the connection to his soul, the telephone was his connection to the real world that he had to return to from time to time.

If Billy Two didn't step back into his persona now and then, he was in danger of becoming another crazy old sun-baked hermit wandering the plains and sharing his deepest thoughts with ground hogs.

Billy Two measured his recovery by how well he compared to his former self—the self that was a die-hard SOB.

He played back the taped message that waited for him on his answering machine.

The booming voice of Alex Nanos chased away any spirits that might have been lingering in the neighborhood.

"Billy, this is Nanos! Quit playing with that bird of yours and get your ass to Copenhagen!" Nanos laughed, then spoke in a normal voice. "That is, if you don't mind."

Billy Two shook his head as he listened to the rest of the message. If anything could bring him down to earth it was his friend Alex Nanos.

He played the message back one more time to make sure he got the correct name of the hotel where the SOBs would be waiting for him.

Copenhagen, he thought.

Perhaps more than the SOBs would be there. Perhaps the creatures from his dreams waited for him in Copenhagen. And perhaps he could slay them once and for all.

CHAPTER SEVEN

When the ax fell on Lillian Reykling's neck, Magnus Koll was sitting hundreds of miles away in his dark wood aerie high above Tonsberg, one of the oldest, if not *the* oldest, town in Norway.

The natives liked to claim it was the first town in modern Norway, and Magnus Koll liked to believe that.

Koll had lived for years in a sprawling wooden house partially carved out of the steep hills that rose above Tonsberg. The original builders had made the baronial mansion as much a part of the landscape as possible.

The home of Magnus Koll looked almost as natural as if it had grown timber by timber from the surrounding woods. At one time it had been a church, and though Magnus had kept the steeples, gables and crucifixed eaves, he had made a few subtle alterations to the exterior that belied its pastoral appearance.

Sculpted dragon heads lurked around the crosses, and lushly carved fertility goddesses added a pagan touch to the spiritual home and headquarters of the Varangian Guard.

A long gallery with a ceiling in the shape of an inverted Viking warship connected the rear wings of the building. The gallery doubled as an armory for the relics of war Koll had collected during his reign as one of the premier mercenary captains in Europe.

Mounted like trophies on the wall were throwing axes, Danish, Norman and Saxon swords; shields emblazoned with winged dragons; crossbows, spears and helmets; and dozens of more obscure one-of-a-kind weapons.

The wide floor planks in the gallery were worn smooth from the steady volume of traffic. In addition to being an exhibition hall, the gallery was wide enough to be used as a training area.

The weapons were not there for looks alone. On many a night the hall echoed with the sound of ancient armor being put to the test.

Behind the relic-strewn wall was a more covert armory. This collection of weaponry was of a more recent vintage, containing everything from machine pistols and submachine guns right up to grenade launchers.

They were tools of the trade, a trade that had allowed Koll to return to his native Norway as a conquering hero. As yet he was an unsung hero, but that would change in time.

For now, his deeds were carried out on a quiet level. Only a select few knew the acts for which he was responsible—although an entire country would soon feel their effects.

Until that time Magnus Koll was simply a man who had done well. He had a military background, that much was known. His American father had brought him and his mother to the States after the war, where he misspent a good deal of his youth. But he seldom talked about this American era, treating it as if that part of his past had been chopped off, severed with a sword stroke.

Overall he was a polite, well-off man who had no quarrels with anyone. Of course, sometimes he seemed to entertain a fair number of people—but that was to be expected of someone with his wealth.

Koll had been drawn to the Tonsberg area because of its history and its strategic location. Situated on the west side of the Oslo Fjord, the shipping port of Tonsberg provided easy access to a number of areas. Although many of the inhabitants of Tonsberg lived there because of its established trade routes, Magnus Koll liked it for a different reason entirely. Tonsberg was within striking distance of anywhere in northern Europe.

Denmark and West Germany were just a quick jump south across the Skagerrak Channel.

Sweden and the Baltic were to the east. And because of some of his more discreet mercenary assignments, Koll even had underworld contacts in the Eastern bloc countries on the Baltic.

To the immediate north was Oslo, a short trip in case his business, covert or otherwise, took him to the Norwegian capital.

Farther north were the past and future targets for more military actions. Trondheim, Bodo, Narvik and the military installations along the Norwegian Sea.

All in all, Tonsberg was the perfect staging area for the political and military wings of the Varangian Guard.

But there were other reasons that brought Koll to Tonsberg. The steep hills, dark forests and strategic harbor held a sense of history. It was a history that could still be read in ancient Viking burial grounds and cairns. A history that Koll felt destined to relive.

From this area many of the first Viking fleets had sailed a millenium ago. Remnants of their warships were still found now and then in the area. The famous Oseberg ship on display in Oslo had been discovered nearby.

All through the region were former ceremonial sites and battlefields where Viking chieftains had established their claim to the throne.

Closer to Koll's own dominion were castle ruins and crumbling foundations of a fort that once stood guard over the country of Norway—foundations that were being rebuilt one stone at a time from the regal abode of the VG leader.

Magnus Koll had come home from the war for good, and he had brought the war home with him.

In the style of the kings who had come before him, even as he lounged in the pagan grandeur of his Tonsberg retreat, acts were being committed in his name...

WHEN THE AX FELL, Lillian Reykling was directly beneath it, sitting at her teak-topped desk in the second-floor study of her home in Old Uppsala, Sweden. She was poring over a catalog of antiquities that would soon be made public by an art auction house.

It was an advance copy, closely guarded, and nearly impossible to get unless you had some clout in the field. Lillian Reykling, known to many in the art world as a master restorer, had a lot of clout.

What was little known about Lillian, except to those who availed themselves of her services, was that she was also a master forger. She specialized in fake paintings by Grünewald, turning out his "lost altarpieces" at a discreet pace. She also created fake Grecian ceramics, Etruscan bronzes, gold Thracian drinking vessels adorned with ferocious griffins and whatever was in vogue in the semilegitimate world of collectors.

To make her duplicitous life even simpler, she was often hired as a consultant to establish the provenance of "new finds," finds that she created herself or were made by contacts of hers.

Naturally she'd verify the fakes as real, and it only stood to reason that she grew richer.

She spent the money on other objects of art. Because of the quick decisions she often had to make in the thieves' market, she sometimes got burned herself. But she took it well, passing on the fakes to her usual customers when she could, suffering the losses quietly when she couldn't. It was all part of the game she had chosen to play.

Lillian also dealt in real pieces whenever they came her way, but her nature was such that she couldn't resist knocking off a duplicate fake to sell on the underground art market.

It was a simple business, really. Many collectors were blind to art, unable to tell a real work from a cheap knock-off. More important was their craving for "unattainable objects,'' those legendary pieces stolen from legendary collections.

Since these collectors couldn't go around showing their stolen pieces, they kept them to themselves, making it that much easier for art forgers to pass off fakes.

Lillian was always one step ahead of her peers in the field, anticipating when the market was getting crowded with certain types of forgeries.

Sooner or later there was bound to be an overload of bogus paintings or sculptures by a certain artist. Eventually even the densest collectors grew suspicious. By then, a master like Lillian Reykling would be long gone, leaving other forgers to get caught trying to peddle fakes in an overworked market.

The key to survival in the business was to keep moving, spot the next trend before the competition, and then exploit the illicit market before it got flooded.

Lately Lillian had been dealing in a growing demand for Viking artifacts, and true to form, she had manufactured a couple of artifacts on her own. She thought nothing of it, except for the money that came into her pockets.

She thought only of the future. There was no other way to go on with her life. To look back was to invite her long-lost conscience to return. And with conscience came danger. There was no room for such a troublesome commodity in her life.

So she sat at her desk, with her collector's eye scanning the catalog of ancient masterpieces for ones she could create on her own.

Lillian wore a pair of stereo headphones while she studied the catalog, listening to Swedish opera on the compact disc player that squatted on the far corner of her desk. The chrome-and-metallic-blue player was one of the few exceptions she'd made in her antique decor.

Lillian liked to work with the opera booming in her ears. When she had the headphones on she felt as though the performers had been transported inside her head, performing on stage for her pleasure.

From the back, with her headphones on, Lillian Reykling looked somewhat like a pilot charting her course across the wide open catalog.

WHEN THE AX FELL on Lillian Reykling, Frederick Mannenheim was wielding it.

The cherubic-faced mariner swung the long ax with the sure hand of a hooded executioner.

The razor-sharp blade bit into the back of Lillian's neck in a downward arc, slicing through muscle and bone, making a dull *thwack*. Then it made the scritching sound of a man hoeing his garden as the metal ax head proceeded on its course.

This kind of gardening, this ultimate weeding process, was Frederick's specialty.

Until tonight he'd never used such an ax. But the designated weapon was part of the contract. So he practiced with it until he had acquired the grace of a lumberjack, a grace that Lillian herself might have appreciated if she had been alive to witness it.

But Lillian hadn't heard his approach. Even without the headphones on, she probably wouldn't have noticed his entry into her home.

He'd worn soft-soled black shoes, black gloves that left no prints, and had spent no more than thirty seconds rifling the lock on her door.

The lock was her secondary defense. Her first line of defense, on which she had depended for years now, was sleeping like a puppy along the inside of the iron-spired fence. Frederick had dropped her huge Great Dane with one narcotic-tipped fléchette fired silently from a dart gun.

He had been summoned from his home in Hamburg's notorious Saint Pauli district, where he debauched away his days between jobs with an endless parade of prostitutes.

The youthful-faced hatchetman ransacked Lillian's place, setting aside relics and paintings, until finally he found the object he was looking for in a metal jewelry box hidden in her bedroom.

The object that Lillian Reykling had died for was a gold finger ring with amber and onyx stones set in a dragon-claw mount. Swastikas and rune staffs were carved on both sides of the band, along with serpentine knots of stylized naked warriors and priestesses. The miniature figures had been carved by a pagan craftsman hundreds of years before.

Frederick wrapped the ring in a handkerchief, knotted the ends together, then buried it deep inside his jeans pocket.

He returned to the woman's body.

The neck had been hewn clear through to her clavicle by the ax head that now rested like a serving tray beneath her splattery throat.

Frederick couldn't help wondering at her greed, that she'd had so much going for her and she still had to steal.

Overkill had done her in. She'd stolen by reflex. But she'd stolen from the wrong man. The man who hired Frederick had used a series of cutouts to contact him. They were a higher class of crooked men who were able to pay a higher than usual fee.

Whoever the hidden employer was, he had been grievously insulted that Lillian had tried to pass off a fake to him. She'd made a duplicate of the ring for him and tried to keep the real one herself.

Obviously this man was not easily fooled. He was not one of the bourgeois collectors she was used to dealing with.

No, this man was out of the ordinary.

He had paid a substantial amount of money for the ring, enough for her to make a good profit for the short time that it was in her possession.

The ring had come from a hoard of other Viking relics found in a Norwegian peat bog. The team that unearthed it never listed it among its discoveries. Instead, its existence and availability was whispered about through the discreet society of underworld art lovers until finally it passed into the hands of Lillian Reykling.

She couldn't resist the lure of the ring, nor the challenge of duplicating it, creating a fake that was nearly a masterpiece in its own right.

The fake ring had been given to Frederick days before so he would know exactly what he was looking for.

Following his instructions, Frederick now placed the fake ring on the finger of the woman who created it. It gave him a ghoulish sensation, as if he'd just wedded a specter. A specter of his own making.

He spent several moments looking at the work of art he'd created and thought it too bad that no one was there to witness his craftsmanship. The only ones who would see it were the ones who would shortly try to catch him.

Lillian was collapsed over her desk, a sluice of red still painting the catalog she'd been spinning dreams over.

Frederick made a quick tour of her home, taking a few small items that looked easy enough to dispose of.

Then he left as quietly as he'd come, intent on carrying out the rest of his contract.

After walking the short distance to his car and calmly driving off, Frederick entertained the thought of keeping the ring for himself.

It was obviously worth a lot of money.

But if he kept it, he wouldn't be able to return to his haunts in Hamburg.

The person who hired him in the first place definitely had the ability to track him down wherever he went. Soon there would be someone just like Frederick himself hunting *him* down.

Frederick decided to stay honest. The people who hired him for this job had hinted there could be plenty of similar jobs in the future.

He was hooked on the high-pay, high-risk occupation. After every performance he could purchase his fill of wine, women and weaponry—all he asked out of life.

It was almost like being a rock star, he thought, except that there could never be an audience. The closest he would ever come to getting fans would be the people who bought the sensationalist tabloids about his exploits.

Frederick drove south to Uppsala, ready to make the dead drop of the ring. He wanted to hand it over quickly. Before the curse got to him.

Something told him that a lot of people had already died because of this ring. Perhaps a lot more would die before too long.

It was possible that Lillian Reykling was just the first in a long line of victims.

Whatever happened, Frederick didn't plan on being around when her grisly corpse greeted the Swedish police.

He wanted to be long gone by the time the body was found, by the time the reviews came out.

The newspapers would remark on the unusual method by which she was dispatched and maybe they'd even mention the unusual ring she wore.

The art world would mourn her loss.

And Frederick Mannenheim would have crested another plateau in his promising career.

THE MORNING AFTER the ax fell, Magnus Koll received a visitor at his Tonsberg home.

It was Telik Wulfson, who had been keeping a low profile since the first overt acts of the Varangian Guard.

He'd brought a present.

It was a ring, the ring of a great chieftain.

In the early light that shone through the shoreside windows, Magnus Koll slipped the onyx-and-amber ring onto his finger.

It was nearly a perfect fit, only cutting into his finger slightly.

He held the ring up to the sunlight, bathing his eyes in the glinting reflection of Viking gold.

"Fit for a king," Koll said.

CHAPTER EIGHT

"ELF appears in Copenhagen!" Nile Barrabas said, mimicking the step-right-up voice of a street-corner news vendor in an old Hollywood movie. "Thousands of demonstrators gather at Environmental Liberation Front rally."

But instead of a movie set, Nile Barrabas was reading the newspaper headline out loud in a secure hotel suite Walker Jessup had booked for them in Copenhagen.

Overlooking the old city moats, the hotel was a haven for well-off tourists, international businessmen, and from here on in, an elite group of soldiers of fortune temporarily masquerading as hi-tech troubleshooters for a multinational integrated-software firm.

Barrabas tossed the English-language newspaper with the screaming headline onto the oval conference table.

"Take a good look at this," he said to the five SOBs gathered around the conference table. "The circus is in town."

"Who's running it?" Lee Hatton asked.

Of all the SOBs, Barrabas thought that she was the only one who looked really relaxed—as if she had actually taken it easy during the time since their last operation.

The other SOBs looked as though they still had to recover from their recuperation.

"That's one of the things we're here to find out," Nile answered. "I doubt Barnum and Bailey are running this circus. But you can bet that Ivan and Boris have a hand in it, even if it's not their show entirely.

"Thousands of protestors don't put on running shoes all at the same time by coincidence—especially for a group that just came out of the woodwork weeks ago."

Liam O'Toole scanned the headline, then briefly studied the photograph of the protest rally that had taken place in the center of Copenhagen.

"Looks like the sixties have come to Denmark," O'Toole said. The red-bearded Irishman quickly surveyed the rest of the article, then passed it on.

Nanos barely studied it before handing it over to Claude Hayes, prompting a look from the merc leader.

"I realize it doesn't have a nude photo spread like the tabloids you usually read, Nanos," Barrabas chided, "but I was hoping you might look at the article just the same."

"Already did, Colonel," Nanos said.

Barrabas cocked his head. "That's a hell of a trick," he said. "The paper just came out."

"I read it in the native tongue, sir," Nanos said. "The Copenhagen papers were full of articles on the rally."

"You speak Danish?" Barrabas asked.

Claude Hayes laughed. "*Eating* Danish is more like it. We haven't been able to keep the Greek away from the *stroget*. But as far as speaking it, Nile, the only thing I've heard Nanos utter is 'Skal.'"

Nanos flexed his arms, then stretched his fingers flat on the table. "Laugh if you must," Nanos said with wounded pride. "But I've been expanding my language base lately. I do more than chase women, you know."

In tandem, all the SOBs gave Alex Nanos a look of disbelief. Although Nanos was fluent in German and Russian, as well as Greek, the SOBs weren't about to let him off that easily.

Although language was often a survival skill in the places where the SOBs journeyed to, it was hard for them to imagine Nanos taking the time off from his Key West sojourns to add another lingo to his belt.

"I swear it's true. I *can* get by in Scandinavia. It's close to German, and what with my other languages, I can figure out what people are saying here."

Barrabas nodded. If the Greek said he could read it, he could. "Then you know what we're up against already."

Nanos nodded. "Our friends in the Environmental Liberation Front—or ELF, as they like to be called—are screaming out for social justice, clean air and the un-American way. Get the U.S. of A. and NATO out of Scandinavia."

"Close enough," Barrabas said, giving the other SOBs time to look over the news article before continuing with the briefing. He'd been filling in the crew for the past hour on the Varangian Guard, transferring some of the information that Walker Jessup had already given him. And now he was filling in the blanks that connected the Environmental Liberation Front to the VG.

The Varangian Guards were still a shadowy outfit with little known about them except a few cryptic comments made by anonymous callers. Right now there was still a lot of mystery around the group of hard-core guerrillas. The mystery was designed to build up the mythos of these shadow warriors who were sworn to drive the poison merchants out of Scandinavia. Soon they would be heroes, except to the innocents who stood in their way.

The string of assaults on chemical sites in Norway and "accidental" releases of deadly chemicals into the atmosphere had been impossible to keep out of the press. Especially since the government's stories were always followed by anonymous tips to the news media that told a totally opposite tale.

And though no one could penetrate the cloud of rumor and misinformation that shrouded the issue of chemical stockpiles, sabotage and reckless training exercises, there were enough critics to make sure it stayed on the front pages.

The most vocal was the ELF, which gathered a number of environmental and political causes under its chemical-free umbrella.

"ELF opened up offices in Oslo and Stockholm at the same time as they did in Copenhagen," Barrabas said. "Protests in those cities have matched the one that nearly started a riot here.

"ELF is no doubt funded and guided by the Varangian Guards. It's the same old story: a political entity supports the high ideals and principles of a movement. And then the action arm—the terrorist group the political front claims to denounce—commits outrages in the name of their cause."

Lee Hatton scanned the article one last time, then folded it into a tomahawk and sailed it back down the long table to Barrabas. "Are you saying that everyone in ELF is knowingly linked to the VG?"

"Not at all," Barrabas said. "There are a lot of genuine 'elves' who want the Garden of Eden to come back, but you don't get an army of demonstrators to act simultaneously in three countries on the spur of the moment. There's considerable organization behind it. Someone has spent a lot of time building up this group. It's no coincidence that they came on the scene the same time as the VG."

Lee shook her head from left to right. "I don't get it. From what you've shown us so far, the main protests have been in Oslo, with satellite groups building up support in Stockholm and here in Copenhagen. So why aren't we going up there?"

"Some of us will be," Barrabas said. "Soon enough. But we're going to go in with different teams."

He briefed them on the situation in Norway.

A movement such as ELF, which looked as though it was going to be a popular cause, was always taken seriously by internal security forces, according to the colonel. And though Denmark and Sweden were certainly taking it seriously, the Norwegian government considered itself to be almost on a war footing. The covert war had hit them in too many sensitive areas for them to dismiss it as just random acts of terrorism.

Since it was obvious the VG were playing for keeps, the Norwegian government was doing the same. They'd activated a coordinated task force of intelligence-gathering teams and action squads from military and police units.

"A couple of you are going in solo," Barrabas explained. "The rest of us are going in straight ahead. But before that starts, I want everybody to know who the players are."

Barrabas gave them a quick rundown on the security forces that were even now making a bid to snare the Varangian Guard.

"As you can imagine, the group that got hit by the VG is out for blood. The Norwegians have a Marine Jaeger platoon that specializes in underwater demolitions, amphibious operations and recon. They lost nearly ten percent of their unit in their first engagement. They'll be looking to even the score."

"What if the VG stay away from the water from here on in?" Nanos asked. "Or worse? What if they decide to walk on the water?"

"They're good, all right," Barrabas said, "but they're not gods."

Barrabas suddenly caught an odd look on Billy Two's face as he mentioned the word *gods*. It was there for just a moment, but it was still long enough to register with the leader, who was usually highly attuned to his soldiers' state of mind. The Osage normally kept his inner feelings in check, but here among his friends they had slipped out.

Nile decided he'd have to check out Billy Two before too long to see what pantheon of gods and demons were battling inside him. Everybody had his demons to slay, but if Billy Two was dueling with devils, or whatever currently possessed him, Barrabas wanted to know. For now, however, it would have to wait.

"The Marine Jaegers are part of a combined antiterrorist unit," Barrabas continued. "They work hand in hand with the Parachute Jaeger group. So to answer your question, Nanos, whether the VG come in on water or wings, the Jaegers can reach them. Their recon teams will go anywhere."

"So why are we here?" O'Toole asked, tugging at his bright red, well-trimmed mustache. "If these Jaegers got their act together, and they know the terrain—"

"We're here because we're invisible," Barrabas said, cutting him off.

Claude Hayes cleared his throat. "With all due respect, Nile, I think I may be just a touch noticeable way up here in the Great White North."

Barrabas laughed. "Invisible in the sense that if we screw up, no one gets in trouble. Although we're unofficially sanctioned, we're deniable. If we get blown, as far as the public is concerned, we're just another group of wild-eyed goons with guns. Eminently disposable.

"Besides, the Jaegers are under close scrutiny. Even though they were the ones hit, they're being labeled as aggressors in ELF and leftist circles. Until this blows over, they've got to walk softly—softer than usual, that is."

Although the SOBs were familiar with the ins and outs of police and intelligence work, it was vital for Barrabas to give them a "Who's Who" book on the covert community. They had to know who their real allies were.

Many intelligence agencies used the term *animals* when referring to free-lancers or contract players like the SOBs. And though there was a world of difference between the SOBs and rank-and-file guns for hire, they were lumped in the same category until they proved otherwise.

Barrabas now clued in his troops to the tense atmosphere on the Norwegian side. So far they hadn't been able to strike back, and they wanted to hit somebody.

"You're saying we might not be welcomed with open arms," Claude Hayes speculated, after hearing the colonel's view of the situation.

Barrabas's response was short and to the point. "We'll be welcomed with *automatic* arms, unless we do this right. That's why we cover all the bases before we make our run."

Then he continued his crash course on the Scandinavian services who would have their people in the field. "A lot of our intelligence—aside from what the NSA vacuums from the air for us—will originate from the Norwegian surveillance police and narcotics officers."

Barrabas had spent long hours with Walker Jessup going over his opposite numbers in the Norwegian agencies, finding out what kind of restraints they operated under and what they could do in a pinch.

The group that handled internal security and plainclothes operations, somewhat along the lines of the FBI, were the *Overvaakingspolitiet*, known as the surveillance police. The *Politiet's Narkotikaavdeling* were the Norwegian counterpart to the DEA. Their considerable resources were brought to bear on the VG search because the sole VG casualty had been traced to a drug cartel that had been dealing in synthetics.

Then there were the Beredskatrop, police commandos with a strong military capability. They formed the "Readiness Troops," which worked on a secrecy level akin to SAS antiterrorist squads.

"Tactical support will originate from the Jaegers and the Beredskatrop," Barrabas said. "Plus whatever goodies the Norwegians allow us to use from Uncle Sam's footlockers."

"Could you repeat that in Greek?" Nanos said. "I think I missed something. What was that about footlockers?"

"The Norwegians have underground fortresses and tunnels stocked with matériel for use in wartime. Some of these tunnels are stocked with U.S. ordnance. If the level of the threat is considered serious enough, we can appropriate some of the big-ticket items stored there. The ordnance is kept there to supply a Marine landing. And right now, the only Marines I see are you and me. So let's handle the native spy guys the right way. Our lives could depend on them."

The SOBs were not going to be waltzing around these men as if they were crossing guards. Barrabas needed to win some of their key people over if they were going to carry out the mission.

"Those are just some of the crews we're going to encounter on the Norwegian side," Barrabas said. "But the traffic will be heavy from all of the services. We've got to know who they are and where they're coming from."

"So we can stay out of their way?" Claude asked, obviously not looking forward to playing diplomat.

He could do it, but the Detroit-bred SOB preferred the straight-ahead approach. Sometimes it had near-fatal results. Claude would have been right at home in some of the early battles between Cromwell's Roundheads and Prince Rupert's Royalists. They were fond of marching head-on into each others' ranks and firing until everyone on one side died or left the field. It was a strategy that Claude had relied upon on more than one occasion.

Barrabas leaned over the conference table, spreading his palms on the smooth surface. "That's exactly what I mean, Claude," he said. "We either stay out of their way—or we take them out. Whatever has to be done. Along with the friendlies, there's bound to be a lot of Russian bears sniffing around."

Hayes smiled, placated somewhat by the promise—or threat—of action by hostile intelligence agencies.

"Now, listen up, people," Barrabas continued. "Here's some more 'Who's Who in Scandinavia' for you."

Nanos groaned and buried his head in his hands. "All these polities and bearstraps!" he protested. "How are we going to keep them straight? There's not enough room in my head for all these names."

"There's more space up there than you think," Billy Two said, breaking his near silence.

Normally Barrabas would have chewed them out for carrying away the briefing. But he knew that despite their apparent horsing around, each man and woman there was committing everything he said to memory.

Besides, soon enough, there wouldn't be much room for laughing.

"Now," Barrabas said. "About the Danes. They won't be sitting still while a Viking army gathers in Norway. They'll be looking to neutralize whatever comes their way..."

The Danish counterterrorist group, *Politiet's Efterretningstejeneste*, the PE, operated within the Danish State Police Intelligence Service, whereas the *Fromandskorset*, the main military counterterrorist team, was recruited from the Royal Danish Navy Combat Swimmers.

The Danes and the Norwegians had strong ties with one another because of their joint NATO commitments, and they shared a steady flow of information. Although the nonaligned Swedes proudly went their own way in military and intelligence matters, SAPO and IB, their intelligence services, were cooperating with the other Nordic agencies. Neutral or not, Sweden had the same enemies.

"And lastly," Barrabas said, "we come to our old friends from the Pickle Factory."

"The CIA is jumping in on this?" Hatton asked.

"With both left feet," Barrabas said.

Relations between the CIA and the SOBs fluctuated a lot, usually depending on who aced who in their last meeting.

Some of the cliques in the Company cabal were top-notch. Others were suicidal, judging from the operations they launched.

"Anyway," the Colonel continued, "we're just looking to the Company for some assets on this operation. Like everybody else, they'll be nosing around, trying to infiltrate the ELF. Hopefully we can use their assets to piggyback one of us into the political stew. They'll also try to infiltrate the VG. But I think that's something only we can do."

He looked around at the SOBs, his eyes settling on O'Toole. "How are you on politics these days?"

"Same as ever," O'Toole said. "Ballots or bullets— whatever it takes to make my vote count."

"I think you'll fit right in with their political action committee," Barrabas said. "You'll start here in Copenhagen, make a few friends and enemies in ELF, then drift up to Oslo as a known commodity. Let them think you're a rabble-rouser who wants more than political action. Sooner or later you'll be recruited into the Varangian Guard."

"You mean I have to act crazy?" O'Toole said. "Maybe even a bit violent?"

"Try and fake it," Barrabas said. "Force yourself to have a drink or two."

The other SOBs laughed. O'Toole's fondness for searching out bars was complemented by his knack for destroying them. Beneath the sensitive soul of a poet, there lurked at times the senseless soul of a madman. Now he would become a madman with a license.

"Who's my contact?" O'Toole asked.

"Walker Jessup's worked out a couple of phone numbers and safe houses for you," Barrabas said. "Places to go, people to see in case you get in a bind. We'll go over that later."

O'Toole looked surprised. "The fat man's here? Did they airlift him in?"

"Jessup's running interference for us up north," Barrabas said. "Enlisting the right chiefs and trying to isolate the others."

"Throwing his weight around," O'Toole suggested.

"That's his speciality," Barrabas agreed. "But back to business, Liam. I want you to go in deep and stay there. We may be able to get a couple people in there to watch your back, but play out your cover to the end. You're on your own until you find us a target, or we pull you out."

O'Toole nodded.

"Who's the other undercover?" Lee Hatton asked.

Barrabas stared at the black-haired beauty, who just then looked as if she could be right at home in a boardroom, a bedroom or on a battlefield.

"You are," he said.

She lifted her eyebrows. "Do I get to play Viking, too?"

"If it comes to that. Your task is to identify their political command structure and discover their chemical inventory—what they have, what they're after and how we can protect ourselves from it or neutralize the threat. You're the one with the medical background to find out what the hell is going on. And there's another thing in your favor. They won't suspect just how dangerous you can be. You'll be just another doll in their collection."

She flashed daggers at Barrabas for a second, reminding him that she belonged to no one's collection. But then her gaze cooled. She would play the Barbie Doll if it came down to it.

Barrabas wrapped up the meeting with some background on the bogus software company Walker Jessup had created for their use. The supposed product was Translator, an integrated software package that could convert documents into multilingual formats.

Many software packagers had attempted to come up with the right package, but so far the resulting translations sounded as if they'd been made by robots with warped senses of humor.

Translator was the chief product of Trans-Europe Telekom, a heavily financed software company making a bid for international stardom.

From here on in, Jessup's temporary conglomerate would be based in the hotel, complete with a small staff to handle invoices and accounts for the surprisingly energetic "executives" scouting out clients for their very specialized business.

"All right," Barrabas concluded. "The rest of us are going into Norway together."

"How far north?" Nanos asked.

"Oslo, Trondheim, probably northeast to the Russian border," Barrabas said. "Why?"

"Just wondering if we'd see the northern lights, you know, the areola."

Lee Hatton laughed at the Greek, wondering if he was putting them on again. "If anyone is going to see a giant areola in the sky, it's you, Nanos. The rest of us will have to settle for the aurora borealis."

"That's what I said," Nanos protested.

"Besides, it's too early for the midnight sun. We won't be seeing that unless—" Lee paused and looked steadily at Barrabas "—unless we're here for a hell of a long time. Any make on the length of our stay, Nile?"

"We're not getting paid by the hour," Barrabas said. "We stay here until the VG are dead and gone."

CHAPTER NINE

The man who knew where the Norwegian Security Service kept its skeletons buried was waiting for Barrabas by the sixty-foot obelisk in Frogner Park.

He had a copy of *Aftenposten* folded beside him on the park bench, seemingly oblivious to the afternoon crowd that streamed through Oslo's main park. The man was stocky but his well-tailored clothes gave him a streamlined look, and he appeared to be intent on filling in a crossword puzzle.

His lapels were flapped around by occasional flurries of wind and his straw-blond hair was tousled. The unmanageable shock of hair made him look almost boyish, even though he sported a neatly clipped, newly grown beard.

When Barrabas sat next to him the man looked up for the first time. He was a bit younger than Barrabas, maybe somewhere in his late thirties. Despite his earnest jottings on the puzzle, he didn't have the eyes of a man who spent his afternoons doing crosswords.

In fact, the cool, arrogant eyes that studied Barrabas regarded him more as an enemy than a potential ally.

He greeted Barrabas as if they were old acquaintances who often met at the bench. After flashing a disposable smile, he said, "You're just in time. I'm stuck." He waved the crossword puzzle around, and the wind raced through the billowing page, nearly sending it airborne. He folded it tighter and then smoothed it flat out on the bench. "Maybe you can help me out."

"I could use the excitement," Barrabas said.

The blond man smirked. "Let's see how well you do," he said. He looked down at the puzzle as if he were reading one of the clues. "A river in Africa. Four letters."

"Nile," Barrabas said.

"Ah, that was much too easy. But wait, here's another one. Brother of Christ..."

"Barrabas."

"Nile Barrabas," the man said, weighing the name and finding it acceptable. "The long-lost brother. Welcome to Oslo. I'm Eric Thorne."

"Sure you are," Barrabas said, finding the name a little too pat to be believable. But nom de guerre or not, it was the name he was expecting. "It's nice to see that cloak-and-dagger is still alive and well here. What next? Does everyone start to wear paisley ties and tie-dyed shirts?"

"I was told to meet with you," Thorne said. "But I wasn't told you were a funny man."

Barrabas shook his head. "I'm a serious guy," he said. "Dead serious. That's why I'm here."

Thorne tossed the newspaper to his right, then folded his arms in front of him. He looked up at the sky, his eyes automatically drawn to the obelisk.

The monument was supposed to be a sign of man's eternal struggle, presenting a crowd of naked human figures winding skyward, one on top of the other in a linked procession to the top. To Barrabas the sterile naked figures seemed like a love-in that just got word about AIDS and was having second thoughts.

Barrabas was a mercenary, not a critic. Still, he knew what he didn't like, and he didn't like the obelisk any more than he liked Eric Thorne. They both had the same warmth about them.

"We don't need the U.S. Cavalry," Thorne said. "Or whatever it is you're supposed to be. We can take care of our own here."

Barrabas studied his Norwegian counterpart. As the main action man for the Ministry of Justice and Police, Thorne was coordinating the deployment of the Jaeger units and the Readiness Troops. It was a personal matter for him. Since he had had friends among the Jaegers who had been eliminated, it was only natural to resent Barrabas's presence. If he hadn't been instructed to liaison with Barrabas, the two would have never met.

"Look," Barrabas said. "Let's get something straight here. At the very least we accomplish one thing by meeting. We can recognize each other's faces so we don't kill each other in the field."

"Perhaps," Thorne said. "I'll know your face and you'll know mine. There will be other troops in the field."

Barrabas shrugged. "Why don't you show them the pictures your crew has been taking of this meeting?"

Thorne's face showed genuine warmth for the first time since they'd met. "You noticed my people? I'll have to reprimand them."

Though foot traffic in the park was relatively sparse, there had been a number of people walking by, and a few of them had taken more than a casual interest in Barrabas. He'd seen a couple of scruffy men in bomber jackets and an apparent pair of young lovers who by all rights should have had eyes for each other and not for the leather-jacketed man with a shock of nearly white hair.

The thought occurred to Thorne that he wasn't the only one to resort to subterfuge. "And you?" he asked. "What about your compatriots? Are they out for a stroll, too?"

"I wouldn't be surprised," Barrabas said. The SOBs were present in Frogner Park. But Claude Hayes, Alex Nanos and Billy Two had disguised their interest in the rendezvous better than Thorne's crew.

"Let's take a walk," Thorne said, folding the paper under his arm.

He and Barrabas strolled through the park like old friends, walking over the grass and making their way between the randomly placed statues. The park was populated by bronze and granite figures of naked men, women and children. Like the huge obelisk, they had all been created by the sculptor Gustav Vigeland. Long after his death the life-size creations "lived" in the park—running, fighting, loving, carrying on as though they were his offspring, his family line in bronze.

The net effect was that even without a human soul in it, Frogner Park would never appear deserted, Barrabas thought, and he could easily picture Eric Thorne standing there among them, a granite welcome frozen upon his face.

As the two soldiers passed an open-air restaurant, Barrabas noticed Alex Nanos sitting at a table, practicing his charm and his Norwegian on a brightly clad waitress.

With his polite but indifferent voice, Thorne made his position clear to Barrabas. As far as he was concerned the SOBs were unneeded. But they would be tolerated because of the orders that had personally come down to him from the loftier regions of the Norwegian government.

"What is it that you expect from me?" Eric asked.

"For starters," Barrabas said, "how about the matériel I was assured you would loan to us."

Thorne nodded, reached into his pocket and withdrew a set of keys. "These belong to a touring man. You and your fellow tourists can see the country in it."

Barrabas unzipped a side leather pocket and dropped the keys into them. He waited for the Norwegian to continue.

"You will find maps in the van. You will also find an assortment of weapons."

"Swords and spears?"

"The weapons that were requested will be there."

"Thanks," Barrabas said. "How about a few magic words to go with them?"

The SOBs could have acquired sufficient weaponry on their own, but the reason for going through Thorne was to get an unofficial license. In the event that the wrong authorities found the SOBs carrying lethal weapons in awkward circumstances, Barrabas wanted a get-out-of-jail-card.

"Use my name," Thorne said. "And this number." He recited a phone exchange which Barrabas committed to memory. "Just the fact that you have that number will take some of the heat off you." The Norwegian operative glanced at Barrabas's white hair for a moment, then said, "To identify yourself, use the code name 'Wise Old Man.'"

"Should be easy to remember," Barrabas said.

"There is one more thing. The plates on the van have a special designation recognizable to our people. Unless you are found carrying nuclear devices or some such thing, you probably won't be interfered with."

Barrabas nodded. "You've given it a lot of thought," he said. "Thanks."

"Just following orders," Thorne said.

"Same here," Barrabas said. "Different army. Same side. We can work well together."

The man shrugged it off.

"Or maybe not," Barrabas said. "But like you say, we each have our orders."

"My orders have been followed," said the Norwegian, turning back and heading toward the obelisk where they first met. His brusque manner indicated that their meeting was over.

Barrabas walked beside him, his hands in his pockets, his eyes scanning the park for Thorne's team, as well as his own. There was another element he was looking for. The chances were good that either one or more of the Norwegian counterterrorist teams had been penetrated by a VG mole or that an ex-officer whose knowledge and contacts were still current was working with the VG.

Someone had to be close to the group. Otherwise the VG wouldn't have been able to pull off the Trondheim hit. To carry out that operation had required a detailed knowledge of the time and place for the training exercises, along with the location of the research institute.

Those same people might have knowledge of an outside force being called in. And it would be in the VG interest to take out that outside force as soon as they could.

The two covert commanders had already discussed the likelihood that Thorne's group was compromised. Thorne admitted the possibility, but countered that he was only using a small crew, people he trusted with his life.

Dusk was creeping over the park by the time they were halfway back to the huge Vigeland monolith. In the dim light the other statues took on a more lifelike appearance.

It was disconcerting to Barrabas at first. Were they humans or statues? He kept scanning the park, even though he had other eyes doing the same for him.

Billy Two was walking on a diagonal to them, his longish hair flapping above the collar of his peacoat. His hands were in his pockets and a cigarette was dangling from his mouth, the puffs of smoke swirling away in the breeze.

It was a perfectly natural tableau, a man out for a walk, seeding the crisp, cool air with a cloud of tobacco. It was natural except for one thing.

Billy Two didn't smoke.

He was signaling Barrabas.

A phalanx of trees to his right caught Barrabas's eye. It was the same direction in which Billy Two had been pointing his cigarette a few moments ago.

Surrounding one of the statues a small grove made a natural shrine for the gleaming gray idol. Barrabas gestured to the side of the path they were taking, as if he were taken by the sculpture. He led Thorne over with him.

"See something you like?" Thorne asked.

"Not exactly," Barrabas said, but he kept up his feigned interest in the statue as he moved closer to it.

Thorne stepped with him.

Barrabas spoke softly. "Tell me something, Eric. These people you trust with your life..."

"Yes?" The man looked annoyed. "What is it?"

"Do they watch you through sniper scopes?"

Eric Thorne was suddenly all business. "Of course not," he said. "What did you see?"

"Just up ahead of us," Barrabas said. "In the boughs of one of those trees there's a man with a rifle. Sitting there in camouflage, aiming at us right now. He had a perfect line of sight on the path we were walking on. I made it a bit more difficult for him."

Waving and bending in the wind, the branches of the tree moved in a random pattern, screening the two men from the sniper in the tree.

Eric Thorne hadn't broken the pleasant facade he'd been maintaining since the beginning. As he nodded his head, smiling, he said, "If there is somebody there, he's not one of mine."

"There's somebody there, all right," Barrabas said. He felt his chest tightening, his blood racing. The self-preservation instinct was kicking in, making it almost impossible to stand still. It was time for flight or fighting.

"Unless we get back on the path in a few moments, he'll probably do a rock-and-roll reconnaissance," Barrabas said. "Spraying the area in a wide arc just to see what he hits. A lot of citizens could get hurt."

There was still a slim crowd meandering through the park. The constant wind and the approaching darkness hadn't yet chased them out.

The park had been built around the sprawl of woods, offering plenty of shelter to the sniper. Whoever he was, he'd been very cool. He'd let his quarry walk past him the first time to make the guards feel secure that no one was here.

And now that they were coming back, he'd try and take them out, then vanish into the gloom.

"Any of your guys in position to take him out?" Barrabas asked.

"Not in enough time to keep him from getting off a few rounds before they locate him."

"I got it covered," Barrabas said. "Just give me the word."

Eric Thorne studied the soldier of fortune next to him, searching for the man hidden behind the stony gaze. "It could blow up in our faces if this goes wrong."

"It's your ballpark," Barrabas remarked.

Eric nodded and clapped him on the back, keeping up the guise of old friends. "It's settled," the Norwegian said. "You're up."

"All right, let's go," Barrabas said. He walked back toward the path, knowing that he'd be stepping into the sniper's sight for a few critical seconds.

But judging from his patience so far, the sniper was a pro. Barrabas figured he would take time to zero in on his target. Or so he hoped. Those few seconds would decide his fate. It was out of his hands, but he had to take the risk.

He stepped onto the path, walking a few steps while he searched for Billy Two. The Osage had been strolling slowly through the area, looking like an off-duty bar-crawler killing time with a smoke or two in the park before the night got serious.

Barrabas nodded, and Billy Two spun around in a blur, his right hand unsheathing a suppressed Ingram MAC-10 machine pistol from the slashed pocket of his peacoat.

His left hand gripped the leather sleeve on the sound suppressor as he raised the 9 mm Ingram skyward and squeezed the trigger.

Scything through the leaves, the 9 mm slugs punched a half dozen holes in the sniper's body.

The *phyyt-phyyt-phyyt* sound of the silenced spray was followed by the groans of the sniper as he crashed through the branches, snapping some of them off on his downward flight.

One of his arms cracked under him, awkwardly raising his body as it folded beneath him like a clipped wing.

He got a mouthful of dirt as the earth silenced forever his last shout of surprise and thirstily soaked up his blood.

Falling slightly after him, caught for a few moments in the tree limbs, was a G3SG-1 sniper rifle with a 20-round box magazine and a quick-release Zeiss-glass scope mount.

It could have done a lot of damage, but the Osage had nailed him before he got a shot off.

Right after the body thumped onto the ground, Billy Two tossed his suppressed Ingram in the air, sailing it butt over barrel before it landed harmlessly in the grass.

At the same time Billy Two opened his arms wide and lifted them up in the sign language of peace and love and universal brotherhood and said, "Don't shoot."

The action saved Billy Two from getting aced by the submachine guns displayed by Eric Thorne's backups as they materialized from all directions.

"He's one of mine," Barrabas said to Thorne.

"Thank God for that," Thorne answered.

"So are those two." Barrabas nodded at Alex Nanos and Claude Hayes, who had instinctively taken up cross-fire positions to support Billy Two in case someone didn't get the message and tried to take him out.

Thorne passed on the information to one of his subordinates, who quickly calmed the Norwegian strike team.

Barrabas exhaled the tension that had built up inside of him. It hadn't been easy walking into the wrong end of a rifle barrel, but he had the confidence in his men that let him place his life in their hands. So far it had worked wonders. And if it ever stopped working, he'd be the last person to notice.

The split-second hit had gone off as smoothly as shooting a bird off a wire.

Except that this bird had come crashing down like a prehistoric pterodactyl, extinction courtesy of the SOBs.

Barrabas joined the plainclothes officers and intelligence ops who gathered near the body as police moved to cordon off the area.

"I thought you guys needed arms from me," Thorne said.

Barrabas shrugged. "We always dress for the occasion. But the additional weapons will be appreciated."

"Judging from today's performance, they'll be put to good use." Thorne looked around the park at the startled faces peering from the distance. He knew that human nature being what it is, soon the curious onlookers would swarm to the assassination site to bathe in the safe danger of the gory aftermath. "This is going to make a lot of noise," Thorne said. "Explaining how this happened."

"What's to explain," Barrabas said. "One of your guys gets to be a hero for a while. The way I see it, you got a PR coup here. The headlines are endless. Security Policeman Stops Slaughter. Or, Police Ambushed by Assassin in Park. Escaped Murderer Dies in Stakeout."

"If he fits the bill," Eric said.

"A guy like this, with a sniper rifle—hell, you can pin a hundred unsolved crimes on him. Mass Murderer Silenced Forever. Hey, I don't have to tell you this. You know the score."

"Yes," Thorne acknowledged. "But I wanted to hear it just the same. So everyone agrees what happened here."

When the three other SOBs drifted over to Barrabas, he said, "I think it's time we left."

Thorne and a couple of his people walked with Barrabas to the edge of the hit scene. The Norwegian commando's manner was entirely different now that he'd seen the SOBs in action. Their performance wasn't that of cowboys who had come to shoot up the town. They were pros. He gave

Barrabas the location of the van and made arrangements to fill him in on any leads from the slain sniper.

Then Thorne turned to his men and said, "Take a close look at these faces. They are our friends. Look out for them. I have a feeling we'll be seeing a lot of them."

CHAPTER TEN

Liam O'Toole placed the crude helmet upon his head, seeing the world for the first time through the eyes of a Viking—a Viking who was about to prove himself on a sodden field of combat deep in the Danish marshlands.

It wasn't a jeweled helmet or a ceremonial one with horns or stags gracing the crown. Nothing like the finely crafted ones Liam had seen in museums, those worn by ancient chieftains. Those helmets would come later—if he rose through the ranks and survived the weaning process to enter the kingdom.

The helmet Liam O'Toole wore was a helmet made for war. It was a blunt metal mask with a horizontal visor's grate for him to see through; it looked like an iron thimble for a giant's thumb.

There was padding on the lip of the helmet, a thoughtful addition that kept the wearer from being decapitated by a sword stroke slapping the helmet against the neck.

As he waited in the stall in the manner of a bull about to charge into the arena, he felt like a heavy metal goalie, carrying a fighting stave instead of a hockey stick.

Their choice of weapon was the sword or the staff. Normally combatants in the Norse Clans practiced for months or years before venturing into this kind of tournament. But O'Toole was familiar with staff fighting from his martial arts training. The hardwood staff was about the length of the Japanese *bo*, which he'd mastered long ago.

O'Toole had never gone in much for the sword forms of the marital arts, figuring the odds were one in a million against ever facing an opponent with a sword.

Sticks, clubs or staves, yes. Swords, no.

So much for his career as an oddsmaker, he thought.

The audience outside the corraled combat area was in period costume, and they avidly watched the contest taking place before them as the tired warriors neared the end of their combat. Sooner or later one of them would fall.

One fighter had a red dragon emblazoned upon the back of his helmet, the spiny wings flapping forward and stretching above the visor. His shield was similarly marked, but the red color had faded from the sword strikes it had taken.

The other fighter was unheralded, unless the plain green color of his shield stood for something. O'Toole wasn't certain yet. He was still new to the field, and though nearly everyone in the clans spoke English, it wasn't a favorite practice at medievalist gatherings. So he asked his questions sparingly and gained his knowledge piecemeal.

It was in the city that he could find out the most, over a table full of drink in one of the numerous taverns that seemed to serve as the ELF's home away from home. It was through some of the rowdier members of the ELF that he had first learned of the Norse Clans. And it was by means of those clans that he would find the Varangian Guard.

Here in the woods, in the field of combat, actions were more valued than words. A talkative man was acceptable to the Norse Clans, but a man well-tried in battle was preferred. Like the kind of men who fought in front of him right now.

Both combatants were using swords, and as they thrust and parried, there was a steady stream of *thwapping*, *whumping* and clattering sounds made by blows landing on armor plating, wooden shields, leather arm guards or an opponent's sword.

With each flurry of attack, there was a chorus of cries from the audience, followed by stunned silences.

And like everyone else gathered at the arena, O'Toole found himself wondering how the two combatants could still stand after all the punishment they had taken.

He turned from the combat for a moment to study the crowd, all dressed for the part and living out their chosen masquerades.

But for some of them, O'Toole knew, it was more than a masquerade. It was a way of life. This was the real world for many of them. The world they desired was beyond understanding to society at large.

Some of them were over the edge, flailing around in an escapist fantasy life.

Others took it seriously, seeing it as a discipline to enrich their lives and keep them strong despite their lax and easy way of life back home in the city.

And then there were the fighters like O'Toole, aspirers to a warrior caste. Escapist or not, the Viking combat was real. This was the genuine entrance to the Norse Clans. The sword was the heart of it.

It was mock combat in one sense only: the combatants didn't fight to the death. But they did fight grimly and furiously with their swords, shields and staves, though the swords were blunted and wrapped with leather and wooden sheaths, and the bosses on the shields were smoothed over so no one would be slashed badly when struck by them.

The clans had their own rules of combat. The goal was to vanquish the enemy, knock him to the ground where his life was forfeit. It could be ritual—with a series of strikes to designated areas counting as wounds; with each wound the fighter would yield some of his ability. First he would be reduced to fighting with only one hand. Then he'd have to fight on one knee. Then both knees. The combat continued until the final coup could be delivered.

This clan, the one that O'Toole had discovered through his Copenhagen undercover life, went for the more primitive style. There were no partial wounds. No points. The combatants battered until one of them was knocked off his feet and put to the sword.

A marshal was assigned to keep the combat from turning fatal. In caged arenas, even the best of friends could get carried away in battle frenzy—with the danger that one of them would be carried away for good.

Casually and without being obvious, O'Toole scanned the crowd again. His vision was limited by the helmet, but at the same time that was an advantage that allowed his curious gaze to roam freely.

Although he wasn't looking for anyone in particular, he wanted to spot the chieftains of the clans who were rumored to attend some of the festivals.

Every kingdom had its ruling court, but so far O'Toole hadn't noticed anyone who seemed connected to the invisible royalty so often whispered about in the Norse Clans.

Just the usual crowd of unusual people. Many of them had come from the Copenhagen area, but there were a good number who'd traveled farther, abandoning the present and embracing the past with every step that brought them closer to this stretch of the Zealand coast.

Liam O'Toole had come down from Copenhagen with a small caravan of ELF members who had helped him get his armor, as well as find a place for him in the lists.

The armor was heavy but it wasn't the weight that really bothered him. It was the heat from the armor that was oppressive, enclosing him and resting heavily on his rough-woven tunic, capturing the sweat from his pores as it trapped the air inside.

The expression "heat of battle" actually stood for a little-known reality. The danger of heat prostration was just as much of an enemy to the armored warrior as his armed opponent was. Perhaps that was why many of the Vikings fought without armor, O'Toole thought. They preferred to protect themselves with amulets and the swiftness of their own attack.

Although O'Toole was sweating, the wintry wind was taking its toll on the spectators outside the wooden fence. The icy autumn air carried the wild scent of the bogs as it tugged at their costumes, raising goosebumps and blowing their hair in golden and red banners, while clutches of leaves scattered around their feet in endless swirling circles.

While there was a lot of dampened vegetation in the nearby marshlands, luckily for the chilled spectators, the arena, the living quarters and the craftsmen's tents were set up on the drier stretches of the raised bog.

O'Toole waited, his staff in one hand, a short sea ax sheathed by his side. It was a requirement for that event for very sensible reasons, and also for the sake of authenticity. While a man would go into battle with a spear, or in this case a staff, he would carry a secondary weapon for use once the spear was hurled or the staff broken.

The wood-blunted sea ax, the ancestor of the Saxon name, would do little against the large swords favored by the other fighters. But as a last resort, it was better than going in barehanded.

A sudden howl from the crowd quickly got O'Toole's attention back to the battle.

The man with the green shield had been staggered by a sword slash that had clanged violently against his helmet.

He backed up several paces, his sword arm wavering as he sought to recover his defensive stance. Finally he managed to stand still and position his shield in front of him. He raised his sword over his head, stepping slowly to the attack.

The dragon-helmeted fighter advanced undaunted, jumping into the air despite the weight of his armor. When he landed solidly on his feet, he flung his shield like a disk at his opponent's face. Then he risked all on a two-handed all-out sword strike at his opponent.

With the full weight of a powerful body guiding it, the sword struck the opponent's shoulder with great force. His shoulders scrunched down, the sword flew out of his hand and his shield dropped boss down into the dirt. Then he tumbled straight down, arms flapping by his sides. The dragon-helmeted swordsman stepped over to deliver the ritual kill stroke. With both hands on the hilt of his sword, he powered the blade down toward the fallen man, stopping it inches from the bottom ridge of his helmet.

He did it with such power and grace that O'Toole figured the man would have had little trouble in real life, looking for all the world like a knight who'd taken this form of combat to the ultimate bloody conclusion.

But instead of running the sword up under the helmet and through the underside of the man's chin, the dragon-helmeted fighter paused long enough for the marshal to register the "kill."

The marshal signaled the end of the combat with a loud shout. Then he raised the dragon fighter's sword arm in acknowledgment.

The crowd roared their approval.

The victor took off his helmet, breathing out the fire of combat from his lungs and gasping in the cold fresh air. He had a high forehead and blond collar-length hair knotted in the back in the customary style of medievalists.

He saluted the fight marshal with his sword, then made the same gesture to the crowd while a group of men and women carried the stunned fighter off the field.

The marshal spoke to the victor, then looked over in O'Toole's direction.

They were obviously talking about him.

The two men continued their conversation, then the victor nodded, leaning on his sword to catch his breath. His eyes searched the visor for O'Toole's gaze, as if he were trying to stare him down through the metal slits. O'Toole had seen that kind of look before—it was the look of a man who was about to kill his prey.

The marshal nodded to O'Toole, then to the man with the dragon helmet, who now placed the helmet back on his head. He had agreed to fight O'Toole.

The marshal had been giving the victor of the previous match the option to continue, or to let somebody else from among the gathered fighters take his place. This was one of the practices of the hard-core members of the Norse Clans, because in a real battle the opposing sides didn't stop fighting when somebody got tired.

With this man there was no choice. He would stay until he dropped.

The marshal approached O'Toole and pulled aside the long wooden post that had barred him from entering the arena.

O'Toole stepped to the middle of the fighting area, digging his leather shoes into the earth, getting his center and feeling his balance.

His opponent did the same. He stood with his shield raised in his left hand, his sword in his right.

The marshal stood between both men, saw to it that they were ready, then shouted. He stepped back. The combat had begun.

There was no fancy circling as the swordsman charged immediately with an overhand strike coming right down on O'Toole's head.

O'Toole had two choices. If he held the staff up with both hands it would stop the strike, but the blow might snap the wood in two. He went for the riskier move. Stepping to his left, he dropped into a gondolier's stance, looking as though he was poling downstream. Left arm down, right arm raised, both hands clenched the weapon.

He snapped his right hand down, swinging the staff like an ax. It connected with the swordman's wrist, pushing the sword into the ground and pinning it for a crucial second. Then, before his opponent could recover his balance, O'Toole snapped the staff back into his face.

The wooden staff smashed into the forehead area of the man's helmet, literally rattling his cage.

O'Toole grunted in satisfaction, but before he finished congratulating himself, a sledgehammer crashed into his ribs and sent him reeling backward.

The sledgehammer was actually just a shield. O'Toole's armor kept his ribs from caving in, but the impact stunned him just the same.

The swordsman had recovered, and he was now on the attack again.

O'Toole spun his staff like a spear, stopping the advance with a rap to the helmet.

O'Toole's breath came fast and hard as his heart pumped in increasing rhythm. His chest heaved beneath the armor, and his sore ribs told him that he was alive.

He felt good, as though he was in the right place, among friends. Or at least among the right kind of enemies.

O'Toole thought that maybe it would be better to hold back. If he displayed his martial prowess, it could make him a stand out. He wanted to be accepted, not lionized.

Just as he was thinking those thoughts, the swordsman closed in on him. He kicked O'Toole in the stomach. The strike wasn't meant to hurt him, and it hardly could through all that armor. Instead it was meant to position him and set him up for the finishing thrust.

O'Toole instinctively dropped to the ground, taking the brunt of the fall on his shoulders and kicking up with both feet, spinning at the last moment. His scissors kick swept the swordsman's legs out from under him, and the man fell down to his knees.

The Irishman continued his spin, bounding to his feet and readying *his* finishing strike when the sword swung straight for his eyes. It was a backhanded slash but it caught him square.

O'Toole saw the end coming. He had that sick feeling in his stomach and the momentary clarity that comes when the body flashes a damage report to the brain. As his vision began to blur, the signal was clear. All systems shut down.

But even as he fell, the Irishman struck out, half in rage, half in instinct, throwing himself onto the kneeling swordsman and clotheslining the back of his helmet with the staff. He hit him with the force of an upside-down bench press as he landed on top of him.

As O'Toole thudded against the damp earth, he had a mental image of a dragon flying away from him, just before he fell unconscious.

He had no idea how long that state lasted and came to just in time to hear a query tentatively addressed to him.

"Are you all right?"

It was a woman's voice, soft and with the rising lilt that those of the Scandinavian tongue have when speaking English.

"I'm all in one piece," O'Toole said, opening his eyes. He sat up and felt a stab of pain shoot through his temple. "Make that pieces," he added, then sank back down into the soft makeshift pillow of furs he'd been sleeping on.

He'd been able to make out that he was in one of the tents. It was the more permanent kind of structure that he'd seen at the edge of the encampment.

"We were worried," she said.

O'Toole groaned. He checked himself out slowly for damage, and understood he'd been hammered but suffered no drastic injuries. It felt like the concentrate of a dozen hangovers was swilling around in his brain.

When he closed his eyes, he felt disoriented again. He opened them and concentrated on the sight in front of him. Her hair was also a bright red, and it was braided in a thick coil that snaked down her back.

She was dressed much like the spectators, and the costume didn't look drab on her. It clung to her in a fetching way. And, O'Toole noted with interest, her eyes were a warm bewitching hazel.

"Is this Valhalla?" he asked.

She laughed. *"Valholl,"* she corrected him. "But no, it's not. You're still on earth."

"Lucky me," he said.

There was the sound of a heavy-footed tread just outside the hut, then a scarred hand pushed aside the coarse hanging over the doorway and the marshal looked inside, his eyes immediately locking onto O'Toole. He nodded his head in recognition. "You fought well," he said.

As he approached O'Toole, the woman withdrew to the back of the hut.

O'Toole lifted his right hand and waved away the compliment. "Not all that well," he said. "Otherwise I wouldn't be lying here right now."

The marshal crouched down next to him, looking at his temple. "That shot could've cracked your skull. Normally a guard wouldn't fight with such force against someone new to the clans. That kind of fighting is usually reserved when we are among our own. Not when there is—" he searched for the word "—when there is potential new blood . . ."

"I didn't expect a love tap," O'Toole said.

The marshal laughed. "Then we matched your expectations," he said. "As you did ours."

O'Toole realized the man was checking on more than his health. He was about in his mid-thirties, and though he looked simply like a brawling medievalist out there in the arena, in here he looked more like a thinking man.

"You did better than you think," he said. "The man you fought is not very happy. As a matter of fact, he too was out for a while."

"Glad to hear it," O'Toole said. "Like deserves like."

The marshal nodded. "Where did you learn to fight like that?" he asked.

"Errol Flynn," O'Toole said.

"Who?"

"Errol Flynn, an actor. I watched a lot of movies when I was a kid. Errol Flynn, Richard Widmark. The Vikings."

The marshal lifted O'Toole's callused hand, examining it like a fortune-teller. But here he was telling the past. "This kind of skill didn't come from Hollywood," he said.

"You're right."

"So where did you learn to fight?"

"The old country," Liam O'Toole said. "A land where it's dangerous for me to live."

"Ahh," the marshal said, his voice granting approval. "And you're looking for a new country..."

"I don't quite know what I'm looking for," O'Toole said.

The marshal clasped his shoulder. "I think, my friend, that you may have found it."

He looked at O'Toole's bruised temple and shook his head. "All that black and blue with all that red hair. It suits you fine," he said. "Katerina works wonders with men like you." The marshal stood up and backed away. "You'll stay the night," he said.

O'Toole pushed himself up on his elbows. "I've got to catch a ride back to Copenhagen," he said. "There's an ELF rally—"

"For some of us there are more important things," he said. "And you won't want to miss the feast we're having later. After all the outsiders go."

"I'll stay," O'Toole said.

The marshal nodded, his look making it clear that O'Toole had no choice.

O'Toole was an insider now, and though he was just stepping into one of the outer kingdoms, it was clear that he was on the path.

The marshal left, and once again O'Toole was alone with Katerina, who'd returned to his side as soon as the marshal had gone.

"Sleep," she said.

O'Toole felt his senses returning, and knew the best way to shake off the pain and the grogginess would be to get outside into the open forest and feel the air upon him.

He didn't want sleep, but then again, there was nothing all that painful about staying and receiving the soothing ministrations of Katerina.

"Who was that?" O'Toole asked.

"The marshal. You do remember that part, don't you?"

"I meant his name. Who he is. He seems to wield a lot of power around here."

"Of course he does," Katerina said. "He is one of the kinglings. The small kings."

"And you?" O'Toole questioned. "His queen?"

"I'm no man's," she said. "Yet." Her eyes had a roguish look to them.

They were like windows of opportunity, Liam thought as he looked into them deeply. Then, for a moment, he was worried that his poetry had left him. Maybe his senses had been knocked loose. Faced with a hazel-eyed beauty like Katerina . . . and he could only think of her eyes in military terms.

"Who was the man I fought?" O'Toole asked.

She regarded him more seriously than before, making him think he was asking too many questions too quickly.

"His first name's Telik," she said. "He's one of the Wulfings clan."

"Will he be at the feast?" O'Toole asked.

"No," she said. "He's got business. We're lucky he was able to come to this gathering. In the past he tried to make them all, but lately . . . lately he's been occupied with some important matters in the cities."

"Good," O'Toole said.

"Why's that?" she asked.

There was a frown on her face. Perhaps she was thinking it was cowardice that prompted the question.

"Less competition," he said.

"In the arena?" she asked.

"No," he said. "In your eyes."

TELIK WULFSON WALKED along the grassy ridge that marked the edge of the encampment.

He was no longer wearing armor, but with his loose-fitting cloth shirt and his thatch of hair hanging over his collar, he still had the aura of an untamed Viking warrior about him.

The wildness of this particular site appealed to him. It differed from Denmark's restored sites, where actors played out the roles of their Viking ancestors, living in huts that were replicas, following a regimen dictated by archaeological and sociological chieftains from the universities, academics who decided what was authentic reenactment.

Those sites were interesting to some, but to Telik they were museum pieces. They might have been living and breathing museum pieces, but they were still lifeless.

The Norse Clans would have nothing to do with them. It was here on their own site that the old ways were brought back. Unlike the wearisome rules of the scholars, the rules in the Norse Clans came from the heart—the heart of the warrior cult that was beating once again.

Telik felt at home in the medievalist camp. This was just one of the outposts of the Varangian Guard with no overt connection to the group. It wasn't as austere or regal as the real VG camps, but he still felt better here than in the cities.

More and more the guises were changing. In the beginning, when he first teamed up with Magnus Koll, the Viking ways seemed like an escapist dream, but the more he was drawn into it, the more the real world instead seemed like a dream.

But all that would change soon, he thought, then turned when he heard his name called.

"Telik."

Christian Andreasson, the marshal, was returning from the hut. He'd been checking on the newcomer. "He's come around," Christian said as he approached.

"Good," Telik said. His concern wasn't so much for the man's health as it was for his own needs. The ranks of the VG were getting strong, but not quite strong enough to carry out Koll's dream. "He wouldn't be much use if he couldn't survive a hit like that."

"He's a tough one," Christian agreed. "You gave him a hell of a rap."

Telik continued walking along the ridge, measuring his words as he paced himself. "It was hard enough," he agreed. "Nothing special. Besides, the sword was wrapped."

The marshal must have a point to make, Telik realized, as the man continued in the same vein. "Hit a man with an iron bar and he'll drop, even it it's wrapped in silk."

Telik stopped walking. He turned to squarely face the other man and said, "Just what is the marshal getting at?"

"You couldn't hold yourself in check during the fight. You were fighting nearly full strength."

"He fought in kind," Telik said. "But there's something else. I sensed a danger in this man. He fights good. Maybe too good."

"If he hadn't fought so well, would we want him?" the marshal asked. "No, I think not. We need his kind."

"*If* he's playing no games with us," Telik said. "But I want you to watch him."

"He's being watched already," the marshal said. "Katerina is looking after him."

"She seems quite taken with him," Telik offered the observation.

"Red hair, red beard. Strong. Looks like a born son of Odin. Katerina's been looking for someone for a long time."

Telik's eyes flared. He'd been coming to this site more often than the other Norse Clan sites. Not just to encounter potential new members, but to see Katerina. So far she had managed to avoid him.

"And he's quite taken with her," the marshal added.

"All the better," Telik said. "She can bring him in gradually."

There was silence for a moment, then the marshal made a cautious statement. "Things may move faster than you expect."

"As long as we find out what he's made of," Telik said. As Magnus Koll's man, he had to make a number of decisions, and the most important was to recruit the right type to join the Varangian Guards. It was a slow process. First they were watched in the outside organization, the ELF. Then, if they passed the first test, they were steered to the next step—a gathering of the clans. If they proved themselves worthy, then they were brought to a much harsher proving ground. This man looked as if he would make it. It was up to Telik. He had seen him, and now he had to judge him.

"Christian, find out where he came from."

"I already know," the marshal answered.

"Where?"

"He came out of the blue, an unheralded champion—"

"You read too many fairy tales, Christian."

"And you, Telik, not enough.'

Telik shook his head. He gazed back at the encampment. The fires were being set. Soon it would be dark and the old members of the Norse Clan would sit around the flames to tell tales of the combats they'd seen, to whisper about the dangerous things in the woods.

But tonight Telik wouldn't be there. He had business to take care of in the real world and wouldn't see Katerina's red hair lit by the firelight. He couldn't just take her. Not her. Not yet. But the new man would be with her...

"The Irishman's good, but he's no champion. Not yet. And he didn't come from a fairy tale. He's had his training

somewhere. He could have killed me. That was a lethal
strike, but he held back. You don't learn that unless you've
been in the business.''

"He hinted that he was a wanted man in a few places. On
some hit lists.''

"Those are good credentials,'' Telik said. "If they're true.
Have them verified.''

"I'll have him checked out on a police data base,''
Christian said. "Just like the Vikings of old.''

LIAM O'TOOLE SAT wrapped in sheepskins that draped over
his shoulders. His back was propped against a tree and his
hand was lifting another stone cup of honeyed ale.

The rich mead had been made by Norse Clans brewers
who'd heavily sugared it to boost the alcohol content. It was
a point of honor to drink it, and Liam O'Toole was an
honorable man.

With the homemade brew curling his beard and warming
his heart toward Katerina, he felt that he was home once and
for all, that he had found the place to be.

O'Toole was alert to the dangers. He knew that the camp
was unobtrusively guarded by a clan warden, perhaps by the
marshal himself, Christian. His name didn't quite suit him,
judging by the bawdy songs he'd regaled the crowd with.
But the Irishman thought that Christian was acting a lot
drunker than he was, while he himself was drunker than he
showed. A good deal of that was due to the presence of Katerina, who sat beside him.

She had nursed him back to health, or so he had let her
think. To a man of O'Toole's experience the crack on the
head was minor. He would have shrugged it off any other
time and kept going about his business, but he didn't want
to act any more capable than the clans expected. Better to
let them think he needed to be coached, guided along step
by step until he was ready for a real fight.

The trail that led him to the camp already seemed like a shallow dream. As Barrabas had instructed, O'Toole had made his presence felt in the ELF movement. Crusaders liked to have a good time just like everyone else. They couldn't go around being saints twenty-four hours a day, and O'Toole was always ready to lend a hand or buy a drink.

He had gravitated toward some of the wilder members of the ELF, touring the after-hours dens of Copenhagen with them when they had finished with the endless rounds of political meetings in storefront headquarters and run-down apartments.

He had made himself known as a man with good intentions but a short attention span. An action man. That was why he had been led to the marshlands, where he now partook of the ritual drink.

As evening crept over the camp, the surroundings took on a timeless quality.

The thatched roofs of the primitively constructed huts recalled the dark picture of medieval times. Here, far away from the cities and the crackle and hum of electricity, the only light came from the stars and from the roaring fire of the torched peat.

There were piles of peat that had been cut from the bog and dried out to be used for fuel. Now there was enough for a bonfire—or perhaps for a sacrifice. Both normally occurred near bogs.

That much O'Toole knew from his recent study of Viking culture.

The bogs were mysterious and holy places to the Vikings. It was where they disposed of criminals, outcasts and traitors. In the past decade a number of well-preserved bodies had been dug up from the bogs, their grayish features often still frozen in grimace. Many of them were found with nooses around their necks and several stab wounds in their torso, marking them as victims of an Odin cult.

A cult, in fact, that was very much alive, O'Toole thought, and he was at one of its hidden shrines.

And to all eyes in the camp, O'Toole was one of the worshipers.

There was something else about the camp that O'Toole liked. The Norse Clans revered their poets. Known as skalds, the poets' task was not only to create great legends about their warriors, but to become warriors great enough to have epics made about them.

Warriors and wordsmiths were held in great esteem. To be accomplished in both martial and poetic skills was an ideal they all aspired to.

That was something O'Toole could relate to.

But even better than creating a poem, O'Toole thought, was living in one.

Right then he felt as if he were almost living inside one of the great epics, Beowulf.

As some of the lines of the poem passed through his mind, he saw them through Viking eyes—eyes that peered in the darkness for the monsters who lurked just beyond the shadows of the fire, the ones who "dwell in the secret lands, haunt the hills loved by wolves, the windy nesses, dangerous marshy paths, where the dark moorland stream sinks in the somber earth."

He'd long conjured up such places in his mind, but tonight was the first time he'd ever visited one of them. In such good company, too, he thought, as another skald began his tale . . .

CHAPTER ELEVEN

"Film at eleven," Barrabas said. Tired from a night of surveillance of suspected VG targets, he planted both elbows firmly on the long table in front of him and propped up his head. The grim visage across the table must match my own, he thought.

"Again?" Alex Nanos complained.

"Again and then some," Barrabas said. "After we get up to par with this film on 'The Ten Best Chemical Hits,' then we meet with a superspook from one of the Norwegian chemwar programs."

"How enchanting," Nanos said. "Or maybe I should say *enchanted*, with all these spell-casting drugs we've been learning about."

They were sitting in a sterile-looking cafeteria in a lower chamber of a small military base just west of Oslo. The lights in the room were artificially bright, and though it could have been any time of the day, it was ten in the morning.

Claude Hayes and Billy Two were standing in a nearby chrome-and-steel alcove, helping themselves to their usual transfusions of coffee.

All the SOBs were dog tired. Although Eric Thorne's task force was also conducting a large-scale surveillance operation against likely ELF and VG targets, the SOBs had their own intuition to follow. They didn't like to sit around and depend on someone else's intelligence.

So far they had turned up about the same number of leads as their counterparts. Not a whole hell of a lot, Barrabas thought. There were some promising people to check out, people who might lead them to their real targets, but there was no great breakthrough.

While they were waiting for that breakthrough, the SOBs were arming themselves with one of the most important weapons in the arsenal against terrorism—knowledge. It looked as if the only way they could gain an initial engagement with the VG was by anticipating how and where they would strike, and then to be hopefully in a position to launch a counterstrike.

The current visit to the base was yet another part of their education.

The base was unnamed. It was known to the Norwegians who worked there simply as "the facility."

Aside from the endless supply of coffee, what the facility had to recommend it was its close proximity to the Allied Forces North Europe headquarters at Kolsas. The AFNORTH headquarters always had a complement of high-ranking military figures and civilian experts on hand.

The United States, Great Britain, Canada, Denmark and Germany staffed the headquarters group along with the Norwegians. Since contingency plans for the defense of Norway, as well as all of northern Europe, were hatched at AFNORTH, there were always a considerable number of support staff available.

A satellite community of spooks, diplomats and "civilian" brain trusts had grown up around AFNORTH, and one of the scenarios they were all working on was the chemical crusade of ELF and the VG.

Barrabas was getting a steady dose of their intel on it and hoped that knowledge would serve as the antidote when the time came. And if only it came soon, he thought. He was tired, running out of patience. The VG were playing a cat-and-mouse game with the SOBs and the Norwegian populace, who were cast in the role of mice about to get exterminated with an arsenal of high-tech poisons.

Like most successful guerrilla operations, the VG were infuriatingly unpredictable. After a flurry of sudden strikes, they lay low, hiding out and regrouping.

There was no place for the SOBs to strike back yet. All they could do was predict the possible strike targets and be prepared to move out.

Until they got their sights on the target, Barrabas was determined to explore every avenue, which was one of the reasons he'd taken Eric Thorne up on his suggestion to meet with a Norwegian scientist who specialized in chemical warfare.

After a few minutes of waiting, while the SOBs inhaled coffee, Eric Thorne arrived.

"Good morning," the covert commander of the Norwegian task force said. He grabbed a seat next to Barrabas. "Are you ready?"

"We've been ready since the day we got here," Barrabas said.

"So I noticed," Thorne said. "That was quite a show you put on in the park the other day."

Thorne's attitude had changed a good deal since the assassination attempt. Initially he'd chafed at the slightest hint that someone had penetrated his service, but the shots fired in Frogner Park proved that someone knew about their mission. Fortunately the shots had come from one of the white hats.

Billy Two's calm marksmanship had taken out the assassin. Now the only thing that had to be plugged was the leak that had led him to the park.

The leak could have come from higher channels in the Ministry, or maybe from someone in the lower ranks. Whatever the source, it was obvious that it had come from the Norwegian side. If anyone had been shadowing the SOBs, they'd had plenty of opportunity to hit them before they rendezvoused with the Norwegians.

"Any luck with the assassin?"

"Yes," Thorne said. "Some. It appears that someone imported him from Germany. He wasn't really from the mercenary network, but from the underworld. It was more like a murder for hire."

"They could be using throwaways," Barrabas said, "bringing in outside hitters with no connection to the main battle group. If they get caught, so what? There won't be any traces to the parent organization. And if they get killed instead of caught, all the better."

Thorne blew away the steam from his Styrofoam cup of black coffee. "You've been reading my mind," he said.

"No task too small," Nanos vowed.

Thorne looked at the Greek.

"Or too large," Nanos said.

"Don't mind him," Barrabas said. "He's in training to be funny."

"Send him back to boot camp," Thorne said, "for the jokes, that is. His military maneuvers seem fine. All your men did a hell of a job out there. But to get back to the killers. I tend to agree with your throwaway theory. The man who fell from the trees wasn't a singular case."

"You've got other leads?"

Thorne nodded. "We contacted SAPO and IB immediately after the Trondheim massacre. The Swedes have one of the most comprehensive computerized dossiers in Europe. They helped us trace the single Varangian Guard who has been identified to date. He was killed by a Jaeger just before they both went into the water."

"Identified as a pure wacko," Hayes said.

"Pure," Thorne agreed. "But the man was not what you would call a wacko. He was an accomplished mercenary with a number of scrapes. He'd been involved in the drug trade in the past, although his service in the Norwegian Army was exemplary."

"As far as you *know*," Barrabas said. "He could have made his contacts there. Or he could have turned bad somewhere after his hitch."

"Right," Thorne said. "But wherever and whenever it happened, one thing is certain. He was committed. It was a medieval type killing, obviously. Committed by someone who identified completely with the original Varangian Guards."

"That much we know," Barrabas said. "What else have you discovered?"

"There's been another killing that may be connected to this matter."

"Where?"

"Sweden," Thorne said.

"That's great," Barrabas said. "That means we only have a couple of thousand more miles to search."

"Not really," Thorne said. "This was connected, but in a peripheral way. Not an actual VG operation, but one carried out for them."

"Another throwaway?" Barrabas asked.

"In effect, yes. It happened in Old Uppsala. Although it was a murder it was also a robbery and the Swedes think that was the primary motivation here."

"Any special reason?"

"Yes," Thorne said. He leaned forward, opening his hands as he slid them over the table like a poker player showing his winning hand. "The man who hit that house entered quietly. First he took out a guard dog, nice and neat, then came in quietly. He murdered the woman, then went though the house, opening safes, discovering all her hiding spots, all in all doing his job in a calm and relaxed manner. He spent a lot of time in there."

"So?"

"So the Swedes think it wasn't a merc because mercs like to come crashing through doors, make their hit and then exit with guns blazing if they have their choice."

"Hey, we'd use keys if someone gave them to us," Nanos said. "But you're right. Get in, hit the target and get out. That's how the usual merc would do it."

Thorne nodded. "This guy came in like a ghost. No one even knew anything had happened for two days—until she failed to show up for an appointment at the university. He got what he was looking for and then some. There were a number of items known to be in her house that were missing. And there was another item rumored to be in her house. A relic, supposedly a ring from a recent Norway excavation."

Thorne briefed them on Old Uppsala. Not only was it the site of one of the oldest known Viking temples, the area had a goodly share of burial mounds and Viking ships. As a result, the region attracted some of the best-known specialists in Viking history.

For centuries it had been the home of pagan kings, and even after the temple was burned and replaced by churches, the pagans had come back.

The struggles between the old gods and the new one had never quite ended in Uppsala.

Rich in lore, it was the kind of place that attracted a specialist like the Reykling woman. A well-accepted authority, she was also considered by many to have a few lock picks in her antique hope chest. An occasional dealer in relics, she was a likely candidate for having the relic in her possession.

According to the rumors, she sold the ring in question. But obviously something went wrong along the way.

"You think she was involved with the VG in some way?" Barrabas asked.

"In the wrong way," Thorne said. "They certainly had her taken care of. The way I see it, they sent in a professional to do the job. A professional who the Swedes have been after for some time. Apparently he's one of several specialists in the underworld trade of artifacts. But this time he left something behind that connects him to the VG.''

''What's that?'' Barrabas asked.

''He left an ax in Lillian Reykling's neck. It's a modern version of one of the old Viking battle-axes. Long handle, sharp blade. It was left as a warning.''

Barrabas drank the rest of his lukewarm coffee, then set the cup down in the middle of the table, where it made a hollow sound.

''And you think the ax is meant as a signature,'' Barrabas said. ''That the VG put him up to it.''

''Yes,'' Thorne said. ''The man has killed before when he had to, but never like this. The ax marks him as someone working for the VG. Still, it was a gruesome way to go for the woman. It takes a certain kind of ghoul to use a weapon like that.''

''Let's hope we meet them soon enough,'' Barrabas said.

Thorne looked at Barrabas. ''I've given you all I've got so far,'' he said. ''Within reason, of course. Now it's my turn to ask. Have your people come up with anything?''

Barrabas was silent for a moment. The remark about ''his people'' could refer to the six SOBs—or the thousands of men and man-hours the NSA was bringing to bear on the search for the Viking camps. In addition, Jessup was squeezing what he could from the CIA.

''No need to hold back,'' he decided. ''We have somebody who is well on his way to joining what looks like one of their paramilitary groups. He should work his way up fast. There's a danger in moving that quickly, of course. Getting noticed by the right people and getting their interest means you also raise a lot of suspicions. But in the couple of contacts we've received from our man so far, he's been able to inform us about a network of medievalist groups. Although it's moving slowly, we don't want to push it and send in more people just yet. We don't want to show too much interest in them.''

Thorne sighed. His disappointment was obvious. "The medievalist groups? They're scattered all over Norway. And you can find them throughout Scandinavia. Naturally they were considered and studied."

"And our man is in one of them," Barrabas said.

"That may be helpful," Thorne agreed. "But there's no proof that these groups are involved with the VG. A lot of them are tough outfits by nature. They appeal to a certain breed. Even some of our own people have participated in the medievalist groups in the past. It's good sport. And the people, overall there's a lot to be admired in them..."

"Some of your people are already involved in these groups?" Barrabas asked. "On their own?"

"Yes," Thorne said. "It's a great diversion. In recent years it's become as popular with some of our people as football is with yours. I think when we find the people we're looking for, they'll be buried much deeper. Not something you can just walk into through a group of escapists."

"True, it could just be a diversion," Barrabas said. "But there's also the chance that a few weekend warriors have become full-time warriors, keeping their military careers as cover."

"As I said, all of this has been considered," Thorne replied. "We've checked out the people in our groups and our initial investigation shows them to be legit. As far as we're concerned they'll probably be cleared through all phases of the investigation. But just to be on the safe side, we have a few of our people cozying up to some of the outfits."

"Would any of them be the Norse Clans?" Barrabas asked.

"Of course," Thorne said. "The Norse Clans are the most well-known. And respected. But let me explain something to you: there are perhaps fifteen to twenty thousand members of these clans. Those are a lot of suspects. It would take perhaps a hundred thousand men to watch them, which we can't really spare at the moment. Besides, we can't picture all or any as being members of the VG. It's a lead, but not a definite one. Don't get your hopes up.''

"They're not," Barrabas said. "We just like to consider everything under the sun."

"Good," Thorne said. "Then you'll like what our distinguished professor is about to show you. Shall we go to the screening room?"

"Yeah," Barrabas said. "Let's go see what this mad doctor has to show us."

"Mad doctor isn't quite the word," Thorne said. "She's a bit angry perhaps, but not mad."

"She?"

Thorne led the SOBs out into the hallway, then down a series of drab corridors.

"Don't worry," Thorne said. "She'll be just as surprised to see you. Until now she'd been briefing brass and civilian head honchos from around the world. They usually just sit there and mull things over for ten years or so. This will be her first action briefing. You'll be the first real live troops to get this information."

Thorne was right on the money. The mad doctor was surprised to see the SOBs troop into the screening room with the leader of the Norwegian task force.

The SOBs were dressed in fatigues and there wasn't a general among them, to her disappointment. Obviously she'd been expecting another cabal of bureaucrats and had dressed accordingly.

Resting a slender arm on a wooden podium at the side of a small stage was a woman in a soft brown, high-necked dress. With her severe gaze, she looked like a red-haired lioness with a long mane sweeping out to frame her face.

The kind of woman you take to embassy affairs, Barrabas thought. More importantly, she was the kind you wanted to take home afterward. She was in her late thirties, maybe early forties. A sophisticated and worldly woman. Barrabas thought it likely that she had seen everything, except, judging from her disapproving and stern expression, a troop of soldiers of fortune penetrating the hush-hush haven.

The recessed screen behind her was small. Obviously this screening room wasn't meant for large groups. It was used for select audiences, Barrabas thought, those who could be trusted to keep what they saw to themselves.

He also doubted that many people would mind being confined with her in such a compact room.

"There seems to be some kind of mistake," she said, addressing Thorne.

She spoke the King's English. Barrabas figured she would use the same flawless enunciation in half a dozen tongues. Her work as an adjunct to NATO demanded a fluency in languages and a high tolerance for bullshit.

"No mistake," Thorne said, ignoring her obvious discomfort while making introductions. He swept his arm toward the redhead onstage and said, "This is Dr. Gudrun Bjoner." He continued the sweep of his arm, indicating the SOBs. "And these are the Americans I want you to show your work to."

"Might I remind you . . ." She paused, obviously searching for the right thing to say, aware that Thorne's word opened doors that by all rights were locked to men. His word could also shut doors that were open in the covert community. "Might I remind you, Mr. Thorne, you said to prepare a showing for an American delegation. These men look like soldiers."

"Perceptive, Gudrun," he said. "And if they wore white Stetsons, I'll bet you'd say they looked like cowboys."

Her face reddened as she spoke, half in anger and half in embarrassment, but there was a certain curiosity there also. The men who stood before her, whoever they were, were out of the ordinary. "Mr. Thorne," Gudrun said. "You yourself have stressed the importance of keeping this material guarded. These are restricted films—"

"R-rated or X?" Nanos joked.

Gudrun ignored the Greek. But she stared at Barrabas in a way that said she really didn't mind that he was there at all. Sparks were flying between them, but they were grounded by the presence of the Norwegian security man and the other soldiers.

"No one on the outside is really supposed to get a look at this kind of information," she said, still looking at Barrabas.

Barrabas nodded his head as if he understood perfectly that he wasn't supposed to see the film. Then he sat down in the front row of black-cushioned seats, ready for the screening.

Nanos, Hayes and Billy Two dropped into the remaining front-row seats.

Gudrun seemed slightly flustered. She turned to Eric Thorne for more of an explanation.

"There's no problem at all," he said. "If you'll take another look around this room you'll see that no one is here." Thorne waited as Gudrun lifted her eyes skyward. She then scanned the room, looking over everyone's head.

There was a clear smile on her face when she turned back to Thorne. "You're right," she said.

"And what's more," Thorne said, "there's no one in this room on my authority."

The Norwegian had made it clear. If anything happened and there was a ruckus about not following channels, it would be on his head. Eric Thorne had more things to worry about than making sure he got the right kind of tickets to admit an audience of SOBs for a special screening.

Barrabas laughed quietly. It was the same the world over. The people who really needed something, whether it was weapons, money or information, were usually the last ones to get it. Meanwhile, the people who got their combat experience by sitting behind a desk reading situation reports, or toadying to the right bureaucrat, were given carte blanche access to the most privileged information.

That was the reason for Thorne's double-talk and Gudrun's initial reluctance. Whatever uniform they wore, everyone had to cover their ass.

And as he waited for the film, Barrabas couldn't help thinking that Gudrun covered hers well as she prepared to show them the top-secret films in this theater of the absurd.

"Well then, if everyone is ready," Gudrun said, "we'll begin." She turned a couple of switches on the control deck built onto the podium, lowering the lights and turning on the recessed screen. They were all plunged into shadow, like apostles before a brilliantly lit screen.

It took Barrabas a few moments for his eyes to adjust to the darkness, and to help him along he used Gudrun Bjoner as a focal point.

Gudrun gripped the joystick speed control and pushed it to the right. She fast-forwarded through several blank frames and test-color patterns, and finally brought the tape to a stop on a light blue kill frame, which was logoless.

There were no credits on this movie.

"What you are about to see is a compilation of footage I've assembled over the years. Interspersed with the footage will be charts, data, whatever is relevant to presenting the most accurate picture of chemical warfare today. Confirmed incidents as well as suspected incidents. Some of the episodes are quite old but they must still be considered important because those same techniques might be used today or tomorrow."

"Before you start," Barrabas said, "I'd like to ask a question."

"Go right ahead." She seemed slightly perturbed at the interruption but still gave him the floor.

"Thanks," Barrabas said. "I'm sure you're good at history, Gudrun. And so are we. Most of us have a basic familiarity with the subject at hand. The key question here is this: how are you at predicting the future? My main interest right now is to find out what's going to happen or what can happen with future guerrilla attacks. What are the potential targets? What kind of sequence can you predict judging from the chemicals they have available to them? What additional chemicals do they want? Can you give us that?''

His main interest had been stated clearly. He didn't want to waste time viewing a collection of chemical-warfare-related footage unless it was going to be useful in fighting the VG. His other interest—Gudrun Bjoner herself—was spoken in a silent language.

"I understand you are an action team, but if you can sit still long enough . . .'' her voice took on a delicate scolding quality ''. . . then you'll be able to see what you're up against. If you manage to stay awake through it all, then perhaps I'll be able to help you predict the future. That is *my* main interest.''

She looked around the room, her eyes patrolling every face for any further objections.

Seeing none, she pushed the joystick forward and Stonehenge appeared on the screen, the circular stone megaliths standing atop Salisbury Plain in England like a prehistoric timepiece, a sacred clock that stopped ticking centuries ago.

"This is Stonehenge," Gudrun said. "A number of scholars believe that prehistoric shamans cast their spells here. Later Celtic priests and Druids used potions and herbs to stir their warriors into a homicidal frenzy or stun and disorient their sacrificial victims so they would go willingly to their deaths.''

"Sounds like Sunset Strip," Claude Hayes said.

The next scene showed a huge military installation, a small city of modern buildings. "This is Porton Down, still on Salisbury Plain," Gudrun said. "During World War I the British created one of the world's largest chemical-war development centers and proving grounds. But that has long since been dwarfed by the U.S. and the Soviet Union. They've mixed enough potions to turn entire armies homicidal or practically disintegrate them from the inside out.''

Barrabas took it all in, thinking for a moment that this was beginning to sound like an ELF rally. But then again, none of the speakers he'd seen from surveillance and news footage of Environmental Liberation Front rallies offered a speaker as effective as Gudrun. Even if he hadn't been interested in her presentation, she still demanded his attention.

Gudrun went through the long list of poisons, potions, gases and grenades that Porton Down had offered to the world and had been prepared to unleash on the Germans at certain stages in World War II. The British finally decided against offensive use of the weapons, not because of any humanitarian concerns, but because they no longer *needed* to use them. The tide had turned in their favor.

But apparently the British had had no qualms about bombarding the Germans with chemicals defensively. If the Nazi forces had succeeded in crossing the channel and invading England, they would have been hit with everything in the arsenal.

The film moved to the grim industrial heart of Germany during World War II, where the huge chemical combines produced the first generation of nerve gases, gases that were still being manufactured decades later by several other countries. Gudrun made the point that although there had been incredible, in fact, inhuman advances made in the science of chemical warfare, the original products were still lethally effective. Those relatively primitive weapons could eliminate populations and contaminate the earth for hours, weeks, months, and in some cases, years. ''You can literally name your poison these days,'' she said. ''The selection of chemicals is endless.

"Hitler was stricken by poison gas during World War I, which was fortunate in the sense that even he considered it too horrible to use. There's no reason to suspect this was out of the goodness of his heart. Hitler believed the Allies would use the same thing on him, forcing him to go through that hell all over again. Even so, Hitler's 'alchemists' went on producing new and better chemical agents."

Gudrun's narration faded in and out. Many of the scenes needed no description. Other than identifying the name of the agent used, there were often no words she could provide.

The footage she showed was exceedingly rare—compiled from filmed experiments that were still considered too ruthless for the public to stomach.

The Japanese germ- and chemical-warfare experiments on American and Chinese prisoners in Manchuria were little known to the world—except to the few survivors who described their experiences years later. Towns were sprayed with airborne disease clouds. Infected carcasses were dropped near water supplies.

Carried out by Japan's notorious 731 Regiment, the experiments on POWs and civilian populations were meticulously observed and reported, although the records were as invisible as the brutalized corpses that carried those secrets into the grave.

Inheriting the Japanese records, the U.S. managed to keep them secret from the world at large until most of the perpetrators were dead and buried, face-to-face with the victims they'd sent before them.

Even when one of the Japanese experimenters was later involved in a bank robbery that employed fatal chemicals, the lid was shut tight. And the results were not destroyed or discarded but marched into the secret annals of warfare.

Gudrun's film brought her select audience up to the present with a mild case of yin and yang.

"This is the overnight train from Moscow to Leningrad," she said, as the Russian express roared over the screen. The next scene showed a group of Japanese citizens who'd been riding on the train.

"These men are nuclear scientists who specialized in low-temperature physics. On their way to an international conference, their sleeping car was sprayed with an anesthetic gas that gave them more than dreams. When they finally came to, they were sick and disoriented, and their papers had all been ransacked. The Soviets, in their subtle way, said that a couple of criminals had somehow got possession of the chemical and . . ." She paused. "As you can see, the excuse is flimsy, but the gas was potent. Chemical warfare does not have to be fatal to gain results."

A nerve-gas plant loomed on the screen, near Baghdad. Built by West Germans, the Iraqi "pesticide" plant had all the necessary chemicals for the production of nerve gas. Both mustard-gas attacks and nerve-gas attacks were allegedly launched against Iranian soldiers and Iranian-controlled Kurdish villages within Iraq's borders.

It was a classic problem. Although every country with chemical weapons swore not to use them, when faced with an invasion and no way out, what could they do?

The answer seemed to be in nerve gas. But when footage of the aftermath reached worldwide audiences, there was a shocked gasp.

Some villagers had horrible burns from the mustard gas that had seared their lungs and bubbled their skin. Just as horrifying were the mothers sprawled in the dirt, still holding on to their infants, trying to protect them to the end.

Inevitably the poison clouds settled over the child. Both mother and infant lay in the dirt, their tormented bodies curled up in frozen husks—looking like upended beetles that had been sprayed with insecticide.

"Iraq was faced with an impossible decision," Gudrun explained. "After years of fighting, with the enemy invading their land and taking over strategic areas, they responded with what they considered the surest way to stop it. The use of chemical weapons. Now its easy for everyone in the West to point a finger at Iraq and condemn them. But then remember that the West was—*is*—prepared to use chemical weapons if they have to. The Iraqis decided they had to. And if one side uses one weapon, what's to keep the other side from doing the same? Then, gentlemen, Pandora's Box is open, and there is no way of closing it.''

Gudrun continued to focus on the region, highlighting Iran's offensive and defensive capacity to wage chemical warfare, then Libya's limited arsenal for use against Chad.

Syria's nerve-gas facility in the desert north of Damascus was portrayed in three-dimensional computer-generated video assembled from several different satellite passes made over the complex. Layered one over the other, the satellite images had compiled a total picture of the plant. Next on screen came the Syrian missiles that were ready to deliver the chemicals.

Syria's SS-21 missiles had a 75-mile range, and their Scud-B missiles had a 170-mile range. Armed with chemical warheads, the missiles could easily reach most targets inside Israel.

The missiles and chemical-delivery systems came from the Soviet Union and Czechoslovakia.

Countering the Syrian chemical capacity was the Israeli complex at Dimona. The Israelis had been working on nerve gas ever since they discovered that enemy tanks captured in the 1967 and 1973 wars were prepared for chemical warfare.

Barrabas and the SOBs were now treated to an alchemist's nightmare on screen.

Some of the footage was familiar, coming from news crews on the scenes. Other footage came from government operatives covertly filming production sites or the somber battlefields after the chemical attacks. There was also clinical footage provided by the scientists who'd carried out the tests.

The extremely raw footage had been assembled over a long period of time and put together quite rapidly—due to the covert chemical war threatening Norway in the immediate future. So far, only a couple of skirmishes served as warning, but every indication pointed to a higher-intensity action.

The completeness of the film was itself a bit of a coup for Gudrun.

Although the NATO countries shared information with each other for planning purposes, what they chose to divulge was up to them. What they volunteered depended on their own interests and the perceived needs of the countries they were sharing the information with.

As a result, items of interest became available only after they were known around the world because of the media. Other data, though available in the press, was held back because in the light of some other bit of information, it might have explosive results.

There was also the matter of airing dirty laundry, or in this case, dirty weaponry. No country liked to admit that it used the stocks. No country liked to parade its mistakes and disasters for the rest of the world.

Consequently, the major catastrophes were glossed over or referred to as failed tests. When thousands of sheep were killed because a valve stuck when a plane made its test run over a proving ground, the incident was referred to as "accidental animal fatalities."

Every country had such horror stories about its secret arsenals. The horror stories were used in the film but presented in such a way that only what was considered a suitable or relevant detail was included: the quality and quantity of the chemical, the duration, the long-range effects.

Even with the restrained method of reporting, the film still offered an accurate picture of what the world's arsenals contained and what the SOBs might be up against.

The current openness and willingness to update one another was due to the fact that nearly all the NATO countries stood to face the same situation as Norway.

Whatever information might assist Norway in countering the threat was as strategically important to the commander-in-chief of Allied Forces Northern Europe as it was to the commander, Allied Forces South Norway, and his counterpart, the commander of Allied Forces North Norway.

As a link in the NATO chain, Norway's performance would directly affect the operations of the commander-in-chief, Allied Forces Central Europe, and the commander-in-chief, Allied Forces Southern Europe.

With so many people on the firing line, the word came down to cooperate with the production of a literal sneak-preview film, a film that wasn't supposed to exist.

The end result Gudrun produced was one of those rare bits of intelligence summary that paved the way for NATO operational plans.

For Gudrun it was a major step forward in her covert career.

Rather than gather the information themselves, NATO intelligence operatives analyzed information given to them from the other member countries. Since the West was an open society, a lot of the material was available from newspapers and broadcast files.

But no one had been prepared for the scope of the film, and it became a "must see" for those in the know, as well as those with the "need to know," such as the group of soldiers gathered before her.

The footage covered the U.S. installations that multiplied after World War II just like some of the viruses they created inside of them.

The sites appeared one after the other, huge desert complexes, entire cities carved out of rock. Air strips, caverns, high-tech dungeons guarded by barbed wire and electrified fences.

Rocky Mountain Arsenal, Colorado. Edgewood Arsenal in the Aberdeen Proving Grounds, Maryland. Pine Bluff Arsenal. Fort Detrick, Maryland. Dugway Proving Grounds, Utah.

The U.S. Chemical Corps picked up where the British left off, conjuring up enough lethal poisons for friends and enemies alike.

The U.S. arsenals were matched poison by poison, gas by gas, by the Soviets, who eventually surpassed them with concoctions destined for clandestine battlefields.

Kirov, Sverdlovsk, Moscow, along with Wrangel Island and a half-dozen other sites provided a Russian mirror image to the Western factories.

Both sides specialized in creating arcane names for their arcane products: mycotoxins and mustard gas, Blue-X, sarin, soman and tabun, VX, VR-55, and T2 toxins.

The alchemists didn't restrict themselves to man-made chemicals. A good deal of their potions, sprays and powders came from shellfish, reptiles and toxic plants.

Just like the wizards of old, the modern chemists worked with "naturals." They extracted poisons and hallucinogens from salamanders, puffer fish, frogs, newts, mushrooms and coral.

Chinese battalions were hit by the Soviets during border skirmishes that literally knocked out the Chinese troops. Later the Vietnamese struck the Chinese with chemical weapons during one of their frequent flare-ups.

Since World War II the French had quietly created an immense chemical combat capacity and were ready for state-of-the-art offensive or defensive warfare.

Gudrun brought the military aspects of chemical warfare to an end with a survey of delivery systems, from disease-ridden rats to aerosol sprays, land mines and warheads.

"Now we come to something a bit more explosive," Gudrun said. "The civilian sector."

The film closed in on a factory in Paderno, Italy, where a leak from a dye plant actually turned the local population various shades of blue, red, green and violet. Colored spots appeared on their skin in bizarrely hued blotches. The food and plants changed color.

"This was caused by a zinc-based dye mixture released into the atmosphere. A cloud fell upon the city and besides the coloring effect, the irritant affected the eyes and mucous membranes."

Paderno was replaced on-screen by another Italian town. Seveso. The chemical factory exploded a deadly white cloud of dioxin into the air. The town was evacuated and sealed off. Years after the explosion it was still uninhabitable and could be safely approached only by using protective gear.

"These chemical accidents have lasting effects," Gudrun said, "scarring the population with immediate effects of contamination, and shadowing the rest of their lives with birth defects and disease.

"But sometimes, the disease is already there—"

Anthrax spores were believed to have been released into the air after an explosion at Russia's Sverdlovsk germ-warfare plant. A massive evacuation and vaccination program was carried out, but even then there were thousands of casualties.

"From accidents to intentional use is a short step," Gudrun said. "These shots come from Afghanistan..."

The next photos showed Red Army troops returning from a battle with Afghan rebels. Chemical troops were spraying armored troop carriers.

A parade of ARS decontamination vehicles swarmed through the area and a series of decontamination tents were set up for the troops to progress through.

And in the hills the Afghanis were dying from chemical rain dropped upon them.

That particular footage had been hard to obtain. The Soviets treated photographers and reporters in Afghanistan as though they were combatants, and in a way they were. The photographers who made it out of Afghanistan with the chemwar shots dealt the Soviets a hard blow. But as the presence of chemical troops increased, satellite photos picked up and trailed the chemwar vehicles.

The next scene was a swank hotel room. Then faces of well-dressed prostitutes appeared on-screen.

"These troopers also used chemical warfare on their targets," Gudrun explained. "Once they got their men into the room, either before or after the act, they laced the client with scopolamine."

The former covert drug of choice for interrogation purposes was a current favorite among prostitutes, who though professional in one calling, frequently screwed up with their dosages. Several fatalities of prominent businessmen and politicians were directly related to scopolamine-laced drinks.

"Pay attention, Alex," Barrabas said.

Nanos shrugged his shoulders. "I only sleep with girls I know for a while."

"Yeah," Claude said. "For at least fifteen minutes."

Gudrun continued showing a smorgasbord of lethal possibilities to the SOBs. It was overwhelming but necessary to understand. If the SOBs were going to prevent it from happening in major proportions, they had to know where it was going to start.

"The people you are going against have the capacity to wage just about any kind of chemical warfare they want," she said. "The technology exists in third world countries, as well as in terrorist groups. What it comes down to is for you to stop them before they exercise that skill.

"The last section of the film shows where Scandinavia is vulnerable, Norway in particular. Before we move on to that, are there any questions or comments?",

"Yeah," Alex said. "Where can we get some of those white chemical warsuits. And do you know a good tailor?"

Gudrun smiled. "Just keep watching," she said, then continued showing them the travelogue of man-made hell.

CHAPTER TWELVE

Freda Stensgaard strolled through Oslo's sleek, modern international airport with an air that seemed casual but thoroughly purposeful, as though she had a most natural reason for being there.

But even though the airport was the major point of departure or arrival for Scandinavian and European travelers in the Oslo area, Freda was doing neither. She may have looked like one of many passengers coming and going, but she was about to go on a trip of another kind.

No matter how casual her movements seemed, her stroll took her through a carefully mapped-out circuit of the facility.

Freda was dressed in a smart businesswoman's outfit, a gray tweed jacket with matching skirt and powder-gray stockings. Beneath the jacket was a snug white sweater that diverted attention from the calf-leather suitcase she was carrying.

A tantalizing picture of success, Freda Stensgaard looked confident, businesslike and beautiful. She presented a challenge that some hard-driving men could never refuse.

As she walked on the smoothly polished floor of the terminal, her high heels tapped out a slick cadence that served to trigger the attention of a number of men who then turned to watch her.

Freda pressed a soft-touch button just below the handle of her suitcase. Phase One had begun.

She stopped at a newsstand and picked up copies of *Dagbladet* and *Aftenposten*. Then, after folding the tabloid and the late-edition newspaper under her left arm, she continued on her way.

Freda swung the suitcase in a slow back and forth motion in her right hand, delicately but deliberately mixing the contents inside.

Then she pressed a second button—one on the underside of the handle grip—which she held down as she walked. It took a steady pressure on her part but the effort wasn't enough to be noticeable.

A barely audible hissing sound escaped from a false rivet on the side of the suitcase. From a nozzle tip embedded in the false rivet a steady stream of vapor shot into the air. Phase Two was in effect.

Freda blended in with the crowd, dispersing the finely blended aerosol spray with every step she took.

A man in a gray suit brought her to a halt just as she rounded a bend. They nearly collided, and the slightly flustered blond released her finger from the button, stopping the spray as she studied the man in front of her.

Security! she thought. He was a square-jawed type, his hair thinning, his eyes boring into hers. His short hair looked as though it had been styled in a barbershop that catered to old-school policemen.

She'd seen too many of the type back in her native Denmark.

Freda's senses were alive, taking in everything about him in a split second. It was the same instinct that animals often displayed when somebody intruded into their territory, and it was at work inside Freda, ready to call on the surge of energy that was coursing through her.

Everything about him marked him as a plainclothesman working airport security, one of the silent but not too secret men who looked for passengers out of the ordinary. They all had certain revealing mannerisms to the knowing eye—excessive edginess, too great an awareness of the other travelers. Airports had profiles to fit smugglers, fugitives and thieves—the type of men she used to travel with.

If he tried to detain her, the man was as good as dead.

"Sorry," he said. "I was wondering if you had the time."

Freda smiled. "Of course." She pointedly glanced at his shirtsleeve, which no doubt harbored one of those Dick Tracy watches with alarms, time zones on four continents and perhaps even a microcomputer.

But this wasn't the first time she'd been stopped and asked for the time by a man who had something altogether different on his mind.

Setting down her suitcase, Freda raised her left hand then peeled back her jacket sleeve with her finely manicured nails.

"It's just past three-thirty," she said.

"Thank you—"

With a stream of people passing them on both sides, Freda gave him an impatient nod then started to step around him.

The man was searching for something to say. He scanned the crowd as if someone would give him the perfect words. He'd stopped her by impulse, thinking this could be one of those magic moments. A chance meeting. The right word. The right phrase.

"That's a stunning perfume you're wearing."

She dazzled him with a smile and said, "Thanks," certain that it was lust rather than watchfulness that controlled this man.

"May I ask what kind it is?"

BZ, she thought. By Magnus Koll. It'll really knock you out. "No," she said.

He looked hurt for a moment until she said, "After all, there are some things a woman has to keep secret—if we're going to keep on luring men like you."

"Of course," he said, mollified by the slightly teasing response that confirmed he still had what it took.

"Now," she said, "I'm sorry, but I must be going." She lifted her suitcase in front of her, then followed it away from the man with the throbbing heart.

Whatever he was, he hadn't turned out to be a threat.

Freda glanced once behind her, as if she was giving the man a parting smile. Actually she was looking for Koll's right-hand man, who'd been tagging behind her, ready to deal with anyone who stopped her.

The suitcase was outfitted with a genuine interior, complete with an adjustable mirror on the padded surface. There were business papers inside a folder that indicated she was in the real estate business, with several brochures and tip sheets on luxury-class estates, the kind that only someone of her breeding would handle.

Another item in the suitcase, designed to catch the gaze of anyone who opened it, was a semisedate red satin chemise with black ribbon trim and embroidered marquisette heart-shaped rib cage.

It was something a businesswoman might wear for a little excitement, but nothing that smacked of her past profession. Perhaps it might discourage an inspector who would be embarrassed to run the silky garment through his fingers for too long.

It would have been impossible for any man not to picture Freda in the lingerie.

All in all, the suitcase was designed to fool a cursory inspection, but a more detailed look would reveal the aerosol mechanism hidden inside.

However, if she got led away toward one of the interrogation rooms, Magnus Koll had men stationed in the airport to act before anything happened.

Freda locked eyes with the man assigned to cover her. He wore wood-green corduroy pants and jacket and a canary yellow tie that, judging from her past experience with the man, was probably lined with a wire garrote.

To her Telik Wulfson looked like a man in disguise. She was used to seeing him in the Viking camps in much more primitive clothing. But the world at large hadn't seen that side of Telik Wulfson yet, so to them he looked like just another traveler. His hair was tucked under his collar and was neatly smoothed into place. He appeared innocuous, perhaps a traveler who'd toured one of the bars in search of a traveling companion.

His eyes were roving, taking stock of all the women in sight—including Freda.

Wulfson would have killed the man if he'd posed any danger to her, Freda thought, or maybe he would have killed Freda herself. That certainly wouldn't have bothered him one way or the other. He'd done worse. She knew that for a fact. The images were still burnt in her mind.

It was hard to say what Magnus Koll's plans were. He gave the orders and she followed them.

She pressed the button again, releasing the vapor once again into the closed-in corridors.

After all, she was just following orders.

TELIK WULFSON DRIFTED back into the crowd, surveying the other suitcase-wielding Vikings. A team of four was patrolling the airport, and each suitcase contained the same amount of aerosol and was equipped with the release mechanism.

And each suitcase-wielder was closely watched by yet another man who served as backup.

If anything happened, the VG would make a good account of themselves in the airport.

But Wulfson was convinced that nothing would happen to his people. Arrangements had been made to shepherd all of the VG out of the airport grounds in waiting cars and vans.

What might happen to the rest of the crowd, the civilians filtering through the hallways...well, that was up for grabs.

The mixture they were now being exposed to had been created by Koll himself.

Koll had a lot of experience from his days working for one of the underground drug cartels.

The effects of the aerosol spray were unknown even to Koll's people, including Telik Wulfson. For all he knew, it could be a lethal spray.

But Magnus Koll was a fanatic and not a lunatic in his designs. The cause of the VG would hardly be helped by a mass murder.

At least not under these conditions.

One thing was sure though. The vapor wouldn't take effect right away, otherwise there would be an entire squad of VG left behind in the airport.

When Wulfson had asked for some of the standard antidotes or tranquilizers used to combat the effects of the chemicals in the VG arsenal, Koll had refused.

They had to learn to operate under the influence of the chemicals whenever possible.

Consequently, today's action served as field training besides being a hit. Unless, of course, it was all a test to see if the teams would follow through with their orders.

It was hard to tell. Koll was a merc. He'd done exhaustive preparations on the free-lance missions Telik had worked on with him.

There was no reason to suspect it was just a dummy strike. If that was the case, then Telik Wulfson and the rest of the team were the dummies.

But Telik was beginning to feel a bit off. Part of it was elation, and the rest was expectation. His internal chemistry was starting to cook.

This was a real mission, his sixth sense told him as it kicked into gear.

A battle was imminent, he thought, even if it was only a battle of wills with hallucinogenic ordnance. Koll had an abiding interest in BZ gas, or quinuclidinyl benzilate, as he referred to it in chantlike tones.

The gas had been deep-sixed by the military units in many countries because it had too many unpredictable effects. Nevertheless some of the officers and agents who'd voluntarily conducted maneuvers and field tests under the influence of BZ learned how to control the effects, but only in a limited way.

One of the side effects was that the BZ made them violent to an uncontrollable degree, which made it all the more attractive for Koll's elite unit of berserkers, though even Telik was growing somewhat weary of being around them.

Koll was creating his own private order of assassins along the same lines as the original *hashshashin* of Persia and Syria. Many times Wulfson and Koll had talked late into the night, discussing the order founded by Sheikh al-Jabal, whose liberal use of hashish and mystic training had produced a conquering army ready to embrace death.

And now, once again, an army was being created to charge headlong into that same great warrior's deathlands. *Valholl* awaited.

Telik felt himself getting a bit light-headed. Yes, it had to be the BZ. But how potent was it? And how long before its effects kicked in?

He fought to maintain a calm appearance as he patrolled the airport, but an urgency was building up inside him.

He was carrying a news magazine in his hand. It had been selected not for its contents, but for its thick spine, and it was the only visible weapon Telik Wulfson carried.

Rolled up like a scroll, the magazine could certainly core a man's Adam's apple, or stun him with a quick jab to the gut or the head.

It was an old trick, but even so, not too many people ever expect to be swatted like a fly, and certainly not by a man carrying an innocent-looking magazine.

But it was like anything else, Telik thought; you had to be able to read between the lines.

CHAPTER THIRTEEN

Of the two airports serving Oslo, one was full of crazy people. Their insanity was only temporary, but few of them were in a condition to realize that, especially those who had lingered for a while, getting higher doses of the aerosol droplets filling the teeming halls.

Koll had targeted the airport near the center of Oslo because, unlike the more distant airport at Gardermoen, he could inflict a maximum amount of damage at that location.

The passengers from the airport laced with BZ gas didn't need to get to the harbor or the red-brick town hall that sat at the peak of the fjord in order to affect the city. Busy government offices, shopping districts, parks and streets full of restaurants and theaters spiraled out from the center, and they were places that would soon be visited by all those passengers.

Although the city itself was a relatively small capital in population, with a half million people, it was huge in size. Oslo stretched out from the harbor along forest-studded coastal arms that embraced the fjord on both sides. Attractive villas flashed their windows from the evergreen timbers of the lovely natural setting.

The city spread out from its perch on the fjord, then backed uphill to the high cliffs dotted with ski lodges and restaurants overlooking the capital.

Oslo was capable of expanding into the surrounding wilderness with little problem. Whereas most capitals had a park in the middle of the city, Oslo, in effect, was in the middle of a huge park.

Despite its population, it was the fourth largest metropolitan area in the world.

And the panic was spreading through it like a forest fire—a blaze that had been sparked at the airport.

The madness spread slowly at first, with isolated incidents occurring seemingly at random as the effects of the chemicals overtook individuals and they were stricken by disoriented feelings. But then the number of incidents swelled as the BZ gas took full effect.

It had been timed to act in a relatively short time and calculated so as to give enough time for the victims to *almost* get to their destinations.

SHORTLY AFTER TAKEOFF the pilot of a jetliner on a scheduled Oslo-to-Stockholm flight began to feel uncomfortable, as if he'd been injected with novocaine all over his body. He wasn't quite sure if he could feel certain parts of his body at all.

Ahead of him, beyond a jumble of clouds, he could see that the sky was falling. Clouds dropped like pieces of a puzzle that was suddenly broken apart, hit by the invisible hand of God. Funny it could happen like this, he thought. He'd never noticed this kind of pattern before.

He signaled the first officer to take control of the plane. Or maybe the first officer had signaled him. *Someone* had been yelling in the cockpit a moment ago.

He really wasn't sure about when or how he relinquished control. Whatever happened, one thing was clear. He wasn't flying the plane anymore.

He felt tired as he sank back into the captain's seat, closing his eyes for a moment to shield his brain from all the lights that were flashing.

But it was no good. When he opened his eyes, the radar altimeter merged with the barometric altimeter, playing tricks on him, as was the overhead switch panel. It began pulsing. Then the navigational computer switches started to grow, creeping downward like stalactites.

It was time to close his eyes again; the thought came to him vaguely, just long enough to erase all of the haywire impressions that were assaulting his senses. His mind took up another idea, but it seemed vague and distant, as though it belonged to somebody else.

Passengers. He had better make an announcement to the passengers.

But his mouth wasn't working right. He couldn't say anything. He couldn't even scream.

It was looking pretty bad. The first officer was excited, but he'd managed to keep things under control, even with that angel that was flapping at the windscreen. Looked like an archangel. Or a swan. Then the wings changed from fluffy white to a rich shade of black.

Something was wrong with the plane, he thought, and he shook his head.

"What's wrong?"

The words spun around in circles, echoing his question over and over. "What's wrong?"

Drunk. Someone said he was drunk. Who was it? The first officer or that air steward who normally had a pretty face but tonight it kept on changing, telescoping into strange moon-shaped cheeks.

"I'm not drunk..." he protested. The words got lost on the long journey up from his vocal cords to his mouth. "I'm nottt unrkk. Noddrunk."

Oh god, get me out of here...

The pilot scrambled from his seat then left the flight deck under a hundred watchful eyes. Everyone was watching him so hard that they grew into multiples, clones that came out of the eye stalks and followed his progress.

"Here...all...an injection."

An injection. Yes, they were going to give him an injection. He stepped back toward the upper lounge, but a hand caught him by the elbow.

He didn't make it to the lounge but he could hear voices back there. Somebody else was saying barely coherently that he was seeing gremlins, too. That made him feel better.

So did the announcements.

The first officer informed the passengers that they were returning to Oslo airport.

The pilot couldn't hear why. He was listening to the soft but controlled chatter from air-traffic control about all flights from Oslo halted.

Thank God the first officer was still in control, the pilot thought, but then he didn't think much of anything as the jab of a needle brought with it a welcome stab of pain, and suddenly he found himself thinking about the waitress he'd stopped off to see for a quick cup of coffee...

THE WOMAN in the coffee shop screamed.

Scalding coffee splashed over her from the shoulder down to her hip. It felt like hot glass searing away her skin bit by bit, then scraped altogether into one horrendous burn.

The waitress looked on as if she didn't know what had happened. She had an empty look on her face and a carafe of coffee in her hand.

THREE MINUTES AWAY from the airport, a blue Opal gave chase to a taxi.

The driver of the Opal rammed into the back bumper of the taxi. There was a curt metallic sound, just a brief little crunch.

Not enough, thought the aggressor, who stepped on the gas and back-ended the taxi again. The taxi accelerated, and through the back window a pair of angry frightened faces were yammering at the Opal driver, who'd been in a foul mood ever since he left the airport. However, he'd concluded, it was nothing that a little demolition derby couldn't fix.

THE AIRBUS WAS SCHEDULED to take the new arrivals from the airport to Oslo's Central Station.

Instead it drove around in circles without depositing any of its human cargo.

The passengers began to suspect something was wrong when the driver suddenly pawed furiously at the steering wheel and pulled over to the side of the road. He began pounding his hands on the steering wheel.

"What in heaven's name is wrong with our driver?" a white-haired matron asked, her hand tightly gripping her purse as though she wanted to derive some assurance from it. Her eyes darted over the gallery of passengers in search of a response.

"Stop shouting!" the driver yelled, turning around, his head spasmodically swivelling on his scrawny neck.

It was like something out of a movie, a movie no one wanted to see.

The passengers screamed back at him in an absolute fury.

The white-haired woman was suddenly overwhelmed by the years of indignities heaped upon her. All the accumulated slights were suddenly acutely alive in her mind. No one ever listened to her anymore or paid the least bit of attention to her complaints. She had sat by politely and took it over and over, year after year, but now there was no stopping her. She had reached her limit. As the passengers were jostled along in the airbus, she marched and staggered up to the front.

She swung her purse as though it was a bolo, building up the momentum with a sidearm swing. The pointed bottom corner of the leather bag slashed the driver's cheek, drawing a neat red line that held its form for a moment, then changed into jagged splotches as blood ran down his face in bright red droplets.

Whack! The purse gashed him again on its return journey, goring his neck like the horn of a bull.

The blow snapped his head back. He went with the motion and backed out of range of her next slash, then ducked under the onslaught of the weighted purse and hit her in the stomach with a meaty forearm. That brought her back to her senses, and she doubled over, gasping for breath and staggering back in the direction of her seat.

"Watch your step!" the driver shouted, cackling as she stumbled against another passenger who was trying to get up from the seat.

Next he stomped on the gas pedal and threw the standing passengers back in a swirling trample of swearing, sweating and panicky bodies.

Despite the frantic motion of the airbus and the press of bodies, one man doggedly moved forward, prying his way through flailing elbows and grasping fingernails. He lurched forward, hand over hand, seat by seat, until finally he got within striking distance. He stretched his hands out in a strangling motion and darted for the driver's neck.

The driver stomped on the brakes, filling the bus with a violent screeching sound.

"Ohhhh!" His would-be throttler uttered a weak protest just before his head smashed into the windshield. Not heavily enough to crack the glass, but it certainly did a number on his head. The man's hands fell to his sides, and he collapsed to the floor.

The driver was in his glory. No one could touch him. This was his province.

He lurched the bus around in a poorly executed turn, like the kind he'd seen on the television shows where the wheelman expertly whips the vehicle around.

The van lifted up onto two wheels, almost tipping over. Then it came back down on all four, the tires suddenly grabbing the road and hurling them all forward in a chorus of screams and screeches.

Even before the airbus was totally under control, he stomped on the pedal again and sliced through oncoming traffic.

As though he were sitting in an arcade booth in a video racetrack game, he spun through the traffic, honking at pedestrians, clearing everyone in the field out of his way.

Except it wasn't a game.

The oncoming drivers cursed at him in livid fury while their vehicles emitted a squawking, irritating cadence of sound.

A cream-colored Volvo cut in front of his path, ran off the road and scrunched metal on concrete for ten yards before sailing into the brick pillar of a parking lot. The man jumped out of his car and waved his fist at the driver of the airbus.

The airbus drove on, leading a herd of screeching, honking cars, all of them containing enraged passengers. Looking in his rearview mirror, the bus driver saw the afternoon sun glinting off a phalanx of cars. All pursuing him. He chopped at the rearview mirror, then flung it onto the floor.

The blond came to his mind then.

The blond in the airport that he'd been following. He'd ducked in to pick up a newspaper while he was waiting for his passengers. Then he saw the woman carrying a suitcase. He trailed after her, not thinking for a minute he could strike up a conversation with her.

But still, he could dream.

And so he walked behind her—and began to dream. Oddly, at first it appeared to him as if she didn't quite know where she was going. She backtracked a couple of times, and when it might have started to be evident that he was following her, he broke off his idle pursuit.

He couldn't understand why he was thinking of the incident, but it was almost as if a part of his mind made some connection with her and this cloud of craziness that had settled over him and over everyone. His passengers all going crazy.

He slammed the brakes on with another jarring screech. The white-haired woman was shouting into his face again. He grabbed her by the elbow and pushed her off the bus. The other passengers piled out too, jumping at the chance for salvation. The driver kicked at one of the men, missed him, then jumped back into his seat and spun the wheel, thinking that he was going to get back to the airport and take care of that stuck-up bitch...

THE AIRPORT SECURITY MAN was reeling. He felt light-headed, as if he'd been hit with something. Somebody had cracked him one, he decided, and he had to arrest somebody.

He grabbed at a man in black jeans and a denim jacket. "You'll come with me—"

The man skipped away, brushing off the detaining hand with the ease he would use in dealing with an insect.

Insects.

The corridor was full of insects. Lobster-backed insects beneath those suits, their antennae pointing at him.

He called for the rest of the security staff to come to his rescue. They came running at the sound of his voice. Safe...he was safe. But when they reached him, it wasn't to help him. They were grabbing him, hauling him down the hallway.

Only now did he realize that they were disguised as security men. In reality they were some kind of scaly creatures, with red faces, claws sticking out at the end of their hands...

PETER L. HARRACK chugged into the media room of Elsk-bern Unlimited like a locomotive, his pipe billowing out wispy puffs of smoke in his wake.

He was a bit more animated than usual.

The marketing executives had been sitting patiently in the soundproofed, light-proofed room, reviewing potential advertising pitches for their latest line of sporting gear into the Scandinavian and Northern Europe market.

They looked bored.

Half-empty coffee cups, crushed cigarette butts and stale soda cans littered the top of the table.

But by unanimous consent, each of them was imprisoned in the Oslo headquarters until they came up with the proper approach. The wise old men of the company were gathered in the smoke-filled room for one of their legendary caucuses. No one would leave until they'd agreed on the right advertising campaign and the right advertiser. Blocks of time had been mapped out for each agency to come in and do their best—the usual dog-and-pony show.

There wasn't much new to be said about sporting clothes that hadn't been said during the last couple of hundred years. Most of the ad men had pitched variations of those same nothings.

And now Peter Harrack stood in front of them, acting as if he was pleased to see so many distressed faces once again.

Peter had once handled a fair amount of their advertising, and had come to win it back.

He set up his carousel tray of computer-generated slides, ready to roll out the smorgasbord of advertising slogans he was known for. He did series commercials, each one a sequel to the previous one building to the grande finale that was supposed to hook the audience, making them all think they shared a private joke.

"Gentlemen," he said.

The noble heads who'd long overseen an empire of sweaters, socks, ski pants, hats, exercise apparel and apparatus, all looked up at the advertising man who'd just called them to order.

But something was wrong.

He wasn't saying anything, but just stared at them all as if he'd never seen them before in his life.

True, he'd just flown in to Oslo after a grueling round of business in London, but that was no matter. Not during the pitch. The pitch was sacred. Nothing stopped a scheduled advertising pitch except an act of God.

But Peter Harrack was looking godlike—or looking like he was seeing a god at the moment.

His eyes were glassy. He had the countenance of a man who was about to issue a tablet full of commandments.

Yet he didn't say a word.

Some of them thought he was acting out his pitch, setting them up for a knockout punch.

But he remained silent and instead of talking he unclipped the carousel slide tray from its stand.

If he was trying to get their attention, he got it. All eyes followed his hand.

They followed his hand as he flung the carousel across the room. It spun like a black discus directly at the balding skull of the head of international marketing, who threw himself out of the chair to avoid getting his head bashed in by the heavy round tray.

"What are you looking at?" he demanded.

He had their undivided attention now as to a man they rose from their seats.

It took nearly all of them to restrain him.

PHONE CALLS flooded into the Oslo police station. Reports of accidents, assaults, hysteria. At first it seemed a lot of celebrating was going on. But then the number of incidents grew and grew, and the disorderliness took on horrendous proportions. It wasn't just drunkenness or an isolated celebration that had got out of hand.

It was an endless parade of misery and suffering.

First the victim would feel giddy, then stumble around drunkenly. Next came the hallucinations or paranoia. Then others in turn became victims as those affected by the chemicals exploded in rage.

Ambulance crews patrolled the streets, chasing or being chased by the people they'd been dispatched to help. But there weren't enough crews to keep up with the demand. An army of men in white coats simply wasn't enough. Even with calling on backup personnel, there was no way they could handle the situation adequately. Injuries and madness multiplied.

Hotel rooms suddenly had an influx of apparently drunk guests. But there was more at stake than the loss of decorum. Many of them were violent.

There were smashings in lobbies, in restaurants, in bars. And it wasn't just glass that got smashed, not just replaceable items. There was an epidemic of violence as fists connected with vulnerable skulls, as seemingly peaceful guests suddenly went berserk.

All of it related to and started with new arrivals, and finally the airport was shut down.

All personnel—those who weren't affected—were sequestered in separate waiting rooms. Rooms where they waited to go mad, perhaps.

Security personnel, suspicious even of their fellow officers, tried to make sense of what had happened in the airport, beginning a series of interrogations that pointed to no flash point. It just seemed to happen spontaneously and randomly.

There were a few holdouts among the cargo handlers who had gone on a freewheeling rampage, damaging some of the goods that came into their hands, but mostly just running wild, fleeing from the approaching security men and hiding out in the spots they knew best.

It all added up to a somewhat subdued panic that had the city firmly in its grip.

No one quite knew what was going on, but the signs were clear that something uncontrollable had happened.

The word quarantine passed from mouth to mouth. People talked about a mysterious disease, a homicidal contagion spreading throughout the capital.

Rumors spread like wildfire, feeding on the increasing incidents of violence, and swamped the newspapers, radio and television, hinting at some dark conspiracy, some monstrous oversight on the part of the government.

But no matter what rumor one listened to, the effect was the same and made one thing certain.

Nothing was safe anymore, and nobody could trust in the reassuring, calming aspect of the commonplace things in daily life.

CHAPTER FOURTEEN

Magnus Koll followed the progress of his field test on television.

The Norwegian Broadcasting Company was bringing a firsthand look at the "airport incident" into Koll's living room at his Tonsberg estate.

The newscaster had several bulletins and could hardly keep up with new reports filing in, and the usually cool and suave looking man had a flustered and perplexed air. The initial reports mentioned a number of accidents near the airport, and then it became clear that large-scale paranoia had struck normally placid and peaceful Oslo.

No one seemed to know what caused it, except for Magnus Koll. It was a modified BZ gas. A type that had been disavowed by the Western countries because it was too outlandish for them.

The newscaster strived to regain his professional tone, and his voice took on a comforting quality. It was no accident he'd been selected to handle these bulletins.

"The illness is believed to have come from tainted food on one of the flights coming into Oslo..."

The screen showed a busy newsroom as up-to-the-minute reports were coming in.

The chaotic view of the news bureau was reassuring in a strange and misleading way because it made the airport incident seem like just one more show for the public to digest: it was being seen across the country, it was being handled, and it signified that it was business as usual. Another crisis under control.

MATCH THE SECRET COMBINATION NUMBERS ...AND RECEIVE FIVE FREE GIFTS!

HOW TO SCORE **5** INSTANT FREE GIFTS:

1. The Combination Lock on the front cover is yours. First, CHECK the numbers on this Lock against the three numbers on the right.

2. If you have a MATCH, Peel off your Combination Lock from the front and attach it in the space provided across.

3. RETURN the attached card and we'll send you your Free Gifts: 4 of the hottest Gold Eagle novels ever published—**FREE**—plus an *extra* Surprise Gift—**FREE!**

"UNLOCK" YOUR BEST DEAL EVER!

Once you've read your free books, we're betting you'll want more of these DYNAMITE stories delivered right to your home. So we'll send you six brand-new Gold Eagle books every other month to preview—Two Mack Bolans and one each of Able Team, Phoenix Force, Vietnam: Ground Zero and SOBs.

OUR IRON-CLAD GUARANTEE OF SATISFACTION!

As A Gold Eagle subscriber, you come FIRST. That means you ALWAYS get: 1. **Brand-new,** action-packed novels 2. **Hefty savings** off the retail price 3. **Delivery** right to your home 4. Hot-off-the-press books **before** they're available in bookstores 5. The right to cancel **at any time!** 6. Free newsletter with every shipment.

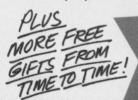

PLUS MORE FREE GIFTS FROM TIME TO TIME!

DON'T MISS THIS INCREDIBLE ALL-FREE OFFER!

The Secret Combination Lock is in your hands now. Find a perfect match...and get yourself FIVE FREE GIFTS! RUSH YOUR REPLY CARD TO US TODAY!

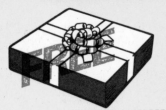

"Several hospital personnel have taken up residence near the airport to help those stricken by this mysterious flu..."

Koll laughed at the next series of images that came onto the screen. The men in white coats had arrived. Men like gods. The sacred doctors, the new priests in charge of mens' souls. Witchfinders, Koll had come to call them, and he thought them no different than shamans or exorcists. But their magic wasn't good any more. It was obsolete.

Where was the witchfinder general? Koll wondered. Which man was the one in charge?

He scanned the faces on the screen, knowing there was a good chance he would recognize some of the security men from his past work.

"Government officials are investigating even now..."

The cameras focused on several serious-looking men who were busily searching for clues to the person or persons responsible for creating such chaos.

And all the time the man responsible was looking at them. Safely. From a distance.

The field test had gone off perfectly.

So had the "spontaneous" shouts of outrage from concerned environmentalists throughout Scandinavia.

The newscaster had been logging in their protests all along, mixed in with coverage of the disaster.

"...Spokesmen for the Environmental Liberation Front have denounced the reckless disregard for human life shown by government authorities. They charge that the government has allowed dangerous substances into the country. According to Una Siglund, the ELF coordinator in Oslo, the effects seen at the airport are similar to experimental chemical-warfare gases used by the military in other countries."

The newscaster shook his head, as if in disbelief, but then continued. "ELF claims its researchers have discovered that several unstable chemical agents have been stored in Norway and are often transported by civilian carriers.

"Government spokesmen have branded such claims as absurd inventions of insensitive malcontents looking to make political progress out of such a tragedy..."

Koll nodded his head in response to the broadcaster. "Yes," he said. "It *is* a tragedy. But act one is far from over."

FREDA STENSGAARD was feeling giddy by the time she reached the Tonsberg hideaway.

Two men had shepherded her all the way from Oslo, one driving the Mercedes, the other in the back seat to keep her from trying to jump out of the car.

Not from fear, but from ecstasy.

She was feeling the effects of the BZ she had so deliberately laced the airport with.

Unlike the unsuspecting victims at the airport, the chemical hadn't taken her totally by surprise. She had been exposed to it before, conditioned almost. But no one ever really got conditioned to the hallucinogenic free-fall state she was in.

One of the men walked with her up to the villa entrance just to make sure she didn't wander around aimlessly and tumble off a cliff into the sea.

Koll had made plans for each member of the VG team, making sure that they would get home to their safehouses.

But he had made special plans for Freda Stensgaard, and he reviewed them as he waited for her in the dark wood library that had in effect become his throne room.

Tooled cordovan-leather wall coverings matted the upper half of the room above the dark wood paneling that gave it a touch of the Black Forest.

On a long table in the center of the room were scrolls, old books, and more important, hidden books, the latest works of a Norwegian supremacist who had stopped publishing in the aboveground press.

But he was still doing work for a limited audience: Magnus Koll and company.

There were also maps spread about the table in an apparently random fashion. Maps that portrayed the strongholds of the Viking kingdom—the future kingdom. As of yet there was precious little territory on those maps that belonged to the Varangian Guards.

But all that would come in time. It was a matter of setting the stage, and right now, he heard one of his best actresses returning from the stage.

He heard her high heels clatter on the parquet floor in the hallway. They moved with an off balance rhythm, as if she were drunk or out of control.

She bypassed the room.

Koll pushed aside the maps, deciding there were more timely things to conquer, and stepped out into the hallway.

Freda had walked past him, but still she turned at the sound of his approach.

"You're supposed to report to me," he said, "immediately upon your return."

She laughed and tossed her head, her blond hair swirling about her shoulders, her hands in her pockets.

She looked disheveled, delightfully so, as if she'd been in a windstorm—as if she still *was* in a windstorm, one created by unleashed and primitive urges in her mind.

Although her eyes had an intoxicated glow, Koll's gaze unsettled her. She stepped back down the hallway, bringing with her the last shreds of concentration. She'd been determined to go her own way. Until now. Until she'd been caught.

Freda laughed. It was her best defense, a way to defuse the anger, or at least the scorn coming from his eyes.

"Are you so weak that you can't follow orders?"

"Weak?" she said. "I am what you made me. Following orders got me into this state."

Koll nodded toward the library he'd just left. His eyes showed her the path she was supposed to take.

Freda played on her condition, backing farther away and heading for her room—rather, the room he occasionally let her stay in when she was needed at the estate.

She looked like a beautiful but cunning madwoman who was trying to pretend sanity, aware that she could be taken away and committed somewhere. To an asylum.

The only asylum she really craved was with Magnus Koll. But the BZ dose she'd been exposed to gave her a license to roam, a chance to test the boundaries of his control.

"Come here," Koll said.

"I'm not a slave."

He shrugged off the statement, then said, "No, you're not. Not anymore."

She looked defiant, pursing her lips. Radiant. A wild woman.

"But come here anyway," Koll said.

Freda stepped up to him. Koll smiled as he took her elbow and then steered her into the room.

"What do you want to know?" Freda asked, looking up at the amused expression of the modern Viking. She saw him as a kaleidoscopic image, a dozen smiling clones of Magnus Koll. His white teeth glistened like a wolf's, she thought. A white wolf. He was standing just a couple of feet away from her. "Whatever it is," she said. "Don't ask me. I'm not in the right condition."

"You're in perfect condition," he said.

He dropped his hands to her shoulders and slowly turned her left then right, studying her as if she were a sculpture he'd created. And in a way she was.

He had fashioned her into the woman she'd become. A woman who had previously lived only in her dreams, hidden far away in the untouched recesses of her mind.

Two windows were open, letting the wintry air seep into the room, swirling in cool invisible currents around her exposed neck. Hissing flames roared in the fireplace across from the window, the dry heat meeting the icy streams of air midway in the room.

Koll dropped his hands down to her elbows, pressing them inward, pinning her arms to her sides.

He lifted her up on her toes, his grip tightening as he pulled her lips to his mouth.

And for a moment they seemed transported to a wilderness. The wood around them seemed to be alive. She felt like she was in a wildwood arena in a grove, a sacred grove where the sacrament was lust.

The BZ blend created by the man in front of her triggered another round of hallucinations that she could almost guide with her emotions. The wind seemed to snap at his hair even though they were inside, lifting it over his shoulders. And suddenly it was a thousand years ago. Instead of standing inside a warm house, he was standing atop a sheer spine of rock, looking down onto the water.

One after the other, the images changed. Magnus Koll the Viking. Magnus Koll the mercenary. Magnus Koll the soldier. She slipped in and out of time, in and out of lives, but always it was the same face gazing back at her.

Koll seemed to understand what was going on inside her mind and anticipated her desires. He peeled her jacket down her shoulders, then he kissed the hollow of her throat. His mouth found hers in bruising kisses, and they clung to each other roughly, with a sense of urgency.

Like birds of prey, she thought. Like eagles, proud and fierce even when in the throes of mating.

Freda dug her hands into his back, scratching him with her nails and drawing blood.

He growled and took off his shirt, then hers.

His hands scooped up her flesh as if it was gold running through his fingers. He bent his head down, his hair falling over her skin in golden tendrils. A shaggy-headed centaur.

A beast of the forest. A Viking wolf in mercenary's clothing. Then just a wolf, unclothed.

Words rushed through her head, fleeting thoughts leaving only the barest imprint on her mind. Then, like an endless loop, came the thoughts of god and goddess. She wasn't sure if she'd spoken the words out loud or had only thought them.

"I feel like a goddess," she said. It would have seemed crazy any other time. But now that she was crazy, it seemed perfectly rational.

"You *are* a goddess," he said. "Again. I've come back for you."

As he spoke, a certain craftiness revealed itself in his eyes. She really couldn't trust him. He would always say what she wanted to hear or only what he wanted her to hear. Behind the provoking gaze was a calculating man, one who manipulated her and was always in control.

For a moment she doubted him, but it was only a fleeting doubt. And like all good cultists, when doubts came to mind, she banished them.

"Goddess," he repeated.

The god pushed her down near the fire, wrestling her across the heat-scorched carpet, then positioned her in every ungodlike way imaginable.

Magnus Koll didn't make love.

He took it.

FREDA LOLLED ON THE BED in Koll's room afterward. Her mind was clearing slowly as the BZ dosage was winding her down plateau by plateau, slipping out of her system.

She eased in and out of dreams. Some were based on things she'd experienced with Koll, and others were actual memories, rushing through her mind unbidden.

All were about Magnus Koll, the man who had and still possessed her. He had taken her from another life, lifted her up as if he were a god suddenly granting her not immortality, but mortality. He granted Freda her own life, or as close as she'd ever come to having a real life...

"I love you like sin, but I won't be your pigeon..."

The Blue Oyster Cult song had become Freda's own personal anthem.

It was playing on the jukebox the night Magnus Koll first spotted her, and it was still playing in her mind whenever she had dealings with men.

"I love you like sin, but I won't be your pigeon..."

It was a solid philosophy, but one she couldn't always live up to. Beauty had been her entrée into the world ever since she had been in her teens, and beauty had been her prison, one with red satin bars.

It happened in a seaside bar in Stockholm. The tavern was so close to the Baltic Sea quays that there were often a number of drunks splashing about after they'd had too much to drink. Or sometimes the reluctant swimmers were tossed into the drink by the heavy-fingered types who prowled the waterfront, upset that their marks didn't have enough money in their pockets.

The man she was living with, working for, and now and then hiding from, wasn't actually a pimp. He was a man who introduced her to people. They weren't always classy men, but they always were the "right people," people who could do something for him. People who could get him and Freda out of the stagnant X-rated waters they were drowning in and into the legitimate cinemas.

The Dane, as he was known in Swedish and German haunts was going to make her a star. If anything it was a shooting star, burning bright and burning out fast.

He'd taken her only from Copenhagen to Stockholm, broadening her horizons and shrinking her chances, turning her on and chaining her down to a variety of drug dealers, drunks, and now and then a diplomat on the hook.

Freda was afraid to leave him. She'd seen what had happened to others who'd tried, and she'd seen what happened to men who stood in his way. Axel fancied himself a surgeon with a knife. He was a cruel man, and though he did most of his damage himself, he always traveled with a few others in his crew to look out for him.

The Dane had a regular table near the back of the bar where he held court. It was a round table shared by his crooked confederates on those rare nights when he wasn't scamming somebody or lying low.

Magnus Koll had come into the bar well toward three a.m. He ignored the stares, scowls and mutters tossed his way. So did the man who'd come in with him. A man called Telik Wulfson.

All that Koll paid attention to was the outrageously beautiful blond who sat quietly at a booth near the Dane. She was parked in the splintery drink-sodden booth like a Silver Cloud on display, engine running, lips glossed, ready whenever the Dane wanted her to take off.

The Dane had been fueling her with beer all night, and Koll had the bartender send over a bottle of wine with his compliments to her.

After bottle and glass were placed in front of the blond, the Dane studied the fair-haired, long-limbed Norwegian as if he were measuring him for a funeral suit.

Koll ignored the man and looked only at Freda.

"Takken," she said, thanking Koll a bit too loudly, overstepping the thugs' sense of decorum shared by the Dane and his dockside cohorts.

They stood up, walked over to the booth and backhanded the bottle of wine to the floor. Some of it spilled onto Freda's blouse like a bloodstain, and when she started to wipe it off, the Dane grabbed her hand and held it still. He twisted it back until their was a light cracking sound of the joint being strained, then he flung her hand down onto the square booth table. He was certain she'd gotten the message that she was to ignore and put up with the spreading wine stain.

It was a mark of disobedience to do otherwise.

Koll ordered the bartender to send over another bottle, but the man shook his head, then craned his massive neck to check out the lead pipe he used to sweep the place clean during brawls. He wasn't about to offend the Dane.

Koll then ordered two bottles for himself and when the bartender placed them on the table, the Norwegian pushed one of them away. "Send this one to the lady," he said.

The bartender ignored him.

Koll picked up the second bottle and politely said, "Or send this one up your ass."

The bartender opted for the first suggestion when he saw in Koll's eyes a promise that he would carry out his threat. It was a difficult decision, but one that had to be made. Trouble now or later—at least he'd gained some time.

The bartender stepped lightly around the suddenly quiet tables.

The Dane pushed his chair back from the table.

Koll speared his fingers around the stems of two cheap wine glasses, then curled his thumb and forefinger around the neck of the wine bottle. The bottle and glasses clinked together in his left hand as he and Wulfson sauntered over toward the blond.

As he neared the table with the dockside roughs, all of them conspicuous for their bulk and visible evidence of bruised brains, the Dane signaled the man closest to Koll's path.

A stocky fullback-sized man with a shank of unruly black hair and a bushy eyebrow twisted by scar tissue, the man shoved his chair away from the table and directly blocked Koll's passage. Then he opened his mouth in a jack-o'-lantern grin, daring Koll to try something, armed with the knowledge that he had nearly sixty pounds on the newcomer and was surrounded by the Dane's crew.

Koll stopped abruptly. He stared at the Dane across the table, then his right hand moved in a blur. He smacked the man in his path in the back of the head. Grabbing his hair, Koll pushed the man's head forward and plunked his forehead squarely onto the wooden table.

The impact made a loud thumping sound and its force imprinted the pattern of the cheap, cracked Formica onto his forehead. Still holding the unconscious man by the hair, Koll tugged him backward, then threw him aside.

He kicked the chair back against the table, then sat down in the booth across from Freda.

Wulfson leaned against the side of the booth, as comfortable as if he and Koll had just walked into a church social.

The Dane looked at the bartender and jerked his head in the direction of the bar's entryway. The bartender looked away, busying himself with drying some beer glasses while he inched his way down to lock the door.

Freda looked across at Koll, wondering what kind of madman had come into the den.

And Koll looked at her with a steady bright gaze that washed away the gloom clouding her eyes for the long cruel years of her descent.

She had once been something beautiful, inside as well as out, and Magnus Koll could still see that.

He had the gift of transforming the surroundings where they were together, as she came to find out. She was no longer in the low-life bar she'd been accustomed to. It would become the place where she met Magnus Koll.

The Dane wasn't nearly as impressed.

He stood up from the table, smoking a filterless cigarette, punctuating his anger with puffs of smoke. Four other men at the table imitated his action. Normally they were good at this kind of work, but they didn't like the way that Koll had matter-of-factly removed the man who had been in his way nor that he looked relaxed and unworried about the rest of them.

The Dane came over to the booth and stood slightly behind Freda. He rubbed her shoulder while he glared at Koll. "What is it you want?"

"From you?" Koll said. "Nothing." He turned to Freda as he poured her a glass of wine. "From you? Everything."

"Then that means you do want something from me," the Dane said. "She's mine."

"Are you?" Koll asked her.

Freda stayed silent.

"Answer him," the Dane demanded. He stepped to the middle of the booth's table and folded his arms in front of him. He flexed his meaty forearms below his rolled-up shirtsleeves for Magnus Koll's benefit.

As far as Koll was concerned, the Dane wasn't even there. Just Freda.

She still held back. There was fear in her eyes. But she had a feeling that the Norwegian just might be one of those people who could pull her from the nightlife swamp she'd been floundering in. She'd been trading on her beauty for too long. If things kept up this way...

"Let me put it another way," Koll said. "Do you want to be his?"

The hint of a refusal parted her lips. She answered breathlessly, soundlessly, so the Dane couldn't hear.

But it was loud enough for Koll. "Me and the lady are talking," he said. "Leave us alone."

The Dane glanced behind him. His crew stood there like statues, waiting for their instructions. The one that Koll had already felled was sitting up on the floor, groaning and wiping the blood off his face.

"You want her that bad?" the Dane asked. "Bad enough to risk life and limb?"

"The risk is yours," Koll said.

The Dane ignored him. "Everything has a price."

Girls who sold themselves, willingly or not, were just as often put on the market like a piece of property by the men who controlled them. If someone wanted to improve his string of girls—or replace one who ended up in the morgue or a detox chamber, he could always shop around and buy one from another pimp.

The price he paid depended on the draw the girl commanded.

Freda was the Dane's top draw. He wasn't about to let her go that easily. "If you can afford it," he said, "you and the lady can walk out of here. If not, you can crawl out."

"The woman is free," Koll said. "From here on in, she is free to do as she pleases."

Koll had the money. In fact, he had enough to buy the bar and the people in it, tear it down and put up a quayside hotel in its place. But money had nothing to do with what was happening between him and the blond girl from Copenhagen.

Koll looked once more at Freda. "You want out of this life?" he asked. "Come here. Nothing can stop you . . ."

The hard, set faces on the Dane and his crew said otherwise as Freda looked at the path she would have to take to first join Koll, then get out of the bar.

But it was worth it. Koll had seen that she was at the end of her rope. Ready for a move. Up or out.

She slid to the edge of the booth.

"Ummph!"

The Dane's largest cohort dropped to his knees, stricken by a kidney punch from Telik Wulfson. Koll's man had moved silently the moment the larger man tried to close in on Freda.

She could hardly follow what happened next.

One moment the Dane made a grab for her and twisted her arm, bending her head down to the table so that her blond hair trailed over it as he prepared to fling her across the room.

The next moment Magnus Koll swooped out of the booth and smashed his cupped hand into the Dane's face. He ground the smoldering cigarette into the Dane's mouth with his callused hand, pounding tobacco and glowing embers into his face.

The blow and the burn brought a howl of rage from the Dane, a howl that was cut off just as suddenly as it began when Koll whipped his elbow into his breastbone.

Both of the Norwegians moved swiftly and with an economy of motion she had never seen before—just short powerful strokes, none of the usual flailing arms of a barfight.

They moved like professionals.

As the Dane's men fell in heaps on the barroom floor, she knew that Koll hadn't gone to all this trouble for a night of joy with her.

An eternity perhaps, but not just a night.

From that point on she traveled with Koll. He made no demands on her in the beginning. Nothing she didn't want to do. He hired top notch doctors to bring her back to full health, restored her to the beautiful woman she once was.

She had become more of an idol than an idolater. Instead of a sex object, she was an object of worship—at least in the beginning.

As time progressed, Koll groomed her. He brought her into his organization bit by bit, showing her how things worked in the big leagues.

She still felled men with her looks and whatever stories she concocted to gain their confidence, but it was for a cause now. A cause that had become her own.

Freda wasn't averse to the drastic methods that Koll's group employed. She'd been exposed to too much of a wild life already to object.

And though there were times when she felt she had just exchanged one tyrant for another—the times when Koll's commands gave no room for options or refusals—she looked on it from a military standpoint.

Different master, different methods. With the Dane she had been a veritable slave. With Koll, she was still under his control but occasionally she had a voice. She had a share in Koll's plan. More like a consort than a courtesan.

Freda Stensgaard was given a chance to use her hardened soul for the Viking movement.

There was no turning back. Once in, an initiate had to be with them to the end.

There were only two ways out of the hidden kingdom. The preferred way was through the gloried gates of *Valholl* after dying in battle. The other way was the one given to traitors, cowards and deserters—an eternal swing from Odin's rope.

MAGNUS KOLL SAT in the darkened room, looking out at the sea. A low fire in the hearth provided the only wavering light in the room.

When he wasn't in one of the Viking encampments, Koll liked to be as close to the elements as possible. Here in the Tonsberg home on the side of the hills the wind blasted against the walls and the water seethed below.

It was one of the rare times he felt at peace with himself. There would be more VG actions soon, but for the moment there was nothing that had to be done. The latest operation was a success. There would be a brief lull and then, while the authorities were still trying to figure out what had happened at the airport, Koll would strike again.

Right now all he had to pay attention to was the wind-shorn quiet of the rocky aerie.

He tilted his wood-slated chair back, pressing his soft leather boots against the wall board beneath the oval windows that eyed the sea. Koll absently rocked back and forth in tandem with the tide crashing on the rocks below.

He watched the watery horizon with the calm of a king surveying his property.

He'd left Freda sleeping in her room. Now and then he heard her turning in the old bed, sighing out the last weary gasps of her hallucinogenic trip.

She was sated.

So was he. She'd done well.

There was nothing that needed attending to now but his thoughts. Mulling over his destiny. It wasn't pride. It was simply fact. Some men were born to lead. Some were born to rule. It didn't happen by accident but had to be planned all along. All the right moments had to be seized and the wrong ones had to be shunned. Before any conquest, the roads had to be built for the armies to march upon.

Like the lords who went before him a thousand years ago, Koll was setting the stage. The final struggle for the throne was always bloody—and the actual battles for it were brief in the grand scheme of things. Reaching the point where battle was possible, that was the hard part.

Other men who dreamt the same dreams as Magnus Koll would have precipitated the war earlier.

And they would have lost.

Koll was building up his support politically, militarily and psychologically. Soon the time would be right. Soon the country would welcome a man like Magnus Koll.

If they wouldn't welcome him with open arms, then he would meet them with a different kind of arms.

The important thing was to be prepared for anything and to wait.

Like Harald Hardrade himself, the original captain of the Varangian Guards, he needed fortune and fame to put him on top of the throne.

He had the fortune. At the moment his fame was covert. But soon that would change. Soon he would make a public bid for the throne.

Just as Harald Hardrade had done before him.

He shared many parallels in his life with the original leader of the Varangian Guards, he thought.

As a mercenary captain, Harald left Norway and fought for the Russian King Jaroslav. He then served under the Byzantine emperor at Constantinople, accumulating wealth, prowess and a reputation that spread through the Middle East, the Balkans and Europe.

A king without a country when he returned to Norway, Harald campaigned for the throne. He took it bit by bit, with gold, alliances, negotiation and the sword. Finally, when Harald was the last claimant alive, he took all of Norway for himself.

Next he fought the Danes.

Then he took up arms against the English in 1066, losing his battle and his life to the English King Harold, who in turn lost England to William of Normandy. The English campaign was Harald's fatal mistake.

But unlike Harald, Magnus had no ambitions beyond Scandinavia. All would come in time.

Norway first. Denmark and Sweden would follow. Then the womb of all nations would be intact once again.

Finland would remain as it was now. On the surface it was passive, especially when viewed against the heavy-handedness of Russia, its neighbor, but beneath the placid facade it remained a stubbornly independent nation.

Moreover, like Harald, Magnus Koll had worked for the Russians from time to time and a certain friendship existed. He'd helped them in the Middle East and in Europe. Working as a mercenary, he saw little difference between the Russians and any other potential employers, though connections were always useful. Trafficking in arms and drugs was all part of the East's destabilizing program—just as trafficking in arms and drugs had been part of some Western agencies' stabilizing programs—and Koll had had no qualms about lending a helping hand. It was a free-world circus, anyway.

Defense technology was another area where Koll had played a part. Some Western mercs tried to protect the technology from the East, others tried to sell it, and Eastern mercs tried to take it or buy it. But it was all business to

Koll. Once he entered the arena, it didn't matter who was paying, as long as they paid well.

Like Harald, he had an international reputation by the time he returned to Norway as a triumphant lord. And he had an elite cadre of men working for him. Some were strictly for hire. Others were fit for the modern Varangian Guard.

Koll let the chair fall onto the floor with a thud.

He leaned his head back against the chair, letting himself slip into a well-deserved rest.

Even kings slept. He dreamt of who he'd been, who he was now, and who he would become...

MAGNUS KOLL WAS a child of war. His natural father fought in the Norwegian secret army known as MILORG when the Germans occupied Norway. Koll Sr. helped set up one of the camouflaged arms factories that kept the thirty-thousand-strong resistance army in weapons. Working in a sabotage team that specialized in blowing up railroad lines one step ahead of the Germans, he survived in the secret army until the Gestapo zeroed in on Televaag.

Britain's Special Operations Executive had worked with MILORG to set up a clandestine radio station and an underground armory in Televaag. But the SOE were discovered, and after a short battle, the Germans struck in force.

The Gestapo killed more than fifty members of the Norwegian secret army in Televaag, Koll's father among them, before destroying the town itself by putting it to the torch. The rest of the townsfolk were sent to concentration and internment camps.

And Magnus Koll's father never returned home to Oslo.

He and his mother, a graphic artist, survived the war like stunned mice, wondering if and when the German cats would come scratching for them.

Toward the end of the war the CIA's forerunner, the OSS, sent in several of their guerrilla specialists to help MILORG harass the Germans retreating from Norway down to Denmark and Germany.

It was one of these OSS men who married Koll's mother at the end of the war and took them both to the States.

Koll grew up strong and independent. He was well-liked by women, respected by men, but there was a certain part of him that remained an outsider. For one thing, he kept the name Koll, using it all through childhood, to the confusion and consternation of his teachers.

His stepfather understood that Magnus was different and he wasn't going to change him. The boy would grow up to be his own man.

He wasn't an all-American—he was a Norwegian living an all-American life while his roots stayed behind in Norway, and he just wasn't emotionally committed to the West.

In Koll's mind, Norway was still occupied, and in fact had never stopped being occupied.

It was a benevolent occupation and almost unnoticeable. Economically and politically it was tied to the West. But it wasn't independent. It had to accept the long arm—and arms—of NATO in order to protect itself from Russia.

The signs were obvious.

First Russia swallowed Czechoslovakia after assuring the Czechs it had no designs on them. When the Russians started giving assurances to the Norwegians, Norway felt compelled to polish its shield. It saw NATO as the only stalwart shield in sight.

There had been a way, Koll thought. Even then there had been a way out. But no one wanted to take the only path that could let them stay independent, let them choose their own course, and the rest of the world be damned.

No one dared take that path. Yet.

All through his stay in the U.S., Koll followed the progress of his native land. Although he became Americanized in some respects, it was only superficial. He still dreamed in Norwegian, walking through the woods of home at night, but always in the morning came the painful awakening that he was still in America.

He prospered in America. Like his father and stepfather, he became a soldier. After an eye-opening stint with the Special Forces, he returned home to Norway.

But the Norway he'd cherished was no longer there.

Not the Norway that had lingered in his dreams.

It was no longer a wild country. It was a tamed, machine-run, indebted country, owned by industries that brought them progress and took away dreams.

There was only one course to follow. He had to dream that lost Norway back into existence. To do that he had to return to his roots—the roots of the past, when Norway wasn't invaded, when it did the invading.

He served his time in the military and joined the Marine Jaegers. A counterterrorist specialist, he served as liaison with the National Police's Beredskatrop. By the time he embarked on his mercenary career, Magnus Koll had experience and contacts throughout the Norwegian services. He had identified potential recruits for his mercenary work and for the Varangian Guard.

He knew the pillars that the Norwegian security services were built upon. More important, he knew how to take those pillars down.

As much as he loved Norway, it wasn't that hard for him to leave it to make his fortune.

It had been, if not Americanized, then Westernized. NATO shrouded Norway's own security efforts. NSA listening posts or posts staffed by Norwegians who funneled information to the NSA, sprouted up all across the country. Just like bugs, he thought.

He knew where most were located. And he had ways of finding out other spots: the four interceptor locations in Vadso—like metallic bugs with huge antennae pointing toward the Russian bears across the border, tapping into Murmansk and the Barents Sea activity.

Then there were the stations at Viksjofjell and Vardo.

He also knew of the chemical storage sites. The development complexes.

Magnus Koll knew where most of the secrets of the kingdom were kept. They were all secret keys waiting for someone to turn in the lock.

He knew where the hidden airfields were and knew the bases in the Arctic Circle.

The Nike missile bases.

It was his business to know, and his obsession.

There were other facets to his knowledge. More obvious than the military links were the economic ones.

The North Sea oil finds had brought wealth to Norway. It also brought a lot of Americans who somehow seemed to become synonymous with oil, or at least the technology for finding oil, drilling it, distributing it. All of those modern arts had been perfected by the Americans years ago.

The offshore oil platforms. The underwater pipelines.

It was as if it had become their calling, and as a result some of the oil towns in Norway were as American as Houston.

Koll didn't dislike the Americans. He got along fine with them, in fact. It was love for Norway, a Norway that no longer existed, that made him what he was. A Viking.

He wanted and was determined to see a Norway where no foreign power would dare enter. A country where no child would have to wait for a father who was never going to come home from a secret army of desperate men.

Koll was prepared to go to any length to see that it couldn't happen again—that Norway would never again have to raise a secret army to fight foreign troops.

Although in the beginning Koll appeared to be just another mercenary to those who employed him—a ruthless fighting man with little on his mind but his pay—he was actually paving the way for the Varangian Guard. Every operation he undertook had a reason. Either he would learn from it, or it would swell the coffers of the kingdom.

His credo of "Have machine gun, will travel" gave him a quick education in the raising and destruction of overt and underground armies from Africa to South America and Europe. His leadership in the field quickly attracted the mercs who wanted a captain capable of bringing them safely out of action once he'd gotten them lucrative assignments.

The tall blond Viking had little trouble assembling crews whenever the need arose. He paid well. And his temporary enemies paid in blood.

After establishing his credentials with high-risk, high-profit mercenary tours, Koll learned all the tricks of the trade. The drug trade.

He became familiar with just about every kind of drug on the market. Narcotics, tranquilizers, hallucinogens, mescaline and amphetamine labs. Concoction and combinations that culminated in new effects especially interested him.

He even learned how to create drugs that rather than working magic on the street, worked sorcery. Like DOB or as it was most appropriately called, DOOM. It was a psychotomimetic amphetamine that often provided violence with a glimpse of heaven.

Some variants of it could make an ordinary man berserk. Others could make a berserk one even more so.

DOOM was a triple-length hallucinogen that was touted as being superior to LSD. But it paralyzed the mind as well as the body. The nightmare stories attributed to LSD use were more likely a result of deception. DOOM, the drug frequently passed off as acid, helped a good many unwitting users pass away.

Koll had learned how a five-hundred-dollar investment could purchase enough precursor chemicals to turn out a batch of LSD that would make a fortune on the street, that is, if the lab workers didn't walk off the face of the earth first. He acquired firsthand experience in setting up cocaine labs. Ether ore, he called it. Mining the veins of the rich and poor alike who wanted to numb their senses and alter their consciousness with paranoia, heart attacks or strokes.

Koll had also become a near-expert in the art of heroin trafficking from the ground up—from the cream, white and gray opium seeds sown in the Bekka Valley in Lebanon, or the Soviet-controlled crops from Afghanistan, to their eventual ports of call in the European capitals.

He became a knowledgeable chemist versed in the relatively simple alchemy of crystal, brown and cream heroin. The necessary tools of the heroin trade—anhydrous ammonia, sodium bicarbonate, sodium hydroxide, charcoal and white pharmaceutical alcohol—were readily available.

Koll discovered in himself an aptitude for clandestine chemistry, and he soaked up all the information he could. He had never liked to hang back in any of the drug operations he got involved with. He was the boss who wanted to get hands-on experience with everything.

He particularly excelled in the use and abuse of the hallucinogens like LSD, mescaline, BZ and its multiple-effect cousin, S-341, as well as the deadlier dosages of saxitoxins and other toxins.

Throughout his underworld tour he always stayed clean in his native land.

His lasting refuge was Norway, and he wasn't about to jeopardize his plans with criminal charges back home. As far as Norway was concerned, he was clean. His mercenary work was on the up-and-up. And in the other European countries, his full range of activities wasn't known. They knew him as a merc of the West. Not a merc working entirely for himself.

Whenever there weren't military operations to engage his services, Koll gravitated to the drug cartels. Financing some deals, setting up labs and protecting them. He worked as the go-between for drug and arms transfers.

Personally he disliked drugs. He disliked anyone who used them or relied on them. It was strictly business, and the money without fail went for the empire he was going to build.

As far as he was concerned, there was nothing wrong with giving people what they wanted. If they couldn't stand up without their drugs, that was their problem. But he had no use for druggies. He saw little difference between handing them heroin or giving them a rope to hang themselves with. It was suicide just the same. Their choice.

Drug warfare was simply another tactic to be used by the strong to vanquish the weak. Every government in the world was involved in its use in some manner, looking the other way if an ally used the drug trade to bring in hard currency. Self-righteousness was only displayed when that ally crossed it. Then the tolerant government would suddenly topple an arrangement or two—until the incumbent ally learned how to tow the line.

He certainly wasn't concerned about the fate of a few addicts when he was prepared to use drugs against the population at large.

Even so, he was glad to be out of the drug circuit now. He'd made a reputation as a man to be trusted, and he had his contacts with the underworld groups when he needed their services. But he no longer had to rely on building up his fortune from the drug harvest.

The fortunes he'd amassed were steadily amassing interest. He had money in legitimate businesses, and he had a steady income from the almost legal trade in artifacts that the VG had jumped into wholeheartedly.

In a way Magnus Koll had followed in his father's footsteps—even if he had taken a few crooked turns along the way.

But it was all justified in his eyes. Norway had become a vassal state dependent on the United States NATO alliance. And it still had to fear its Russian neighbor—in case NATO ever decided to sacrifice its northern frontier in the event of a conflict.

Sweden, on the other hand, had achieved a neutrality of sorts. It fortified its independence with a strong armaments industry and one of the most respected military organizations in the world.

If Sweden could stand alone, Koll reasoned, a united Sweden, Denmark and Norway could present an even more formidable front.

Especially if it had the right leadership in the person of someone who dared to confront any and all enemies with the ultimate defense and offense.

Sweden, Denmark and Norway could face down the Russians with the advanced chemical-warfare facilities in Norway. If someone knew how to employ them.

People would be hurt but that was unavoidable.

His concern wasn't for the casualties of war. It was for his own people. The people of his kingdom to come.

CHAPTER FIFTEEN

Nile Barrabas swooped down over the Helmark Forest like a hawk hunting its prey.

The prey in this case were the Varangian Guards, and the claws to pluck them from their wilderness lair were bayonets and ice picks packed away in the equipment storage rack of the Powerchute Raider.

Instead of relying on wings, Nile Barrabas was flying a Powerchute Systems International motorized parachute. It looked like a flying tricycle with an overhead roll bar, the lightweight frame and undercarriage powered by a Rotax 477-cc 2-cycle engine with a twin-blade propeller.

Keeping him aloft was a 9-cell canopy, controlled by the two overhead steering toggles in his hands.

Slices of wintry air whipped at his face, quickly finding the patches of skin not covered by the white thermal face mask.

Barrabas eased his foot back on the throttle, descending until the powerchute skimmed just above the treetops.

The airborne SOBs behind Barrabas followed suit and dropped to the same level.

The VG camp was straight ahead, a few miles away. As the birds fly, Barrabas thought, then amended it to as the SOBs fly. So far they were flying pretty good.

They'd spent several days training at the Rjukan Mountain and Arctic Warfare Center, taking a quick refresher course in skiing—which had turned out to be a *crash* course—and traveling in snowshoes. It had been a while since the SOBs conducted winter war.

And to go into it cold was taking one too many steps toward suicide.

Norwegian instructors put the SOBs through the paces with units from the 3 Commando Brigade from Britain and the Dutch Amphibious Combat Group, who were training at Rjukan.

After the SOBs regained their ski legs, they practiced with the Raiders. A few days of training got them airborne. A couple extra days of training had made sure they wouldn't be blown out of the sky.

Fresh snow had fallen recently, looking like a mantel of bright white clouds speared by the green spruce and pine treetops. There were a lot of gusts in the area, snapping at each other in the higher altitudes.

The SOBs were coming in low and slow and quiet.

They were traveling in a diamond formation, Nile at the forward point, Claude Hayes and Alex Nanos on the sides, and Billy Two at the back.

The VG had been tracked ever since they hit a bank in the resort town of Lillehammer, surprising not only the vacationers who'd been robbed and laced in the bank, but also the local police.

In a coordinated move that combined a heavy armed presence, knockout gas and the abduction of a bank employee, the VG had outmaneuvered their pursuers, finally making good their escape after a brief standoff.

Or so they thought.

The best HUMINT and ELINT available had been used to trail the Viking guerrillas.

Billy Two had provided the best possible source of human intelligence, his Osage tracking ability guiding him and the SOBs almost by instinct on the path of the Varangian Guards.

The electronic intelligence had come from the eyes of SR-71 Blackbirds, Norwegian Orion P-3s and KH-11 satellites, whose priority list had included a number of Norwegian sites ever since the arrival of the SOBs.

The eyes in the sky had been scanning the wilderness terrain the VG were moving through. Given the intensity and number of electronic eyes blanketing the area, it wasn't all that hard to pick up the VG exodus. There weren't that many bands of Vikings moving southeast through the wilderness region between Lillehammer and the Swedish border, leaving infrared paths in their wakes.

Previous reconnaissance passes had already picked out a number of potential sites that met the requirements for the typical Viking settlement. While working undercover, O'Toole had passed word through Jessup about the possible existence of one of the VG camps in the area. Several sites had been identified and marked for further study.

Now that it was proven that the VG were in the area, the final exams were about to begin. Coming out of one of them alive was a passing grade.

Barrabas eyed the horizon above the treetops. In the distance he could see a couple of specks coming out of the clouds. It was another flock of Powerchute Raiders homing in on the VG camp.

Coming in from the opposite direction was a trio of similarly equipped Jaeger commandos under the direction of Eric Thorne, the Norwegian action man Barrabas had previously met with in Oslo.

They knew the Helmark area well, and perhaps only the VG terrorists knew it better, for they had chosen to live there in the wilds.

And, Barrabas thought, perhaps they had subconsciously chosen to die there, as well. There was no escape for them now. If by some chance the VG made it out of the pincer movement formed by the SOBs and Thorne's troopers, the guerrillas would run into a waiting Beredskatrop group, the Norwegian SWAT units of the National Police.

The Beredskatrop had formed a well-armed picket line to seal off any avenue of retreat.

Getting out wasn't going to be nearly as easy as getting in.

The VG had been allowed to make their getaway as long as they headed deep into the woods.

The goal of the operation was to prevent the VG from knowing they were under threat of attack until that attack was in progress. For that reason the Norwegian choppers were being held at bay until the VG were engaged.

It had to be a surprise.

And it was imperative the confrontation take place at that location.

Better to fight them away from civilization just in case they made good their threat to release nerve gas, as they'd threatened to do in the early moments of their escape from the bank. Some canisters had been shown, though they could have been filled with whipped cream for all anybody knew. But chances were good that it was the real item.

And if the canisters were legit and the VG unleashed them, this was the best spot to contain it.

In the wild places.

Barrabas stepped on the throttle, picking up the pace, eager to be on the ground again.

He felt too exposed and vulnerable, with his weapons lying out of reach, temporarily out of action in the storage rack beneath the engine.

One thing was in his favor, though. Unless the VG were waiting for them at treetop level, they wouldn't be able to get off a good shot at the SOBs.

He scanned the forest, then looked from side to side at the other SOBs.

Each one of them was flying like Icarus from Greek mythology, he thought—Icarus with a machine gun.

Soon it would be time for Icarus to descend.

The recon photos had shown several strips of snow raking through the forest, indicating bald spots. They were just slim patches of rough ground between trees.

But that was all they needed.

The Powerchute Raider needed only ten to twenty yards to land, thirty to forty yards to take off.

No matter how wild the country, the powerchutes could be flown long enough to find a suitable landing area.

The 2.3-gallon fuel tank had been replaced with a ten-gallon tank that gave the motorized chute a range of nearly 250 miles.

Like birds of prey homing in on their quarry, the flock of mercenaries headed for the battlefield they'd been looking for ever since their arrival in Norway.

The hour was finally at hand.

EVEN THE GODS have to sleep, Nils Hendrik thought, closing his eyes for a moment.

The shaggy-haired Varangian Guard chieftain leaned back against the dark, cold walls of the dugout.

He opened his eyes again.

Nils was sitting on a clay ledge that had been carved out of the earth when they first made the dugout. It was covered with deerskin and brush, serving as bed, table and weapons rack.

The sunken room could shelter four warriors comfortably, keeping them protected from the cold and hidden from their enemies. The hearth was lit only when the temperature dipped too low for them to operate at their best.

Near the hearth there were a lot of freshly snared game, sacks of dried grain, flasks of water and a lot of cash.

There were two other dugouts nestled beneath the canopy of spruce gathered above them.

The shelters were simple and safe.

They'd piled treetops and brush over the thatched hut, cutting down its visibility by making it blend right into the surrounding woods.

The outpost was on a raised hillock in the forest, protected on the slope by a natural stone fortification. At least it appeared natural at first.

The cairn of rocks had been built up slowly in an apparently haphazard fashion. But each seemingly random design protected the approach to one of the dugouts. All in all it was a disguised fortress in the woods.

The temporary camp had been fortified long ago for just such an occasion when they needed to hide out. It felt like home, and for that reason he was relaxed.

He forced himself to open his eyes again, just to check around.

The bank employee "hostage"—a VG supporter who'd been charmed into accepting a more "active" role in the military arm of the group—was already sleeping comfortably. Although most of the VG were hardened to the wilderness trek, she had been totally unprepared for it. She'd been hurried along, roughly at times. No one was going to be left as a marker for the pursuers.

And right now she slept the sleep of the just. Or at least the truly exhausted.

It was hypnotic almost, to watch her sleep. Nils felt that he was also sleeping, with his eyes open. Every breath she took produced a similar rhythm from him. He breathed in and out along with the rise and fall of her body.

Tired, he thought. So tired...

A couple of VG guards were standing watch, and there was little more he could do at the moment.

He still felt guilty about giving in to the exhaustion that had stalked him throughout the flight into the woods. But now that they had reached the prepared hideout, he could at last obey his body's call for rest.

They had eluded their pursuers way back in Lillehammer, using a series of cars commandeered from their owners and hostages to keep the police at bay.

In the confusion, the VG had diverted a substantial part of their haul to a bank "customer" who'd easily passed himself off as one of the panicked citizens during the pandemonium.

Even now the courier was driving down to Oslo in a station wagon owned by a female member of the ELF who knew nothing at all about the VG. She and her young daughter offered perfect camouflage to the courier in the event he was stopped.

But Nils preferred the camouflage of the wild.

The forests of Helmark covered the eastern region of Norway like a blanket of dark green spires. Spruce and fir trees filled the valleys, then marched uphill on the mountains, with clear patches where some farms flourished with strips of cultivated land.

The large forests in the southeastern region of Norway made the wilderness area just right for the VG camps. There were farms, small villages and deep valleys, and some resorts on the perimeter of the wilderness.

It was an area easy to get lost in, but hard to get found in.

That was one of the reasons why it was chosen for a Varangian Guard encampment.

The Swedish border lay to the east and so did some of the wildest country in all of Norway. There were plenty of lakes in the region, all of them providing a source of food or means of flight to a mobile force like the VG.

But at the moment they weren't too mobile at all. Most of their energy had been spent on evading their pursuers. The pressure of running when it was in their nature to stand and fight was wearing them away psychologically. Over and over with every step they took they were going against their first instinct—the killing instinct.

But orders were orders, and Magnus Koll had clearly outlined what was supposed to be done. And Hendrik would see that Koll's design was carried out.

Out here he was the commander of the regular VG, as well as the berserker unit. His word was law.

Law number one was that the hostage stayed with him.

Law number two was that no one surrendered in the event of battle. Battles were won or their lives were lost. There was no other way. The mission was not only to acquire money from the bank but also to demonstrate how accomplished the VG was.

Some of the guerrilla raids were, in a way, auditions for the public. They were to show how adept a force the VG was, that it could attract high-caliber recruits.

So far the action had been a success. They had had no fatalities yet, and the money had been liberated. Even if they were eventually tracked down, they would go out in a blaze of glory.

This was how it should be. In the eyes of Odin there was nothing more sacred than a warrior fallen in battle. It was so sacred that he would bring his soldiers to life again in *Valholl*. Just as the soldiers in the woods had brought the god himself alive again.

He'd been sleeping for too long. It took soldiers like the VG to wake him again.

THE SOBs ARRIVED like ghosts, white-clad figures suddenly dropping out of the sky.

Barrabas was the first to reach one of the rough-terrain landing strips they'd selected.

He pulled down on the steering toggles and pressed the throttle at the same time, flaring the canopy to come in for a soft landing.

The Powerchute Raider landed on the skis fitted to the undercarriage, rode down a slight snowy decline, then coasted silently into the woods.

Barrabas snapped free of the harness, picked up his gear from the storage rack, then covered the descent of the other SOBs.

They landed without incident, riding their lightweight powerchutes to the edge of the woods.

The SOBs emptied their equipment racks of sniping rifles, submachine guns, small arms, thermal-image goggles, the Carl Gustav gun and other ordnance selected for the mission.

They draped the canopies over the frames of the Powerchute Raiders, then trekked into the woods, stepping lightly through the snow.

"Hope I don't run into any of my friends out here," Claude Hayes said. "Ku-kluxing around like this wouldn't go over none too smooth."

"If you met any friends out here," Barrabas said, "they wouldn't be your friends."

Alex Nanos laughed. "No one likes these snowmen suits. They're abominable. But we all have our crosses to bear."

"Or burn," Hayes said, still finding it a bit unusual to be in the midst of armed men in white hoods.

"Not in this outfit," Barrabas said.

The SOB chief lifted his field glasses and scanned the countryside. The forest was sparse in some sections, dense in others. Their target was less than a mile away. They'd dropped with this much of a distance between them to cover the sound of the powerchute engines. Though the engines put out a low noise level, the sound carried far in the crisp white stillness of the Norwegian wilderness.

"Okay, let's keep silent from here on in. The next voice you'll hear will be the sniper rifle. Then commence firing."

Both teams carried small streamlined transceivers with lightweight headsets.

The Norwegians were coming in from the west, the SOBs from the south.

The attack had to be simultaneous if they were going to contain the VG or push them into the waiting arms of the Beredskatrop. The Norwegian SWAT troops had taken up a stationary position to the east to keep the VG from slipping over the Swedish border.

Whatever happened was going to happen inside the boundaries of Norway.

Ten minutes of travel brought them to the outskirts of the VG camp. Snow was thrown up from the ground by the persistent wind that alternately hushed any sound and shrieked close to the base of the trees. It covered the noise made by their fur-wrapped boots, keeping them from clopping through the thin crust of snow.

The SOBs spread out as they neared the encampment. Billy Two took up a position closest to the camp. They all had silent skills, but the Osage's past made him right at home in the woods. And hand-to-hand combat was his speciality.

Claude Hayes dropped back a bit and took out the transceiver.

Barrabas scanned the area once again. He could make out two armed sentries in the distance.

Barrabas unslung the tools of his trade. It was time to go to work.

ERIC THORNE MOVED IN as close as possible without risking detection.

The SOBs were going to be the hammer strike, laying down lightning rounds of fire to scatter the VG.

Thorne's Jaegers were to act as the mop-up team, charging forward, beating the bushes for Vikings, turning them toward the waiting Beredskatrop.

At the same time Thorne was going to call in the two choppers at his command. He had flares to signal them at the right moment. As soon as the operation commenced and there was no more need for silence, the choppers were coming in.

All in all, Thorne was using only a fraction of the forces available to him. He could have fielded a small army if he'd wanted to. But then there was the matter of trust. The services could have been penetrated.

In fact, they had to have been. The VG had too much privileged information. Too much expertise.

Thorne limited his men to only those he'd used on previous operations, men he knew he could count on. And if not, if he'd made a mistake with any of them, then he was no longer a true judge of character and it was time to get out.

These men were his very best.

With the SOBs he had another small army in the field. It was going to work, Thorne thought.

Or it wasn't, he thought again, a man used to seeing both sides of the question.

A fatalist, he couldn't help thinking that if something happened and this operation went wrong, it was the right way to go for him—taking on the Nordic nationalists who were going to take apart the nation.

He waited for the signal.

CLAUDE HAYES WORKED the transceiver when Barrabas gave him the go-ahead. They'd been holding their position long enough to give the Norwegians time to get there. If they weren't ready now, the SOBs were going in alone.

Hayes raised their Norwegian counterparts. "Rathouse, this is River Nile," Hayes said.

"This is Radhuset," the Norwegian Jaeger responded. "Go ahead, River Nile."

Hayes shrugged. Rathouse, Radhuset. These guys were so formal, he thought. However you pronounced it, it meant town hall in Norwegian, their agreed upon designation for the local commandos. "We're in position," Hayes said.

"We have two sentries lit up. We see three dugouts, possible trenches, and a fortified bunker. Do you see the targets?"

"Targets seen and identified. One of the sentries took part in the bank robbery. We're ready for them."

"Okay, Radhuset, we're gonna take 'em in sixty seconds. Out." Hayes clicked off, then nodded to Barrabas.

HIS WHITE HOOD OFF, thermal face mask off, Barrabas was breathing easy as he lay prone in the snow, holding the Model PM L96A1 sniper rifle steady.

The Accuracy International weapon was designed to work under any weather condition.

With the right hands and a 10-round magazine, the L96A1 could do a lot of damage.

Nile Barrabas had the right hands. At the moment his left one gripped the underside of the bolt-action sniper rifle. The high-impact plastic stock was nestled against his shoulder, and his trigger finger was ready to pull.

Only two Varangian Guards were visible. They had no face masks, respirators, none of the bulky CW gear they'd be expected to wear that would indicate their readiness to employ chemicals if they were attacked.

The SOBs and the Norwegians had early on been issued protective nuclear/biological/chemical warfare gear, but a commando team in an NBC suit wasn't likely to do much surprising, so they were just in whites, and though the suits were of the latest, lightest material, they were still somewhat bulky.

The SOBs would take their chances on a quick hit to take out the VG before they had a chance to employ an CW ordnance.

The chances were even that the VG had some kind of chemical weaponry available, even if it was just a form of the BZ they'd used back in Lillehammer. While Barrabas doubted they'd be snuggling up to a canister of nerve gas, the way those things leaked it would be good night forever if they did get too close. Probably the best place to stash it was in one of the trenches, he thought. And it would take some time to get to the canisters. Time enough to kill.

The sentry to Barrabas's left scanned the forest. Perhaps the man had been alerted by instinct. He felt he'd been spotted but wasn't sure enough to give the alarm. Through the scope Barrabas saw a bearded face, the beard neatly trimmed. A man not too long out of the city.

Like the SOBs, the sentries were in camouflage cloaks, white with a stripped-bark design that blended in with the brush and snow at ground level around the camp.

Same tailors, different gods, it occurred to Barrabas. What needs did some modern men have that made them return to old beliefs and ways of life and caused them to almost deify a berserk, war-for-war's-sake god? He shook his head in puzzlement.

Barrabas tracked the sentry with the Schmidt & Bender PM 6 x 42 mm sight, saw him step forward and seemingly glance Barrabas's way once more.

Then he pulled the trigger, drilling the sentry with a 7.62 mm NATO subsonic bit. It cored his temple, then ran a river of red onto the white cloak.

The sentry's legs crumpled beneath him and he dropped in a staggering motion, a motion that Barrabas didn't watch to the end.

Still keeping his eye on the scope, Barrabas swiveled slightly to his right, working the smooth bolt action with a reflex motion.

The second sentry was just reacting to the suppressed shot that dropped his partner when Barrabas squeezed off a second round. It caught him in the chest and flung him against the tree. He was trying to curl around the tree and get to safety when Barrabas dispatched another round.

Two down and an entire clan to go.

Barrabas scanned the encampment. They wanted to take out most of the VG and save the girl if possible. The money from the bank was of little consequence. They were interested in the data banks inside the VG heads about to roll. They wanted leads to the other camps.

Rather than just smoke them, he was going to use selective fire. If they had just wanted to eliminate every enemy, they could have called for an air strike. But then there would have been nothing left to trace them to the rest of the VG empire.

A head popped up from the dugout, emerging through the brush.

Barrabas selected it. He fired. The man quickly sank back down into the dugout, from where came cries of rage that suddenly were drowned out by a machine gun rain that began to fall. It came from the side of the granite wall that had been built into a bunker by the VG.

The Norwegian team had moved in and opened up with automatic weapons fire, forcing the enemy to be inactive for a while as they sought cover.

But they were swept back when the light machine gun opened up. It was firing from a well-protected location and the gunner doing the shooting into the forest full of SOBs was a professional for sure.

He'd chosen the location well and had scrambled to it under the fire, definitely a man to be concerned with.

By now the VG were recovering from the first shock of battle, grabbing their weapons, preparing for a counterstrike.

Little more than a minute had passed—along with three or four lifetimes that were now soaking the snow-covered ground with streams of dark red blood.

The heavy 5.56 mm cartridges blasted the treeline like a rapid-fire shotgun, capable of chopping through wood and steel helmets with the same ease.

Barrabas rolled to his left as heavy SS-109 5.56 mm cartridges chopped up the countryside above and behind him. He dropped down out of sight, then looked over at Alex Nanos, who'd been moving to the right.

"Take out the MG!" Barrabas shouted. "Or we're stopped dead in our tracks."

The Greek crab-walked along a low ridge, carrying the 84 mm Carl Gustav recoilless gun they'd brought along to dig out the VG from their holes; the Swedish gun could knock out a tank, or perhaps even dig a hole to the center of the earth if that's how deep the VG were dug in.

The latest Carl Gustav gun weighed only seventeen pounds, half of its former weight, letting the SOBs bring it in with them without adding too much to the powerchute payload.

Claude Hayes crouched next to Nanos, readying the loads for the gun. They'd brought HEAT and smoke rounds.

"Give me some HEAT, Claude," Nanos said.

Hayes loaded the HEAT round into the Carl Gustav gun, then dropped to the ground to avoid the backblast.

Nanos homed in on the light machine gun...

And the machine gunner nearly took off his head.

The Greek ducked in time when he saw gouts of snow flakking the air, kicked up by the stream of heavy projectiles coming his way.

"Bastard," Nanos said, knocked off his feet by the sudden scramble.

"He's not the politest fella we met," Hayes said.

Nanos moved to the left, looking for a better cover from which to strike.

He had to get the light machine gun before much more time passed. If the VG recovered their balance right away they just might turn the tables. Judging from the screaming he heard—screams of rage that got closer and closer as they forged out of the dugouts—they were ready to lock horns.

Both teams were prepared to die.

But unlike the VG troops in the encampment, dying wasn't Alex's idea of a good time.

Nanos had to risk a shot. Either he could knock out the machine gunner before the gunner dropped him or the machine gunner could hold the SOBs at bay.

Nanos jogged to his right, carrying the recoilless gun effortlessly on his stocky shoulder. He dropped down onto the ridge and sighted the target.

The gunner in the bunker had been keeping a special watch for Alex, and as the Greek appeared, he swept his gun toward him.

Nanos held his ground and triggered the Carl Gustav gun.

The FFV HEAT rocket-assisted shell hurtled straight for the bunker.

Nanos dropped as hot lead spit over his head.

Then the shell hit home. Unlike the slow-moving projectiles of most recoilless guns, the flight-to-target time was almost immediate as the HEAT warhead detonated.

The warhead struck the cairn of rocks right where the gunner had set up his granite portal, pulverizing rocks and disintegrating the gunner in a spray of red. Boulders flew into the air, then descended on the camp.

The CETME 5.56 Ameli MG was silenced, the barrel twisted like a swizzle stick. Nanos had canceled out the suppressing fire of the 100-round box magazine.

"That taught him some manners," Hayes said, loading a smoke projectile into the gun.

"Yeah," Nanos said. "But his friends didn't quite catch on."

The Varangian Guards streamed out of their encampment like hornets.

There were men of two worlds countering the SOB attack. The real-world soldiers of the VG opened up with automatic weapons. The warriors from the old Viking world charged through the forest, heedless of the fire pinning them down.

ERIC THORNE HAD FIRED three Ferret penetrating cartridges into the dugouts with a Haley & Weller 12-bore shotgun, spraying the interiors with liquid irritant. But by the time the cartridges disintegrated inside the dugouts, most of the VG were already up and running. The pulverized hail of rocks had spurred them on.

"How many are there?" Thorne asked, setting down the 12-bore shotgun and picking up his Heckler & Koch MP-5 SMG. He sprayed a 3-round burst toward the encampment.

"More than recon showed," the Jaeger trooper beside him said. He flicked his selector to full-auto and squeezed off a burst to cut down the advance. Thorne continued firing 3-round bursts.

"They got reinforcements from somewhere."

"Send up the flare," Thorne called to the remaining Jaeger moving out to his left.

The man ducked behind a tree, sought a clear space above the treetops, then fired a signal flare.

At the same time the flare burst in the air, another round from the Carl Gustav gun struck home.

Smoke billowed from the encampment, quickly shrouding it from view. The VG staggered about in the solid smokescreen, stumbling into trees, roaring with rage.

Some of them made it out of the smokescreen.

"Look out—" shouted the man next to Thorne.

A Viking appeared out of nowhere, chopping air with a long battle-ax. He swung it right for the Jaeger's head, but the commando swung his emptied Heckler & Koch at the ax. The rifle barrel deflected the blow, preventing an almost certain kill.

The Viking dropped his ax and went for the Jaeger's throat with both hands, his weight hurtling both of them down to the ground.

"Aghhh!" the Jaeger screamed, his cry of pain mingling with ripping sounds as the berserker was biting, clawing at him and choking him.

Thorne dived into the pile and locked his arm around the Viking berserker.

It was like trying to stop a bucking horse, but Thorne managed to hang on. He pulled back on the thick neck trapped in the crook of his arm.

An elbow smashed into Thorne's left temple, momentarily bringing down a sweep of darkness into his vision, but a part of him realized that if he gave in to the pain and accepted the merciful seconds of unconsciousness then he might never come awake again.

With his head spinning and ringing and his eyes watering beneath a galaxy of white-hot stars, Thorne changed his hold. His left hand palmed the Viking's chin, then pulled back as his right hand freed his blade from its sheath.

The Viking bit into his hand, crunching bruising skin to bite through flesh and draw blood. But Thorne held on long enough to draw his blade from hilt to tip across the cricoid cartilage of the Viking's exposed throat.

The trachea folded outward, and four seconds later the Viking gasped his last breath, falling on the snow-covered grass, a lake of red blossoming around his shaggy head.

Thorne stood over the dead VG. "Like something from a nightmare," he said.

But the nightmare wasn't over yet. The wild berserker dream was casting its spell all over the forest, drawing everyone in to the same crazy world that had come back to haunt modern man.

The fallen Jaeger was bloodied but still alive.

Thorne's left thumb and forefinger had been mangled but the world wasn't about to stop and wait for him to recuperate. He turned to confront the first shock troops of the nightmare. They were brandishing submachine guns, spears, axes and knives.

Thorne tore up the advancing dream with a 3-round burst. One of the Vikings fell. Two more closed in. And there were more coming.

Behind him he heard the cry of the remaining Jaeger trooper. A pair of camouflaged VG had come from the back, wearing torn and shaggy earth-colored cloaks. Instead of helmets they had crowns of leaves and thorns. Their faces were smeared and streaked from charging through the woods.

One of them swung an ax. It caught Thorne's trooper in the back, the blade making a horrible rending sound that rose above the hue and cry of battle.

The Jaeger dropped to the ground with the ax protruding from his back.

Thorne emptied his magazine into the newcomers, dropping one of them.

Then he felt something hit him on the back of the shoulders. It was a war club with a stone head. As he tumbled to the ground, he saw a stone-age warrior towering above him.

Thorne couldn't tear his gaze away from the club, and he watched as if hypnotized while it was hefted for a downward blow.

BILLY TWO FOUGHT tooth and nail, SMG and combat knife with the Varangian Guards.

It wasn't the first time he'd faced such foes.

As he closed ranks with them, picking them out one after the other, charging into battle head-on, Billy Two had a glimpse of the past.

Through Hawk Spirit's eyes he saw a similar battle taking place.

Between Indian and Viking.

Only it had been on another continent hundreds of years ago. When the Vikings first came to North America, they landed on its shores and without thinking twice about it, exterminated the first Indians they found.

Skraelings, the Vikings had called them.

They looked on all the natives as primitives suitable only for slavery until the *skraelings* fought back and chased them from the continent. Now one of the *skraelings* was invading Norway, returning the favor.

Billy Two whipped through the woods, barreling into the cluster of Vikings bearing down on the Norwegians.

He reached Thorne's side just as the war club was swishing through the air with deadly finality.

Billy Two launched himself off the ground, his feet moving in a slow, graceful motion until he struck the club wielder with a flying kick that caved in the left side of his chest.

His black hair flying, his right hand first carving air, then skin as his sharp knife landed, Billy Two induced the same kind of nightmare in the VG as they'd tried to do with the Norwegians.

Thorne looked up briefly at the wild-eyed Osage. He nodded his thanks, then rejoined the fray.

BARRABAS SWUNG the empty sniper rifle in a rowing motion. Working it like an oar, he pulled down on the barrel with his left hand and snapped the stock up and out with his right.

The whipping motion of the stock stunned the knife hand that was coming down toward Barrabas's chest. He'd detected the motion of the Viking at the last moment as he hurtled through the forest behind the SOB chief.

The stock batted away the long knife, then crunched into a mouthful of teeth. Blood and cracked teeth sprayed over the bearded man's visage.

But he wasn't done yet. Even as the blood fountained from his mouth, an ecstatic rage glowed from his eyes. This bloodied man was in his glory, still swinging.

Barrabas dropped the rifle, then back-fisted the man's forehead just over the bridge of his nose. His bare knuckles cracked into the skull. It was a hard blow, but the only one open to Barrabas. Besides, to stop the onslaught he had to hit the command center. These berserkers were going on willpower, on magic, and it took a magic wand of bare knuckles to break the spell.

Barrabas picked up the Heckler & Koch MP-5 that had been lying in the crook of a tree just before he'd been ambushed, and waded through the brush.

The VG were spreading all over the encampment, all over the woods.

Now the white-haired chief knew how Custer must have felt. Where had all the VG come from?

There must have been a returning war party. Or perhaps another group had planned a rendezvous at the camp all along and the SOBs happened to drop in just in time for the reunion.

Coming in ones and twos through the forest, the VG could have evaded the photo recon before they gathered together. Or maybe the recon had picked them up and it wasn't forwarded to the right people.

Barrabas couldn't help thinking of Custer again. Just before Custer led his 7th Cavalry into the three-mile-long gathering of Sioux and Cheyenne at the Little Big Horn, he was reported to have said, "Now we've got them."

And three thousand braves extinguished the luck that had carried G. A. Custer through the Civil War.

There weren't three thousand of them in the woods today, but there was a hell of a swarm of crazed, as well as quite rational VG troops.

Had he led his men for the last time?

No, he thought.

Now we've got them, Barrabas told himself. There was no other thought allowed into his mind. He certainly couldn't permit himself to think *Now they've got us.*

Wherever they *did* come from was beside the point. Barrabas was more concerned with dispatching them than determining their origin.

And there was one advantage.

The SOBs had been in these kinds of battlefields before. They knew the rules and regulations and how and when to break them.

Right now their carefully prepared plan of a surprise attack had to be abandoned.

The SOBs instinctively moved toward the weaker flank where Billy Two and the Norwegians were drawing a lot of fire. It was hit and miss. Hit and run. The VG were concentrating on their quarry until the rest of the SOBs came in shooting.

The field around Barrabas was awash with madmen and blood. Cordite clouds mixed with the smokescreen. Yells of defiance mixed with yelps of pain. The white snow was stained with red. The trees that had been growing so straight and tall in isolated splendor were now pockmarked, trashed and chewed up by automatic fire.

The original objective was to recover the hostage and take one or two VG prisoners to shake for information. The current objective was to stay alive long enough to do that. Unless they saved their own troops they wouldn't have enough firepower left to haul their own asses out of the fire.

Barrabas sighted on a VG who was sprinting through the woods in a blur, SMG in hand.

The colonel looked ahead of him, then triggered a 3-round burst.

One smacked square into a tree, another singed through the cold air, and the third kicked out the legs from under the running man. He tumbled face first into the ground, howling as his face smashed into the cold earth.

Thorne stepped over and finished the man with his PS7 automatic.

CLAUDE HAYES had been separated from the SOBs during the firefight. The conditions had led him right in the direction of the bunker's remnants.

His Heckler & Koch SMG was on semiautomatic, picking out his targets one by one, moving through the rubble of rock and ruin.

He glanced over toward the SOBs and saw Alex Nanos preparing to fire another round to disperse a gathering of VG. But at the same time there was a wild-eyed, wild-haired Viking bearing down on Nanos, running through the trees and ducking behind cover.

With all the bedlam around him, there was no way that the Greek could hear a shout of warning, and there was no way Claude could zero in on the attacker. The man was coming in from an angle.

Claude took aim at a thick spruce behind Nanos and squeezed off a shot.

The bullet cracked into the bark.

Nanos turned his head at the motion, his trigger finger on the Carl Gustav gun. But there wasn't enough time to drop the gun and escape the attack.

Nanos swung to his right and fired the missile. The rocket went wild, thrashing through the trees. But the backblast caught the VG right in the face, ripping off the skin.

Nanos picked up his SMG, ripped a shot into the near-dead VG, then took aim at another...

BARRABAS HAD MADE IT over to Thorne's side. The Norwegians, Billy Two and Alex Nanos had made a small defensive line on a raised part of the forest that commanded a clear view of attacking VG.

It was the kind of view that made an ordinary man want to write up his will.

There was no end to them.

"Where's the damn cavalry?" Barrabas shouted. "I thought you called in the choppers."

"They're coming," Thorne yelled.

A burst of automatic fire scythed through the trees right above Barrabas's head, and he dropped down, moved to the right, then returned fire.

And then from above they heard the cavalry coming.

Two choppers whined above the treetops, scanning the forest.

A Sikorsky MH-53H/J Pave Low helicopter had come in on time to unleash the special-operations troops and the rescuers.

One of the crewmen on the armor-plated chopper opened up with a 7.62 minigun, shredding the tops of the pines and the ranks of the VG.

Barrabas and the SOBs jumped down from the hill, hitting the scattered VG with a steady barrage of automatic fire and driving them back toward the encampment.

The second chopper hovered above the camp, dropping a team of commandos to reinforce the operation.

CHAPTER SIXTEEN

Three Norwegian Beredskatrop commandos dropped from the second chopper, a CH-53 "Knife" that hovered above a small clearing. They used the fast-rope technique, gloved hands and boots shooting down the rope. The first team of commandos didn't come under any fire as they slid down the two-and-one-half-inch-diameter rope—until they neared the ground.

A swarm of berserkers streamed out of the woods.

They were dashing into the open, oblivious to the deadly fire of the SOBs. Like human buzz saws they chopped and hacked at the commandos with knives and battle-axes.

They were as good as demonically possessed, and their frenzy grew stronger with each bloodletting.

It was a massacre on both sides. As the berserkers fell, they climbed over their fallen clansmen to get at the newcomers.

The first two commandos were cut in pieces.

The third was clinging to the rope his two compatriots had just slid down.

He was firing with his pistol into the throng, needing little time to aim. By just pointing downward and pulling the trigger he was bound to hit something.

Barrabas leaped into the swirl of berserkers, kicking and hacking away, and Claude Hayes was right behind him.

One by one the SOBs waded in.

Barrabas wrenched an ax from the hands of a falling berserker, then swung it as though it was a mallet. It connected with solid skull, cleaving it down to the bone with a loud thwack.

The berserker Barrabas struck had been attempting to scale up to the chopper but counted no more in the scheme of things.

Barrabas pulled back on the ax that was stuck in the man's head and flung him off the scaling wire.

The commando on the rope slide down into the midst of chaos, firing away.

Thorne and another Norwegian commando pried the SMGs from the harnesses of the rescue team that lay in a bloody heap on the ground. They cleared out a space and then three more commandos dropped.

The other attack chopper circled above the treeline, letting loose with miniguns and machine gun fire, dispelling the berserkers whenever they gathered.

Finally the commandos got the upper hand, driving away the VG force, but only the regular soldiers moved away.

The berserkers stayed to the end, relishing their pending fate.

The SOBs complied, emptying their magazines clip after clip, always moving forward, chasing in the footsteps of the dead Viking force.

When the smoke cleared, all that remained near the encampment was the berserker who'd seemed to be directing everything throughout the fight.

He was a stocky and powerful-looking man, and despite his zeal for the battle, he had a certain air of control about him.

As the SOBs and the Norwegians closed in, he caught up with the female bank employee, her face streaked with tears from the gas and from the terror caused by the inferno that had broken out all around her.

More important, though, was the look of surprise on her face. Obviously she had not been expecting the berserker to turn on her. As Barrabas approached, he recalled how smoothly the bank robbery had gone.

The VG commander made a grab for the woman's arm, twisted it, then yanked her off her feet. She went down in a sprawling heap, rolling on the ground to get away from him.

But no one was going to be left alive to talk to the enemy, especially not a recent recruit who lacked any real commitment.

He ignored the advancing commandos, perhaps inviting them to take him out. Death was his punishment and his reward.

He acted as if they weren't there or as if he were invincible.

Wielding a compact 9 mm Walther, the VG commander stood over the woman and pulled back on the cocking knob.

Barrabas ripped him off his feet with three smacks from a freshly loaded magazine in the Heckler & Koch SMG, then he hurried forward.

The man was three-quarters dead, but there was a chance to save him.

"You got a medic?" Barrabas asked Thorne, who looked pretty well mangled himself.

Thorne nodded.

"Good. Save this one, put him in a deep freeze for a while. Resurrect Florence Nightingale if you have to. We gotta keep him alive long enough to get some information."

Thorne called out to the Norwegian medic who'd arrived in the chopper, and the young brown-haired man hurried over to the fallen VG commander with his kit.

Barrabas looked at the VG chieftain. Either he was in shock or he was gone. It was hard to tell. He was very still. Whatever happened, from here on in the man was going to be on an enforced regimen of painkillers and soothsaying drugs. The brain-burning drugs would do the soothing and the VG commander would do the saying.

The SOBs secured the area around the encampment while the choppers scoured the forest.

Now Barrabas looked down at the woman.

She may have been pretty before the action had started, but her composure, along with her city beauty, had been washed away by her christening in fire. The firefight had shredded the last veil of deception about what the VG were truly about. It was more than a political environmental group. It was a terrorist network and they had been fully prepared to unload some of that terror on one of their own. She would have been dead if it had not been for the white-suited commando.

The arctic-white camouflage was streaked with dark, glistening blood, a gruesome canvas painted by hand-to-hand combat.

These people lived and died in a different world. A world she wanted no part of.

Right now she looked like a stricken animal. No longer was she *Norwegius Amazonus*.

Terror-stricken eyes met Barrabas's. "You saved my life," she said.

The merc leader looked around at the carnage, then down at her. "It couldn't be helped," he said.

THE ENCAMPMENT WAS torn apart, rock by rock, uncovering caches of weapons. The search revealed money from the robbery, a robbery no doubt facilitated by the "hostage" Barrabas and company had just rescued. Supplies of food were located, indicating that the VG had been prepared to stay put for a while. Weaponry, both modern and Viking age, was heaped in the center of the camp. Enough for a small army to wage war.

The SOBs had jumped their timetable a bit, but all things considered, the VG had performed admirably.

Though they'd lost this battle.

The VG bodies would still do some talking. Prints, photos, clothing, body condition. All of it would tell a story.

The forensics people would be on the lookout for every possible clue to their past whereabouts.

Several canisters also came to light. They were unmarked or their designations were scratched out. They were placed in large sealed containers. Again, that was work for the scientists to do. Nerve gas, BZ, or good old-fashioned CS, whatever it was, no one in the attack party was eager to get a firsthand knowledge of it.

Within an hour after the battle, the SOBs were flying to Oslo in the CH-53 with the wounded VG commander and the rescued "hostage" in tow.

The Norwegian superspook was also accompanying the SOBs on the air trek to Oslo. Other cities were closer, but the Norwegian capital had the best facilities to accomplish their objectives with the prisoners.

Throughout the flight the brown-haired woman tried to maintain the fiction that she was an innocent taken by these savages and that she was overjoyed to be rescued at last.

The farther away from the battle they got, the more her civilized ways came back. She looked calmer. She looked a bit more groomed, like a cat who'd licked her ruffled fur into place.

But she was ignored. No one spoke to her, and no one registered any of her grateful thanks.

The first phase of her interrogation wouldn't begin until they got her into the right place. But until then she was being softened up with a psychological pounding—the stony silence of all these men who'd done the work of hell back there in the encampment.

They treated her as though she were a ghost or soon would be one. A ghost to join her fellow VG who would walk no more in the Helmark woods.

Thorne maintained a thoughtful silence during the flight. He'd lost some of his best men in the action, and they too were flying back to Oslo. But they were on the other chopper, ferried along with the other dead men. Instead of welcoming families, all that waited for them at the end of the flight was shrieks and burial.

He'd left some of his Jaegers in the woods to live up to their names. Jaeger meant hunter. And the Jaegers were staying behind to hunt down any remnants of the VG, looking for clues to lead them to another nest that needed exterminating.

SANNA MIKKALSEN did not take well to captivity.

Once she realized she hadn't deceived her captors, she demanded access to lawyers. She wanted to be interviewed by members of the press, particularly the leftist ones.

She'd expected to be a cause célèbre, touted in the newspapers as the heroine of the revolution. A martyr, in fact.

In her fantasies, she had envisioned herself being held up as an example to the country of what a bold woman with strong ideals could do if only she took a stand.

Most definitely she had not expected to be cut off from the outside world for lengthy interrogations, kept in an all-white soundproofed room in a small country house in the middle of Oslo.

But then again she wasn't even quite sure she was in Oslo. It could have been anywhere, and her captors were in no mood to educate her.

"I'm innocent," she said once again, switching her tactics. "No one can prove otherwise."

"It's already been proven," Barrabas said, "to our satisfaction at least."

She was sitting handcuffed in a bare wooden chair that faced Nile Barrabas. A copious amount of tears had been shed by her, and so far they had received admissions of guilt from her, admissions that she immediately flip-flopped on and denied.

Part of her tactic was to tacitly admit her guilt—then claim that her confession was made under duress. She was a chameleon moment to moment, changing her role from one of a frightened victim to a defiant revolutionary. The farther away they were from the battlefield, the braver she got.

The defense-of-the-realm acts were not in the picture as far as she was concerned. She was a patriot and not a traitor.

She couldn't understand why the man with the nearly white hair and a no-nonsense stern expression was questioning her. She wondered where the Norwegian was, the blond man who'd led the attack on the camp. Surely he could do something for her.

"Innocent?" Barrabas said. "The proof is on the film taken by the bank."

She'd seen the film several times. It showed the Varangian Guards swarming into the bank—after the knockout gas had been introduced into the ventilation system. It was an inside job, and she was the one who worked in the area with access to the vents.

She was the one the bank robbers chose to empty out the vaults, the teller drawers. Naturally she made sure she gave them the largest denominations.

It was also convenient that she had been chosen as a "hostage." When the Varangian Guards hauled her out of the bank, the security men from the bank and the police couldn't fire at them for fear of hitting her.

"Officially the only people who returned from the bloodbath in the woods were the Norwegian security force," Barrabas said. "And the dead VG." He paused for a moment, letting her comprehend the situation. Then he shook his head as if he were overcome by sadness. "Officially there was no sign of Sanna Mikkalsen."

"Why is that?" she said.

Barrabas leaned against the wall. His arms were folded in front of him. "In case it has to turn out that you died back there in the woods. Victim of the firefight, innocent victim, of course. If you're dead, there's little point to ruining your name. If . . . when you're dead, we'll just let the world think of you as a hero . . ."

Sanna bit her lip. "Why are you doing this to me?"

"A lot of people died because of you," Barrabas said.

"*They* did the killing. Not me."

"You were just along for the ride," Barrabas suggested.

"I had no choice," she said. "I was a . . . a hostage." The word was getting harder and harder for her to say.

Barrabas had been patient all along. He was also waiting for the information that came from the wounded VG commander. Eric Thorne and some of his Norwegian specialists were questioning him in another room.

Really they were questioning what was left of him—just a frame of mind, actually. He was going fast. But he was pumped with the tongue-freeing drugs, and he was spilling what he knew. The questioners were posing as friends, as sympathizers, as leaders of the movement, following whatever cue Nils Hendrik gave them. A skilled interrogator could get anything from anyone. There were a dozen ways. Narcohypnosis. Gratifications. Punishment. Fear. Barrabas had seen just about all the methods at one time or another.

Time-consuming though it was, they would glean some information. Until then, she had no way of knowing whether he talked or not.

"Nils Hendrik has explained everything to us," Barrabas said. "Names, places. He told us all about you. You are implicated in the planning as well as the execution. According to him, you were the impetus behind this operation. He said you thought it would establish you in the movement."

"That's a lie," Sanna said, then her face assumed a scornful look. "Nils?" she said. "He'd never do such a thing."

Barrabas laughed. "Don't make him out to be so noble. Just a short while ago he was ready to blow you away."

Her face screwed up in bitter contemplation. There was no denying that she'd been betrayed by the very people she was supposed to be serving with. She'd been used.

"Even if he hadn't told us a word, there would still be enough to connect you to the robbery. The moment you were taken 'hostage,' the Norwegian security services went to work. They searched your apartment. Built up a dossier on you. Matched your photos to photos at the ELF demonstrations."

"That's not a crime—"

"No," Barrabas said. "Of course not. Demonstrations aren't illegal. But subversion is. Bank robbery is. It all adds up." Barrabas stepped closer, looking down at the disheveled woman. "And what it adds up to is the fact that you've been caught dead to rights."

"I would like to speak to my countryman," she said.

"So you can make another confession?" Barrabas asked. "Then retract it when you feel like it?"

"I want to speak to one of my peers," she said.

Barrabas nodded. "Most of your peers were killed in the forest. And rightly so. If you would like to join them," he said, "it can be arranged."

She laughed.

Barrabas had little time or inclination to terrorize the woman who'd been duped into working for the VG. She'd come through the ELF, which as far as he was concerned was just a vague umbrella for run-of-the-mill malcontents. Its real purpose was the recruitment or entrapment of people such as Sanna.

As far as its legitimacy went, the group might as well have been called the Nebulous Liberation Front. Norwegian intelligence was finding leads to huge Soviet contributions, as well as funding from nostalgic former radicals who were always on the lookout for movements to join.

Sometimes it took the shocking truth to make them understand what the score really was. She'd just participated in a major bank robbery, aided a group of terrorists and sparked a firefight near the Norwegian/Swedish border. Astonishingly enough, through a weird twist of logic, she was the one who felt she was being persecuted.

"I have a right to speak with someone from my own government."

In a moment she got her wish as Eric Thorne entered the room, catching her last bit of conversation.

"You lost your rights when my men lost their lives," he said.

She shook her head and sighed, as if she had to put up with more of the same treatment.

Thorne spoke to Barrabas as if the woman weren't there. "Hendriks gave us everything we needed," he said. "We have no more need of her." He jerked his head to indicate the captive ELF woman who'd made her bid for greatness and lost.

Barrabas nodded.

"Perhaps it's best if you do not see this," Thorne said. "Witnesses, you understand."

Barrabas shrugged.

The Norwegian security chief made a big show of unholstering his Heckler & Koch 9 mm pistol. He inserted a 9-round magazine and pulled back the slide to chamber a round.

Barrabas made for the door with the determination and blank look of a man who doesn't want to be a witness. What really went through his mind was that stock in Heckler & Koch was definitely going up after this operation. Like the British SAS, whom the Norwegians patterned many of their operations after, the Nordic operatives leaned heavily on the H & K weaponry, especially the MP-5 SMG. The nickname "Hockers," which the SAS used, also made the passage from Britain to Norway.

Then again, Barrabas mused, it wasn't so odd after all. Heckler & Koch spoke a universal language.

"I'll leave you two alone," Barrabas said.

"The three of us will do the talking," Thorne said, holding up the pistol.

The girl stiffened. Her eyes dropped to the pistol, staring at it like a mouse at a snake.

Barrabas closed the door behind him. He had no doubt the woman would talk. There were a dozen ways to do it, but it was best if she came over of her own free will—or at least think that she was.

There would be fewer complications that way.

The soft approach was best. The function of the cuffs was to act more as a psychological restraint than anything else. There was little harm she could do, given the circumstances. The danger she could inflict stemmed from her pretty little head, and her former position at the bank. Average people trusted her, and so placed their necks on the block.

But Barrabas and Thorne were far from being average people. Their necks had been on the block frequently enough for them not to trust too many people.

Barrabas sat in the adjacent room, which was a twin of the interrogation room. Sparse and functional, its only extravagance seemed to be the two-way mirror from which Thorne had been watching.

It would be a while before Nils Hendrik was in proper shape for more interrogation, but there was no reason for Sanna to know that.

It was a very simple routine. Barrabas was there to be a threatening presence, a foreigner unsympathetic to her. Then, when she thought that one of her own would be easier on her, in comes Thorne with a loaded gun, dashing her last shred of hope into pieces.

Together they would get the information they needed, and with luck that would lead them to safe houses, Viking camps, or at the very least, people who made up part of the underground chain between ELF and the VG.

He dropped into the chair positioned by the mirror and watched the rest of the interrogation.

"What's my way out?" she said to the Norwegian operative in her best pleading voice. There was always a bargain in the offering. That much she knew. Otherwise, why would anyone waste so much time on her?

"There's no easy way out for you," Eric Thorne began. "So you can forget that right now. To forgive may be divine, but in some cases it's idiotic. I am not a forgiving man."

He holstered the pistol. "But I am a reasonable one," he continued. "If you are prepared to cooperate, we can always say that you were in effect brainwashed by these people. You went overboard with your political zeal, and before you knew it, you had become involved in criminal conspiracy. And you were manipulated by some very sophisticated types. No matter how much they play up this simplistic hunter and warrior image, they are well-versed in our civilization's vices. They are skilled in all the ways of espionage."

She sat back, as if playing over the opportunity in her mind. "Do you think it will be credible that I was controlled that easy?"

Thorne laughed. It was a cold, mirthless laugh. "Of course they'll believe it," he said. "Because it's true. It's no coincidence they sought you out. You were the key to the bank. You were just waiting to be used."

"And now I'm going to be used again..."

"Correct," Thorne said. "You help us, then we can do something for you."

"What exactly do you want?" she said. She looked up at the Norwegian operative with an expression that said she'd seen it all before. That she had received a great many difficult requests from the VG and carried them out. Whatever they had been—she must have, to be still alive.

"I want you to remain a member of those noble Vikings," he said. "Contact them, as if you and Nils got away."

"Even if I admit to being with them voluntarily, if I contact them again they'll never believe I could get away—"

Thorne cut her off with a gesture of his hand. "Two points," he said. "First point is that you will voluntarily confess your part in this entire escapade. If not voluntarily, then you will admit it under the influence of drugs to our pharmaceutical people. There's a drug for everything these days. But you should know that. There's even a drug that lets you rob banks."

She smiled for the first time. It was clear that even if she had been misled originally, her basic temperament was to be calculating. The only other alternative was that she had become warped by her experience. "What's the second point?"

"The second thing is to keep in mind that from here on in you do whatever we tell you," he said. "That's the only way out. No questions. No hesitation."

"They'll kill me."

Thorne nodded. "Perhaps. Sooner or later they probably would—unless we stop them. At least our way you've got a chance. The other way—" He handed her a sheet of paper, placing it gently in her cuffed hands. It was a draft of an article that would appear in the newspaper.

The headline read: Hostage Dies in Shootout With Abductors.

The story went on to describe how Sanna Mikkalsen was killed during the face-off authorities had with her captors.

"You would do this?" she said. "You, a man of the law, would have me killed?"

"The past is easy enough to change," Thorne said. "It's the future that gives us problems."

She looked into his eyes to search for sympathy, but saw none. "You're deliberately exposing me to those—those…"

"Peers?" he suggested.

"Murderers," she said.

"That is correct. But only because you have entered into a much bigger game than protest and parties. A game you now have to play out."

"Or you'll kill me?"

Thorne fell silent for a moment, as if he were contemplating the question seriously, then a look appeared on his face indicating a decision to tell her the truth and lift a burden from his own shoulders at the same time. "Actually," he started with a grave intonation in his voice, "that isn't necessary. All that is needed is to let it slip out just a bit in the media that you have given us some leads, and hint at things only the VG would know, then release you and watch them come and get you."

Just then the door opened, and Barrabas appeared on cue. He deliberately looked tired and cross, which wasn't far from the truth. After all he'd been through, playing games with Pollyannas was not on his Top Ten list.

"Of course," Thorne continued with a meaningful look at Barrabas, "if I found it too hard to carry through with my plan, there is always my friend here to convince me."

She looked into the eyes of Barrabas with the unconscious appeal of one who is seeking an ally but saw regions of coldness that he had masked from her before. Her lips tightened in annoyance.

"You're not fair to me," she summoned up her major irresistible defense. "I'm just a woman who has been misled..."

Barrabas was tiring of the refrain. "You should have thought of that before. It didn't make much of a difference to those whose deaths you've contributed to that you're a woman. Didn't ease them any as they lay dying. You gave no quarter and you can't expect special treatment now. You deserve even worse."

"You are a son of a bitch," she said bitterly.

He nodded his head, accepting the dead-on compliment.

"What happens if I live through this assignment you've cooked up for me?" she asked Thorne.

Thorne removed her cuffs and said, "Then you try and do what we all do," he said. "You live free."

CHAPTER SEVENTEEN

Snow swirled outside Gudrun Bjoner's farmhouse in driving gusts that sometimes ended on a drawn-out, faint wailing that was like a forlorn sigh through the trees.

It had a nice melancholy sound to it, Barrabas thought, the kind of sound that made him pleased he was on the inside. Basking in the warm dry heat of a stone Norwegian wood stove, the bitterly cold wind coiling around the exterior of the house was the music of the wilderness.

He'd been out chasing through that wilderness long enough to appreciate the contrast as he sat in a low-slung pine chair, his forearms resting on the broad, flat arms, his legs stretched out casually before him.

"Another drink?" Gudrun asked.

"No," Barrabas said. "Just sitting here looking at you is fine enough."

The redhead smiled. "Thanks," she said, and there was something slightly mocking about her manner. "But a man like you doesn't have to use lines, Nile."

"I know," he said. "That's why I don't use them."

She slid forward on the rug, setting her drink down on the wooden table in the center of the room. With her back to the wall of warmth from the wood stove, she looked cosy and at ease.

"Well, then, Nile," she said. "Thanks for real." Her face was flushed, but it wasn't from the drink. Although she'd had more than a couple of glasses of liqueur, they really hadn't gone to her head.

Something else was at work on her senses.

"You know," she said, "when I first saw you, I thought you were the same as the rest of them."

"The rest of who?"

"The spooks who haunt Oslo. The soldiers. The cowboys...and Indians," she said.

He shrugged and gave her a conspiratorial wink. It appeared that Billy Two's Indian heritage had left its mark on her. But then again, few who encountered the Osage were likely to forget his presence.

"All these people playing with their guns," she said. "Saving the world, or at least pretending to. I thought you were just one more Don Quixote, clanking around with your body armor, your holsters, all the equipment you guys always carry with you."

"I've tilted a few windmills in my time," he said.

She laughed again. She had one of those light Hollywood laughs, a throaty, sultry call that was coveted by starlets anxious for attention. It was the kind of tone he often associated with a young Katherine Hepburn, her voice alone a siren.

Barrabas placed a lot of faith in voices. They revealed much about a person. And now, tonight, not only did Gudrun's tell a lot about her, but it had a telling effect on him, as well.

"What made you change your mind?" he said. "For that matter, what made you invite me out here to have dinner with you?"

"Don't get me wrong," she said. "I'm not knocking the military. I work with them. There's a lot of good soldiers out there. A lot of fine men. But there are a lot of chiefs who just want to play war—to rattle swords behind closed doors—and never do anything about it. When I showed you that film about chemical warfare, I thought you were just another bunch of chiefs who would mull it over for a year or two before sitting down to watch yet another film and start all over again."

"The circle game," he said.

"The circle jerk," she said, laughing. "As you Americans call it. Don't think you have to be polite on my account. Believe me, politeness is the farthest thing from my mind."

Gudrun sent an experimental smoldering look his way that was designed to heat up the atmosphere. It was the kind of look that could make men walk across hot coals, Barrabas thought as he acknowledged that he wasn't unaffected.

"Anyway," she said. "From what I've heard, you and your men are the kind that go out there and do it. And then say little about it."

Barrabas tapped his fingers on the arm of the chair. "Somebody's been talking about us?"

She nodded. "Eric mentioned a few things."

Barrabas raised his eyebrows.

"Nothing compromising, of course," she said, "but since I had to know about the Helmark operation, Eric told me what he could. He said that you were more than a match for the Viking brigands."

"What little we've seen of them so far," Nile said.

That would change soon.

The Norwegian intelligence services were closing their net on the political and military arms of the Varangian Guards. Soon the Jaegers and the SOBs would be able to hit them hard, roll up the safe houses and launch a series of strikes right at the camps.

The interrogation of Sanna Mikkalsen had given the Norwegians a number of strong leads to pursue. They were closing in on the VG already and sooner or later would have come across the names and places given up by the burned-and-turned Amazon.

But it was nice to have some intel fall into your lap now and then. It would be evaluated, cross-checked with the intel they already had, and then if everything was legit, the info would be acted upon.

But not tonight.

Tonight there was a lull in the campaign.

A lull before the firestorm.

Barrabas sensed the pattern. You went into the territory, beat the bushes, dug up what you could, and sooner or later you'd draw fire. Then all you had to do was put it out.

They'd come here in the late fall, riding out the first storms of winter, digging in for the fight that was about to come. And now all signs showed that everything was on the verge of coming together.

A lot of missions did reach the same point of culmination, Barrabas thought, just before they fell apart.

"We came out of the first scrape okay," Barrabas said. "But it was close. And this was just one outpost."

"And?" she said.

"And they earned a lot of respect today," Barrabas said. He had no illusions about the skirmish they had just won. If the rest of them were this good then it was going to be a hell of a war. "These people could win," he said.

Fear touched her eyes for a moment. "Do you really think that?"

"I can't close my eyes to it," he said. "They're good. We have to recognize that. Just because they're underground doesn't mean they're not good soldiers."

"They're nationalists," she said. "So far they've done a good job of getting sympathy for their cause."

Barrabas nodded. "What terrorist doesn't consider himself a nationalist? They're all willing to make sacrifices for the greater good. The problem is, they want to make sacrifices of anyone who doesn't agree with them."

The damnedest thing about it was that, other than their disregard for people who got in their way, there was something in them that was admirable. Under other circumstances, he thought, in another time...

"Excuse me for a moment, would you?" Gudrun said.

"Sure," Barrabas said.

She left the cozy room.

Barrabas wondered if he had managed to break the spell that had been settling over them with all this talk of war. But there was little he could do. It was always there, always on the edge.

In fact, the reason he was here tonight had a lot to do with the work they'd done earlier in the day.

Gudrun was in charge of the canisters the SOBs had recovered from the VG camp. It was her job to analyze them, then attempt to trace where they'd been manufactured and stolen from. It turned out to be BZ gas, a potent new variant, but not the nerve gas they'd dreaded.

Barrabas had gone over to her office to wait for the report, and Gudrun ended up inviting him to dinner.

He'd followed her Volvo out to her isolated farm on the eastern side of the Oslo Fjord, the Ostfeld area.

Right now the spook van that Thorne had given him was parked outside. The van had taken him and the SOBs all over the wild regions of Norway, from Trondheim down to Oslo, searching for the VG, making contacts, planning their moves in the event they uncovered the trail of the VG.

It would be a letdown at that juncture if he climbed back into the van and left the farmhouse.

She'd served him sautéed salmon, seared on one side. And later there were the glasses of Swedish Punsch liqueur, and it all served to create a welcome lull before—or between—battles, Barrabas mused.

The farm was an appropriate place for such a respite. Very little farming had been done there the past few years, Gudrun had informed him. She had used it as an escape more than anything else.

The storm was growing stronger, piling up the snow in drifts by the house.

It was an unusually severe storm for that time of year. Usually the interior of Norway took the brunt of winter, far away from the warm gulf current that kept the coastal regions of Norway at a moderate temperature.

Most of Norway below the Arctic Circle was milder than the northern Adirondacks where Barrabas had been spending some of his free time lately.

Free time away from Erika Dykstra.

He had nearly forgotten her.

Erika was back in Amsterdam, recuperating from one of their recent outs. It was hard to tell which was more painful—when they were on or when they were off. When they were on, she wanted him to drop the life he led. When they were off, it was because of the life he led.

There was no solution. He couldn't run away from what he was. He could only run with it.

He forgot Erika again when Gudrun stepped back into the room. She was barefoot and wore a light brown robe that was tied loosely around her statuesque frame. Her long red hair hung over the collar in back and in front, spilled down to the slightly opened robe.

There were a dozen stupid things he might say, so Barrabas kept quiet.

She had a large robe in her hand. "This should fit," she said. "Come on." Her voice had a lilt to it. The siren in her had come back.

"Where are we going?" he asked, catching the robe in midair when she tossed it to him.

"Outside," she said.

Barrabas looked at the snow tap-dancing on the frosted windows. "Outside?"

Challengingly she put a hand on her hip. "Outside," she repeated.

"In these?" Barrabas said, shaking the robe.

"In these. It's all we need. Now hurry and follow me." She turned and left the room.

Barrabas pushed himself up from the chair. "All right," he said. He shrugged out of his shirt and dropped it onto the floor. "When in Norway..."

A few moments later, clad in just the robe, he followed her voice to the back of the house, where she was waiting for him.

She opened the door.

Gusts of snow streamed toward the door, taking the warmth by surprise.

Both of them were rocked by the wind. It smacked at his skin but was invigorating more than irritating.

A wooden ramp several feet off the ground led to another wooden building well away from the house. Snow surrounded the walkway like a moat.

Steady streams of aromatic smoke poured into the night sky from the chimney.

This was where she had been disappearing to, on and off through the evening, stoking up the wooden cottage. "A sauna," Barrabas said.

"Of course," she said. "What did you think?"

"Nothing," he said. "Nothing and everything."

She walked down the dark wooden planks.

Barrabas stepped out with her.

The snow melted on contact with his feet. Both of them hurried through the night, then stepped inside the sauna, shutting the winter out.

There was the odor of birch smoke, and four wooden benches long enough to stretch out on lined the walls. In the center of the room was a thick stove fired with spruce, and on its top a bed of stones radiated heat.

And most important were the hooks by the door.

Gudrun wasted no time shedding her robe. She held it out to Barrabas like a flag of surrender—or a declaration of war. Actually, he thought, a declaration of love.

Modesty was the furthest thing from her mind, and Barrabas the closest. The only thing she wore was her glossy red fingernail polish. Sweat immediately sheened her full breasts and on her smooth stomach.

Gudrun swept her manelike hair back over her shoulders and rested her hands on the flare of her hips.

Barrabas draped her robe over the hook, then dropped his down his shoulders and placed it on top of hers.

When he turned around, her little intake of breath made him look at her questioningly.

"You've been hurt," she said. She reached out, and her fingers traced the fresh bruises from the fight in the Helmark region. But aside from that there were the other lines—transparent scar tissue that crisscrossed his body. "And not for the first time."

Barrabas had easily dismissed the injuries from the clawing, gnashing hand-to-hand combat between the SOBs and the VG. No one had escaped damage, but the cuts, bruises and splintered bones of the living were minor in view of the number who were carried off the battlefield.

His body carried signs of a hundred such clashes, but it also carried signs of the strength, perseverance and skill needed to come out of them alive.

As she traced the wounds on his shoulders, he stepped closer. And he traced the soft paths of her life-style. His hands moved down the back of her thighs, taut from the regular outlet of skiing.

He leaned down and kissed her on the lips. They were moist. Hot. Their skin was subjected to twin fires—one from the heat of their bodies, one from the warmth of the sauna.

"Mmm," she said. "We're getting ahead of ourselves."

"A nice place to be."

"Getting there's half the fun," she said. "Let's get there the right way." She stepped softly away from his embrace.

The sauna bath was getting to their skin now, opening up the pores, releasing the sweat, and then starting the process all over again.

It was a good release, and it was the right time for it as there was little they could do about their problems in the real world now—except try to forget them.

Gudrun took a bucket and threw some water on the hot stone bed on top of the stove. The stones immediately began hissing and spitting, casting streaks of steam into the air.

"Here," Gudrun said, dipping a switch of birch leaves into the bucket. Then, almost as if it were a part of a religious ceremony, she whisked the branches onto her shoulder. She made an ecstatic face as the sweat streamed out of her. "Good. Now you try it."

She handed another switch of thin birch branches to Barrabas. He flicked the branches onto his shoulders. The motion opened up his pores and covered him with steam at the same time.

"Now," she said, turning toward him, "do me."

Barrabas flicked the leaves at her, and she joyously shook her whole body at the motion. Then he moved a bit closer.

"You always go in for flagellation?"

"Mmm-mmm," she moaned. "It's not kinky at all. This is traditional."

"Uh-huh," Barrabas said. He whisked the branches over her lower back, then over her taut cheeks.

She trembled slightly. Her skin glowed, and when she turned slightly, her breasts were like gently rotating pearls.

"I'm a hell of a believer in tradition," he said.

Gudrun laughed, then she faced Barrabas fully as she swished the birch leaves across her breasts.

For a moment she seemed like a wood spirit, clutching the leaves to her, using them as camouflage one instant, then lifting the switch and bringing it down the next. There was a slight hissing sound with each stroke, the hiss of steam and the moan of pleasure that streamed from her lips.

She held the switch out to him.

Barrabas smiled, but he dropped the leaves to the floor. Though the whisking was undeniably pleasurable, he had another pleasure on his mind.

He stepped closer.

Her breasts were slippery to the touch as he lifted them as softly as his callused palms would allow. Then one of his hands slipped around her back, and he drew her forward slowly. He pulled her closer until finally her silkiness was meshed tightly against his chest.

Tossing from side to side, she rolled against him. She had flung back her head, exposing the vulnerable, tender curve of her neck.

Barrabas pressed his lips against her flesh, then his mouth trailed down her neck to her shoulders.

She arched her back, leaning away from him like a ballet dancer.

He lowered his head, then delicately feathered her breasts. His hands swooped down to her hips to pull her close, and they seemed to be fused together, the heat of their bodies merging with the heat of the sauna.

And then they moved down onto one of the hardwood benches.

They didn't feel the hardness of the bench beneath them as they became lost in starting a tradition of their own.

CHAPTER EIGHTEEN

An army was afoot in Oslo.

"Free the Children of Chernobyl!" Lee Hatton shouted, her voice mingling with thousands of other voices as she marched down Karl Johansgate.

The raven-haired SOB wore leather boots and a cheeky pair of tight blue jeans to the demonstration. She also wore a short fatigue jacket that easily concealed the weapons she was carrying.

It was her standard uniform for the ELF rallies and festivals she'd been infiltrating ever since she joined up with the group in Copenhagen. Lee had moved throughout Scandinavia, often on short notice, stopping in the capitals and throwing off a few sparks, organizing, hitting the streets, making the rounds of folk clubs—going anywhere she could find support.

And Lee Hatton was the type who could bring in followers, especially among the males.

Bearded men, long, straight-haired women, wizened ecological guerrillas and jaded thrill seekers filled the ranks as the army of protestors flowed down the main thoroughfare of the city.

If they wanted to, the unruly throng could easily shut down the city. They could launch riots.

But that wasn't on the schedule.

Not yet.

The struggle was still a political and economic one. Every rally always brought in an influx of cash, as well as services rendered. Volunteers came out of the woodwork after most of the manic protest fests.

Cash also flowed in from drug deals, political rallies and clan gatherings disguised as folk festivals. All of it came uncounted into the underground cash registers. To handle money like that, the ELF needed a lot of people it could trust.

It needed committed members. Bold organizers. People who gave a damn and could be counted on to carry out some of the shadier tasks of the ELF.

People like Lee Hatton.

She'd shed her wealthy past and was living out a cover as a card-carrying member of ELF.

Lee Hatton was a rising star in the Pan-Nordic movement.

Though she was working under an alias, like many undercover operatives she kept her own first name in case someone recognized her and called out to her in a crowd.

Although it wouldn't be too far out of line for someone in the underground to have more than one name, it usually garnered unneeded attention and had to be explained.

As the march spilled down Universitetsgate, a crazed shaggy-bearded protestor hurried up beside her, staring into her face as he lifted his placard.

Inwardly she shuddered, but outwardly she kept up the dedicated appearance.

The clown was trying to pick her up. He was one of the bozos that went along with any demonstration, seeing it as a good place to "pick up chicks." Even if the protest was for the purpose of banning protests, he would have marched along.

Lee was saved from any further approaches from her ersatz suitor when the cry went up from the marchers again. "Children of Chernobyl..."

The cry spread from mouth to mouth and was uttered in many languages. Just as the signs they carried were in Norwegian, English, French, German and Russian for the benefit of newspaper reporters, the slogans they shouted were also in these languages so the broadcast media could get their spots in the appropriate tongue.

Protests—even "spontaneous" ones—made use of equal opportunity. Besides, the message often got lost if it appeared in subtitles on news broadcasts.

Lee forged ahead and pushed her way through the crowd. They were moving faster than usual. It was almost a festive atmosphere. There was also a religious undercurrent to the march. An earth movement, true, but it was rigid, fascistic in nature. Everyone had to share the same beliefs or they were considered unfit for the movement. Heil Mary, she thought.

Although Christmas was approaching, the weather was mild. Just enough to keep the snow on the ground.

Just enough to keep everyone's mind on the sloganeering.

As the usual chants made the rounds of the crowd, it was almost like a sing-along for children. Except the message was a bit stronger than usual.

"Free Scandinavia."

The simultaneous shout filled the square. Even the bystanders who stood in awe—wondering if they should boo or applaud the protestors—seemed taken by that chant. What harm could there be in people who wanted a free and united Scandinavia?

That slogan was relied on regularly, but today there was a slight variation in the usual theme. First had been the Chernobyl bit. That was new. Until now the ELF had slammed only the West.

And now the usual, "Stop the NATO War Machine," was supplemented with another slogan: "Stop East Bloc Agitprop."

Lee Hatton jabbed the protest sign skyward, moving it in the same rhythm as a hundred other placards in the square.

Slogan-on-a-stick, she thought. Instant political awareness.

They'd been professionally printed. Slick artists had come up with sufficiently gruesome illustrations to add punch—and blood—to the slogans. Like magic, the well-oiled ELF machine moved forward, propelled by the best propaganda money could buy.

A lot of that money had come from the Soviets, who'd used their usual tactic of tiptoeing into a peace movement one lead foot at a time, gradually turning it into an anti-West slugfest.

Today the massive rally in Oslo had a wide range of supporters, like most of the other ELF rallies she'd attended.

Some of the protestors were professionals. For them the protest was the thing—as long as it was against *something*, and as long as it was even vaguely radical.

About half of the people milling about were true believers in the always shifting ELF platform.

But a good number were provided by the KGB.

The Soviets had tried to cloak their presence more than usual this time around but the Norwegians were onto them from the start.

In the past, antinuke and anti-NATO peace marches that struck simultaneously in Oslo, Copenhagen and Stockholm had been exposed as being largely Soviet conceived and executed.

The KGB operative in charge of fomenting the protests had been expelled after he was overheard boasting how he could bring out 100,000 protestors in any Scandinavian capital at the snap of his fingers. Though it was the truth, the reason he was expelled was because he admitted it, bragged about it, in fact.

Since then the Norwegians had scored a few other hits against the KGB but they also lost a major battle. A Norwegian company that developed computer-aided machine tooling for submarine propellers had sold that technology to the Russians—via considerable subterfuge on the part of a Japanese company.

In effect, the Norwegian technology allowed the Soviets to lower the noise signature of their submarines to such an extent that they were almost impossible to detect—making obsolete the Norwegian underwater listening stations that tracked the submarines.

The thing that stung the Norwegians' pride the most was that it wasn't any great intelligence coup on the part of the Soviets. The KGB simply paid for it. They used kroners rather than cunning to rob the West of yet another defensive weapon in its arsenal.

As a result the Norwegians were determined to get back at the Soviets, and so far they'd kept track of the KGB influence in the ELF movement. But they hadn't acted yet, hoping to use the presence of so many Soviet agents as a chance to identify as much of their network as possible before they struck.

Lee came to a halt, packed into the middle of the surging crowd. Although they were no longer marching forward, there was still a surge of electricity jolting through the crowd. Once the energy had been turned on, it was hard to turn it off.

She saw the reason for the halt up ahead, as one of the old-guard speakers suddenly clambered up onto a stone wall where a mike system had been set up.

Surrounded by loudspeakers, the wall made a perfect platform.

After waiting for a sufficient number of reporters to make their way through the crowd, holding their microphones aloft like scepters, the speaker began in a loud and deep voice filled with sorrow and rage.

"We lived through Chernobyl!" he shouted. "But more than 200,000 other living creatures didn't make it."

He cited some of the chilling statistics that had come out of the aftermath of the Russian nuclear accident.

More than 200,000 reindeer had to be killed and then buried in deep underground trenches in Norway.

The Chernobyl explosion had contaminated the Norwegian reindeer herds with the radioactive isotopes caesium 137 and caesium 134.

In some areas the contamination level was hundreds of times greater than the safety level. Sweden's herds were also affected. And the fauna of Scandinavian countries had been severely damaged by the explosion, as well. Fishing was banned in many lakes. Vegetation was savaged, with entire crops of berries having to be destroyed. Strontium was found in the milk supply.

And in Greenland, caesium and strontium were detected just inches below the surface of the snow.

The crowd reacted as expected to the statistics, recoiling in horror and shouting in anger at the death toll.

Then the speaker moved on to the presence of dangerous chemicals in Norway itself.

And simultaneously, speakers in Stockholm and Copenhagen were warning crowds about dangerous chemicals harbored inside Sweden and Denmark.

All that posed a risk to Scandinavia. A risk that only a united Scandinavia could fight—with the Environmental Liberation Front at its head.

Lee Hatton thrust her placard into the air once more. Around her the other protestors did the same. As she gazed around the multitude, she felt as if she just had a glimpse of the future—seeing an uncontrolled horde slashing the sky with their swords.

CHAPTER NINETEEN

Grim Swann stood by the window of the real headquarters of ELF, watching the KGB officer building up a head of steam on the snow-swept street in the middle of Trondheim.

When the officer was less than half a block away, a smile crossed Grim's face.

Given the phony expression of serenity chiseled on his granite face, the barrel-chested Russian looked like a walking monument. It was probably modeled after the last time the man really was calm, Grim thought. Maybe thirty years or so ago—before Leonid Davilov joined the KGB.

Now he looked as if he was on urgent business. He always did, but on this occasion even more so.

His upper torso and thick arms were held rigidly, giving the lie to his placid square-jawed face. Even his dark black hair looked rigid—rusted iron falling away from the machine works of his head.

Three houses away, Comrade Leonid's composure began to fade. There was fire in his eyes, fire beneath those thick smoky eyebrows. Not very comradely at all, Grim thought.

The man seemed ready to kill someone.

But certainly not there in the exclusive Market Square district of Trondheim.

Grim's offices—his lookout—took up the upper floor of a brightly painted wooden house just off of Erling Skakesgate, the long thoroughfare near the center of the old town.

The bottom floor of the house was for showcase purposes. In the event they were visited by authorities, Grim's people would be able to display legitimate work to prove they were a commercial art agency.

Drafting tables, compugraphics desks, VDTs, slide developers and printing equipment filled most of the rooms on the lower floor. Recently designed corporate logos graced the walls, and there were company brochures story-boarded on the drafting tables.

Overall it looked like an average, prosperous agency.

It had nothing to indicate that it was the heart and soul of the Varangian Guards.

Then again, Grim Swann looked nothing like a Viking—on the outside.

His straw-blond hair was cut short and in a conservative manner. The suit he wore marked him as a rising young executive type. But the hands and eyes revealed someone different.

His hands weren't strong and powerful from training at a health spa. They had acquired skill and strength from his periodic training in the camps. And the cold blue eyes that had watched the KGB's approach were not the greed-washed eyes of a mercenary businessman. They were the cold eyes of a mercenary.

A mercenary who had managed the coup of being concealed in plain sight. Right in the heart of Trondheim, where he had his finger on the heartbeat of the country.

Cash flowed through here, pouring in from conduits all over Scandinavia. Grim controlled a network of trusted operatives who could be counted on to deliver the goods. They were the ones who were in deep already, the ones who were being groomed for entry into the real organization.

Thoughts of one particular recruit jumped into his mind.

Her name was Lee. She had shown a talent for deception and manipulation. As a result she rose quickly through the ranks. She had good ideas, and she was a natural when it came to drafting effective propaganda.

Grim was her sponsor. Soon he would take her into the heart of the group. Then he would lead her through the door into those secret rooms that so far she had only had glimpses of.

Perhaps, he thought, when she came up here... Maybe it was time...

All thoughts of the woman vanished when the streetside entrance to Grim's agency opened.

He heard the gruff voice of Leonid Davilov speaking with Anna, the one-woman welcoming committee for Grim's aboveground as well as underground visitors.

"But it's urgent!" Davilov protested. "I must see him now."

A moment later the soft but firm voice of Anna Dolvina put him back into his place.

Grim's instruction had been to detain the man for a while, just long enough to break the rhythm of his planned attack.

Leonid Davilov's arrival was expected, right down to every last fluster.

Grim glanced at the half-open door to his office suite, then returned his attention to the window. It was his favorite view, looking out at Trondheim.

All the roots of the Vikings were here, and as he looked out at the old medieval city, he imagined the roots were growing once again, bursting through the sidewalks, snaking toward the fjord.

This was the spiritual center of the VG. There were other important locations to the movement, especially Magnus Koll's Tonsberg estate and the wilderness camps. But the driving force behind the philosophy of the VG was here.

Every movement has a philosophical leader and a military leader. It is rare for the two to be combined in one person.

Charlemagne had his peers of the realm to help him brand his combined pagan and Christian stamp on his kingdom.

Hitler had his black magus.

And Magnus Koll had his own counsel, though his personal priest was a well-kept secret to many of the VG. He was known only to Grim and a few other trusted insiders.

The chieftain's counsel lived right in Trondheim, a once-honored man who was scorned by the world at large but welcomed by the Varangian Guard. They were the ones who mattered.

His name was Hrolf Anker and he lived nearby, close to Nidaros Cathedral, where Viking kings had often been crowned in the past. Hrolf was completely supported by VG coffers, and he lived a sequestered life.

They based him here in the middle of the country, within striking distance of the capital at Oslo and north to the bases at Bodo and beyond the Arctic Circle.

In Trondheim Hrolf had access to the library of *Det Kongelige Norske Videnskabers Selskab*, Norway's Royal Society of Sciences. It was situated right on Erling Skakesgate, just a short walk away.

The old manuscripts of the library were some of the most prized in all Scandinavia—outside of Hrolf's own collection, which had multiplied ever since Koll found him.

Despite his apparently invisible public role in the VG, Hrolf's planning had covered just about everything.

Even the visit from Leonid Davilov, or a similar KGB operative, had been expected. It was only natural after the latest demonstration that cited the Soviets as well as the West.

It was like a grand plan. The course had been charted and they were all following it to their destiny.

Anna knocked on Grim's door before stepping into the room to usher in the next stage of the grand plan.

"*Comrade* Davilov is here," she said. "He says that it's a very urgent matter."

Grim heard a cough or a grumble from the hallway. Davilov had followed the woman upstairs. If possible, he was growing even angrier at her use of the word *comrade*.

It was only natural. Davilov had carefully guarded his connection to the Soviets from one and all, and resented that a woman would so casually bandy about his background.

"Send him right in," Grim said jovially, playing out his pretense of welcome. He walked over to the door to admit the sturdy KGB officer who had been cooling his heels in the hallway.

"Leonid," he said, shaking hands. "Please come in."

Leonid's hand was cold and felt rigid. He shook hands but quickly tore his hand free. At Grim's inviting gesture he barged into the room and strode over to the desk.

Grim closed the door, and Leonid nodded approvingly. They would need privacy.

Then Grim locked the door.

Leonid became alert for a moment. He studied the man he'd come to regard as a professorial type—a blue-blooded academic with a talent for conspiracy.

Grim waited behind his desk. "Something has upset you."

Leonid unleashed the fury that had been building up inside of him for so long. He pounded his hand on Grim's desk, the blow sounding a dull thud.

Grim stared calmly at the KGB officer's hand. Then up at the eyes.

"Can you put that in words?" he asked coldly.

"You have betrayed us!" Leonid bellowed as he smashed his hand on the desk one more time. "Have I made myself clear to you?"

"Perfectly," Grim replied. His demeanor hadn't changed a bit. Leonid's famous bellow may have been able to make KGB underlings quake, but Grim wasn't in thrall to the KGB.

"You just stand there?" Leonid demanded. "After what you've done to us?"

Grim shrugged his shoulders. "Would you like me to run down to the cathedral and make my penance?"

The Russian stared at the Norwegian like he was mad.

"Oh," Grim said. "I forgot. You don't believe in such foolish things as religion. Well then, perhaps I should go and bow down before a picture of Comrade Stalin."

Leonid Davilov had been struck several blows at once. First was the mockery itself, always a sore point for rigid men who could not tolerate any questioning of their beliefs. It was something they couldn't admit. The second blow was the simple realization that Grim was willing to go against him and all he represented.

It eliminated his position of strength. Davilov had been planning on intimidating the Norwegian with threats of using the might of the KGB against the ELF, but he'd been preempted.

"We cannot tolerate any more rabid political attacks," Davilov said. "Using the tragedy at Chernobyl is impermissable. No more mention will be made of such things in the future."

"Or?" Grim asked.

The KGB officer glared at him. It was infuriating that Grim hadn't lost control, hadn't even blinked. Not only that, but he was also being taunting.

"Or..." Davilov began, "or we will withdraw our support."

Grim nodded. "Yes, we counted on that."

Davilov fell back on his old methods. He leaned forward on the desk, both hands firmly spread out as if he were going to launch himself at Grim. His heavy cheeks shook like a bulldog's.

"You presumed to judge our actions? Before we committed ourselves..."

The shock was taking hold of the KGB officer. Gradually he realized how well planned the ELF movement was and how solidly the Varangian Guard was entrenched. They hadn't been led by the Soviets at all—they had been doing the leading.

Leonid shook his head from side to side. "How could you do this to me...to us! After all the money we gave you, now you dare to attack the Soviet Union."

Grim folded his arms in front of him, perfectly relaxed, his composure adding salt to the Russian's wounded pride. "We told the truth, comrade," Grim said. "We are warning the world about the dangers it faces, wherever they come from. East. West. In our own country. It makes no difference. We are after truth. At least that's what I recall you saying at some of our earlier meetings. We are after peace, are we not? If we are all for peace, then we must cut down tyranny wherever it rises."

"But we planned on—"

"No," Grim said, cutting him off. "*You* planned on. That is the trouble. America has plans for Norway. Russia has plans for Norway. But until now, very few Norwegians have had plans for Norway. And now, comrade, we are taking the reins. *We* have plans for Norway."

"But you used us," Davilov protested. "You deceived us to get our support. We made great sacrifices to help your organization develop." Davilov shook his head as if he were taking an unruly student to task. "If you dare to offend us, your lives are forfeit."

Grim laughed. "Sorry, comrade. But you are sheep in wolve's clothing. We are the wolves and we are hungry. If any forfeiting is done, it will happen on your side."

"You can't mock me like this!"

"Actually, comrade, it's really quite easy to do. Now, go. Please. I have work to do. If we wish to talk to you anymore, I will contact you. But don't count on it."

Leonid hurtled over the desk, his stocky forearms pushing into Grim's chest. It wasn't smooth, but it was sheer force, the force of an old soldier who saw no other way.

The wall shook when Grim fell back against it. But the assault had been expected. He took the blow, spread his hands against the wall to share the impact, and then struck at the huge KGB man.

First he chopped both hands down in circular motions, sweeping away the bull's outstretched arms. Then, as Leonid staggered, Grim flung both hands out again, cracking the Russian on the face.

It wasn't a hard strike, but it had been delivered with a smooth economy of motion. The execution of the two-handed strike was a matter of instinct, and that instinct sent Leonid Davilov crashing to the floor.

Davilov recognized that he was outgunned. He had the presence of mind to realize that at this stage in the game he was in over his head. Perhaps when he was younger he could have done some damage in return.

But now he was on the floor.

Grim was the soldier that Leonid had once aspired to be. But Grim's soldiering was hidden much deeper. Even Davilov hadn't been aware of the Norwegian's capabilities previously, though the man had been checked out as thoroughly as possible.

The Soviets knew only of Grim's standard tour with the military. He served his time and then got out. There was nothing spectacular in his record. But that was only the visible record.

They knew nothing of the advanced tour around the world that Grim took—with Magnus Koll as the guide.

While working on missions with Koll, Grim had become something of a diplomat. He used his newly discovered talents as a negotiator to help the opposing side see reason. Or, if they continued to oppose Koll, then Grim helped them see nothing at all.

He was a very quiet and controlled assassin who accomplished his tasks like a true professional. He excelled because he liked his work. It gave him a chance to use his artistry.

And it was well concealed in the very professional way he ran Koll's propaganda division.

Grim helped the older man to his feet.

"I didn't mean to hurt your pride, comrade," Grim said. "You *have* helped us and that help is appreciated. But when the time came for you to move on, you didn't take the hints. When I tried to be subtle, you didn't understand, or perhaps you refused to understand. We are moving beyond any plans you could possibly have for us, comrade."

Davilov brushed off his gray suit. He eyed the man who stood before him and acknowledged that he had been greatly underestimated.

"You have made powerful enemies today," he said. "There are plenty of us who are not as old as I. Or as slow."

"I'm glad to hear that," Grim said, "otherwise you would be in much worse trouble."

Davilov lumbered to the door. He unlocked it, shaking his head with the realization that if the fight had been for real, perhaps he might never have walked out of the room.

"This is not over between us," Davilov said.

Grim held the door for him. "No," he said. "It is not over for any of us." His eyes held the glow that at the moment even he could not successfully conceal. "It has all just begun in earnest now. Until now, very few have realized what has been going on. Soon, everyone will know."

"Fanatic," Davilov said. "This could have worked well if only—"

"If only we played along," Grim said. "If only we did what we were told by our Russian masters."

He accompanied the Russian downstairs, then out to the street.

"You will regret this the rest of your days," Davilov said. "Luckily it won't be all that long."

Grim watched the man go down the street. As he closed the door slowly and thoughtfully, he acknowledged that from now on he would have to watch his back.

But even so, he'd experienced a promise of excitement there. He had been living out his role too placidly, too securely.

Soon the Viking would emerge.

CHAPTER TWENTY

Trondheim offered a dozen avenues of retreat for Leonid Davilov. None of them seemed particularly pleasant at the moment. He needed time to consider everything.

As he walked by the port at the mouth of the Nidelv waterway that circled through the city, the KGB officer thought of shipping out. It would be so easy to sail away and avoid the storm that was coming his way. At the moment he was at the eye of the storm, but soon the terrible backlash would strike out at him.

His carefully orchestrated campaign was coming undone. There was hope of salvaging it, but that meant escalating the peace war he'd been waging. The KGB operatives who'd infiltrated ELF had identified many of the leaders and could easily liquidate them.

The hit teams could cut away the malignant leaders who wanted to run ELF on their own and hopefully replace them with people who could be controlled.

Like Afghanistan in a way, he thought.

By now most countries in the west had heard of the Spetsnaz commando team that went into Kabul, assassinated the president who wasn't kowtowing to the Soviets, then replaced him with a puppet willing to play by Soviet rules.

It was a *Glavnoe Razvedyvatelnoe Upravlenie* operation. GRU, the military intelligence service, sent in the Spetsnaz team to Afghanistan, then directed the war from then on.

Leonid smiled.

There weren't too many boasts about Afghanistan making the rounds of the GRU.

Now Leonid faced his own Afghanistan.

If the KGB excised the ELF troublemakers, ELF would certainly strike back. There were plenty of others like Grim involved in the movement.

Their Viking cadres would be hard to put down.

Leonid saw the struggle getting out of hand with the Vikings hitting back at the KGB. There would be a series of counterattacks, assassinations, skirmishes...

And sooner or later GRU would step in. If they already weren't involved, he thought.

Military operations were the province of the army. When bullets started to fly, GRU would soon muscle in and direct every aspect of the operation.

Leonid would be buried unless he could outfinesse them.

GRU had dominance in some countries and the KGB were their vassals, political minions falling subordinate to the military. But in other areas KGB could dragoon GRU operatives. As a result there was an endless secret war between their own secret services.

There was always a score to settle.

As long as Leonid's operation brought in some returns, the KGB could hold sway in Scandinavia—at least in this particular peace war.

And Leonid might survive.

He lingered by the wooden warehouses on the pilings. It was peaceful and relatively deserted. The air was crisp and steady as it swept in from the sea. But to a man in love with Russian winters, the cold was nothing.

His overcoat was unbuttoned, in fact.

He'd been sweating so much after his struggle with Grim that he actually needed to cool off. His heart was thumping. He was out of shape for confrontations like that. It had been years since he'd been in anything other than a mental struggle.

Grim showed him the score. Now he would have to even the score or, if possible, abandon everything.

Leonid Davilov walked slowly away from the port. He wandered through the old town and passed by the huge wooden cathedral that had drawn so many pagans, Vikings and Christians throughout the centuries.

He kept on walking until he found his own temple.

It was a weathered and well-trafficked bar that concentrated on food and drink rather than decor. Leonid headed toward the front of the bar and took a seat a few booths away from the streetfront window.

It was too early for anyone to be coming after him, but he liked to cover himself whenever possible.

"What would you like?" the waitress said, giving him the soft smile she reserved for regulars.

A reprieve. A fast boat to China, Davilov thought. But he said, "A gallon of vodka to start."

She scolded him with a laugh, then brought him a glass of vodka while he pored over the menu.

He took his time ordering after he'd decided that the last supper of Leonid Davilov should be special. Finally, after the first vodka took off the edge, he ordered a cut of beef, some slices of *knackebrod*, Danish cheese, sausages and some strong lager to wash it all down.

After a few beers he began to think clearly, or at least it seemed there was a clarity to his thoughts.

First, he had been taken totally by surprise.

Second, it would be nearly impossible to come out of it intact, but he could put off the inevitable by contacting his superiors and going through the motions of limiting the damage. Acting as if he was still on top of matters. It would be impossible to explain how the anti-Soviet sentiment took him by surprise but he could try.

Third, he had to cut his losses. He would be summoned back to Moscow and a couple of KGB guardians would come to make sure he got on the plane. They would be thoughtful, full of good cheer, and they would blow his head off without hesitation if he made any move to evade the return.

He ordered another beer.

It was so unfair.

He'd done everything by the book. And still he'd practically signed his own death warrant.

Leonid was a prime mover in the beginning of the ELF peace movement. He was instrumental in gaining support for the operation from the head of the First Directorate. He'd received all the necessary approvals and acquired the necessary funds. It was costly, but the KGB considered peace movements, disarmaments and high technology transfers of greatest importance.

They were always prepared to loosen the purse strings for any of those high-priority operations, but they would watch the money closely and demand an adequate return.

Leonid Davilov had taken a giant step up in the ranks with this operation, although now it looked as if it was a step off a cliff.

He'd been discovered before, had even been expelled from Third World countries, but he always surfaced under different names, working out of different embassies with different covers.

But the current situation was not like a Third World crash. Those countries didn't have the manpower or skill to track the KGB and share information with their neighbors for the simple enough reason that they were usually cutting their neighbor's throats at every chance.

If the operation in Norway was blown, however, there would be no other chances. Back to Moscow on a hook.

Leonid had one more drink, then he began looking at the telephone booth in the bar. More and more it seemed to him like a lifeboat.

He walked calmly over to the phone and made three calls.

One of the calls was to his KGB cutout in Norway. Using an outwardly innocent code, he turned it into an emergency call, which meant that Leonid had to go into hiding. It also transferred the reins of the operation to a backup KGB officer, who would be given all the necessary information by his superiors.

Another call was to a cutout operative who was told to activate the assassins who'd infiltrated the ELF. It had to be now. Grim had given every indication that the anti-Soviet onslaught was just beginning. That could not be allowed.

And then Leonid made a third call, just in case his other calls didn't bear fruit.

The third call was to a friend in Norwegian security, a man who ran most of the internal covert-action operations in Norway. He wasn't a friend really. Leonid barely knew him. But anyone who could save him from his own comrades was to be considered a friend at a time of crisis.

The man wasn't in, and to the rather demanding voice on the other line asking about his identity and how he got hold of that number, Leonid simply said he would call again—if he could.

THE ASSASSINATION of key members within ELF had the earmarks of some degree of success. With one slashing stroke, the KGB could have eliminated their wayward opposition.

Except for one thing.

The assassination team was beaten to the draw.

Overnight the ranks of the ELF were purged, but they were purged of KGB officers.

Many of them vanished.

Some of them met up with "accidents," leaving their bodies too mangled for identification.

Others were victims of robberies.

Leonid Davilov discovered it the following morning when he tried to contact the team leader and found no trace of him. Next he attempted to reach the support team for the hit squad. There was no sign of them.

Then he decided to see if he could get in touch with the leaders of the ELF who were slated for execution.

They were all there. When he got them on the phone they sounded fully alive, definitely cheerful and infinitely menacing.

He was a marked man on both sides. The ELF or VG, whoever had done the preemptive assassinations, were after him. So were the KGB, and possibly the GRU.

It made a man absolutely patriotic.

For his newly chosen country, that is, he amended the thought.

Leonid Davilov made a number of frantic calls to the Norwegians. He was given several different phone exchanges, and finally got in touch with a man high up enough to help him: Eric Thorne.

"Don't move," Thorne said over the phone, when Davilov explained what he wanted. "We'll pick you up—"

"Shall I go to the police?"

"No," Thorne said. "We'll pick you up."

Davilov hung up the phone. He was calling from a mountain lodge just a short drive north of Trondheim. He'd driven in a car he'd had set aside for just such an occasion. It had been stored in a rented garage, totally unknown to anyone but himself.

Now all he had to do was wait—wait and survive.

MURMANSK WAS THE HOME of the Soviet Arctic Fleet. It was also the home of Nicholas Vrosputin, a lean and wiry lieutenant in the Spetsnaz brigade that had been making regular excursions into Norway for years.

Sometimes they engaged in simulated invasions on Russian soil where Vrosputin would stage attacks on mock-ups of Norwegian targets.

Other times Vrosputin and a team of commandos actually went into Norway, setting themselves up for sabotage and assassination missions. The infiltrations into Norway were dry runs just to see how such assassination operations could be carried out.

Vrosputin had targeted several prominent statesmen, tracked military figures, and conducted surveillance on certain KGB operations that were suspect. There were occasions when rogue agents had to be terminated, and times like that called for men like Nicholas Vrosputin.

Except for a couple of minor incidents that couldn't be avoided they never deliberately harmed any Norwegian citizens.

The Soviets had several plans for entering Norway—either through Sweden across the highway that ran right to Narvik on Norway's western coast, or straight across the border Russia shared with the northeast region of Norway near the Kirkenes.

Recent war games in the Norwegian Sea also demonstrated a capability to avoid the northern installations and sweep down around on the western coastline with the Northern Fleet. A quick push through the Barents Sea and the Soviets would be able to deploy in the North Atlantic.

There was also the chance of going through Finland to get to Norway, although the memory of nearly three-quarters of a million casualties the Russians had suffered when they fought the Finns during World War II was still very strong.

The Finns were a separate species unto themselves.

Though they never did anything to irritate the Russians, they never backed down, either. The ski troops of the Finns were considered among the world's best. They could live in the Arctic wilderness, approach unseen within a few yards of the Russians, then open up with murderous fire. By the time the Soviets were able to respond, the Finns were gone—hitting elsewhere.

Russia had no desire to send its troops marching through a country that could turn an entire population into a skilled guerrilla army in the manner of the one that had fought first Russia, then the Germans, during World War II.

It was better to use politics to defeat the enemy than to have to go through the Finns. It could be done, but it was virtually the same as having the frontline troops commit suicide. And gradually smothering the Finns with their corpses.

But politics hadn't been working all that well, and when diplomacy failed, direct action was called for.

That was the reason for Nicholas Vrosputin putting in an appearance at a dacha in the depth of a forest on the Kola Peninsula early in the afternoon.

The dacha was the extensively guarded retreat of General Kumin, who oversaw operations of the more hidden installations on the Kola Peninsula. He also handled cross-border operations.

Just as the Soviet Air Force tested Norwegian border defenses by sending Badgers screaming toward Nordic airspace until they were picked up and challenged by Norwegian F-16s, the Soviets also tested the land defenses by sending in land forces.

General Kumin was responsible for analyzing and undermining Norway's defenses against sabotage and assassination operations.

He achieved his aims by sending in men like Nicholas Vrosputin.

"Nicholas," he said, shaking hands and wrapping his arm around Vrosputin's shoulder. "Come in and talk with me for a while. Sit down." The general ushered him into a chair in front of his desk, then dropped behind the huge desk as though it was a bunker where he conducted his wars against the West.

Vrosputin had learned long ago that the most effective way to talk to General Kumin was to listen carefully and nod at the appropriate moments.

"I have the greatest faith in you, Nicholas," General Kumin said. "All these years I've watched your progress, and I have heard nothing but good about you. It is a rare man indeed who returns from the battles you have seen."

And so I am sending you to certain death yet again, Vrosputin thought, translating the words. As all intelligence men, the general spoke two languages at once. One language was spoken with words and it was always hard to believe. Then there was the language spoken with his graying eyes. A discerning man could read the cold, hard truth in those eyes.

Vrosputin was a discerning man. As he sat in the wooden chair, he deciphered Kumin's true message from his eyes.

"And so what our friends in the KGB considered an asset has become a liability. It is up to GRU to salvage this operation before it backfires and becomes a huge political coup for our enemies."

Vrosputin's features had assumed an expression of ease and he looked relaxed. Though no one could ever be fully at ease in the presence of the general, the attempt was expected.

The General opened up a bottom drawer of his desk.

Aha, Nicholas thought. The General was offering him a drink. It was a steady ritual that was relied on by Kumin to create a bond. The bond between two equals.

After pouring two glasses of cognac, the general set one down on the desk near Vrosputin. "To your good fortune, Nicholas. And to the good fortune of Russia."

A toast to those who don't come back, Vrosputin thought. Mother Russia will mourn her lost son.

Nicholas poured the first glass down his gullet, where it quickly rushed down and imparted a warm glow, then flowed along to Vrosputin's brain. After two more cognacs he was infused by a maelstrom of bold and boastful thoughts, tapping into the tides of drunkeness where all things were possible. Even impossible assignments from Comrade Kumin.

The general too had a flushed and confident look and filled the glasses again.

Three drinks, Vrosputin thought. Death was thrice as likely. No more drinks needed, general. Just get me out of here. Into the field.

"This Magnus Koll," the general said. "There were great plans made for him. Apparently his were greater. Great enough to cut the throats of our KGB brethren."

Vrosputin was updated about the assassinations of the KGB operatives in ELF. He was also told of the suspected treachery of Leonid Davilov, the KGB officer behind the support of the Vikings. And how the KGB had nourished ELF from the beginning, only to see the seed bear rotten fruit.

No love lost there, Vrosputin thought. There was also no doubt that GRU would have to act. It was an extraordinary chance to prove to the Party who was most deserving.

The triumvirate of the Politburo, KGB and GRU was constantly shifting. Sometimes the balance of power favored military intelligence, sometimes political. But it was the Politburo that helped inaugurate the secret rulers, the ones behind the scenes.

The general wanted to be one of those rulers. That was part of the reason for the mission Vrosputin would be sent on. But there was also the tactical need.

If the Viking fanatics had left well enough alone, Russia might have allowed them to continue. There were other groups who were "encouraged," fueled by the KGB and GRU but not directed by them. Russia provided money, weapons, connections, and then let the groups go off on their own.

That technique helped the Russians distance themselves from later consequences, some of which could become embarrassing. The Vikings could have been another such group, if only they refrained from executing the KGB moles.

"Magnus Koll and his Varangian Guards are a formidable force," the general said. "That much we have seen. Do not underestimate him. And make sure the men you bring with you know what this fanatic has accomplished."

Vrosputin nodded.

Most of the Russian military were kept in the dark about the larger aims leading to certain actions. They were given weapons and shown what had to be accomplished, but never told why.

The Spetsnaz were different. They were the elite, chosen from the ranks of the army and given special schooling and training unavailable to the run-of-the-mill soldier.

Spetsnaz troops were encouraged to think for themselves, to satisfy their curiosity. They knew how things really worked inside the Soviet Union—as well as the rest of the world.

"Are you familiar with the history of the Varangian Guard, comrade?" the general asked.

Of course, he wanted to say. But he simply nodded his head and said, "Yes, General. In fact, the greatest of them all fought for the kingdom of Kiev before heading south to serve for Empress Zoe..."

The Spetsnaz troops were often scholars as well as warriors. Besides being well versed in espionage, many of them mastered other languages and the customs and religions of the lesser countries.

They were allowed access to knowledge and thought that was controlled—banned actually from the average Soviet citizen. It was one of their perks.

The chief perk was the great number of chances they were given to die for their country.

"You are Swedish citizens this time around," the general was saying. "Should you be taken alive by the Norwegians, although that is doubtful..."

The general's eyes met the lieutenant's, telling him that not only was it improbable, it was impossible.

Spetsnaz commandos were expected to "bliss out" their wounded rather than leave them behind for the enemy to capture and interrogate. The eternal bliss was administered with a fatal dosage contained in a syringe they always carried with them in a small emergency field kit. The bliss could be administered to their wounded comrades, or to themselves.

"Should you be taken," he repeated, "the identities are backstopped sufficiently to give you more than enough time to do what you must to prevent us from being compromised."

Next the general got down to the hard details. The main targets were the highly visible members of ELF and the more shadowy VG. Another target was the KGB rogue who hadn't reported back, the traitor who had escaped the intensive search for him in Norway. Of course the KGB would be on the lookout also, but the general had little hope they would find him.

Transportation had already been set up for Vrosputin's commando team via the Russian-controlled freight companies that had virtual free rein throughout Scandinavia. It would be a simple matter to secrete the commandos in the specially prepared trucks—which often carried illegal cargoes—and then drop them at the proper location inside Scandinavia.

The Soviets had a solid support structure embedded throughout Sweden, and it consisted of safe houses, agents, caches, all of the equipment a group like Vrosputin's would need.

The safe houses and contacts could support the "tourists," as Spetsnaz infiltrators called themselves among their own service. But if possible, the Spetsnaz were to involve as few assets as possible. Their activities were going to stir up a lot of attention and there was little to be gained from risking excess assets in the covert network.

Vrosputin agreed with that method of operation. He liked to go it alone. His men, he knew, could be counted on, and the more outsiders that lent a hand, the easier it was to get burned.

Besides, if everything went well, then if and when the Spetsnaz presence was discovered by the West, it would be too late.

Western services were always on the lookout for the more traditional means of covert entry into their countries. Secret parachute drops. Undersea landings.

The intelligence agencies of each targeted country expected Spetsnaz troops to drop behind enemy lines prior to an actual invasion. But nobody fully realized the extent to which many of those Spetsnaz commandos could be in position well ahead of time, merely by coming in on the trade trucks.

It would do just fine, he thought, although there wouldn't be much sight-seeing along the way.

The general softened as he spoke and actually appeared to be sincere instead of just wearing the guise of sincerity.

"Speak freely, Nicholas," the general said after a while. "Give me your thoughts on this mission and its aftermath."

Vrosputin took him up on his offer, voicing his opinion as much as he dared. It was obvious he considered the mission very high risk, because his concerns were mainly about his family. He wanted to make sure they received the extra hazard pay he had coming to him. For every year Spetsnaz troops served they were paid for a year and a half. It built up over the years, especially for a man of his position. But there was always the chance that the hazard pay would be lost along the way, dropping into some paper pusher's pocket.

Vrosputin had no wife, just plenty of girlfriends, and no son or daughter who could use the money. But he did have family he was fond of.

The general nodded. "Your parents will be looked after," he said reassuringly. "They will get everything they have coming to them. Your people will be taken care of."

Vrosputin smiled. He knew they were all considered expendable, no matter how good or skilled they were, and the general's words reminded him of the black market American gangster films he'd often seen on videotapes. The boss sends the enforcer against the opposition and promises to look after the man's family if he gets whacked or sent to prison.

Don't worry, General, he thought with a touch of irony. I'm a stand-up guy.

Vrosputin then talked about the mission and any opposition Special Forces believed to be in the area. They worked out arrangements, timetables, fallback plans and exfiltration points.

After they covered the details, General Kumin dismissed him. The dismissal and good wishes seemed abrupt. Perhaps it was because he didn't want to associate with a doomed man any longer than necessary. It could be contagious.

Vrosputin had one thought in particular on his mind when he left the briefing. How good it would be to see the look of surprise on the general's face when Vrosputin made it back safely.

NICHOLAS VROSPUTIN had assembled his six-man team in a hotel bar in Leningrad's modern city center.

The hotel was usually reserved for tourists. Stocked with the best food and drink on the market, aboveground and below, it was intended to give visitors a favorable impression of Russian life in general and the availability of goods and services to all citizens. To all appearances, it was a typical hotel open to the average Russian.

Tonight Vrosputin's group was not average. Thus they could afford the night out.

Tonight they were "tourists," but they didn't want to see the usual sights. The Winter Palace had little to offer them. Nor did the circus. They wanted to get their fill of food and drink and then stumble along the River Neva.

It was a tradition that Vrosputin always followed. Of course a celebration would follow if they got back—plenty of food and drink for everyone. But this was the celebration for those who might not come back.

"We are going on a vacation soon," Vrosputin announced to the men gathered around a large table in the back.

The room was warm, the drink was steady, and it had been some time since they'd last seen such a feast.

They were all veterans and knew what kind of vacation Vrosputin had in mind. The Spetsnaz had their own language and could talk freely in front of others without fear of giving themselves away.

Vacations. Tourists.

"What shall we take with us, Nicholas?" asked the very sturdy but surprisingly agile sergeant to his right.

"It's being taken care of even as we sit," Vrosputin said. "You need bring only yourself and a prayer or two."

Sergeant Duskovich feigned shock. "But prayers are not allowed, comrade."

"That makes them all the more powerful, doesn't it?"

The sergeant laughed. So did the others. They were used to Vrosputin's ways. Without his brand of humor they would go mad. Better to be out here cutting loose than having to be cooped up, dealing with the tension even before they went on the mission.

Soon enough there would be more tension than an ordinary man could bear. His men were up for what lay ahead.

Like him, they had shed blood before. First bloodletting occurred during their hand-to-hand combat training with the "gladiators" kept in special Soviet prisons. Hardened convicts were spared their immediate death sentences and given chances to stay alive as long as they could. When the gladiators fought the Spetsnaz trainees, there was no holding back. Either combatant might be killed in the struggle.

It prepared the Spetsnaz troops for what lay ahead.

Then there was the actual combat experience.

Afghanistan. Poland. Armenia. South Africa. South America. Wherever special forces were needed, they had participated. Sometimes they were in soldiers' uniforms, other times they fought covertly. They had all seen the world as first-class "tourists."

Vrosputin had the most extensive experience, though he didn't speak of it often. Except to his men, he was known as a "monk," the term used for so many of the secretive types in the Soviet forces.

But to his men he was a "monk" defrocked.

That night they would end up with a suitable number of women. Very unmonkish behavior. The following day they would get ready to go off to war.

In both places, bars or battlefields, Nicholas Vrosputin was the kind of man they could follow.

As Vrosputin relaxed with his men, he was certain they could take care of the targets assigned to them. But there was something else bothering him. Something that the general had spoken of briefly.

Kumin had mentioned a group of commandos who might be in the field for the other side. Vrosputin knew that according to rumors the Americans had a group of elite soldiers who were already on the track of the VG.

More intelligence would come in on them soon, Vrosputin hoped, but what he'd heard so far didn't cheer him.

These American commandos now and then had tangled with some of the mercenaries who worked for the Eastern bloc, and every time the Americans had come out ahead. They had also wrecked a number of Soviet operations—some of them inside Russia itself. And they always got out unscathed.

The "SOBs" they were called.

Special Operations Bureau? Vrosputin wondered. How good could they be?

"Drink up, Nicholas!" his sergeant ordered. "You're too far away."

Vrosputin pulled himself back to the present.

It was time to drink another toast—to good luck, good times, whatever.

Soon they would embark on a covert trek to Scandinavia. Then, whoever or whatever the American commandos were, Vrosputin's troops would meet them. They would find out what these near mythical SOBs were made of.

Vrosputin would destroy the myths once and for all.

Either that, or create another one.

CHAPTER TWENTY-ONE

"Psychedelia" lived aboard the Day-Glo ambulance that had become a regular sight around Copenhagen's "Free City of Christiania."

Bohemians unofficially took over the former military compound and turned the barracks into a haven for squatters, artists and undergrounders of all stripes.

The city allowed the squatters virtual free rein in their artists' quarters, although citizens groups periodically tried to close down the complex. They blamed the wild-living bohemians of Christiania for most of the problems caused by drugs and the wave of crime hitting the city.

But the free city weathered most of the storms, offering a haven to those who wanted to live outside the laws of society.

The Danish army had moved out of the barracks, and an underground army had moved in.

A good number of them liked to hang around with the owner of the brightly painted ambulance.

Converted into a rolling home with a deck added to the roof and a propane-fueled engine, the former ambulance was kept in perfect condition. It could pass any inspection, healthwise or mechanically.

The psychedelic paint on the ambulance that so routinely drove around the Christinshavn district was noticeable, but then so was the driver.

The driver was a leggy blonde with plenty of time on her hands, plenty of money—and she of course had a good word for everyone. Her beauty helped her fit into the scene. She was always welcome wherever she went.

Her real name was Freda Stensgaard, although around the free city she was known just as Lita, the girl with the magic bus.

Early one morning, while the districts around Christinshavn were waking up, Freda drove the magic bus down from Copenhagen along the Zealand coast for her rendezvous with a baby-faced angel and assassin named Frederick Mannenheim.

FREDERICK MANNENHEIM had become adept at moving illicit cargo for his underground employers.

He'd risen through the ranks and was now an auxiliary soldier with some understanding of the Varangian Guard's grand design. He didn't know who the actual leader was, but the man he worked with was near the top of the organization.

Wulfson, the man who gave him his orders, had the air of someone who was used to being in command. He also had the authority to bring people into the fold if they passed muster.

Mannenheim had done well, but others hadn't been so lucky. He understood that a good number of them had been severed from the group much the same way Mannenheim had severed the neck of the woman who had tried to defraud the VG of an artifact.

Since that assignment Mannenheim had done other jobs for his VG masters and was now an almost trusted friend.

He was so trusted that he had been given the task of bringing the canisters of mustard gas to the Zealand coast.

The mustard gas had been moving toward Denmark for nearly forty years now, ever since the Allies dumped thousands of tons of it into the Baltic Sea off the coast of the Danish island of Bornholm after World War II.

Both German and Allied stocks found their way to the bottom of the sea and rested there. For a while. But fisherman had been catching grenades and artillery shells for years, and the Danes who fished off the coast of Bornholm often used gas masks while they pulled up their nets. Too many of them had been burned or blinded by the deposits of gas pulled up from the seabed because a lot of the shells had eroded, spilling the contents of grenades and bombs, which turned into murky, poisonous chunks.

The Danish Navy routinely bought any fisherman's catch that had been contaminated by the spilled mustard gas. Although most of the bombs had totally rotted away, a good number would come up intact and could still explode.

The government handlers would seal up the chunks of solidified mustard gas in nonerodable plastic containers and resink them or pay to have them destroyed in German plants.

But there had been an awful lot of tonnage still down there, and it had just been going to waste until Magnus Koll hired a group of German divers through former underworld connections in Hamburg.

The dive had been carried out in summer and had gone very smoothly and quickly. Divers had gone out on a yacht—with a couple of bronzed, bikini-clad women lazing in the sun—and probed beneath the seabed for the contaminated treasure. It was risky work but they were well paid. And at least no one had been shooting at them for a change.

Because of the hazards involved, the divers had worked slowly. They were meticulous underworld and underwater archaeologists as they carefully uncovered several intact canisters. After sealing them in leakproof containers, the divers had raised them back to the surface.

The yacht had then sailed back to Germany, where the canisters stayed—until the winter day when Frederick Mannenheim was paid to smuggle them through Denmark up to the capital.

The canisters arrived by ship to the Danish island of Mons. An appropriate place, Mannenheim thought. The island was full of ancient burial grounds and prehistoric tombs, popular spots that were often toured by visitors from Copenhagen and other cities on the Zealand island.

Soon, Frederick Mannenheim thought, they wouldn't have to travel so far to see such burial grounds.

They would have enough of their own—right at home.

Mannenheim and another trusted driver took the deadly cargo in two rental cars over the bridge to Zealand and proceeded in the direction of Copenhagen.

They stopped just a short drive south from the city and waited for their meeting with the blond woman.

FREDA STENSGAARD met with Frederick Mannenheim along a roadside that paralleled the Baltic Sea. Though they acted friendly and cheerful with one another, there was nothing even remotely friendly about their rendezvous.

When they parted company a short time later, several canisters and small containers had been added to the storage compartment that housed the propane tanks in the back of the "magic bus."

There was nothing out of the ordinary about them. The canisters were painted the same dull yellow color as the propane tanks. And driving along in the bus was just another beautiful blond woman full of life—and death—riding back to Copenhagen.

WHEN THE WINDS WERE RIGHT, mustard gas could vaporize an entire front line, ripping out their throats with caustic agents.

After the thick yellow clouds of mustard gas wafted across the trenches in World War I, casualties on both sides spread the horror stories about the effects of the gas.

Internal blisters formed and burst inside lungs. Breathing was nearly impossible, and those who inhaled the mustard particles often frothed at the mouth or spit blood before they curled up like roaches and died in convulsions.

More important than the fatalities were the casualties who lived—however shortly—after the attack, as well as the survivors who spread the stories about what they had seen.

Massive fatalities were only the first round of attack.

Fear was the second.

As the general population heard of the effects of the gas, people recoiled in horror. But the image of such a horrendous weapon being used eventually made everyone feel a little safer, too. It was just too inhuman to contemplate inflicting it on anyone.

Some African Zouave troops fighting alongside the Allies in World War I had thought the clouds were supernatural mists carrying demons who destroyed anyone in their wake. They were right in a way. It was a supernatural weapon. Above and beyond nature's worst punishments, mustard was like nothing that had ever hit the battlefield before.

Its use was so awesome that it was finally outlawed.

Actually it wasn't outlawed because of the horror, but because of the fact that the other side would strike back with similar weapons.

So the world thought it was safe from that particular nightmare until 1936 when Italian warplanes sprayed Ethiopian troops with tear and mustard gas, using an estimated seven hundred tons of chemical munitions.

Fifteen thousand people had died, and once and for all the world vowed never to use such weapons again, and repeated that vow again and again.

But the world had not anticipated Freda Stensgaard's magic bus arriving in Copenhagen.

Freda drove back to the Christinshavn district where she had become a regular sight. She parked the magic bus on a side street, then, according to Koll's directions, left the bus overnight. When she returned in the morning, her part was done. The canisters were gone. Another team had stood by, prepared to initiate the next phase of the atrocity agenda.

During the night the two-man demolition team entered the former ambulance and removed the canisters from the psychedelic warehouse.

They then brought them to prearranged and prepared sites around the city, removed the protective domes from the cylinder valves and positioned nozzles where they could do the most damage—in ventilation shafts, or poking through the foliage of indoor plants.

Some of the canisters were sprayers, others bombs.

All of them were set to go off at the same time. At the killing hour.

CHEMICAL PLANTS had multiplied like wildfire throughout Norway, dotting the coastline as well as the interior, producing large quantities of liquid ammonia, sodium chloride, calcium nitrate and heavy water for atomic piles.

The huge manufacturers also turned out a steady stream of chemicals ranging from pharmaceuticals to weed killers.

NorsKemCo was one of the leaders in the field. Owned by a Norwegian/Swedish consortium, NorsKemCo maintained a sprawling complex on the eastern shore of Oslo Fjord.

The company was also one of the most vulnerable.

Though there were many security employees, a good number of them were in place to keep track of people inside the plant. They expected industrial sabotage or isolated instances of theft and were prepared to handle those kinds of cases.

What they didn't expect was an armed attack by a group of guerrillas.

Their location had attracted many top-level workers. NorsKemCo was in the vanguard of the move away from urban industrial centers. They liked to disguise their facilities as retreats and present them as forest-shrouded asylums away from the busy cities.

The choice location that drew in top scientists also drew in top guerrilla fighters who found that the plant was almost designed for a raid.

The VG had bided their time and studied the building from the outside until they knew every entrance and escape route. They also mapped out the interior of the plant by eavesdropping on disaffected employees who shared their woes over several strong drinks after their shifts were over.

They found out the most dangerous spots to work in. The most hazardous chemicals.

With the help of ELF sympathizers working in the company, the VG learned the schedules of the shifts, the location of security and their likely reactions.

They found out enough to enable them to loot the plant and then burn it to the ground, and with that kind of knowledge it was only a matter of time before it was put to use.

The time had come at one in the morning when the thinnest shift was on duty, just settling in for the long haul. The main thing on a good many minds was slogging it out until the morning.

That complacency was ended by a horrendous wrenching noise as an oversize pickup truck raced toward the main gate where security was strongest.

When the pickup truck smacked into the fence, knocking down metal poles, rolling over on its side, it seemed like an aberration, the act of a drunken man. But there was no one in the cab. The driver had bailed out on the access road leading to the gate.

Several guards were scrambling in the direction of the capsized pickup, wondering what the hell some fool was trying to prove, when the explosion went off.

It was a small explosion, but it was enough to splinter the pickup truck and shred skin and bone as the blast ripped through the fence.

An emergency crew was hot on the heels of the security squad, streaming toward the entrance to help the wounded. The guards in the gatehouse frantically called the police and activated alarms inside the plant at the same time.

Attention and energy and pandemonium was centered around a simple diversion while the real attack came at the back of the complex, where black-clad commandos cut through wire fences at the moment of the explosion and hurried to the plant.

It was a small force that worked in total silence. They sprayed silenced SMG ahead of them as a group of startled workers burst out of one of the buildings to be kicked off their feet and shoved out of life with the silenced and deadly volley.

The front men of the team burst into their target building and blew away a confused security guard who'd been thinking that he should make his way to the front gate. The attackers made their way up the stairs.

Nothing stood in their way except the signs plastered all over the corridors on each floor.

CAUTION HAZARDOUS AREA.

GOGGLES REQUIRED.

RESPIRATORS MANDATORY.

DANGER: EXPLOSIVES!

The Varangian Guard commando team followed the signs as though they were street maps. Before they reached any of the hazardous areas they slipped on rat-faced respirators, looking like storm troopers from another planet as they went about their business.

While the inside team worked in their target building, another VG force gathered near the gate and opened up with murderous fire on the rescue and security squads that had arrived on the scene.

One instant the emergency crews were getting everything under control, the next, they were falling over like bowling pins. A steady barrage of automatic fire carved blood-streaked paths through the bodies of the hopelessly outclassed security force. It wasn't a fight at all. It was a massacre.

A third force of VG guerrillas commandeered one of the emergency jeeps, then, lights and sirens screaming, screeched around the interior of the plant, adding to the confusion and taking potshots at the panicked employees who'd emerged to see what was going on.

The attack was very brief.

Perhaps shorter than a coffee break.

The team inside the target building set their plastic explosives, then thundered back down the stairwells and burst out into the courtyard.

They raced back toward the fence they'd cut through and headed for home—deep into the woods.

Five minutes later, while the police and security forces that had been alerted in Oslo were heading for the plant, the plant headed for them.

In pieces.

Steel covers blew off chemical storage tanks and fountains of ignited chemicals leaped into the air.

Toxic vapors streamed into the night like fireworks. Metal, men and chemicals mixed with the atmosphere as explosions rocked the complex, one by one...

The Scandinavian sky was lit up with fire and brimstone as a hellish rainbow of nearly every chemical known to man fell slowly to earth.

And the VG teams vanished into the woods.

COPENHAGEN WAS HIT almost simultaneously.

The mustard gas charges had been hidden throughout the city. Timed explosions went off in unison, sending a shroud of mustard down city streets, blowing in the wind.

The late-night denizens were thrown into panic. Some were screaming, wondering what kind of nightmare they'd woken up to. Others were rolling around in the snow and mud of alleys, unable to scream, unable to extinguish the agony that scorched their insides.

People streamed out of hotel rooms and ran out of bars, looking for someone to help, but no help was to be found.

Explosions trashed street-front apartment windows, sending streams of thick yellow smoke out into the night.

It had a horrible effect on those who were hit. Even with respirators and advance knowledge of a mustard attack, defenders often suffered a great deal.

People who were totally unprepared for mustard gas didn't have a chance against it as the gas wafted through hotels, nightclubs, and canals.

The city went wild. There weren't that many fatalities, but it was the brutality, the sheer terror of the attack that sent a wave of panic through the city.

The panic was contagious.

Chaos reigned.

THE MEDIA WENT AMOK in the next twenty-four hours. Headline writers had a field day:

Chemical Complex Ablaze in Norway.

Saboteurs Reported on Chemical Site.

Automatic Weapons Fired on Industrial Plant.

Clouds of Death over Copenhagen.

The catastrophes brought Denmark and Norway together in mutual outrage, sharing in the calamity and looking for a proper joint response.

Rumors fed the papers and the broadcasting networks with a steady theme of Red-baiting that would have been dismissed as paranoia any other time.

But not when so many lives had been lost.

Peacetime had lulled Scandinavia into thinking that nothing so catastrophic could happen again. The war was over. War was over forever...

But something was trying to bring that war back.

Secret military factions, terrorist cadres and Soviet saboteurs were whispered about at first, but then as the rumors grew, they were shouted about in print and on the airwaves.

A state of shock gripped both countries. At work, in bars, on the streets, they were all trying to figure out what the hell had happened.

The screams of the press were as loud as the screams of the victims.

The rumors and the tips and the informants continued to flood the media.

An increasingly prevalent rumor was that Soviet agents were attacking chemical plants in order to expose preparations NATO was making for chemical warfare. The attack on Copenhagen was attributed to commandos who'd used stocks of mustard gas salvaged from World War II days. Carefully orchestrated VG propaganda hammered out the idea that the Soviet commandos were doing what had to be done to keep these barbaric weapons from being used against their country.

The rumors were propped up by factual material about past "raids" on strategic sites made by similar commandos. Now it was apparent that those raids had been dry runs for the real things. Preemptive strikes.

Another set of rumors fed the media a similar line. But instead of Soviet commandos, these rumors laid total blame for the catastrophes on out-of-control Western intelligence agencies who were conducting a covert war on Norwegian and Danish battlefields.

Both sets of rumors served one purpose: to fan hatred for East and West alike, accusing them in one way or another of trampling all over Norway's sovereignty.

There was only one answer: Scandinavia had to rule itself. It had to protect its own borders from the madness of the superpowers. ELF spokesmen called for the removal of all NATO forces from Scandinavia. They also called for the expulsion of Soviet provocateurs.

Besides the calls denouncing East and West, there were several cries demanding a rethinking of Norway's position in the world.

An overhaul was long overdue.

A group that dared to carry out that overhaul was already working for Scandinavian nationalism, working to prevent the Nordic people from being pawns in a deadly game of international intrigue.

A shadowy spokesman for the Varangian Guard hinted that they were ready to make the ultimate sacrifice to keep Scandinavia free.

Without identifying himself, Grim Swann made several calls to key people in the media, cluing them in to the possibility of a Pan-Nordic response to the latest outrages committed on their territory.

A "spontaneous" movement was sweeping the country.

Soon there would be nothing to stop it, and the seeds had been planted for support of the Varangian Guard, which was going to go into action to save the country from the barbarians who'd perpetrated such outrages.

If Scandinavia were to survive, the survivors had to act now.

CHAPTER TWENTY-TWO

The brightly painted troop carrier cruised through the streets of Oslo.

On the outside it appeared to be just an oversize van or touring bus. On the inside it was outfitted with the latest in surveillance equipment.

The equipment included parabolic mikes to eavesdrop on open-air conversations and camera guns to get a quick zoom and flash on any suspects. It also included several other kinds of guns thoughtfully provided by the Norwegians.

In the front passenger seat Nile Barrabas checked his gear one more time as the SOBs approached the battlefield.

Unfortunately the battlefield was Oslo. It was a bright Saturday afternoon, and the streets and parks were full of strolling people.

One of the walkers was Sanna Mikkalsen. She was killing time until she left for her rendezvous with the Varangian Guard.

The captured VG insider had cooperated fully. She contacted the VG through a prearranged emergency number to ask for help and instructions. Sanna gave them the rundown: Nils Hendrik was barely alive. Both of them had fought their way out of the woods, staggered around lost, and finally made it to civilization. Hendrik was holed up in a barn and wouldn't last much longer before he was discovered or died.

The voice on the other end of the line gave her explicit instructions. Sanna was to come along down Karl Johansgate and then head toward the park. Nobody would meet her there, but she would be observed. After spending ten minutes in the park she was to proceed to the National Theater. Then at the train station she was supposed to take a ride up to Holmenkollen, the ski slope just outside of Oslo. Once there she was to make her way to the huge promontory with the tower looking down on Oslo Fjord. Then she had to start walking back down the road for Oslo.

Somewhere along the route she would be met, then she would lead them to Hendrik.

Barrabas had to admire the plan. The reason for the long stretch was that it gave the VG plenty of opportunity to ambush her. Or they could abandon the attempt if it looked unfavorable. It could happen in the park, on the way to the station, and then once she left the final station, at the ski lift, the lookout tower or any spot along the heavily wooded road.

There was no way to control it. If the Norwegians had insisted on Sanna picking the spot, the VG would expect an ambush. As it was, they would naturally be suspicious of her, but it was still better to follow their own plan.

No one liked to fight in such a populated area, but the VG had shown they were ready to wage war in Scandinavian cities. By meeting them now and attempting to take them out of action, the SOBs hoped to stop worse VG atrocities in the city.

Besides, though it was dangerous, at least the Norwegians were ready.

You couldn't see the forests for the police, Barrabas thought. Undercover units had blanketed the area, and standby teams were ready to take off in any direction.

Barrabas had no doubt that the VG would show up whether they knew it was a trap or not. It was part of their military ethos. The original Varangian Guard never permitted one of their own to fall into enemy hands. It was a matter of honor. They even made it a personal cause to redeem fallen warriors.

That made Nils Hendrik, the captured VG chieftain, a potential draw.

Claude Hayes drove the van past a strip of stores, with new brick-and-glass buildings housing upscale boutiques and glass shops on both sides of the street. "There's something in the air," Claude said.

"It's called snow," Nanos said from the back seat. "You see a lot of that up here."

Hayes ignored Nanos, which from time to time was a shared trait among the small group. "This is going to be more than just a reunion with Sanna," he said. "Anyone else sense that?"

Billy Two sat opposite Nanos. The Osage warrior had been looking out the window, idly studying the civilians. But all along his senses were on the pending operation. "I know what you're talking about. I've seen ahead—"

"Oh God," Nanos said, "the bird has flown again. Don't tell me Hawk Spirit fast-forwarded you into the future."

Billy Two gave Nanos a look that could freeze water.

Nanos backed off. "Whatever works," he said, knowing that each man took his own talisman into battle. With Billy Two it was a bird of prey. With the others it was something not so easily defined. But they all had their own quirks, their own special way of gearing up.

With Barrabas, maybe it was the headband.

Celts and Vikings often wore engraved bronze or silver torques around their necks to keep them from losing their heads in battle. Why shouldn't the headband do the same for Barrabas? It was a fitting talisman, wrapped around his nearly white hair.

Perhaps, the Greek thought, his own talismans were his endless wisecracks. Words to deny disaster, to ward off doom. They had a certain magic to them—even if the others thought they were a bit on the groaning side.

What about Claude? he wondered. It was something different with Claude. Maybe a Detroit Lions T-shirt, he thought. He'd never know. Claude was close-lipped about that kind of thing. Getting through this life was hard enough without bringing the afterlife into it.

Nanos shook his head, listening to Billy Two go on and on about another battle, a greater one than the upcoming one, looming in front of them.

Ragnarok.

The Osage was talking about the Viking apocalypse. Ragnarok. It was also a code name for an ELF operation that Lee Hatton picked up via her undercover work. Barrabas had talked a bit about it to the SOBs, but the bigger picture was still about to come.

What were you supposed to wear to this Viking apocalypse? Nanos wondered. Were combat boots fine or did you need a helmet with a pair of cow horns on it? Wisely, Nanos kept his thoughts to himself.

He figured the rest of the SOBs preferred it that way.

Their involvement in the Viking lore, which they'd studied to some extent, had been taking its toll. It was getting positively mystical. Mysticism was fine, he thought, momentarily clenching his fists to rid some of his tension. But it never hurt if you knew how to kick some ass in the bargain.

SANNA MIKKALSEN WAITED on a park bench for the contact from the terrorists, as she had come to think of them.

She wore a light brown leather jacket, jeans and boots. They were a bit bedraggled, to show she'd been on the streets for a while.

The parkland paths were full of students from the nearby university, but no one seemed to take the least interest in her, though she was aware there were a good number of security agents conducting surveillance over the entire area.

After waiting ten minutes with no contact from the VG, she went to the National Theater and took the entrance to the underground station for the Holmenkolbanen, the train that rode up to the Holmenkollen mountain range.

Norwegian security operatives had already approached the station from an opposite direction and were there ahead of her, flanking her position from a discreet distance.

Riding up to Holmenkollen was a frequent outing for the natives of Oslo, so the surveillance men and women had a good crowd to blend in with.

For the first time in years, Sanna Mikkalsen was glad to be in the presence of so many police and military operatives.

THE SOBS TURNED RIGHT onto Frognervein, drove past the park on Kirkevein, and then left Oslo behind. In just minutes they were on the uphill road that slashed through the forests surrounding the city and hills.

"Enjoy the sights," Barrabas said as the van went uphill, with the SOBs scanning both sides of the road for signs of potential ambush sites.

The problem was there were too many.

The VG could take the woman out with no difficulty at all when Sanna walked back down from the Holmenkollen range. It was about an eight-mile stretch.

"She's going to die," Billy Two said when they were halfway up the hill.

It didn't take a Hawk Spirit to figure that out, Barrabas thought. "She agreed to take the chance," Barrabas remarked, but it had started to bother him. He had no qualms about the risk she had assumed, but he certainly didn't want her throwing her life away, and more important, he didn't want to be responsible for her death.

The only thing in their favor was that the VG would most likely want to take her alive. First, they wanted her to answer questions about the whereabouts of Nils Hendrik. Second, they probably were determined to uncover if she had been turned and revealed anything.

By the time the van reached the heights that looked down over the Oslo region, Barrabas had seen perhaps a hundred good ambush sites. The VG could be anywhere along the way—at the restaurants and shops, in the woods or cruising like sightseers along the main road.

"This isn't going to work," Barrabas said. "We're going to throw her away for nothing."

"God knows," Nanos said, "at least we've got to throw her away for *something*."

Barrabas picked up the radio set and contacted Eric Thorne, who'd been driving along the same route with a handpicked team of Jaeger counterters.

If nothing happened on the train or at the lookout tower, Barrabas proposed a change of plans.

SHE HAD SURVIVED the train ride, and was enduring the usually exhilarating but now terrifying look down onto Oslo, thinking that at any moment she would be hurled over the edge for a bird's-eye view on the way down.

She had to maintain a casual and natural air. But in this case natural meant appearing to be on the lookout for the law.

She knew she should be a bit skittish to escape VG suspicion.

No one had made contact with her, but she was convinced she was being watched somewhere, and definitely not just by the Norwegian security operatives.

In her brief time with the VG she had learned to sense when they were on the hunt, and she knew what it was like when they were after someone or something. It was almost a crusade. Nothing could divert them, the scent of blood always calling them on.

She was like a stag in the hunt, she thought as she started the walk down the road. No, she thought. More like a deer. A panic-stricken deer who might be struck on the road.

"TAKE HER!" shouted the man in the front seat.

The driver screeched on the brakes and skidded off the road, throwing tons of steel in her path.

Sanna stared in amazement, then screamed, "What the hell—"

Two men were leaping out of the back seat, armed with wicked-looking submachine guns. And the man who'd jumped out of the front passenger seat was hurtling toward her.

Blind instinct made her run, and she bolted for the woods, but then felt a collar of steel snake around her wrist and pull her back. It was only a hand, but the ironlike grip was molded to her wrist, almost yanking her arm out of the socket as her momentum still propelled her forward.

Sanna screamed as she tumbled head over heels, then fell into spreading bushes by the ditch. A thick screen of pine forest waited ahead. Freedom. She could get lost in the woods...if she could make it.

Several cars had been passing on the road. Some of them sped up when they saw the girl being chased. Others slowed down and braked hard.

Horns were blaring, and stunned faces peered through their car windows.

"Let me go!" she shouted, but the man who'd grabbed her landed on top of her, pulling her thrashing body away from safety. All she saw was guns and brutal faces, giving her the impetus to somehow wrench free and storm into the woods. She thrashed down a slight incline, slid in the snow, then stumbled to her feet, clawing for support and running into the trees.

The man caught up to her again. He grabbed her around the neck and whirled her back up the hill toward the road.

She spun around and around, losing her footing in a drunkard's stance. Her dazed senses again registered the men with guns—pointed at her, pointed toward the road.

Then the man swiftly got hold of her once more, lifting her to her feet like an empty sack of laundry. He half pushed and half carried her, heading for the van.

They had taken her totally by surprise, and she was filled with terror and a sense of unreality.

Her wildly darting eyes finally focused on the man who'd just abducted her and was dragging her along. He was the very person who'd sent her out here in the first place. The American commando.

"What are you doing?" she screamed, hoarsely, but no one was listening to her.

They were concentrating on the two carloads of VG that suddenly came up on the touring van.

A gray Volvo station wagon appeared to streak by on the opposite side of the road when it suddenly swung over to ram its nose into the side of the transport van.

Claude Hayes gunned the accelerator just as the car screeched toward him, whipping the steering wheel to the left. The snub-nosed wagon barreled into the rear of the van at a slant, its intended impact diluted by Claude's quick angling of the van. The assault car glanced off the back, then slid to the side of the road.

With split-second timing, Claude slammed the van into park, grabbed the Heckler & Koch SMG lying next to him on the seat with his right hand, and pushed open the door with his left.

He leaped out onto the roadway, left foot first, right hand holding the SMG high. As he spun in a semicircle to his right, he lowered the SMG and then unloaded a full-auto burst into the back window of the station wagon.

The rear occupants never had time to regain their balance before they were blasted away.

Claude jumped back into the van's driver seat and put a fresh magazine into the SMG. As the driver, he was supposed to stay put, but he figured that unless he took out the two back-seat gunners when he had the chance, there might not be anyone left to drive away.

Now he turned over the firefight to the other SOBs.

Barrabas shoved the stunned woman through the open side doors of the van, shouted, "Stay down!" and then crouched down as he turned around. While Sanna dove to the floorboards, Barrabas strafed the woods where a pack of heavily armed VG had just appeared, sending a jagged fusillade at the armor-plated van.

Nanos and Starfoot demolished the windshield of the car that had struck the van with quick bursts of 9 mm rounds, silencing the driver and front passenger forever.

Both SOBs then dived down the snow-covered hill, rolling, tumbling and dodging to the edge of the woods as they returned fire at the Varangian Guard contingent. Either the VG had been close by in the woods or they'd jumped out from a car farther down the road and circled around.

Either way, they were in for a blast.

A fifteen-footer with logos marking it as a produce truck produced a Norwegian SWAT team who sprang out of the back like racehorses out of the gate, thundering full-auto bursts into the woods.

The lead rain quieted the VG hitters.

The second carload of VG troops arrived behind the SOBs' van, stopping dead in the middle of the road. Before any of the armed men could get out, Eric Thorne's troops took care of them.

A man and woman had pulled their car over to the side of the road in apparent panic when the melee had started, but now they dropped the panic act as quickly as they dropped their civilian guise and pulled their weapons from their car.

From less than twenty yards away, the woman thumped three 12-gauge slugs into the side of the car, the shotgun cartridges crashing through the glass. The blond-haired Valkyrie worked the Mossberg Bullpup as if she'd been born with it. The CS Ferret cartridges erupted inside the second car.

At the same time, the man next to her darted forward with a flamethrower and hosed the windshield with a dragon's tongue of white phosphorus.

With flame scorching the windshield and CS gas billowing inside the car, the occupants tumbled out, their vicious attack blunted by the carefully prepared tactics of the Norwegian commandos.

Eric Thorne's vengeance-minded Jaegers swarmed all over the scene, strafing any opposition, knocking out the stumbling VG with brutally quick but efficient blows.

Other Viking guerrillas who'd jumped out of their cars farther away from the van were taken totally by surprise as an army of Norwegian Jaegers appeared out of nowhere.

The "trap" had worked perfectly.

Barrabas had figured that the only way to come out ahead was to change the game plan. The VG hadn't expected an "abduction" of their quarry when *they* were the ones supposed to do the abducting.

By choosing the spot for the abduction, the SOBs had turned the tables completely. The most the VG could do was react, and they had reacted in a chaotic fashion.

The Vikings had been forced to assume that the Norwegian security teams had been trailing Sanna and only now were making their move. That meant she was still loyal to the VG.

Their other deduction was that the Norwegian troops were taking her away for good, cutting them off from any chance of finding Nils Hendrik.

There was little debate among the VG. As Barrabas expected, the Vikings chose to go into action and damn the consequences. But that sealed the fate of the encounter's outcome.

The firefight was over in minutes. Some of the VG obviously got away. That had to be expected. Not all of them were as close to the scene as the cars that had been shadowing Sanna, and some of them were even now streaking through the woods.

But a good number of them had been caught in the surprise trap. Dead, wounded or temporarily stricken with CS gas, they were sorted out by the Norwegian security force.

Most of them weren't apparent VG at first. They'd toned down their wild dress and their rangy beards so they could pass unnoticed on the roadway.

But when they went into battle, there was no doubt that they had received considerable training.

Unfortunately for them, though they had had training, they hadn't had enough experience in the ongoing realities of battles the way the SOBs had. The element of shock had also worked totally in the SOBs' favor. Since the game plan hadn't even been devised by Barrabas until shortly before it went down, there was no way to anticipate it.

If the revised plan hadn't worked, the SOBs would have lost little. They would have returned uneventfully to Oslo with Sanna Mikkalsen. But now they were returning with captive Vikings, and their interrogation would be much quicker and harsher than Sanna's.

A thoroughly shook-up Sanna Mikkalsen sat behind Barrabas and touched his shoulder as the van drove off through the debris still being sorted out by Norwegian security operatives.

"You saved my life," she said. "Again."

Barrabas nodded. This time he didn't tell her it was unavoidable. By setting herself up as a potential target for the VG, she made it possible for a hell of an intelligence coup. The new group of prisoners would reveal more about the VG operation.

Sanna's total and obvious shock at being "abducted" by the SOBs was what convinced the VG who'd been surveilling her. She wasn't feigning fright. It was all legit. As far as she knew, the SOBs were going to liquidate her then and there.

That belief sparked off the battle.

Barrabas knew the full details of her fate were in the hands of Eric Thorne, but she'd done well. "You risked your life back there," Barrabas said. "And my guess is that you won it back."

CHAPTER TWENTY-THREE

Liam O'Toole rested his head against the dark oak planking of the Viking hall and closed his eyes. Others around him were still going strong, powered by drink and desperation.

But O'Toole was running on empty.

The strain of living undercover for so long was taking its toll. Not the physical tension—he could handle that. It was more of the mental agony. The trouble with living undercover was that after a while you liked the life too much to leave it.

Wrong became right. Foe became friend.

The woman sitting next to him, Katerina, had stood by him through every step he'd taken into the arms of the Viking movement. She'd helped make armor for him. She'd soothed the wounds he'd received during the progressively harder jousts he'd participated in.

She had kept him anchored to the earth, helped him survive the whole ordeal.

And for that he would betray her. After all, the hazel-eyed Vikingess was the enemy. She was beautiful and she was damned, and Liam O'Toole was the man who held her soul in his hands.

Soon it would be over.

The Varangian Guard was on the move, and Liam O'Toole was moving with it. Like many of the others, O'Toole had arrived in the middle of the afternoon for the rendezvous just outside the town of Tromso.

They'd come north, arriving at the meeting place in ones and twos. The latest contingent of initiates and would-be warriors were about to step into the ranks of the VG once and for all.

The Viking hall was actually just a farmhouse with some walls cut down or removed entirely, with long tables positioned end to end, blankets and furs cast alongside the stone hearth or piled against the wall. It had a certain magic to it, a magic that had cast a spell on the entire gathering.

The farmhouse was blanketed by snowdrifts and perpetual darkness for two months of the year, and so the lamps were always burning brightly. The fires were always lit.

Tromso, like many of Norway's cities north of the Arctic Circle, was always in the dark. From the end of November to the end of January there would be no real sunlight in this part of the world. And so the lights glared from every window in an effort to fight off the depression that tended to come upon people with the deprivation of light.

The VG had come home to the "midnight lands," as it was called a thousand years past, where gods, devils and beings in between roamed in the dark forests.

And now, just as O'Toole was about to drift away into his own dark forest of sleep, the gods came down to earth.

There were four of them, and they came right into the hall without any sound.

The Irishman figured he could take out the Varangian Guard leadership with a full-auto burst the moment they stepped into the hall—if he'd only had an SMG.

Unfortunately for O'Toole, however, the automatic weapons were in the hands of the three VG who'd just arrived at the celebration behind their chieftain.

They flanked the stocky blond-haired Viking who had to bend his head to move through the doorway and grinned at the gathering of men and women.

Magnus Koll had arrived.

O'Toole forced himself to relax. He dropped his arm around Katerina and pulled her closer as the two of them leaned back against the wooden walls of the farmhouse.

Like everyone else, they had acquired a glow from the feasting and drinking, and from the ballads spun by the Norse Clans.

It had been warm inside the hall before, but now that Magnus Koll had arrived there was a scorching in the air.

When Magnus stepped into a room, the women always stared suddenly, as if they heard a voice calling out their names, a voice that had spoken to them only in their fantasies.

Men also stared at Koll, but their thoughts were on their weapons. The impulse was to fight him or fight for him. Either way, his presence was like a primitive current crackling through the firelit hall.

In the past his name had always been whispered throughout the ELF movement and the Norse Clans. But now it was spoken openly. Ever since the first VG captives had been taken prisoner, Magnus Koll had abandoned his Tonsberg home. He'd prepared for that moment all along, moving VG caches across the country to safe hiding places.

Now he was preparing for the final act: Ragnarok Two.

O'Toole had heard more of the grand plan as he went deeper into the organization. Ragnarok One was the political action when all hell was supposed to break loose—towns shut down, factories stopped, communications systems broke—all brought on by ELF sympathizers who held down trusted positions in the real world. O'Toole knew that the political arm had already struck.

Ragnarok Two had to do with the military arm, which only now was being raised overhead to administer the killing blow. And O'Toole would be involved in the strike.

By now O'Toole was well versed in the Viking creeds. Ragnarok was the great Norse holocaust when the gods and the universe were destroyed in a battle that scorched the heavens. But out of the ashes would rise a new race of men and gods.

The Varangian Guard was in place to start that race. Their ranks had been thinned somewhat, but that would be offset by the new members who made it through the combats.

Magnus Koll looked directly at O'Toole. He paused for a moment then moved into the crowd. The entire group had gotten to their feet at the entrance of the Viking chieftain.

O'Toole and Katerina moved through the crowd, stirred once again by the music and the madness. As he held the lithe woman by her supple waist, he almost forgot why he was there—until the man he needed to slay put his hand on O'Toole's shoulder.

O'Toole turned to look at Koll, and saw a trinity standing before him. Soldier, sinner, saint. It was all in the eyes. The hawkish blue eyes marked him as a man of the sword, a man who would rule for all, but would gladly slash his way through anyone to get there.

"Redbeard," he said. "Let's talk."

"I'd like that," O'Toole said. Katerina drifted away into the crowd.

"I wanted to wish you luck in the combats tomorrow," Koll said.

O'Toole nodded. "I'll take all I can get."

"You've done well so far," Koll said. "I like what I've heard about you—and *from* you."

The Irishman had spoken at some of the gatherings, where his best epic poetry had come out, spontaneous and from the heart. And Koll had no doubt at times been listening to O'Toole's brawling voice from the shadows, keeping tabs on his new recruit.

O'Toole had played his part well, allowing his soldiering skills to emerge during the trainings and the combats. He'd been groomed to enter the special ranks of the berserkers. The chosen ones.

"Tomorrow the combat is for real," Koll said. "There will be naked swords. No mock weapons."

"I'm ready," O'Toole said.

"You wouldn't have made it this far if you weren't," Koll said. He gestured with his hand. It was part congratulation, part benediction, the blessing of the shaman. "Everything about you seems perfect. Maybe *too* perfect. Tomorrow, on the field of combat, we'll find out just how real you are."

O'Toole looked at his hands as if he were checking to see if they were flesh and blood. Then he met Koll's eyes and said, "This has been one hell of a long dream if I'm not real."

"This is a dream," Koll said. He waved his hand at the farmhouse gathering and at the town of Tromso beyond. "The outside world is sleeping. Even some of the Varangian Guard are sleeping." As he spoke, a messianic light shone in his eyes, the same light that turned on the hard-core VG. "But at times we really are awake ... And the berserkers, they are awake all of the time."

The Irishman laughed. "You must be the alarm clock that woke them up."

Koll's mane of hair shook as he roared with laughter, then he tilted his head in assent. "Yes. The gong. The chime. The sound of freedom wakes everyone when they hear it loud and clear."

"I'll be listening," O'Toole said.

"Listen well, Redbeard," Koll said. "At this point a lot of men reconsider. It's too big a step for some of them. You could stay on the outside—or you can step into the arena. It makes a man think when he's confronted like this."

"What's to think about?" O'Toole said. "Either I'm in the life all the way, or I'm out."

"In some ways it is that simple," Koll said. "There will be a feast tonight and again tomorrow night. But tomorrow night there will not be so many of us."

It wasn't a shock to O'Toole. He'd been prepared well along the way. But the moment was necessary. Koll was taking his measure, seeing how he acted on the eve of death.

"I'll drink to that," O'Toole said. "Tonight . . . and tomorrow night."

Koll laughed.

"So?" O'Toole said. "What exactly do I have to do?"

Koll glanced across the room at a man with sleek, dark brown hair. Wearing a long leather coat, he'd been lounging against the wall, his eye roving across the women now and then, his mouth clamped shut. By his looks he hadn't been celebrating as much as he'd been building up venom inside himself.

"You have to kill that man," Koll said.

Just then the man's eyes crossed O'Toole's with a coal-black gaze that glistened with ice.

It was obvious that the man was a killer. He was probably from the streets, O'Toole thought. The wrong streets. One of the violent scourges brought into the movement to be shaped and molded by the VG.

Unconcerned, the other man raised his cup.

O'Toole hoisted his mug in return. Then he turned to Koll and said, "When and where?"

"I'll choose the site tomorrow," Koll said. He moved away calmly, as if he had been having just another conversation rather than arranging a gladiatorial combat.

O'Toole put down his drink. It would be his last for the night.

He had to check the gear he'd brought along. The armor, the sword, and he had to check on an even more important weapon—his mind.

Tomorrow he had to detach himself from the group. It was kill or be killed. At least one man would die tomorrow, but maybe more.

After that battle—if he survived—he would have to contact Jessup one more time. Throughout his undercover work, Jessup had been receiving the intelligence O'Toole had been gathering on the camps.

The Fixer had a general idea of his whereabouts but nothing concrete. The VG had been very astute about leading O'Toole down false trails, changing cars, changing plans at the last minute. Always making sure that one or more hard-core VG were with him at any one time.

Sometimes what were supposed to have been important meetings had turned out to be just wild-goose chases to see if anyone was shadowing him.

The Irishman didn't doubt that his gear had been searched several times over—which made him glad he hadn't toted along any of the transmitting equipment the Fixer had tried to urge on him. Though it might have made it easier for Jessup to locate him that way, the chances were good that they would also have located a dead O'Toole.

Just like any good cult, the VG had been keeping watch, guiding him, observing him during training and during his so-called free time. It was getting progressively more difficult to slip away to get through to Jessup, difficult but not impossible because many of the VG cut loose in the night haunts of whatever town they were in.

Naturally, O'Toole was no exception. During those night prowls he'd always made the opportunity to contact his man. Now he was due for another one.

Last word from O'Toole had indicated only that he was moving north to the camps. Jessup had wanted to pull the SOB out, feeling he was approaching the dangerous heart of the matter and that the odds were going to work against him perhaps.

"What does Nile say?" O'Toole had asked.

"He's worried, too," Jessup answered.

"But no orders?"

"At the moment he's leaving it up to you."

"I'm staying in," O'Toole had told him. "I'm getting too close to back out now." There were unfinished things he had to see through and find out—even about himself.

According to Jessup, though, the Norwegians had gathered substantial intelligence from the captured VG. Many of the locations of the wilderness camps had been identified. The support people were pretty well known and quite a few of the supply camps were being stalked even now.

But no one had been able to locate Koll. No one knew what his plans were or where his current base of operation was. Until now.

And now no one knew except Liam O'Toole. But that knowledge wouldn't do any good unless he lived long enough to share it.

CHAPTER TWENTY-FOUR

The briefcase was loaded.

Neat paper-stripped bundles of cash were nestled on the bottom. A 9 mm P7M8 pistol was strapped to the lid, concealed behind a velour-covered barricade.

Lee Hatton walked down Erling Škakesgate, then turned down the side street that housed Grim Swann's operation. She looked every inch the smartly dressed career woman, her black hair freshly styled, her step as brisk as the wind that swept in from Trondheim Fjord.

As a courier distributing the funds that poured into ELF, she couldn't wear the same outfits that she wore for the rallies.

She looked up and saw the sentinel at the window.

Grim Swann was standing by his upper-floor window, regarding the streets that would soon be his domain. Part voyeur, part god overseeing his realm.

Or so he thought.

Grim came down to meet her at the door. He looked like the perfect counterpart to her. Matching bookends, she thought, or matching bedmates. His short blond hair was impeccably groomed. The well-tailored gray suit made him look more of an executive than a minister of propaganda.

As he was opening the door, she caught sight of two rough-looking characters in the back near the drafting tables that made the place look like an art studio. Neither one of them looked artistic. The only thing they could draw were their guns, she thought.

"I've got something for you," she said, lifting the briefcase.

"Even if you'd come empty-handed, it would still be more than enough for me," he said.

"Oh, really?" she said, glancing down at the briefcase. "Then you don't mind if I keep this."

He reached down without taking his eyes off her, smiling as if he were going to take the case. His hand lingered on hers long enough to trigger a dozen messages.

The SOB combat doctor smiled, thinking that perhaps she would get more information by letting him play out *his* scenario. They'd flirted before but never had taken it any further.

She pulled the briefcase away from him, making his hand close tighter around hers, prolonging the contact. Then she broke away coquettishly, still keeping possession of the briefcase.

"I've been thinking about you a lot," he said.

She pursed her lips together. "Ahh-hah," she said. "What exactly have you been thinking?"

Grim gestured toward the thick-carpeted stairs that led to the upper floor. "Let's go where it's more private."

She cocked her head. "Whatever you say," she answered.

They passed through the shop where the ELF campaigns were planned and the slogans hatched before being sent down to Oslo, purportedly originating from one of the ELF branch offices.

She stepped into Grim's large upstairs suite, then dropped onto a leather couch and set the briefcase down on a light wood coffee table in front of her.

Grim opened a bottle of aquavit and poured two drinks. After handing Lee her glass, he sat on the edge of his desk.

Lee let herself be led down the guerrilla path. Grim had been steadily hinting that he could do great things for her, initiate her into the real ranks of the VG. Many a man in the VG had plans for her, those plans often having nothing to do with the grand plan.

But she and Grim had talked several times in the past, and each time she realized just how powerful he really was. Now she knew that he was even more important than she first thought—thanks to the revelation of a KGB walk-in.

From what she knew, the KGB operator had been burned by the ELF movement. Rather than face the funeral music from his own people, he had decided to offer his services to the Norwegians. He'd gone directly to Eric Thorne.

One of the first people he offered up was Grim Swann. A killer, a businessman, a diplomat. No doubt the VG planned on putting him in a high position to smooth things over when their kingdom reigned on earth.

But the coronation was still a long way off.

Lee let nature take its course. At least part of the way. She could make a man think he was doing the choosing when in reality she was the one who'd determined the selection process.

"There are some things you should know about me," he said. Then, as part of his seduction, he began to flatter her by casting a net of intrigue, lifting the veil around the organization she'd been working so hard for.

The timing was perfect. The VG were ready to make their move, and so was Grim Swann.

As he spoke, the urgency built up inside him. His face grew taut with excitement and desire—some of it for her, some for the world he wanted to create.

Grim told her more about the organization than she had expected, including information on Magnus Koll's mentor. Hrolf Anker, the man who helped Koll formulate his campaign of conquest, was just minutes away.

But what she most wanted to find out was not the mentor, but the whereabouts of Magnus Koll himself.

Grim hinted at it, giving her the general direction up north, but he always held back precise information. That was the carrot. That was the key to the kingdom, but before he was willing to share that with her, she had to become one of them.

There was little doubt about how that could be arranged.

Every king needed a queen, every priest a priestess and every bard a muse.

"It's time to make your decision, Lee," he said. "It's time to make the commitment."

"You're right," Lee said.

He smiled. He was sitting on the edge of the desk, a noble lord who was about to admit her to the court.

Lee flipped open the briefcase and said, "Let's start with this—"

Snaking the P7M8 out of the briefcase, she squeezed the cocking lever built into the pistol grip.

A stunned Grim Swann reacted without thinking. Screaming in shock and rage, he swept the half-empty aquavit bottle off the desk, smashing it like a club on her gun hand. Shards of glass and splintery liquid splashed onto her arm.

One shot went off before the pistol dropped from her numbed fingers, but Lee didn't have time to worry about her bloodied arm. Grim, who seconds before was thinking of ways to bed her, threw a windmill kick that would have caved in her face if she hadn't dived to the floor to avoid it.

BOTH MEN DOWNSTAIRS quickly made for the stairwell at the sound of the shot.

A 9 mm scythe of bullets beat them to it, chewing up the stairs and spraying them with splintered wood. The 3-round bursts were accompanied by the sound of breaking glass as Nile Barrabas rammed the barrel of his SMG through the front window to the right of the door.

In that moment of shock, both would-be rescuers of Grim Swann turned toward the door. Claude Hayes blew away the window on the other side of the door and peppered the walls behind them.

Neither man understood what was happening. In the universal language of submachine guns, they were being told to drop their weapons and they would have a chance to live. They were more valuable alive than dead.

But the offer was good for a split second only.

With guns in hand, both VG hitters aimed at the new threats, unaware that each SOB was marksman enough to drop them with their first shots.

Barrabas strafed them off their feet, then dived through the smashed window.

Barrabas and Hayes had been on foot. Billy Two and Nanos had been listening to Grim's conversation with a laser mike from a second-floor apartment on the other side of the street. Grim's frequent practice of looking out the window and thus not covering it with a curtain made him vulnerable to the laser bug.

As long as the window was uncovered, the laser beam could pick up voice vibrations from the glass, then bounce the beam back to a receiver that demodulated the beam and turned it into conversation.

Billy Two had given a prearranged signal to Barrabas the moment the situation went into red.

LEE HATTON WAS USED to being on her own. She didn't count on help arriving before her time with Grim was through. There was still one card she could play.

For all Grim knew, she could only handle herself with a gun, and not very well at that, considering that he'd disarmed her so quickly.

That made him sloppy with the strikes he aimed at her.

Lee rolled and jumped and scrambled away from the attack, playing the panicked woman to the hilt. With the back of her hand starting to swell from the blow and nausea creeping up to her brain, it wasn't very hard to act. She had that same familiar sensation that came when bones were broken and the body was going on automatic pilot.

Grim's rage stoked itself to a higher plateau with each missed strike, until finally the corporation man had reverted to a creature of the wild.

He stiff-armed her, throwing her off balance and crashing her against the wall. The paneling rattled and so did her rib cage as the wind was knocked out of her.

Grim followed through with a right-elbow strike, his fist curled in toward his shoulder, his elbow swinging like a hammer.

Lee dodged to the right, snapped her left hand up in a short circle block and slapped her open palm against his elbow.

Using the momentum of his unsuccessful strike, she pushed hard. The follow-through of her strike forced Grim off his feet as he lost his balance and whirled around.

Lee straightened him out with a left backfist to the head. He went down to the floor. Then he slithered like a snake, going for the pistol she'd dropped.

His hands curled around the grip as he half raised himself from the floor. As he started to track Lee with the gun, Nile Barrabas flew into the room and drop-kicked him in the middle of the chest.

Grim rolled over onto his side, the trauma of the kick paralyzing him for a few moments. His eyes locked onto Barrabas's, showing anger and hatred, but most of all surprise as he keeled over on his back and went out.

"You all right?" Barrabas asked.

She lifted her bloody right hand gingerly, as though it was a precious artifact or something that didn't belong to her.

"Right enough," she said. "Thanks for coming in on time."

Barrabas gripped her shoulder. "Thanks for going in."

She started to fill him in on the intelligence, but after she covered the major points, Barrabas raised his hand.

"That's enough for now," he said. "Nanos has it all on tape. We'll scan it, then share it with the Norwegians. They can add it to their armory."

Barrabas glanced at her hand again. "You'd better have somebody look at that."

She gave him an amused look.

"Actually," he amended, "you'd better look at it yourself. You're the doc."

NICHOLAS VROSPUTIN leafed through the gold-edged pages of the old leather-bound volume that Hrolf Anker had been reading shortly before Vrosputin killed him.

It was an oversize book of maps spread out on an old scarred wooden table. Many of the maps portrayed Norway as it was a millenium ago.

There were notes filling the margins, indicating that Anker hoped to see ancient Norway reborn with Magnus Koll at the helm.

Vrosputin turned the pages and scanned the annotations in Anker's calligraphic scrawl. Notes to himself. Notes for Koll.

Ragnarok. That was their dream, a dream they all were willing to die for.

Hrolf Anker had resisted at first. But he was an older man. A defeated one who had seen his chance for victory in Magnus Koll, perhaps the only man who would take his ideas of a Pan-Nordic nation seriously.

The gray-haired sage eventually broke his silence and opened up to the Spetsnaz commander. It did take some persuasion—quick and brutal demonstrations that Vrosputin was not a man to deceive.

Anker talked.

And Vrosputin rewarded him with a quick and neat death, with relatively no pain.

Vrosputin had stood behind Anker and swooped his left forearm around Anker's throat, striking his trachea with the ridge of his hand so that he involuntarily gasped. He continued the movement until the crook of his elbow trapped the man's neck. His left biceps crushed from the left side, his forearm from the right. Then he added his right hand and forearm to the equation of the shrinking triangle.

It was a classical strangle move taught in many of the martial arts. But not many lethal artists practiced it these days—not the way Vrosputin did.

The man was gone in a matter of seconds, the blood cut off from his brain.

In a strange way, Vrosputin thought, Anker had seemed to anticipate his end, as though it were fitting in some way. He was out of it now, crossing the bridge into Asgard.

"Fairy tales," Vrosputin said, looking around at the other books that Anker had written privately for the Varangian Guard. "All fairy tales. You should have stuck to the old stuff."

The dead man was sleeping peacefully on the other side of the table, sleeping forever.

Vrosputin knew all about Anker, about the moderately well received books he used to write before he became alienated and branded as a crank, a *fringe* writer too far over the line of reason. Anker had been one of Grim's favorite subjects. Always talking about him. And everything that Grim talked about was picked up on the spike mikes the Spetsnaz troops planted in his offices.

Vrosputin's crew had climbed up the ladder of ELF and VG members throughout Norway, using each one to lead them to the next. By now the ladder was full of bloody rungs that had led them all the way up across Trondheim.

And there was little chance of discovery or immediate retaliation.

The Norwegians were hitting ELF and the VG just as hard, swooping down on their safe houses, striking at the wilderness camps. Arms caches and chemical dumps had been seized. The Viking troops were being attacked at every turn with an unprecedented ferociousness.

Special Forces teams, army squads, police units and mercenaries were finding targets with an awesome regularity.

It was only natural. The Norwegians had been waiting to strike back ever since the first VG attacks. Once they got their first leads, they retaliated with a vengeance. Each strike forced a number of new leads, and the battles raged on in cities and in the country.

Vrosputin's Spetsnaz soldiers used the very same tactics.

Vrosputin glanced over at the dead sage. The high priest was dead. The soul of the VG had been quieted.

Now it was time to strike at the head.

Vrosputin pushed away from the table and was ready to dig into the treasure trove of books when there was a pounding on the door, immediately followed by the excited voice of his sergeant, who should have been monitoring the listening devices planted on Grim.

"What made you leave your post?" Vrosputin asked, admitting the sergeant into Anker's room.

"It's the Americans," he said. "They're here. They just hit Grim. They know about this place now. And what's more, they've found out a good deal about where Koll is. Up north. Near Tromso."

"We must go," Vrosputin said. "But before we do, let us give our good friend a Viking funeral."

While he lifted Anker's body and placed it upon the table—now a funeral bier—the sergeant hurried through the house gathering material to use as kindling.

Just before they left the house that would soon be enveloped in flame, Vrosputin couldn't help letting out a shout. It was a hunter's shout, indicating that the hunt had begun.

CHAPTER TWENTY-FIVE

Helmeted figures moved through the eternal dusk. Torches cast eerie halos around their bearers.

Some snow covered the ground, half shrouding fallen limbs and brush, but a good portion of the battlefield was free of snow, protected by the spiny boughs overhead.

Two Vikings were facing each other, their swords glinting in the flickering light of the torches. They wore leather boots, arm guards and ring-woven shirts of armor and grim-visaged helmets.

Each man carried a round leather-coverd wooden shield with metal rims and reinforcing bands.

The red-bearded one stood still, his broad chest rising and falling as he drank in the cold air. A cloud of vapor hissed through his visor with each exhalation.

The other man moved slowly, but little signs revealed his agitation.

A sparse line of men formed a loose square around them, their faces marked by exposure to the elements, and the tests of difficult tasks.

There were no outside spectators.

This was no ritual.

The only witnesses were the combatants themselves or those who had long before passed through the combats.

Liam O'Toole looked at his opponent. The man who had been pointed out by Magnus Koll, the man who had so recently raised his drink to O'Toole, now lifted his sword.

The marshall stood between them, checking their readiness and waiting to let them go at each other.

He lifted his hand once, then shot it down like a sword.

The combat had started, and it would only finish when one man walked away.

O'Toole's prowess with the sword had sharpened. He had become adept in its use, like other weapons he'd mastered. It was a tool, but not the only one to an experienced soldier of fortune.

The other man charged, sword raised behind his back, ready for a quick chop. Many of the best combats were decided that way. In this bloody trial, the first to strike was often the last one standing.

O'Toole stood his ground and pulled back his weapon as the two-edged sword slashed downward for his head. He moved at the last possible moment, with his attacker totally committed to that one strike.

O'Toole leaped to his right and brought his own sword down hard. Steel struck steel. It was a defensive move only, but the red-bearded fighter wasn't concerned with the sword. That wasn't his weapon. Yet.

Holding his shield horizontal to his body, O'Toole slashed out sideways, smashing it into the man's ribs like a metal discus.

The man choked loudly. He was stunned, and the lip of his heavy helmet dropped down toward his breastbone. He staggered forward but still managed to swing his sword arm. Hurt or not, he meant to kill O'Toole.

O'Toole pulled back his sword.

The other man thrust his blade up toward O'Toole's neck, intending to cut him between his chest and the lip of the helmet.

O'Toole met the sword with his shield boss, flung it aside, then swung with all his might. His arm came down with all the momentum of a guillotine, crashing through the man's raised shield, cleaving his shoulder, moving down through muscle and bone.

The other man was dead on his feet, the wide gap between neck and shoulder a crevice surging with blood. The snow grew dark at his feet.

Lightened by the loss of blood, weighted down by suddenly unsupported armor, the man dropped to his death like a collapsing wall of stone.

The berserkers around him clamored wildly at the sight, giving glory to the fallen man, then sounding an even more resounding cheer for the victor.

Liam O'Toole stepped out of the battle square.

He raised his sword and roared, and the berserker battle cry echoed in the snowy woods.

THE BLOND WARRIOR sat by the fire, and the flickering light cast ruddy shadows over his features.

He glanced at the new faces gathered in the winter camp, members who had made the crossing from citizen to soldier, Viking to berserker.

Magnus Koll spoke.

"We are not like men of old," he said. "We *are* men of old." He smacked his chest with the flat of his hand. "The blood of our ancestors is pulsing inside us. It is the same blood, flowing like a river from generation to generation, and we are still riding on that river."

He spoke in a hushed, reverent tone, the chant of Odin that precursed the voice of battle.

"We had given up our past, our heritage. Now we are taking it back."

O'Toole stared at the Viking across from him. It was like staring a thousand years into the past. And if he'd done so, at that moment, he would have seen a man quite like Koll staring back, with eyes wilder than the fire beside him.

CHAPTER TWENTY-SIX

Tromso was only a two-hour flight from Trondheim, but the island of Senja, lying southwest of Tromso, was a thousand years away.

A bridge on Highway 86 connected the island to the mainland, and a virtually untouched wilderness connected it to the past.

Senja encompassed nearly one thousand square miles of narrow fjords, mountain peaks and deep valleys of wild pine and birch forests. Lakes, tributaries and waterfalls made it a paradise for those who could live wild—such as the Varangian Guard who moved through the wilderness with the same surefooted gait as their Viking ancestors.

They'd been hit hard by the Norwegian counterstrike, with many of their underground depots discovered in the cities. But Koll had prepared a last redoubt for the movement, deep in the gnarled woods of Troll Valley.

Weapons caches, both modern and ancient, had been secreted in their wilderness encampment on Senja. Koll had prepared a sufficient stock of chemical munitions to launch at least one last devastating assault.

Though his army and supplies were depleted, there was still a chance of either lying low and regrouping or launching the ultimate attack that would lead to Ragnarok.

Some of the VG had headed for the encampment from drop points along the road that bisected the island and connected towns on the east and west coast. Others had left their own vehicles in isolated pockets along the road before moving into the wilderness.

They had arrived at different times and locations, but all were preparing to regroup and launch their major assault if possible.

Fortunately the place was easy to get lost in—especially if one was trying to get lost the way Liam O'Toole was.

With every step that took him deeper into the wilderness, O'Toole longed to take a step back. It was time to get back to civilization and contact the SOBs so they could zero in on the small but potent Viking army. The Irishman weighed the odds and wondered about his chances of success.

WINTER WARFARE "exercises" were once again in session. This time the Norwegian forces were concentrating on the area around Tromso, covering the Lyngen Peninsula to the east and the island of Senja to the southwest and the Loftoten island chain farther south—all potential wilderness sites that could harbor the Varangian Guard.

Fast patrol vessels scoured up and down the fjords. Orion maritime surveillance planes scouted the island along with a number of search helicopters.

Senja was the name that had most often come up during interrogations of the hard-core VG captives. But other likely sites were also mentioned in the interrogations. Since the questionees were all under the influence of a wizard's brew of drugs, there was no reason to doubt they were telling the truth—or what they understood the truth to be.

Koll very well could have planted false information among some of his troops for such occasions as this. A group of intentionally misinformed VG could send the Norwegians down the wrong trail.

When and wherever they were found, a platoon of Marine Jaegers was ready to land and a platoon of Parachute Jaegers was ready to drop.

Another group of "marines" was already tracking the VG.

Not only were the SOBs on the trail of the VG, but they were also after one of their own. Liam O'Toole had gone in deep—and now after the brief flight to Tromso, the SOBs were ready to go in and bring him out.

Their first stop had been the farmhouse outside of Tromso. It had been deserted. The Norwegian security services scanned it for signs, but the Vikings left precious little behind. Their exodus had begun.

O'Toole had taken one more chance to contact Walker Jessup from Tromos, right after the drunken celebration for the new initiates into the Viking order. From a tavern phone he'd called the number Jessup had set aside for his communications from the field.

After describing the farmhouse, he'd mentioned the island of Senja as a possible field headquarters for the VG. The name was alive on many a Viking tongue. O'Toole also mentioned something odd, about how some of the older VG were saying that soon the new members would become Trolls. It was an inside joke that O'Toole didn't quite understand yet.

Now that he had made it into the ranks, the VG were not so secretive around the red-bearded Viking.

But even so, they weren't ready to spell things out for him. Like all the other initiates, he would learn in time.

MAGNUS KOLL CAME to a sudden stop.

The sound of footsteps crunching through the newly fallen snow had taken on a different pattern.

They'd passed right behind him, very quick, then fallen back.

He looked back and saw the man he called Redbeard. The Irishman gave him a steady look that Koll did his best to decipher. But all he saw was a mask.

Even dressed in leather clothes, thick boots and white camouflage cloak, Koll looked like a creature of the forest.

"Speak your mind, Redbeard," Koll said.

The Irishman glared back at him. "I've nothing to say to you."

The blond Viking paused, ready to continue the climb uphill. All around him the other VG who had gathered were steadily drifting through the thinning forest as they moved along the mountain pass.

Soon the others hesitated, then halted also.

Their senses were alive. They'd been pursued by the covert forces of the government for weeks now, winning some and losing others.

They knew when their lives hung in the balance.

"Your words have always been as sharp as your sword," Koll said. "I can think of no reason why they should fail you now."

"Nerves," O'Toole said. "Shock maybe."

Koll laughed.

"A man like you is scared of nothing on earth." Koll smiled. "It's the things not of this world that've got you scared."

He turned then and walked uphill, his back crisscrossed with weaponry.

A full-auto SMG and a battle-ax were strapped across Koll's pack. He looked part Guard, part demigod as he moved away. O'Toole followed, thinking that the man was not of this earth.

THE THERMAL IMAGERS on the two Nightfox helicopters picked up three vehicles hidden along the left side of the road. The forward chopper immediately banked to the left and scanned the thick forest for signs of the occupants.

The second chopper radioed the location to one of the ground teams cruising along the road in jeeps and trucks to check out whether the "abandoned" vehicles belonged to mountaineers or mutineers.

THE SOBs and Eric Thorne's commandos milled around the vehicles. One was a Wagoneer with a large cargo bed in the back. The others were compact sedans, big enough to carry maybe four men each. It appeared innocent enough, except for the fact that they'd been pulled off the road and concealed beneath overhangs.

Either there were some all-weather hikers out there in the snow, or a recent group of VG had passed by.

"Blood," Billy Two said, pointing to the back seat of one of the cars where a thin stain ran along the upholstery.

"Could be animal blood," Thorne said.

"Someone was hurt," Barrabas said. "O'Toole mentioned the combats. There were bound to be some wounded. No one comes out of that without a scratch."

Thorne nodded. "We'll use the birds to recon the area."

"We'll use Billy Two," Barrabas said.

The Osage tracker was already at the edge of the woods, moving down into the snow.

Nanos and Claude Hayes kept their eyes on Billy Two, waiting for orders from Barrabas.

Barrabas worked out the approach with Eric Thorne. The SOBs would move in from the left, and Eric's people would come in from the right.

The Norwegian handed the SOB chief a map of the terrain, pinpointing their exact location.

Barrabas scanned the map, then paused. "Wait a second," he said. He looked at it searchingly again. There was a clue of some kind in front of him, something that had registered in his subconscious. Then it came to him. He tapped a section of the map with his finger. "What does this mean in English?"

Thorne glanced quickly at the map and read the word that Barrabas had indicated.

Trolldal.

"It means Troll Valley," Thorne said.

"That's where they are," Barrabas said.

"How do you know?"

"Where else do you go to become a troll?"

Thorne looked quizzically at him.

"It's something O'Toole passed along to us. Said they were all going to be trolls for a while."

Thorne nodded. "We'll find out, won't we?"

"If it kills us," Barrabas said.

VIKING SHADOWS MOVED ahead of him.

Liam O'Toole dropped back, feigning tiredness, as though the rough terrain and the darkness were taking their toll.

As the Varangian Guard closed in on its wilderness fortress, O'Toole took his chance. He stopped dead in his tracks.

All around him the forest stood silent except for the movement of the Vikings.

He let them advance, then smoothly eased himself into cover. A strand of birch trees with snowbound arms welcomed him beneath its shelter.

As the VG made headway, O'Toole moved back. He was armed only with the ceremonial weapon, the sword he'd used to hack his way into the ranks of the berserkers.

Even so, he thought of rushing forward and cleaving the head off Magnus Koll, but there was something that prevented him. He couldn't kill the man so coldly when he had afforded such a genuine welcome. The feeling was misplaced, but still there was something that made O'Toole reluctant.

When he judged he'd gone a sufficient distance, O'Toole paused to take a look for signs of pursuit.

The white-blanketed woodland was quiet.

He'd made it.

O'Toole exhaled a cloud of frosted air, then turned around to head for freedom.

A sudden clanging sound came out of the silence, but O'Toole couldn't even think about it when four swords slashed toward his neck, one from each direction, moving like extensions of the thick muscled arms that wielded them.

The four berserkers had come out of nowhere. One moment there was whiteness all around, the next the swords formed a razor sharp collar around his neck.

O'Toole froze and looked around at the bearded faces. Their eyes held a darker night than the sky above.

Men whom he'd sat side by side with before, men who'd shared song and drink with him were now alien. The feral mask of the forest was on their faces.

It was time for him to die.

The Irishman's hand fell to his own sword. His eyes quickly roved over the men and saw the one he would kill. He was just about to drop down—knowing that one of the swords would cut him, but at least he would go out with bloodied steel in his hand.

"Hold!" Magnus Koll shouted. The Viking chieftain stepped out of the woods. Obviously he'd been on guard ever since O'Toole had come so close to him before, and he'd instructed the berserkers to tend to the Irishman.

"So," Koll said. "It was you. I knew *someone* was in the ranks. My own guard, the ELF folk, all of them were infiltrated. And now we've been shadowed by helos, too. Whoever it was, he had to be good."

The blond Viking chieftain stared at O'Toole for a moment. "I'm only surprised it's you."

"It had to be this way," O'Toole said.

Koll nodded. "Why didn't you kill me when you had a chance?" he asked. "When you stood behind me."

"Not my style," O'Toole said. "It was a matter of honor."

"Yes, there is that among us," he said. "And I believe you. You're an honest man in your own way." He paused, looked at his berserkers who were still ready to put O'Toole down for good. "Whoever you're working for, you can forget them if you want. You can still serve with me. I'm a good judge of character, Redbeard, and you're my kind of man. You wouldn't have made it this far unless a part of you really wanted to be with us... What shall it be?"

O'Toole prepared to die. He gripped the sword tight, ready for the thrust and said, "I serve another captain."

Koll bowed his head, as if he had just encountered O'Toole's captain by looking into the Irishman's eyes. "I would like to meet him," he said. Then he gazed upward into the distance as the soft whine of a Nightfox helicopter approached. "And I have a feeling I will."

O'Toole kept silent. There was nothing he could say.

Koll looked fearless, unconcerned. Whatever lay ahead for him, he was ready to embrace it. "I've sent other scouts out. There's movement in the woods all around us. Another force is coming after us. Perhaps two separate groups. I imagine one of them is your captain."

"I imagine it is," O'Toole said.

As the berserkers held their positions their swords pinning O'Toole, there was an audible and a visible tension in them, and the prickly tension was shared by O'Toole. It wasn't a game. Death was a palpable presence, and any action would be extreme. But Magnus Koll was holding the situation in check with the sheer force of his personality.

"Go to your captain," Koll said.

The swords fell away.

O'Toole could only stare in amazement.

"I owe you a life for what happened back there," Koll said. "And in a way, if I die, I think you can give me another life, Redbeard. You can keep my spirit alive. Speak loudly of it around the campfire—if you should live through this day."

O'Toole stood bewildered in the dark. He couldn't imagine Koll sparing him after what he'd done. But then he remembered Koll speaking about an ancient Viking king who'd trapped another Viking leader he'd battled for years. The king had planned to execute his ancient enemy once and for all—until his enemy composed an epic poem on the eve of his death, a poem about the victorious king. And when he recited it in the great hall, all were silent, all were moved.

And the king let his captive go, granting his verbal art the same recognition as martial art.

Now Magnus Koll was reliving that event from the past. Magnus Koll, the Viking king come again.

"What is your chieftain's name?" Koll asked.

"Barrabas."

Koll nodded. "I'd have to face him sooner or later—and I don't want him chasing us all over heaven and hell."

The Viking chief opened his hand and gestured toward the woods where O'Toole had originally been headed. "Go," he said. "Tell Barrabas I'm waiting for him."

Magnus Koll and the berserkers turned and vanished into the dark woods.

THE SKI COMMANDO swooped over the low hill, then raced across the clear ground.

Behind him came a half-dozen armed Norwegian ski troops, hurtling themselves over the virgin snow with pushes from their ski poles.

They were moving fast and with a great deal of natural ease. This was their terrain.

The scouts had moved far ahead of Eric Thorne's group, searching for terrorists.

And now, in the dark, they found them.

The lead skier was ripped off his feet as he skied into a hail of full-auto fire.

The second one stopped in a crouch, slung his automatic rifle into position, then toppled backward, kicked off his feet by the lead fusillade.

Then more fire came from behind them.

Six of the seven ski commandos were slain on the spot. Only one managed to escape, vanishing back the way he'd come.

THE SPETSNAZ AMBUSHERS moved out of the snowdrifts, white assassins invisible against the landscape.

They'd been closing in on the VG ahead of the Norwegians, and when their rearguard man heard the approach of the ski troops, they set the ambush.

Back in Trondheim Vrosputin had unearthed several of the VG hideouts from Hrolf Anker. The elderly man spoke of them in hushed and reverent tones, especially when it came to the island of Senja.

The isle of the dead, Vrosputin thought.

When he learned the Americans were going north to Tromso, he'd made a calculated guess that sooner or later the VG would return to their home site.

Return home to die.

"WE GOT A WILD MAN on the right," Nanos said.

"I got 'em," Barrabas said, lying in the snowbank, aiming at the trees up ahead.

They'd just reached the top of the hill and had been scanning the horizon when the berserker appeared. They'd been moving fast, with Billy Two slogging through the wilderness, closing in on the trail of the VG.

Barrabas tracked the Viking as he stormed out of the woods, coming right in their direction. His finger on the trigger, he waited until he was close enough for a kill shot.

"Son of a bitch!" Barrabas said, seeing something familiar in the way the figure moved. "It's O'Toole."

"Hell," Nanos said. "He looks dead and buried and back again."

Barrabas aimed the Accuracy International sniper rifle at the woods behind O'Toole in case he was pursued.

Moments later, Nanos flagged the Irishman over to their position.

O'Toole nearly hollered in joy when he saw the line of SOBs. "It's damn good to see you again," Barrabas said to O'Toole. "But unless you want this to be a bullet-ridden reunion, get your ass down."

If O'Toole could make it that far, anyone from the VG camp could do the same.

O'Toole grinned and hunkered down quickly.

"What are we facing up ahead?" Barrabas asked.

"Berserkers," O'Toole said, "and seasoned regulars." O'Toole told Barrabas about the strength of the VG units. "They've even got some women there. Only the real Amazons though. There's a woman named Freda who is just as deadly as most of Koll's men. The other women are back on the mainland, thank God."

Barrabas listened, questioning O'Toole now and then, but letting him tell his story in his own way. Finally O'Toole told Barrabas about how and why the Viking chieftain let him go.

"Even if he loses, he wins," O'Toole said. "He and his men have already died once. They've given their lives to Odin. Now it's just a matter of him collecting it."

"Or us," Barrabas said. He rose to his feet. "Let's go and do what we came here for."

As they moved out Barrabas grabbed O'Toole's shoulder. "One thing," he said. "When we run into them again, can you take him down if you have to? We can't get our asses shot off thinking about chivalry."

"We're even," O'Toole said. "Whatever happens, I'm ready."

"All right people," Barrabas said. "Let's move."

Billy Two continued in the lead, following the trail of VG, though there was no doubt now about their general direction. Barrabas, Nanos, O'Toole and Hayes brought up the rear. Although only one more man had joined them, it was a considerable addition to their force.

Lee Hatton was back on the roadside. Given the broken bones in her hand, she would have been more of a liability in the field than an asset, but she was prepared to doctor any casualties that made it back from the woods.

THE BEARDLESS VIKING was staked to a twisted and gnarled pine tree. A bone-white knife protruded from his neck.

The dark blood glistened, indicating the corpse was relatively fresh.

Another VG sentry, an older one this time, was splashed across the snow, his body spread out as if he'd been making angel wings with his arms.

A bloody trail had left a crimson pattern over the snow. Gouts of blood had landed in a grisly dotted line, pumping out of the fallen Viking like an oil gusher.

The SOBs scanned the area where the VG sentries had been slain. They exchanged looks, then Barrabas said, "This doesn't click. Thorne's people couldn't be ahead of us—not in this direction. And if they were," he said, gesturing at the grisly scene, "this doesn't look like their signature."

Barrabas remembered the automatic fire they'd heard in the distance before. "My guess is there's a team of snake-eaters in the field," he said.

O'Toole nodded. "It probably is Spetsnaz," he said. "Koll seemed to think there was another force in the area. Why not the Russians?"

"Especially the Russians," Barrabas said. "They got burned good by the VG. Now they're coming in to sweep away their mistake."

"Whoever they are," Billy Two said, "they're probably not all that far away. And neither is the VG camp."

Throughout the trek, the VG had periodically dragged branches over the snow to cover their tracks. But as they converged on their forest fortress in the woods, the signs of their presence were harder to miss.

BARRABAS HAD FOUGHT the Varangian Guard in the woods before, and the SOBs had nearly bought it.

Now the Vikings were on their home turf. It wouldn't be so easy this time.

When the Osage came back from a scout and reported that the camp was ahead, Barrabas contacted Eric Thorne on the radio that Hayes carried.

"We've located the camp," Barrabas said, giving the Norwegian their position. "It's immune to a straight hit from the ground. You'll see when you get here. We also tumbled onto signs of another force in the area. We think its Spetsnaz."

The Norwegian reported his own losses. A ski patrol had nearly been wiped out.

The Spetsnaz team was cutting a wide swath through the area, taking everybody out of the action. In the coming face-off, they were the unknown quantity, the dangerous wild card.

But even with Spetsnaz troops operating in the area, Barrabas and Thorne agreed that the VG were their primary target and they were going to take them out.

THE VIKING STOCKADE had been carved out of the woods and built to accommodate the terrain. A thin trail spiraled up and around the earthen ramparts. Like a castle of old, the access ramp had been constructed so that invaders had to climb up a left incline, wielding their weapons with their weaker left arms, while the defenders could strike down with their stronger sword arms.

Stakes speared through the snow, preventing a frontal assault. And all around the fortress were banks of trees to provide cover.

Barrabas scoped out the fortress with a Barr & Stroud thermal imager.

He could see the men moving around, preparing for battle. They showed up white against the darkness, like afterimages of themselves. Dead men not quite dead yet.

Eric Thorne was also scanning the Viking redoubt. His men were spread out to the right, carrying a variety of weapons.

"Everyone set?" Barrabas asked.

"It's a go," Thorne replied.

"Okay, let's light 'em up."

Barrabas fired a round of the Accuracy International rifle. A VG soldier became a ghost for real.

The Norwegians fired several flares into the fortress.

At the signal, the Nightfox helicopters popped up over the treeline and zeroed in on the flare-lit fortress.

Powered by Allison 250-C30 engines and four-blade quiet rotors, the Nightfox choppers seemed to come out of nowhere to fire their thunderbolts.

The first chopper unleashed a 70 mm rocket into the entrance of the fortress, blasting it and several occupants into the air. Snow, earth and blood sprayed the trees.

The second chopper opened up with its 7.62 mm chain gun, hot lead burning through the camp like a forest fire. With a 4000-round capacity and a rate of 1200 rpm, the chain gun swept the VG off their feet.

After the first pass, when the VG staggered from their fortress, the SOBs commenced automatic fire and employed smoke and gas grenades.

The Norwegians opened up to their right, sending a full-auto 9 mm spray into the fortress.

When the Viking force was knocked back by the murderous fire, Alex Nanos thumped in an illuminating round from his Carl Gustav recoilless gun.

The stockade was lit up like the aurora borealis come down to earth. It was a firsthand glimpse of Ragnarok as the chain gun chopper swept in for another pass, firing off a lethal barrage into the lit-up encampment.

The combined American and Norwegian commando force closed in under cover of more smoke grenades.

Thorne scurried over to Barrabas's side as the SOB leader advanced.

"One of the copilots radioed us about another team moving up a good distance behind the VG."

"None of our boys," Barrabas said. "Must be the Terrible Ivans themselves." The Spetsnaz team had obviously circled the VG and were planning to take them out at the end—picking up the pieces.

"That's what I figured," Thorne said. "The Nightfox is going to pay them a visit to keep them back for a while."

When the smoke cleared near the fortress, the woods were alive with the VG. Regular VG soldiers and berserkers streamed into the woods, laying down a barrage of full-auto fire, as well as attacking with sword and ax as they closed in for the final battle.

Barrabas pushed forward. The SOBs advanced with him, slipping through the ancient and twisted pines, diving to the snow as they invaded the haunted forest. They fired round after round until finally they were face-to-face with the surviving Vikings themselves.

The berserkers howled and roared, leaping through the air, oblivious to the lead flying around them, intent only on burying their axes and swords one more time before they went down.

They were Odin's own, hanged men still walking the earth, still fighting on, convinced that the moment they died they would fight in another army, an army that could never be defeated.

This battle was just a transition period, a bloody fight in the darkness.

Barrabas saw a woman running with the VG. She moved like a huntress, a shield maiden. She emptied her SMG into a line of Norwegian commandos, threw it down when it was empty, then faded out of sight.

Barrabas was looking for Koll when a berserker came flying out of nowhere at him, somehow moving soundlessly through the trees.

Barrabas dropped to the ground, avoiding a sword slash that would have taken his head off. He pushed himself off the ground while the berserker was still trying to find his balance. Barrabas planted a kick to his knee, knocking him back. As he fell, Barrabas backfisted him in the temple. Berserker or not, the man saw stars.

Barrabas picked up the berserker's sword and swung it two-handed like a baseball bat. The steel chopped into the berserker's neck and the fire in his eyes went out. Barrabas looked around and saw a white-clad commando peering over a small ridge, SMG in hand, looking for a berserker he'd seen hurtling through the trees.

The berserker found him first and screamed in triumph, swinging his battle-ax straight down.

The thick blade buried itself in the man's head, adding a glistening red part to his hair. The blow made the cranium collapse, and the echo of the berserker's war cry chased after him into eternity.

All around the remains of the fortress—the remains of commando and Viking alike—there was blood and smoke and cries of agony, cries of rage.

But finally the ranks of the Vikings thinned out as the modern warriors stood their ground, meeting the berserker frenzy with their own manic battle fever.

Magnus Koll was leaping through the thick undergrowth like a stag in the forest. Surefooted and clear-eyed, he moved through the wood that resounded with the sounds of battle.

He carried a long battle-ax in one hand, an SMG in the other.

Barrabas saw the fleet blond Viking chieftain moving as though he was in two worlds at once, and at home in both.

Beside him was another man, cut from nearly the same mold. That would be Telik Wulfson, Barrabas thought, remembering O'Toole's briefing.

Wulfson suddenly howled. His hands were to his chest in a reflex action, trying to keep the blood from draining out. He'd been hit smack in the chest with a full-auto burst. He cried out and went down.

Koll looked down at his fallen friend, his eyes suddenly going cold, the Viking world almost vanishing around him. But he kept on running, heading straight toward a pocket of Norwegians whose attentions were now on a trio of berserkers charging at them like trolls.

Fighting alongside the Norwegians was Billy Two, his back turned to Koll and the few remaining berserkers who'd gathered behind him.

Barrabas swung the SMG he'd picked up from a fallen commando and aimed it in Koll's direction.

The magazine was empty.

"Koll!" Barrabas shouted.

Magnus Koll was in midair when suddenly he turned his head toward the SOB warrior. This was the leader, he knew, and was pleased that he would go out properly, by meeting his match.

"Barrabas!" the man shouted, almost joyfully.

He threw the SMG into the snow as if it were a weapon fit only for scorn. "I challenge you to settle this the only proper way for men."

Barrabas discarded his weapon. Though a part of him wondered if he were mad, he had been challenged by a man of tradition, a man who believed in a time when king fought against king, when solitary champions on the field could decide who owned the throne.

And though the throne was a bloodstained blanket of snow, it was enough.

Barrabas looked around him. Still forms lay sprawled in the snow, their limbs frozen in haphazard or macabre tableaus of flight or a lethal last dance.

The SOB chief picked up an ax that was still clutched by a berserker who'd swung it for the last time.

The heavy trumpet-shaped blade was washed in fresh blood. The sturdy ash wood was long enough to be wielded in both hands. Barrabas tested the weight of the weapon, then stepped toward Koll.

Both men raced forward.

Like two stags crashing head on, they swung their battle-axes. The heavy blades rang against each other as the hafts crashed and locked together.

Both axes traveled in an arc toward the ground. Barrabas swung his ax straight back, the blunt end whipping toward Koll's head.

Koll dodged but the blunt metal still crashed against his shoulder. It was like hitting a rock.

But Koll looked surprised just the same.

Now, realizing that a battle-ax was not his most effective weapon, Barrabas raised the ax high over his head. As the ax swung back, he released it, letting it fly through the air. His left foot had lifted slightly off the ground with the motion, and now that his weapon no longer took his balance, Barrabas snapped out with his foot, going straight for Koll's face.

His boot heel clipped the Viking under the chin, clacking his teeth together and lifting his head back. The ax fell out of suddenly enervated hands, then Magnus Koll was falling, dropping like a felled tree into the snow.

The other berserkers, who'd been so wild just moments before, suddenly fell silent. They stood still as if they'd been magically struck by the same blow as their chief.

The commandos circled around the last of the Varangian Guard.

Magnus Koll came to quickly. He sat straight up like a god returned to the living. A river of blood ran down the side of his mouth, and a red spray escaped his lips as he spoke.

"I am no man's prisoner," he said.

Barrabas stared at the warrior. The man's gaze was so fierce that it almost convinced Barrabas that the Viking chief had been triumphant on the field.

But Barrabas had taken the man's measure and saw that he would not be a prisoner. He would die before he left the woods, whether by killing himself or by forcing his captors to kill him.

"There is no escape," Barrabas said.

The battered Viking chief stood tall. "If am to die this time," Koll said, "let it be here. Let me go out as a Viking."

Barrabas studied the man who had so recently spared O'Toole's life.

"There is a way," Barrabas said, pointing in the direction where the Soviet commandos had last been seen. "The red dragons are still in their lair. Go and find them if you want."

Barrabas picked up the battle-ax and handed it to Koll. Both the commandos and the surviving VG stared at Barrabas as if he'd gone mad.

MAGNUS KOLL CHARGED across the field of snow.

Three of his men were behind him, their wounds forgotten as they thundered over the clearing, running full steam toward the woods.

Koll yelled, and with that yell a thousand more came to him, voices calling from the past, voices that had once screamed war cries through these same Norwegian woods.

Then the first bullet hit him. It struck him in the shoulder and went clear though. His blood dribbled steadily onto the snow but his feet flew just as fast.

Kings never died easily.

Koll let out a scream once more, the battle-ax raised high over his head as he crashed into the position the Spetsnaz soldiers had chosen to set their ambush.

The Norwegian commandos had spotted them before, but didn't quite know their exact position.

Until now.

Magnus Koll took three more shots in the chest, breaking bone and muscle, but not his will as he leaped into the woods and swung the battle-ax straight down into the head of Nicholas Vrosputin, who died with gun in hand, and at the hands of a man already dead.

Magnus Koll seemed to be suspended in midair for a minute, stock-still as if posing for eternity, then he fell straight to the earth with the heavy majesty of a fallen giant tree.

The other berserkers died at his side, caught in the Spetsnaz fire.

Another barrage ripped through Troll Valley as the SOBs and the Norwegians opened up on the Soviet commandos with everything they had. Now that Koll had made the Soviets give away their position, the joint commando force buried them with a hail of lead.

When silence finally returned to the woodland, one by one they walked over to the edge of the woods.

The SOBs stared down at the slain Viking chief.

O'Toole and Barrabas exchanged a look, then Barrabas nodded once at O'Toole.

The red-bearded Irishman picked up Koll's body, slung it over his shoulder and headed back the way they'd come.

Nile Barrabas and the SOBs stood motionless for a minute and looked silently after the trail of the man who would be king.

Barrabas understood war and its code of honor, and in a way he lived in an old world, too. Not the way of comfort, of a steady job and take-home pay—the cosy pleasures of wife and home. It's too bad, he mused, as he looked away into the distance, that some men in whose blood sings the old hunting songs turn to the wrong ideals.

He shook his head wryly and turned to Nanos and Claude Hayes, then put his hand on the Osage's shoulder. "Come on, you dogs: this war is over."

Out of the ruins of civilization emerges...

The Deathlands saga—edge-of-the-seat adventure not to be missed!

		Quantity
PILGRIMAGE TO HELL became a harrowing journey high in the mountains.	$3.95	☐
RED HOLOCAUST brought the survivors to the freakish wasteland in Alaska.	$2.95	☐
NEUTRON SOLSTICE followed the group through the reeking swampland that was once the Mississippi Basin.	$2.95	☐
CRATER LAKE introduces the survivors to a crazed world more terrifying than their own.	$2.95	☐
HOMEWARD BOUND brings the journey full circle when Ryan Cawdor meets the remnants of his own family—brutal murderers.	$3.50	☐
PONY SOLDIERS introduces the survivors to a specter from the past—General Custer	$3.95	☐

Total Amount	$	
Plus 75¢ Postage		.75
Payment enclosed		

Please send a check or money order payable to Gold Eagle Books.

In the U.S.A.	In Canada
Gold Eagle Books 901 Fuhrmann Blvd. Box 1325 Buffalo, NY 14269-1325	Gold Eagle Books P.O. Box 609 Fort Erie, Ontario L2A 5X3

GOLD EAGLE

DL-A

Please Print

Name: _____

Address: _____

City: _____

State/Prov: _____

Zip/Postal Code: _____

THE *BARRABAS* SERIES

The toughest men
for the dirtiest wars

JACK HILD

" . . . a wealth of detail . . .
gripping . . . (Nile Barrabas)
does the job!"
—West Coast Review of Books

Nile Barrabas was the last American soldier out of Vietnam
and the first man into a new kind of action. His warriors,
called the Soldiers of Barrabas, have one very simple am-
bition: to do what the Marines can't or won't do. Join the
Barrabas blitz! Each book hits new heights—this is brawling at its best!

Mack Bolan's

by Dick Stivers

Action writhes in the reader's own streets
as Able Team's Carl "Ironman" Lyons,
Pol Blancanales and Gadgets Schwarz
make triple trouble in blazing war. Join
Dick Stivers's Able Team as it returns to
the United States to become the country's
finest tactical neutralization squad in an
era of urban terror and unbridled crime.

"Able Team will go anywhere, do anything,
in order to complete their mission. Plenty
of action! Recommended!"
　　　　　　　—*West Coast Review of Books*

More than action adventure...
books written by the men who were there

VIETNAM: GROUND ZERO ™

ERIC HELM

Told through the eyes of an American Special Forces squad, an elite jungle fighting group of strike-and-hide specialists fight a dirty war half a world away from home.

These books cut close to the bone, telling it the way it really was.

"Vietnam at Ground Zero is where this book is written. The author has been there, and he knows. I salute him and I recommend this book to my friends."

—Don Pendleton
creator of *The Executioner*

"Helm writes in an evocative style that gives us Nam as it most likely was, without prettying up or undue bitterness."

—*Cedar Rapids Gazette*

"Eric Helm's Vietnam series embodies a literary standard of excellence. These books linger in the mind long after their reading."

—*Midwest Book Review*

GOLD EAGLE

Available wherever paperbacks are sold.

VIE 1